PENGUIN BOOKS

The Voyage of the Destiny

Robert Nye was born in London in 1939. He left school at the age of sixteen, at which time his first poems were published in the *London Magazine*. Since then he has lived by his writing, at first subsidizing his creative work by writing critical reviews in leading periodicals; he is still the poetry critic for *The Times* and a regular reviewer of new fiction for the *Guardian*. He lived for six years in a remote cottage in Wales, working on two collections of poems which won him a Gregory Award in 1963. His novel *Falstaff* won the Hawthornden Prize and the *Guardian* Fiction Prize for 1976, and was a bestseller in the United Kingdom and a Book-of-the-Month-Club Alternate Choice in the United States. His novels *Merlin* and *Faust* have also been published in Penguin. Sir Walter Ralegh, the subject of this novel, has long fascinated him, and he edited a selection of Ralegh's poems in 1972. Robert Nye is married and lives in Ireland with his wife and children.

D1434889

ROBERT NYE

THE VOYAGE
OF THE
DESTINY

PENGUIN BOOKS

Penguin Books Ltd, Harmondsworth, Middlesex, England
Penguin Books, 40 West 23rd Street, New York, New York 10010, U.S.A.
Penguin Books Australia Ltd, Ringwood, Victoria, Australia
Penguin Books Canada Ltd, 2801 John Street, Markham, Ontario, Canada L3R 1B4
Penguin Books (N.Z.) Ltd, 182–190 Wairau Road, Auckland 10, New Zealand

–

First published by Hamish Hamilton Ltd 1982
Published in Penguin Books 1983

–

–

Made and printed in Great Britain by
Cox & Wyman Ltd, Reading
Set in Linotron Plantin by
Rowland Phototypesetting Ltd,
Bury St Edmunds, Suffolk

I

When Alexander the Great came to the edge of the world of his time, and pitched his camp on the banks of the River Indus, he told his builders to build gigantic pavilions there and to fill each pavilion with a giant's furniture.

Then Alexander instructed his armourers to hammer out swords as long as lances, shields as big and strong as mill wheels, axes like battering rams, and helmets the size of hives for monstrous bees.

When he withdrew and sailed for home, Alexander ordered this vast and ghostly camp to be left standing, with all its huge accoutrements intact.

He wanted to cast a long shadow. He wanted to make people believe that he had been a giant, and that his men had been only a little less, and that this had been a camp occupied by an army like gods.

My son, I am no giant and (God knows) no god.

Here you will find no big chairs.

I write these words aboard my flagship the *Destiny*, anchored now as she is in the bay of Punto Gallo, which the Indians call Curiapan, at the south-west point of the isle of Trinidad. Our position is 10° north wanting five minutes, in a longitude of 62° west. That is, some six miles east of the coast of Guiana. And a world of wild water west of you, Carew.

I kept a Journal for the greater part of this voyage, starting at the end of last August, sixty miles short of Cape Saint Vincent, twelve days after leaving Kinsale Harbour in Ireland. That's five and a half months. For five and a half months I have written of little else than storm and fever, high seas and low spirits, mishap, misfortune, mischance, of sails torn from their masts, masts snapped in two, men dying in as many ways they must, men deserting in as many ways they may.

Not long out of Kinsale and into the Atlantic we sprang a leak that drowned three sailors who were bailing in the hold, and we had to tread down every scrap of our raw meat between the planks to block the cracks that opened in our decks.

I should have known then that this voyage was doomed.

Damned, if you like.

Certainly wrong from the start.

So many ill omens and portents.

I should never have named my ship the *Destiny*. That was high-flown and grandiose and tempted fate. Ah, Elizabeth, how you would have shaken your head and flicked your fingers at such folly. You who disliked all solemn abstract names for the vessels of your fleet, and once made one of your captains change his *Repentance* to the *Dainty*.

'A vessel of five hundred tons,' I told Mr Pett. 'Built to these specifications which I have drawn up myself.'

'In the Tower, Sir Walter?'

'What better place for dreaming of tall ships, Mr Pett?'

Phineas Pett, the royal shipbuilder. I gave him £500 on account. There's £700 still owing. What did I care in those days? I was as confident of finding Guiana gold as I was of not missing my way from my dining-room to my bedchamber.

So my *Destiny* was built at Deptford and launched just nine days before Christmas 1616. A black swan of a ship. Swift, graceful, splendid. Solid English oak throughout, no plank less than five inches thick at any point from stem to stern. Fit to bear two hundred men. With her ports so laid that she could carry out and fire her thirty-six guns in all weathers.

'Why will you have her so heavily armed, Sir Walter?'

'Piracy, Mr Pett.'

'I beg your pardon, Sir Walter?' (Spectacles falling down his nose. Eyes as bright and hard as his bulbous bald head.)

'You ask an old fox a damned innocent question. Piracy is rife, Mr Pett. We live in evil days.'

Ropes, spars, hoists, cradles, stocks, capstans, ribs, hulls, saw-pits, hawsers, vats of pitch and barrels of oakum, davits, transoms, and long timbers all about us.

The great shire horses labouring in their harness, the stubby claws of the launching crab that jerked and stopped, jerked and stopped, the hempen cables singing with the strain, and slowly my *Destiny* inching forwards, rolling and rumbling down the well-greased slope and into the sombre waters of the Thames.

I remember there was snow blown like smoke in the east wind which snatched at our cloaks on the Deptford waterfront. Your mother was there, swathed in furs, my dear Bess, wearing her beaver cap with the ear-flaps. Wat, bare-headed, bright-cheeked, eating an apple in scorn of the cold. My friend Laurence Keymis, tall and thin and scholarly, with a cast in one eye. My cousinly keeper Sir Lewis Stukeley, suffering from a head cold but doing his duty, sipping now and again at a flask which contained an elixir I had prepared for him – powdered betony and balsam of sulphur, mixed with conserve of roses and wine. A brazier ablaze beside us on the quay. I warmed my hands at the hissing coals. And you, Carew, hopping from foot to foot, dancing, cheering, kept warm with your young innocent excitement.

The tarry smell of cordage. The clout of new wet sail-cloth. Pett's mechanicals trimming the yards and bearing down on the helm.

Pett himself with his coat-tails whipped out by the wind. 'A wholesome ship, Sir Walter. She rides well at anchor.'

So do coffins.

My son, you know that I was thirteen years (unjustly) in the Tower, convicted of treason, under sentence of death. I shall have more to say about that in due course. You know also that it was only the prospect of gold which bought me my freedom (such as it is). He enjoys talking and thinking about gold – our King James the Sixth of Scotland and the First of England. Not that I was cheating him when I wrote to Secretary Winwood and told of my plan if released. I have been here before. In '95. On behalf of a lady whom time has surprised. Queen Elizabeth. I can put my fingers on the map of the river Orinoco and point to the places where gold is to be found. Not El Dorado. Not Manoa. No mythical golden city. But potential gold mines. Real ones.

Your father was never quite without friends – especially in Devon and Cornwall, in the West Country, his own country, which has always been loyal to him. There are people there, rich and poor, of high and low estate, who were not blinded by envy even in those (now distant) days when I rose high on fortune's wheel as spun by Queen Elizabeth's right hand and some foppish London fool – Sir Anthony Bagot, as I remember – called me 'the best-hated man in the world'. Well, Bagot, you maggot, the friends of that sometime best-hated man in the world invested £15,000 in backing this little adventure. And my wife Bess (God bless her, your dear mother, my Carew) sold her lands at Mitcham in Surrey to provide me with another £2500. And I called in myself the £8000 which had been on loan since I received it as compensation for my house at Sherborne being taken from me and given to the King's catamite of that time, Robert Carr, Earl of Somerset. And raised a further £5000 from this source and that. So that we had a bit more than £30,000 behind the wind in our sails when we slipped down the Thames in the last week of March 1617, anxious to be on our way before King James changed his mind. And had news of the death of the Indian princess Pocohontas in Gravesend just at the moment we sailed past it.

The sound of Indian drums beating for her funeral there, in England, in the very breath of our setting forth.

Death.

I am not by nature a superstitious man. I have even been called an atheist in my time. (I was never exactly that, though I was once a sceptic – neither affirming nor denying any religious position, but rather opposing it with my powers of reason.) Sceptic or not, perhaps I should have heeded those drums, should have listened to what they were saying.

Death.

For sure I should have known it when we lost one of our pinnaces off Plymouth, before we were halfway into the St George's Channel, the winds so foul and contrary, never such terrible seas since the year of the Armada.

The Devil's sly thumb-prints smudging my sea charts.

Death at the helm.

Forty-two men dead in my flagship alone now, including John Pigott, our Lieutenant General for the land service, and Mr Nicholas Fowler, our chief refiner of metals, and the scholar Jack Talbot, who was my friend and who shared my imprisonment in the Tower for eleven years.

We set forth with fourteen ships and three pinnaces.

The arithmetic of death.

We have ten ships left, and only five of them were light enough to go upriver.

I had to watch them go without me. I am myself too weak to do more than write. When the hot wind blows from the shore I sweat so that I cannot see the words at the end of my pen. The rest of the time I am gripped by a clammy cold.

Even so. I go on. I continue. But you will have understood by now that I am avoiding the issue. That every sentence I have constructed so far has been a tacking this way and that way to keep going while I dodge what I must say. Has been a means – all that talk about money! – to hold my true thoughts and feelings at arm's length. Understand, then: I am not merely going on with my Journal. My Journal is over and done with. Ended. Not finished. What I must write now is what lies beyond its unfinishableness.

I wrote that Journal to and for myself. Now I write to you. For you, Carew, my son. And what I write will not be exactly a Journal. What will it be? I don't know. I am writing it partly to find out. It will have to be something like the truth. Both more than a Journal, and less. No giant or god stuff. But some kind of confession. The story of my days past and the story of my days present. What I was and what I am. What and who. For you, Carew, who do not really know me. My poor Carew, who will probably never read a single word of this. My sad little son, conceived and born in the Tower, christened in the chapel of St Peter in Chains inside the walls, and just thirteen years old today. You didn't think I'd forgotten? That today is your birthday, Carew.

Wat is dead. Your brother. And my only other son. That is the first thing to be said. The thing which I have been avoiding saying. The reason, you will realize, for this present writing. Its spring. Its motive. Its deadly inspiration.

Wat was killed in a battle of some kind with the Spanish near their fort of San Thomé. He was killed in the night of the 2nd of January. He was with Keymis and my young nephew George and the rest of them who set out upriver some ten weeks ago, with never a word until now. They went in our five ships of least draught, five craft light enough to negotiate the tricky shallow waters of the Orinoco delta. With 150 sailors and 250 soldiers. The five ships being commanded by my captains Whitney, King, Smith, Wollaston, and Hall. My nephew George being in charge of the land force. My life-long friend Laurence Keymis entrusted with the search for the location of the mines, and then the supervising of all operations there.

I know, a few gentlemen excepted, what a scum of men George Ralegh and Laurence Keymis have to lead. When I stress that this voyage was doomed from the start, I am not being altogether melodramatic. The truth is that my position in law as an unpardoned 'traitor' merely let out of the Tower to get gold for King James did not attract to my service many men who were better than half-pirates or half-mercenaries. I know for a fact that a fair number of my crew are criminals who didn't so much join me as run away from the justice that still awaits them in England. Even the best of my captains don't trust each other. They refused point-blank to go up the Orinoco unless I remained here with the rest of the ships to guard the river mouth. I am the only one they could all trust not to run if a Spanish fleet comes up after us.

I gave Keymis this assurance:

'You will find me at Punto Gallo, dead or alive. And if you don't find my ships there, you will find their ashes. I will set fire to the galleons, if it comes to the worst. Run will I never.'

So I'm here all right, fevered and sick, eating lemons. Lemons and oranges, quinces and pomegranates. Fruits given to me by the Governor's wife at Gomera, one of the smaller Canary Islands, on the voyage out. She was English, a daughter of the Stafford family. I couldn't have lived without these lemons and other fruits, preserved in big barrels of sand. My stomach is not good. I was unable to take solid food for more than a month. For fifteen days, also, as I wrote to your mother when we reached the Cayenne River last November, I suffered the most violent calenture that ever man did, and lived. The calenture: that's a disease of these tropics, when a man falls into a delirium where he fancies the sea to be green fields and desires nothing more than to leap into it. That passed. The irony was, as I wrote to your mother in the letter borne home by the Dutch vessel, that in all this time of fever your brother Wat kept in perfect health, not even suffering distemper in that hell-fire of heat.

As for me, I am still too weak to walk without an arm to lean on. The arm is usually that of my new Lieutenant General, Sir Warham St Leger. He is sick too. He has dropsy. He remains here with me with the heavy vessels.

Wat died bravely, as one would expect. He died running forward against Spanish pikemen, and shouting *Come on, my hearts!* to his companions. So he died foolishly also, no doubt. And he shouldn't have been killed at all. There was no need. By the terms of my Commission from King James, we aren't supposed to cross swords with any Spaniard. Gondomar saw to that. The Spanish Ambassador. As soon as he heard that I had been released from the Tower (even unpardoned and accompanied everywhere in those early days by a keeper) he went straight to James and complained that the whole of Guiana belonged to Spain. In any case, Gondomar said, he was convinced that I had no intention of doing anything else than turn pirate and plunder the towns of the Spanish Main. As a result, the usual words 'trusty and well-beloved servant' were erased from my Commission, issued to me on the 26th of August 1616, and it was explicitly declared that I was still 'under the peril of the law'. James promised Gondomar that my life would be forfeit if I inflicted any injury whatsoever on the subjects of Spain.

A death trap? Not quite. My plan was to take *French* ships with me. The French could engage the Spaniards while we worked the mines. I sent two Frenchmen, Faige and Belle, to negotiate the matter with Montmorency, the Grand Admiral of France. I still have Montmorency's letter in which he promises me safe haven in any French port if I need it on my return. But what happened to the four French vessels already fitted out for the expedition at Havre and Dieppe? Faige and Belle took money from me, and letters for the French captains, before I sailed from Plymouth. They never came back. I hung around waiting at Kinsale, then in the Canaries, then at the Cayenne River after our torment of crossing the Atlantic. No French showed up. And no French contingent ever yet arrived at the Orinoco.

Keymis counts it an achievement, apparently, that he has taken the Spanish fort at San Thomé. Why he should think that, I don't know. It formed no part of my instructions to him or to my nephew George.

Keymis's letter concerning Wat's death came into my hands

today, your birthday, Carew. It is dated the 8th of January. So it took the wretched man six days to write it, and it took the bearers – an Indian pilot and a sailor called Peter Andrews – five weeks to reach me. San Thomé is more than 200 miles upriver, so there may be some small excuse for the latter. For the former, there can be no excuse I will ever accept. Keymis shall answer for his cowardly heart, by Christ.

And has he opened either of the mines? Got gold?

The miserable botcher says *nothing*.

Not one word of sense concerning that. Nothing at all.

As for Andrews, he is able only to tell me what I now already know and wish I didn't. That our forces hold San Thomé. And Wat's dead.

Vultures over my ship. Her paint peeling. A tropic damp. The weather always hot and misty. The sun trailing a golden hand at noon in the swirling currents of that channel between Trinidad and the mainland which my maps call the Serpent's Mouth.

Ingots of golden water.

And I am as water. For it was Water she called me, the Queen. (Mocking my broad Devon accent, and perhaps a certain infirmity of purpose in my temper.)

An El Dorado undersea, Elizabeth.

Well, Carew, my only son now, I believe in the ingots. Not the city made of gold. Not that imaginary magnificence ruled by a king who was himself covered with gold dust, the legend as looked for by Diego de Ordaz, and Orellano, and Philip von Hutten, and Gonzalo Ximenes de Quesada. That's just a story for children. I tell my child the truth. There *is* gold up the Orinoco there. I have played the world's game for sixty-four years. I'm no slug. I'm no fool. I would not have sailed half the globe over, and put my honour at stake thus, for a lie or a fantasy or a far-fetched hope. The tragedy is that *I* could not lead our actual expedition to fetch the damned stuff back.

My birthday boy, I repeat myself. An old man's privilege. And I am grown suddenly old just today, in the last few hours. Old enough to repeat that this voyage was wrong from the start. Ill-fated. Bad-starred. The sea at the bow of my *Destiny* like boiling copper when it wasn't becalmed and like milk that's gone sour in the churn. Forked lightning following us. Fire-flags of it wrapped round our masts. Tornadoes. Typhoons. Five days we sailed through sweltering tawny mist like a lion's breath. Two days we had to steer by candlelight and the flickering of torches stuck at the stem and stern through fog so thick and black you couldn't see your hand in front of your face. Some of the men swore then that we'd reached the world's end. By God, it made them say their prayers with more attention. And they sang a psalm when we came out beyond the world's end. Like choirboys they were then. Singing a psalm of thanksgiving as the watch was set. Jailbirds as good as gold.

Ingots.

At San Thomé also, Keymis reports in his letter, he found this parcel of papers in the Spanish Governor's house. Plans of our voyage, sent out by King James to the King of Spain via the spy Gondomar. Lists of my ships and my ships' companies in my own handwriting. To be so betrayed by one's own Sovereign Lord . . . I have been a pawn in the King's game with Spain. Very well then: a knight.

Wag – The pen wrote it, the heart spoke it when my head intended Wat. And that's right for I called him the wag in a poem once, and at other times too, for he was a wag, my son the elder, and a wild one.

Wat, as I must make an end of saying, is dead.

And as for Wat's father?

I shall not *soon* be dead. There is no call for me to kill myself. Sir Walter Ralegh is dead already. A man dead in law these fourteen years, convicted of a treason he did not commit, never yet executed by him who most desires his death.

A dead man writes this book.

A dead man writing to his posthumous son.

Big music? Too loud and proud a mouth? Just what my enemies would expect of me?

Carew, once upon a time there was a song they used to sing in the streets of London:

> Ralegh doth time bestride,
> He sits twixt wind and tide,
> Yet uphill he cannot ride –
> For all his bloody pride!

Perhaps they sing it still? Or will again? All the same – Pride?

The first and worst and deadliest of the Seven Deadly Sins, of course. And I have been damnably proud in my day. But it's not my day now.

When my critics said *pride* what did they mean? They meant that I had come from next to nowhere, that my father was nobody, that I had no claim by birth on the world's attention, and no grip on its slippery surface either. I made my own way in the world, and there are those who cannot forgive a man that.

Sometimes I could hardly forgive myself. Yes, there have been moments when that was true too. I'll have to try to come to them as best I can in this telling. But *pride*?

I'd a nag called that once. And her riding was always uphill.

I started life as a bare gentleman, you see. The fifth and youngest son of an English squire. No title. No great fortune. Plain and ordinary as cider. No advantages. Yet sprung from one of the oldest families in Devon.

My father owned a small farm, a few green fields, some boats for fishing. A particular patch of England. He also owned himself. As Raleghs do.

My father married three times. My mother married twice. Katherine Gilbert, widow of Otho Gilbert. She was born Champernown. Daughter of Philip Champernown of Plymouth.

You never knew your grandparents, Carew. I have two stories to give you some hint or print or likeness of what they were. Two stories that say something of our blood. Of what I have inherited from them, and you (perhaps) have inherited from me along with many qualities which properly derive from your dear mother, my wife Bess.

My father, first.

One Sunday morning he was riding to Exeter from our farmhouse at Hayes Barton, near Budleigh Salterton, when he met an old woman with a rosary in her hands. This was in 1549, five years before I was born. The Roman rite was about to be abolished in England, Latin removed from our church services, and the *Book of Common Prayer* introduced. My father took an interest in these matters. No theologian, you understand, he was all the same a man who liked to think for himself, and who was therefore not displeased to see England get out from under the Pope's slipper.

'Madam,' he says, 'you're in danger.'

'What danger?' demands the woman.

'The new laws,' my father explains. 'That rosary makes you look like an enemy of the reformed faith. I'm not criticizing. I'm just warning. No beads. No holy water. I've heard from London. People are going to be punished for such things.'

'Punished?' the woman says. 'How?'

'By death, I believe,' says my father.

My father doffs his hat and he rides on.

The old woman runs into the nearest church flapping her arms and she screams:

'Mr Ralegh! Mr Ralegh! He's going to throw mud on our altars and murder us all in our beds if we don't give up God!'

The people broke out of that church like some sort of wasps. They chased after my father where he rode innocently on his way to Exeter. He had to hide all night in a bell tower, thunder and lightning around him outside, to escape from their foolish fury.

Alas, my poor father. But, Carew, do you understand me any better? And I wonder did I understand him?

Then, when I was three years old or so, and Mary Tudor brought back all the hocus pocus of the Roman Church, another old woman was tried for heresy at Exeter. A very different old woman. Her name was Alice Prest. Alice Prest was not famous. She was no Cranmer, no female Latimer or Ridley. You'll find her in no book of Protestant martyrs. But she refused to go wriggling or crawling back through the narrow Latin gate.

My mother got to hear of the case. She thought that she might save this woman's life. She went to visit Alice Prest in prison.

'Just say your creed, my dear,' my mother begged. 'That's enough. It will do to save you.'

'The creed?'

'Just the creed. There's no harm in that, surely?'

So Alice Prest nods and smiles and recites the creed to my mother and a priest outside listening. But when she comes to the article 'He ascended into heaven . . .' she stops dead.

'Why do you stop?' asks my mother.

'Because I believe it,' says Alice Prest.

'So you should,' says my mother. 'And so do I. So now go on.'

'You don't understand,' says Alice Prest. 'I *believe* it. He ascended into heaven. Jesus did. I believe it. And so I believe that Our Lord's blessed body is in heaven, not here on earth. He isn't here in anything men can make with their hands. The bread of the mass can't be His body, don't you see? Our Lord is in heaven.'

My mother came home to my father.

'I couldn't answer her reasoning,' she told him. 'And she cannot read, and I can.'

They burned Alice Prest.

Two small stories.

My father and my mother.

Who made me, who made you . . .

My only son, now that I have written those two stories down I cannot see the page for tears. They tell it all. My telling. What I have to tell, to define, to tease out from my own life. The infinite capacity we Raleghs have for being misunderstood, or for understanding too well for any useful action. When I was not being chased by ignorant crowds like wasps, I stood with my sensitive back to the burning of the Alice Prests of this world. On these twin poles I have been broken. On this rack I have stretched myself. Nor has it always been to my discomfort. That is my measure.

I'll write no more.

Stop this.

But what *is* Keymis doing up the river? Has he found a mine or not? And is he working it? Can gold bring Wat back? Of course not. But gold is what I need now to fill the ship and justify this voyage to King James. And what do I really care about that? About King James and his satisfaction? Not a fig. Yet my good name is involved.

Good name?

My name is mud.

The mud that fills Wat's mouth.

No more. I shall end my book. End it before it's begun. I can't go on.

2

Keymis came back.

Keymis came back yesterday at nightfall.

The sun goes down suddenly in these latitudes. One moment it is there on the horizon, a great burning ball of fire, a huge guinea nailed into the sky with golden nails. The next moment it is gone. Dragged down. Blotted out. Removed as by some black hand. The sun goes and all is darkness. No twilight. There is never twilight here.

Keymis is dead. My friend. My lieutenant. My old companion.

Keymis killed himself, and I drove him to it.

My son, your father is a murderer. No hero now, as you begin to see. The noble Sir Walter Ralegh conducted himself like a Herod, like a Cain, like a bad actor in a third-rate play at the Globe. Worse. I blamed the whole failure of my life on Keymis.

Between my first entry in these pages, my first writing, and this dark page, many days have elapsed. Hell-hot days, days of raging fever, days when I could not walk the deck of the *Destiny* and peer across the steamy waters of the estuary without Sir Warham St Leger or the Reverend Mr Samuel Jones, our ship's chaplain, there at my side to support me. On any one of those days, or better still in the star-confused nights which followed them, I could and perhaps should have killed myself. I lacked the guts to do it, Carew, and there's some heroic truth for you.

When Edward Hastings died on the long voyage out, our surgeon reported that his liver, spleen, and brains were rotten. By God, my liver must be lily-coloured. My spleen is a lump of hard poison. But, instead of blowing out my own brains, I waited for Keymis and the

17

others to return down the river. And then when he came aboard I gave him the hell of my own anguish.

'Where is the gold?' I said. 'Where is my son?'

He stammered something, but I wouldn't hear him.

'Where is the gold?' I kept saying. 'Where is my son?'

Keymis had a cast in his left eye. He always had that. I was used to it. But it seemed to me then that he was avoiding my looking at him, that he was searching the corners of my cabin for excuses, justifications, anything that would enable him to escape or resist what I saw as my righteous indignation.

'You betrayed me,' I said. 'You did not obey orders.'

He made some garbled noise of protest. I wouldn't allow him to proceed.

'My instructions were that you should bring back gold from one or the other of the sites known to both of us. I did not tell you to attack a Spanish garrison.'

He said: 'They fired first on us.'

'Then you should have retreated. But why were you going for the Caroni mine anyway?'

He stared dumbly at the floor.

'Were you scared to leave the river? Is that it? But damn you, man, even if that's the case there must still have been some way you could have passed San Thomé without a fight.'

Keymis would not meet my gaze.

'Your son,' he said.

There was a silence before Keymis went on.

'Your son died very bravely,' Keymis said. 'He charged a line of Spaniards single-handed. He fell with a dozen pikes in him. After that, there was no turning back.'

I caught him by the neck. I made him look at me.

'Are you claiming it was Wat's fault that you botched everything? A boy in his twenties? A boy who had never before seen military action?'

'He was your son,' Keymis said strangely.

'What do you mean by that?'

'Ask Captain Parker,' Keymis said.

'I will not ask Captain Parker. I am asking you.'

'Your son died, as I wrote in my letter, with extraordinary valour.'

'But he need not – he should not – have died at all,' I said.

Keymis said nothing. He was looking away again. His damned eye was like a crab that crawls for corners.

'Is that what you're driving at?' I demanded. 'Are you blaming the storming of the Spanish outpost on my son's impetuosity?'

Spittle flew from my mouth with the last word spoken. It ran down Keymis's cheek. Then I saw that he was weeping. For some reason, his tears made things worse.

'You fool!' I shouted. 'You went for the wrong mine! You disobeyed orders! You let my son be killed!'

'Forward,' Keymis mumbled. 'He was all for going forward. It was the only word he wanted to hear. Without him, we would never have attempted the attack upon the fort. Ask Captain Parker. He tried to stop him. We all tried to stop him. "Unadvised daringness" – that's what Parker said it was.'

I removed my hands from Keymis's neck. I wiped them on my doublet.

'You are a coward, sir,' I said quietly. 'Strange to have known you so long and only now to have discovered the truth about you. A wilful and obstinate coward, sir. You failed to open either mine. You let my son be killed. And now you stand there blubbering and blabbing like a baby, and trying to use my dead boy as a scapegoat. Will you go, sir? Will you get out of my sight?'

Keymis went.

I sat and watched a candle burn to nothing.

Then there was a soft knock at the door of my cabin, and it was the wretched Keymis back again, with a letter in his hand, the ink still wet on it.

'I have written to Lord Arundel,' he said.

I said nothing.

'He was a chief promoter of your expedition,' Keymis went on. 'This letter sets forth my case. Will you read what I have written?'

I shook my head.

'You had better write to the Devil, sir,' I said. 'He is more likely to understand your explanations.'

'Please,' Keymis said.

'I will not even look at it,' I said.

Then Keymis turned his face away.

19

'I will wait on you presently,' he said in a level voice. 'And I will give you better satisfaction.'

He left me. I heard the tread of his feet along the companionway. Then the sound of his cabin door shutting behind him. Then the crack of a pistol shot.

'Keymis!' I shouted.

His cabin was next to mine on the poop deck. You could hear through the timbers quite clearly.

'It's all right,' he called back. 'I merely fired off my pistol to clean it.'

He had not. He had shut himself up in his cabin, and shot himself with a pocket pistol, but the pistol ball only served to break one of his ribs and finding that it had not done the trick Keymis thrust a long knife into his heart up to the handle and died.

How to make sense of all this? My captains speak of Keymis with implacable contempt. It seems he was never seen to be prospecting for gold. He made himself subservient to my son.

Was Wat truly to blame for the fiasco at San Thomé? It is not important, I think. The taking of the fort was a gross tactical blunder, an irrelevance, but even then – San Thomé once taken – there is no excuse for Keymis. He could easily have left a garrison there, if he wanted, and proceeded to the Caroni mine, which is a matter of just a few miles beyond it. No doubt the Spaniards retreated in that direction, to defend their interests, and he was scared of another confrontation. But then why did he venture so far upriver in the first place? Can it really be true that he feared to leave the Orinoco and march inland to Mount Iconuri, to Putijma's mine?

There, for the first time I have written down the location of it. Why not? I am not as weak as I was, and I propose to lead a second expedition in person, to journey myself up the Orinoco and bring back gold. If I succeed, if I can go home with only a hatful of gold-bearing ore, then at least I shall have some reputation left. And if I fail? Then I ask for no fitter fate than to lay my bones to rest beside Wat's in front of the altar of the church at San Thomé.

Two ingots.

Keymis did bring back with him two gold ingots that he found within the fort. Also a number of documents which seem to refer to the existence of the Caroni mine. Also an Indian, sometime personal servant of Palomeque who was the Governor of the fort. This Indian interests me. He speaks good Spanish. His name is Christoval Guayacunda.

But I do not believe my bones really belong here. I believe I shall lay my bones elsewhere to rest. And my restless flesh and blood and spirit I shall lay out for you, Carew, in these words, these pages, this true book of my life.

As for its style . . . 'Who lists like trade to try?' I wrote that once, long ago, in one of my first poems, penned in commendation of a book called *The Steel Glass*. The idea of that glass of Gascoigne's was that it showed truth, not mere reflections. The inward man, the hidden face, not just the usual surface semblance. And that is certainly my ambition here. But the style? My style? Is there indeed a style of the individual voice? Or a more general style of truth to which individual voices aspire?

I write each sentence as if it were my last. A man might do worse than to write always like that. That's style. That's my style. It is also of course the plain fact of the matter, given the conditions I write in. Besides, I always wrote best under sentence of death. The shadow of the axe gave sharp edge to my sentences.

If I could get just two handfuls of gold –

Wat is dead.

Wat lies lapped and shrouded in unnecessary gold. Damn gold. Damn all thought of gold. Without gold, I would still have my son.

What am I saying? That this voyage was not just 'wrong', but mad? That I should never have left the Tower? This obsession with gold, gold, gold. Where did it start? It has something to do with the Queen. Yes, you, Elizabeth, your finger beckoning me. It's almost as if *you* are upriver there, a glittering golden ghost, Gloriana come back again. And you had my son instead of me. You always liked them young, you glorious bitch. 'Love likes not the falling fruit from the withered tree.' My son, my best piece of poetry, my sacrifice. Water, you called me. You who had nicknames for all your victim lovers. Water and gold and blood; my story. Well, your Water is nearly all spilled now, dead Majesty.

I always needed an end to make a beginning.

So I shall go on writing this book which I said I could not write. I shall go on despite Wat, despite Keymis, despite myself even.

At the very least – supposing it never reaches your eyes or hands or heart, Carew – at that least it may serve to keep me sane, to hold me in my wits long enough to sail this infernal ship, my *Destiny*, either home to England or some other fatal harbour.

One good small detail here: Keymis did bring tobacco in large quantities from San Thomé. I light my long silver pipe with a coal plucked from the fire in a tongs. It is necessary to keep a little tobacco smoke between oneself and the world.

Gold fever? The viper thought so. I mean Francis Bacon, Baron Verulam, Lord Chancellor of England. I consulted him – on Secretary Winwood's advice – before sailing from London. Let me set down the record of our conversation here. I am reminded of it because of this matter of the gold, but I recite it for another reason which will become clear before long.

We were taking the air of an early March evening. It might have been a year ago today. The date escapes me. But every detail of what we had to say, each to each, remains as vivid as if it were yesterday.

The place was the gardens of Gray's Inn, where I had dined with him in his chambers. Over dinner I had talked a great deal about the impending voyage, and Bacon had said little or nothing, busying himself with knife and fork to cut his meat into tiny portions before chewing each piece methodically, as is his usual fashion, or else leaning his long pale face on a long pale hand and staring at me with those eyes which are his most remarkable feature. Bacon's eyes are hazel in colour, delicate, lively, and light. It was my friend William Harvey, discoverer of the circulation of the blood, who first likened those eyes to the eyes of a viper.

As we strolled in the Gray's Inn gardens – two elderly gentlemen, one of them (me) with a limp, and the other (Bacon) like a walking scissors with a tall thin black chimneypot hat – he suddenly turned to confront me and said:

'Sir, your Guiana is like Atlantis – a perfect Platonic idea.'

'There is this difference,' I replied. 'Atlantis is *only* a perfect Platonic idea. Guiana is both an idea and a reality. A perfect piece of Plato and a large, rich, and beautiful empire of imperfections. A golden dream and a place on the map.'

He did not like this answer, I think, though it is always difficult to gauge Bacon's true feelings – supposing he has anything so dangerous, which is not at all certain.

I rubbed in my point. 'King James is never going to give anyone a Commission to sail to Atlantis in search of gold.'

'I was referring,' Bacon said, 'to the quality of your thinking about it.'

'Thank you,' I said. 'But Guiana would still be there if I did not think about it at all.'

'And the gold?' Bacon asked, in a curiously detached and clinical voice.

'What do you mean?' I said.

'You believe Guiana to be highly auriferous?' he said.

'Yes,' I said.

'On what authority?' he said.

'My own,' I said. 'And others.'

Bacon's lips are always dry. I have noticed that. He has this habit of running his tongue over them and making a face as though he does not like his own taste. He did that then. Then he said: 'But no one has seen this El Dorado, this city of gold. Or is it a lake? Or a golden man?' He dabbed at his long nose with his handkerchief. 'I confess that I have never quite been able to reconcile the different tales which have been told,' he went on disdainfully. 'The only thing they seem to me to have in common is that all of them are truly improbable and probably untrue.'

I suppose I felt like taunting him. After all, there are stranger things to be seen in the world than are between London and Staines.

For this reason or that, I said: 'Experience may be improbable but it cannot be untrue, can it? Very well then. In the summer of '94 one of my captains, George Popham, captured a Spanish ship. Among the captured ship's papers were reports of some *twenty* Spanish expeditions to find El Dorado.'

Bacon said: 'Which means they did not find it twenty times.'

I ignored his sarcasm. I remember fixing my eyes on a bright-leaved tree at the end of the avenue down which we were walking, and going on patiently as if telling a story to an inattentive child:

'In the spring of the year following Popham's discovery, I sailed myself to Guiana with five ships. I took captive Antonio de Berrio, the Spanish Governor. He impressed me as an honest man, an old campaigner not given to fantasies. Berrio did not claim to have found the golden city – but he was convinced of its existence. He had in his keeping the sworn deposition of one Juan Martin de Albujar. This man, a Spanish Moor by birth, had been the only survivor of a previous expedition to find El Dorado. He had been captured by Carib Indians and turned native. He swore on oath that he had eventually been shown the way far into the hinterland, where he was allowed to spend seven months in El Dorado, which he described as a vast city built beside a great landlocked lake surrounded by mountains. This city was ruled by an emperor the Indians called the Inga, and this emperor was covered with gold dust . . .'

Bacon stopped me by holding up his right hand and wagging the index finger. 'You believed such testimony?' he demanded. 'A story told by one man about another man's story?'

I said: 'My Lord, I read Albujar's deposition with my own eyes. Then I compelled Berrio to assist me in drawing up a map, using everything to hand – the papers taken from the Spanish ship, his own personal expeditions, the Moor's account.'

'But of course you did not find El Dorado,' Bacon said. 'You did not even discover this lake.'

'The lake, if it exists,' I said carefully, 'must be more like an inland sea than anything we English would call a lake. It is said to be more than 600 miles long and to consist of salt water. Something like the Caspian, I suppose.'

Bacon pushed at the brim of his tall hat, then passed his pale hand wearily across his forehead, which was lightly beaded with perspiration although the evening air was cold. '*If it exists . . . It is said to be . . .*' he repeated scornfully. 'Sir, I find it hard to believe that his Majesty has released you from the Tower to go in search of something so nebulous!'

I stopped in my tracks. I traced circles with my cane on the grass at my feet. Then I chuckled. 'His Majesty hasn't,' I said. 'And you know it.'

Two tiny spots of crimson appeared in Bacon's cheeks. He tried without success to disguise his embarrassment by making his face a puzzled mask. 'So why all this El Dorado nonsense?' he blustered.

'*You* brought up the subject,' I pointed out mildly. 'For my part, I explored the Orinoco pretty damned thoroughly in '95. Old Berrio evidently thought of that river as the road to El Dorado. I found nothing that would confirm his view. On the other hand, I found nothing that would utterly deny it. The next year I sent my man Laurence Keymis back to look again. And the year after that, Captain Leonard Berry. Neither of them could find the lake, although – for what it is worth – both of them reported that the Indians call the lake Parima and call El Dorado by the name of Manoa.'

'I do not see that it matters what names are given to non-existent places,' Bacon said irritably.

I shrugged. I said: 'It was Sir Thomas Roe's expedition six years ago which finally convinced me that even if Manoa does exist it is not worth looking for. Not by an old man, anyway. I subscribed £600 of the £2500 Roe's voyage cost, so I got detailed reports of everything. His brief was to scour the entire Guiana littoral for some tangible evidence of the lake and the city. He went 300 miles up the Amazon, then worked his way north along the coast towards the Orinoco. He spent more than a year penetrating the high country by means of canoe journeys up the various rivers. He followed the Wiapoco in particular, negotiating more than a score of rapids in the direction which the Indians assured him was the way to El Dorado. Roe came back down and home with the usual story. He had *nearly* found it all. But never quite.'

We had reached the end of the long avenue, and stood now in the shadow of the bright-leaved tree, a laurel. I picked a leaf from it and rolled the leaf to and fro between my thumb and forefinger. After a silence, Bacon at last said: 'So?'

'So El Dorado is not my destination,' I replied. 'I have no ambitions to see the Inga. I am going only to collect a little gold dust.'

'You still believe there *is* gold out there?' Bacon asked.

'I know so,' I said.

'Whereabouts?' Bacon asked.

'In the foothills,' I said, 'so to speak.'

'The foothills?' Bacon repeated. 'The foothills of what?'

'Of Manoa,' I said.

The Lord Chancellor took a deep breath. 'Your mind seems disordered,' he complained. 'One might be forgiven for thinking that you must be suffering from some sort of gold fever. In the one sentence, you deny El Dorado. In the next, you speak of its approaches.' He removed his hat and fanned his pallid face with it.

When he went on, he was looking elsewhere. 'As I understand it,' he said, 'you have in fact promised the King that you know the location of certain gold mines. Is that correct?'

'Yes,' I said.

'Where?' he demanded.

'Oh, up the Orinoco,' I said.

'But the Spaniards are there,' he protested. 'They have made settlements.'

'Yes,' I said.

'Yet you have given your word to the King –' Bacon began.

'That I shall not kill or cross swords with any Spaniards,' I said, finishing his sentence for him.

'It will prove impossible!' Bacon exclaimed.

'We shall see,' I said.

I sprinkled the dust of the broken leaf from my fingers. I was enjoying the Lord Chancellor's bafflement. '"Brightness falls from the air,"' I said. 'You recall those verses Nashe wrote in the time of the plague?'

Bacon shook his head, then put his hat back on it.

'"I am sick, I must die,"' I droned. '"Lord, have mercy on us!"' I smiled at his confusion. 'I quote, my Lord. A bad habit.'

Bacon would not look at me.

I said: 'But now it is my turn to question you. I would value your advice as Lord Chancellor. Unofficially, of course –'

'Of course,' Bacon said, still avoiding my eye.

'Very well then,' I said. 'A simple question. What is my legal position?'

'Legal position?' Bacon shivered with false laughter. 'Why, sir, to be master of the sea is an abridgement of a monarchy!'

I flicked at the grass with my cane. I said: 'Don't turn an old friend aside with new aphorisms. As I pointed out to you over dinner, my Commission from King James omits the usual words "trusty and well-beloved" in referring to me as his servant. That can only mean that his Majesty is still displeased with me. My Lord, I shall be frank with you. You know I am forbidden to show my face at Court. Should I not try and purchase a formal pardon from the King before sailing?'

Bacon blinked. 'Not at all,' he said smoothly. 'Money is the knee timber of your voyage, as you have told me. So keep every precious penny you have raised for your ships and their victualling. A pardon is a mere formality.'

I pressed him: 'But would I not be the stronger for having it?'

Bacon said: 'You seem to me to have a full and sufficient pardon already for all that is past – the King having made you his Admiral, and given you his Commission of command. That Commission grants you both freedom to sail and judicial authority over others who sail with you. In doing so, it cancels out your former offences.'

I said: 'But why has the King not added a pardon in so many words?'

Bacon licked his thin lips. 'I cannot speak for the King,' he said. 'However, I say again that it seems to me that the issue of the Commission – which vests in you the power of life and death – is equivalent to a pardon.'

I was still not content. 'Specifically, then, does it cancel out my conviction and sentence for high treason?'

Bacon shut his eyes. Then he said: 'Your Commission as Admiral seems to me as good a pardon for all former offences as the Law of England can afford you.'

'My Lord, I count you as my friend, and no fool,' I said. 'Are you telling me I need not purchase a pardon?'

Bacon sighed. 'Sir, I am sufficiently your friend and no fool as to answer that I never heard that question.'

'Not even when I have asked it of you twice?' I said.

'Have you?' Bacon opened his eyes and frowned, tasting his lips. 'Well, there you are,' he said. 'A proof of my friendship and unfoolishness. I had already forgotten the first time.'

'Shall we go back?' I said. 'My lame leg pains me.'

We retraced our steps through the gardens, moving more briskly now for the air was chill and we walked most of the way in silence. Bacon stopped once to sniff an early blossoming white rose. As he did so he said: 'I shall remember that you took the trouble to consult me. There is little friendship in the world, and least of all between equals.' He let the rose fall back in place in the bush, but carelessly, so that petals flaked from it onto the darkening ground. 'What will you do,' he asked casually, 'if after all this effort and expenditure you fail to find your gold mines in Guiana?'

I laughed. 'Oh, we'll go after the Spanish treasure fleet,' I said.

'You know that it sails every year from Havana to Cadiz with about eight millions in silver.'

'You will do *what*?' Bacon said.

'The Plate Fleet,' I said. 'We'll capture the Plate Fleet.'

'But then you will be pirates,' Bacon said.

'Hardly pirates,' I said, still laughing. 'Who ever heard of men being pirates for millions?'

We had come back to Gray's Inn Court and I was moving to take my leave of the Lord Chancellor, thanking him for the dinner and the advice, when Bacon said suddenly and (so it seemed) on impulse: 'You know, I never knew the late Queen very well. Certainly not as well as I would have wanted to.'

It was an awkward statement, and he stood there awkwardly in the twilight, having made it.

I said: 'Perhaps none of us knew her very well. Perhaps none of us knew her as well as we would have wanted to. I have often wondered. Goodnight, my Lord.'

Gold and blood. Pardons and piracy. I lied, Elizabeth. I knew you as well as I wanted to. Better. Or should it be worse?

Having written the above, I took a turn around the deck to clear my head.

The mainland seems to smoulder in the sun.

I asked Captain Parker, as Keymis asked me to. Captain Parker said Wat was spoiling for a fight. He said my son was very like me when young. He said Wat was envious and ashamed of my reputation and needed to prove himself to himself. He said a lot of other stuff which I forget.

3

'Guattaral,' the Indian says.

I have to keep telling him that is the way the Spaniards say my name. That he must do better. That I am Sir Walter Ralegh.

A lesson he did not learn this afternoon.

'Don Guattaral,' he persisted. 'You are a pirate. You are a very great pirate.'

'I am no pirate,' I said. 'Your Spanish masters may have called me a pirate, but I am not.'

'What are you then?' he demanded. 'If you are not a pirate, what are you?'

A question I found difficult to answer. He asked it in all serious-ness, you see. He is a curious mixture of intelligence and simplicity, this Christoval Guayacunda.

We were standing on deck. The Indian seems to take pleasure in examining the fittings of my ship. Yet it is not so much a matter of their novelty to him. He touches everything confidently, without surprise.

'Do I look like a pirate?' I said.

He shrugged. 'What do pirates look like?' he said. 'I have never seen one before.'

'What *do* I look like?' I said.

'An old man,' he said.

'Go on,' I said.

'An old tired man who has to walk with a stick,' he said.

It's true. And how strange my face must look to him. I know that these Indians have ancient legends which speak of gods with bearded white faces coming to them from the east. But the face which looks back at me from my cracked shaving-mirror can hardly

29

so intimidate or impress. It is more like the face of a ghost than the face of a man. It is assuredly not like the face of any imaginable god. My face is pale and pinched and drawn, the skin so tight across my cheek-bones that you can see them clearly, my eyes like burnt-out pits. My beard is silver and badly cut because my hands shake when I take the scissors to it.

'Let us say that this old man with the stick is some kind of a gentleman,' I suggested.

'What is that?'

'Wholly gentleman, wholly soldier,' I said. I was quoting my own ambitious but evasive description of myself at my trial for treason in 1603.

We had been conversing in Spanish, of course, since that is the language we have in common. But I said those particular words *wholly gentleman, wholly soldier* in English, and now the Indian tried to imitate their sounds.

'What is that *wholly*?' he said.

He made it sound like *woolly*. Or *holy*. Or some bastard cross between the two. Which no doubt, in this context, it may be.

I let it go.

'You then,' I said. 'What are *you*?'

He had been trying his strength against one of the capstan bars. Now he stopped this game and drew himself up to his full height, which is not very high – about an inch or so above five feet, I'd say, and stout in proportion.

'Christoval Guayacunda,' he said. 'A man. What you would call an Indian. A native of what the Spaniards call their New Kingdom, or Granada. Born in the Valley of Sogamoso. Of the Chibcha tribe.'

The sun made his skin shine like copper.

'That is what I am,' he said.

'Not so,' I said. 'That is *who* you are. I could as easily say that I am Walter Ralegh, a man, what you would call a pale-face, a native of England, born in Devonshire, of the Saxon tribe. Those answers would not match the question either.'

The Indian nodded slowly. His head is large and round, his dark eyes full of wit and intellection.

'Very well then,' he said. 'I used to be the servant of Don Diego Palomeque de Acuña.'

'And I used to be the servant of a very great Queen,' I said. 'I was the Captain of her Guard.'

'Yes,' the Indian said. 'I knew that.'

'Did you? Who told you?'

The Indian said: 'It is common knowledge. When I first came to San Thomé in Palomeque's service, I was told that you had journeyed up the Orinoco many years ago. I was told that you had gathered all the tribes together and told them that you had been sent by your Queen to set them free from the Spaniards. They spoke of you with awe. They said that you were the servant of a Queen who was the great Casique of the North, a virgin Queen who had more casiques under her than there are trees in the Island of Trinidad.'

'Casique,' I said. 'It is a long while since I heard that word.'

'It is what the Spaniards call the chiefs of our tribes.'

'I know. What else did the people of the Orinoco say?'

'That you would one day return,' the Indian replied. 'That you had given your word to do so.'

'Which word I kept.'

'Of course,' said the Indian matter-of-factly. 'Men do not give their word often. When they do, they keep it.'

I could detect no irony in his tone. Indeed, his every phrase was straightforward and considered and came with a power of truth behind it. There is a definite nobility about this Indian which strikes me forcibly. I was curious about his background, but held my tongue. For the moment, for my part, I saw my task as to win his confidence.

'I am no longer the servant of that great Queen,' I admitted. 'Queen Elizabeth is dead.'

'Death makes no difference,' the Indian said. 'You are still her man.'

This statement took me aback. There was such truth in it. I found I could say nothing for a while. I put one hand on top of the other on the knob of my cane. Both hands were trembling badly with the ague. I was racked by a spasm of coughing. My cane danced and chattered where it touched the deck.

The coughing fit passed.

'I came back here as the servant of another Casique of the North,' I said. 'King James.'

The Indian looked at me impassively. 'Yet this same King James kept you for many years in a tower, so I was told by Don Palomeque. You were his prisoner.'

'Yes.' I went on hurriedly, not wanting to waste time defending my position by having to explain that the charges of treason brought against me had been rigged by my enemies. 'But you,' I said. 'What are you *now*?'

The Indian brought his big hands together as though their wrists were shackled.

'Guattaral's prisoner,' he said.

I did not like this answer.

I said: 'Keymis said you joined us of your own free will.'

'The man who looked sideways? He is dead.'

'Yes,' I said.

'Guattaral killed him,' the Indian said.

'No,' I said.

'I saw his body go into the river in the sack this morning.'

I shivered in the sun, recalling the funeral service which could have meant nothing to this Indian. The Reverend Mr Samuel Jones had charitably ignored the fact that Keymis, as a suicide, should be denied the proper obsequies of the Church. Somehow, the reduction of that rite to the crude image of a corpse tossed overboard in a sack made Laurence Keymis very vivid in my remembrance. No doubt the sharks would be at him by now. 'These are pearls that were his eyes . . .' A pearl with a cast in it.

I said briskly: 'This isn't a river. This is a channel of the sea. A very great sea. An ocean. The Atlantic Ocean.'

The Indian looked puzzled. I realized that the concept of any expanse of water wider than a river or a lake was beyond his experience. Wherever he had been before he was captured by the Spaniards and compelled into the service of the Governor of San Thomé, it had to have been somewhere inland. His build and stature certainly suggested that his tribe came of mountain stock. But I tried to get back to the point.

'You are not my prisoner,' I insisted. 'You came back down the river because you wanted to. Why did you want to?'

The Indian leaned his broad shoulders against the spindle of the capstan. He did not answer my question. He said nothing for a while. When he spoke at last it was as if he had measured in his head what I had said to him and decided, on balance, that the conversation was worth continuing. All the same, he addressed himself not so much to me as to the spice-laden breeze which blew across the estuary from the mainland.

'Guattaral did not kill the man who looked sideways?'

'That is correct,' I said. 'Keymis killed himself.'

'Why?' the Indian asked softly.

I said: 'Keymis killed himself because he no longer wished to live. Because he had lost his honour. Do you understand that? Honour?'

The Indian looked me straight in the eyes.

'I understand honour,' he said. 'I know honour. My people are a proud people. We had our lands before the Incas came.'

'Where are they?' I said. 'The lands of your tribe?'

The Indian hesitated for a moment. Yet his silence seemed inspired by deliberation rather than any uncertainty. His eyes became incalculable. He said: 'Around Lake Guatavita.'

The word for some reason sent a shiver down my spine. It was not the ague, I swear it.

'Guatavita?' I said.

'Yes.'

'I have never heard of this Lake Guatavita. It must be far away?'

'Yes.'

'Over the mountains? To the west?'

'Yes.'

It was in my mind, of course, to ask him if there was gold in that region. But the moment was wrong. I sensed that by the way his eyes had darkened, the wit drained out of them, as though they now looked inward, dwelling upon some image in his head rather than upon me, his interlocutor. I saw that I would have to win his confidence before I could put any questions to him about the possibility of gold in the lands that he came from. I admit that it occurred to me also that it would be useless to try to torture such information out of him. The Spaniards had crucified Indians in their quest for El Dorado. They had not obtained a single jot of worthwhile information by such methods.

I contented my curiosity by saying: 'Then how is it that you came to San Thomé?'

The Indian said nothing. But he hung his head and for the first time in my brief experience of him there was something like shame in the way he held himself.

'Don Palomeque,' I pursued, 'what was he like?'

The Indian spat.

But he still remained silent.

I said: 'I take it that Palomeque was a bad master. So you are better off now? You were glad that my soldiers killed him? Is that why you came back with Keymis?'

The Indian wears a curious pointed cap on his head. It looks as if it were woven from the grey fibres of some plant – the *cabuya* perhaps. He removed this cap from his head and smoothed his hair with his hand. His hair is as black as a raven's wing, and as glossy, worn long, reaching down to his shoulders.

'Guattaral is mistaken,' he said in a flat voice. 'His soldiers did not kill Palomeque.'

This statement astonished me. I was speechless.

'Palomeque was killed by his own,' the Indian went on. 'There were those in the Spanish fort who wanted Guattaral to take it without bloodshed. There were those who hated Don Diego. Who would have opened the gates for Guattaral's men without fighting. But Guattaral's son ran forward shouting in the moonlight –'

I turned on my heel. I did not want to hear any more. At the top of the stairs leading to my cabin something made me stop and look back at the Indian. He had put his cone-shaped cap back on his head. He was gazing up at the sun with wide open eyes. I never saw anyone do that before without going blind.

This evening I could stand it no longer. I dined in my cabin with my nephew George. He had charge of our land forces that went up the Orinoco. To be brief, he held that command because he was older than Wat, and possesses courage and initiative. But, truth to tell, nephew George has precious little else to commend him. He is a boisterous beef-witted creature, with the manner of an overgrown schoolboy. If he keeps a stiff upper lip it is only to hold up his weak flabby chin.

When I put it plainly to George that Keymis had said that my son was responsible for the fighting at San Thomé, he denied it at first. Then I asked him if it was true that the Governor of the fort had been killed by his own men. He blustered, thumping the table with his clenched fists. I persisted in pursuit of the truth. He grew dangerously quiet, then broke down and wept like a child and admitted all.

It appears that in the first place he and Keymis were dominated by Wat from the moment our party passed out of my sight. It was Wat who insisted on pushing so far up the river.

There was a strong adverse current. They proceeded slowly. Captains Wollaston and Whitney ran their ships aground (George thinks deliberately) on a sandbank. They did not rejoin the expedition until after the fall of San Thomé. Keymis was volubly uneasy but ineffectual. George was brow-beaten by Wat, who taunted him for being a coward when he expressed doubts concerning their venture. As for the men – they were cockscombs and couldn't care less whose orders they half-obeyed just as long as they had a prospect of getting some loot out of it.

As they drew nearer San Thomé, Keymis pulled himself together and conferred secretly with George behind Wat's back. They sent spies on ahead. The spies came back with news that there was widespread and profound hatred of Palomeque, who ruled the fort like a tyrant. There was a faction in San Thomé willing to betray him and arrange a peaceful surrender – especially since the fort contained only about forty soldiers fit for active service, and our forces (even without the contingents aground on the sandbank) numbered over two hundred. The leader of the Spanish conspirators was one Geronimo de Grados. We were to advance and pretend to attack, but the siege would be a game – under cover of which Palomeque could be killed by his own men.

Late in the afternoon of the 2nd of January our squadron anchored at the creek called Aruco some three miles this side of the town. Troops were disembarked. Then the three remaining ships sailed on upstream until they came exactly opposite San Thomé, where they dropped anchor. The ships were promptly fired on by two mortars, no doubt on Palomeque's orders, but the mortars missed, perhaps because Grados had supervision of their firing. Meantime our soldiers marched in battle order straight at San Thomé until they were within half a mile of it. George then ordered a halt. He and Keymis were confident that the faction within the town would open the gates for them.

Darkness fell. Tensions mounted. George found it hard to keep our soldiers in check. It was even harder, he says, to stop Wat from precipitate action. He claims that at this point he told Wat of the plot he and Keymis had hatched with Geronimo de Grados. Wat scoffed at it. But he consented to wait in hope that the dissident Spaniards would either fling open the gates, or give our English some signal for the mock-siege to begin.

Nothing happened.

My nephew claims that Wat then started drinking. It is not impossible. His usual habit, like my own, was not to drink, but I can believe that at this moment, alone with himself in the heart of the dark continent, and about to be put to the test, Wat might have reached for the wine bottle. Impatience would be burning him up, and how was he to know whether Keymis and his cousin had not been misled by the Spanish conspirators? At such a time, in such a situation, had I been his age I can imagine that I could have sought solace in alcohol. None knows better than I, it is terror that holds a man sober. Terror of what is within. When equal terrors threaten from without, then drink can seem a suitable way of meeting them. I can say this because I have been damnably drunk in my day, and lived to regret it. For many years now I have drunk water where others drank wine, and held myself sober when others fell down. Yet, as I say, I can sympathize too much with my poor son to condemn him if indeed it is true that as my nephew says he reached for the bottle.

Drunk or sober, just before one o'clock in the morning of Saturday the 3rd of January it all got too much for Wat. He went wild. He charged forward on his own, sword in hand, straight at the Spanish quietly sitting watching the English line in the starlight. As he ran he shouted, George reports, and the exact words he shouted were: *'Come on, my hearts! Here is the mine that you must expect! They that look for any other mine are fools!'*

According to my nephew, Wat did not die (as Keymis said) with a dozen Spanish pikes in him. He was cut down by a Spanish captain, one Arias Nieto. Our trash of soldiers then lost their heads and flung themselves into attack. Keymis and my nephew did their best to honour the pact with the rebel Grados and his party. Finding that they could not contain their own troops, they shouted out for Grados to identify himself before it was too late. This he did, pointing out (George claims) places and persons not to be fired at. But the men fought and fired indiscriminately, storming the gates, gaining entrance and burning several buildings to the ground. Grados and his followers ran away. We lost their trust, my nephew claims, first because of Wat's wild individual action, and then because our soldiery were plainly out of control.

In any event, our forces outnumbered the Spaniards many times over, and the fort was easily taken. The fighting was over in a matter of minutes.

Keymis found Palomeque dead in the square. He had a hatchet between his shoulder-blades, and the left side of his head had been split open down to the teeth. His body (curiously) had been stripped naked, and his uniform was nowhere to be discovered. An Indian woman identified him at dawn. Also a Spanish priest named Francisco de Leuro, who was a cripple and so unable to run away with the others. There is apparently no doubt that it was Palomeque. He was a great gross man, much larger in girth and stature than anyone else in the fort. George reports that neither the priest nor the remaining Indians and black slaves made any display of grief over his corpse. It seems that the Governor was hated and feared by just about every inhabitant of San Thomé. There had even been an attempt to murder him some weeks before our coming, on the part of a Captain Francisco de Salas. Unfortunately, neither Salas nor Grados nor any other Spaniard was prepared to trust us now. Keymis and my nephew took possession of a fort that was deserted save for the priest, the Indian servants, and the blacks.

Some of our scum were already trying to rape the Indian girls. George claims that he put a stop to this only at pistol point.

It was Keymis who found the Indian Christoval in a room in the Governor's house, where he had been left to guard a chest containing the documents relating to Spanish attempts to mine gold in the region, plus the letters from Madrid sent out to warn the outpost of our coming, which bundle included the lists of ships and men written in my own hand and given to King James who had promptly passed them on to Gondomar, the Spanish Ambassador in London. The chest also contained the two small ingots of gold which were all that Keymis fetched back of that commodity.

My nephew tried to belittle the whole thing. 'A mere skirmish', he called it, reminding me that on our side there were only two men killed besides Wat – Captain Cosmor and Mr Harrington. (Captain Thornhurst was badly wounded, but has made a gradual recovery.) As for the Spanish, George insists that apart from Palomeque there were only two other casualties: the Captain Arias Nieto already mentioned as the slayer of my son; and a captain identified by the Indians as one Juan Ruiz Monge. These seem to have been the only Spaniards who remained sufficiently loyal to the Governor to lay down their lives in defence of the fort.

(So: The dead amounted merely to six persons. But I can take no comfort from such arithmetic. Even if the odious Palomeque was murdered by his own men, that leaves two Spaniards killed by us. Which is two Spaniards too many. And one of our English dead was of course Wat . . .)

I asked George what he thought had happened to Grados and the others who deserted. He replied that he had good reason to suppose that they retreated in the direction of the Caroni Falls. If that is true it would account for Keymis's failure to open up the mine there. Grados was not pro-English, my nephew surmises, he was simply pro-Grados. He was probably using us to help him get rid of Palomeque. George suggests that it might then have loomed in the mind of this Grados that it was important, when any Spanish reinforcements came up the Orinoco, that such reinforcements would not suspect that *he* (Grados) was in any way responsible for the killing of the Governor. Therefore he could hardly have returned to parley with us, even if he had wanted to. Such mental abilities as my nephew possesses are predominantly military, and this reasoning convinces me as likely.

There were a few more 'skirmishes' during the twenty-nine days our troops occupied San Thomé. The history of those days, as recounted by George, is altogether miserable. Keymis went around trying to tease information out of those remaining Indians and blacks who spoke Spanish. He learned nothing of the slightest use from this exercise. He vacillated terribly, knowing that he must write to me but unable to summon up the spirit to tell me the appalling news. On more than one occasion he confided in George, announcing that he contemplated suicide, that he was in the position of one who feels he dare not even shut his eyes to sleep, and so forth. My nephew was not sympathetic. All the captains, he says, himself included, were waiting for Keymis to *do* something. In particular, they expected him to lead them to the mine. But Keymis protested that it was no easy matter to go out into the jungle and locate it. He also remarked to George that if he marched the men out at the head of a column and then confessed that he had lost his bearings, the oafs would go beserk. It appears that he decided to obviate that risk by venturing out one night with a hand-picked squadron of his own, probably up the Caroni River in the direction of the Falls. He brought back a little mineral ore which he showed to George and to the wounded Captain Thornhurst. The ore was tried by a refiner. It proved worthless, and was no more spoken of.

Wat was buried with all military honours in the church at San Thomé. Captain Cosmor and Mr Harrington were also given decent burial.

As for Palomeque and his two dead companions, Keymis instructed some Indian women to bury them. But the ground proved too hard. The three corpses were roped together and left in the town square as a warning to those inhabitants of the fort who remained. One night, my nephew says, someone cut the head off Palomeque. Our soldiers were amused. They used it as a football until it fell to bits.

Keymis spent much of his time cross-questioning the Indians and the blacks. He was obsessed with the idea of getting gold from some deposit already known to the Spaniards. One of the papers in the chest discovered in the Governor's residence spoke of a *barranca* further up the Orinoco where there might be gold. Some of the Indians (but not, apparently, the Governor's servant, Christoval Guayacunda, who would say nothing on the subject) told Keymis that this *barranca* was some six or seven miles upriver past the point where the Caroni flows into it. Two small boats were sent by Keymis to investigate – with gentlemen, soldiers, and sailors aboard. My nephew had command of them. He reports that they got no further than a narrow channel between one side of the riverbank and an island which the Indians called Seiba. There they were fired on. Two of our men were killed, six wounded, and the party retreated to San Thomé in confusion. George gives it as his opinion that this was a deliberate ambush, arranged between Grados and his refugees and the Indians who had stayed in the fort.

Keymis now sank into a state of utter nervelessness and despair. My nephew counts it as some kind of achievement that at this point he decided himself to take action, although the action had nothing to do with the search for gold. He took three launches back up the river. The trip was well-managed, from a military point of view, with one boat kept midstream and the other two keeping to the left and right banks respectively. They passed by Seiba island without incident. They took careful soundings of the river as they went, and urged the various Indian tribes which they encountered to rise against their Spanish overlords and prepare for the coming of a great English army. They got as far as the Guarico – covering, George says, a distance of 300 miles in three weeks going up and returning.

When he got back to San Thomé, he found Keymis openly admitting that all had failed in his quest for gold. He says it was Keymis who ordered the fort to be burned down when it became clear that the whole mission had come to nothing. (The crippled Spanish priest perished in this conflagration.) Wollaston and Whitney had turned up from their convenient sandbank. They jeered at Keymis. There was no morale amongst the men at all. The Spaniards were foraging and sniping quite successfully with a consequence that our people were finding it increasingly difficult to get food. More than anything, George says, Keymis seems to have been terrified by the notion that Spanish reinforcements might cut off his only means of retreat – down the Orinoco. Consequently, as soon as the town had been fired, our ships were loaded with what little plunder there was – chiefly, tobacco, and the contents of the chest found in the Governor's house – and they hoisted sail under white flags of truce, at Keymis's insistence, and began the return journey to the sea.

I asked my nephew why he thought it was that the Indian Christoval chose to join us. He said he had no idea.

As they came back downriver, Keymis sat huddled in his cloak, his hat pulled down over his forehead, barely saying a word. He broke his silence just once, when he stood up suddenly and started 'babbling something about Mount Iconuri' (my nephew's own phrase).

Now Mount Iconuri is about fifteen miles inland from a point some twenty-five miles *this side* of San Thomé. In 1595, on my first voyage here with Keymis, an Indian casique called Putijma told me that this mountain is rich in gold. On that same expedition I picked quartz out of the rock with my dagger from a spot on the north bank of the Caroni River, within sight of the Falls. This particular sample was tried by a refiner in London and found to contain a high proportion of pure gold.

In '96 I sent Keymis back to the Orinoco. He reported that the

Spanish seemed very interested in the Caroni region, for they had now built a fort (San Thomé) within miles of it, which fort commanded the approach by the river. At the same time, he told me that he had been advised by friendly Indians that any gold near the Caroni Falls would be difficult to mine, not only because of the Spanish presence but because the terrain there was not propitious, consisting of hard white spar.

However, although the casique Putijma was no longer to be found, Keymis told me that other Indians had led him inland towards Mount Iconuri and assured him that there was indeed gold there, so much gold in fact that specimens could be brought back *without digging*. He showed me grains of gold they had gathered out of the sand of a tiny shallow river, the Macawini, which springs and falls on that mountain.

When Keymis set out up the Orinoco some three months ago he had clear instructions from me to try Mount Iconuri first, and only to attempt an approach to the other site if all else failed.

Am I really to believe that he disobeyed those orders just because Wat insisted on pushing upriver direct to San Thomé, and only started 'babbling' about Iconuri on the way back when everyone had lost faith in him?

Why did my son not believe in any mine at all?

Keymis alone could answer the first question.

Wat the second.

It is the night watch. A sea of ultramarine darkness. Stars like eyes. I must write calmly and coolly in this tropic lunacy. I must use the past to make sense of the present.

My boy, my boyhood.

Do you imagine, do you fancy, Carew, that your father always thirsted for the sea? Do you picture him in childhood as some avid listening lad, wide-eyed and eager to hear sailors' tales of their voyages, of the great green deep, of mermaids and Tritons, of galleons and argosies?

Nothing could be further from the truth.

I do not care for the sea. I never have.

To be blunt about it: Your father is a poor seaman. As far back as I can remember, I suffered always from the most disgusting and gut-stretching seasickness as soon as I passed out of sight of land.

41

Sir Walter Ralegh, that great captain, would rather go round and about and walk over London Bridge than take a wherry from Southwark to Westminster. It was often remarked on.

Make what you will of it. I say that only fools love the sea for the sea's sake. The sea is negligible when it is not cruel. It is nothing, a nothingness the more to be avoided and despised for its always being hungry to appease and satisfy its own deficiencies by stuffing drowning men into its maw. An element without anatomy or lineaments. A salt indefiniteness.

Drake and the others? Frobisher? Hawkins? Fine fellows. And fools. Let them and their like love the sea. I leave it to them.

For myself, I invariably welcomed the prospect of advancing land with a leap of the heart and a widening of the wits if not the stomach. Besides, the sea is *boring*. I was always too quickly bored.

Elizabeth was crowned Queen when I was four years old. Strange thought. But there are stranger.

4

The dockyard rats! They would not return upriver. I tried everything. I commanded. I cajoled. I even offered bribes to the bolder captains. Result: Perfect failure. Not a man there was who was willing to accompany me back up the Orinoco, even when I told them that there was gold to be got without our venturing again as far as the fort at San Thomé.

The plain truth is that they are all afraid. They refused to return up the Orinoco for fear that a Spanish fleet is already under sail across the Atlantic in pursuit of us. They reminded me of the warnings we had from our old Indian friends when we made our first landfall at the Cayenne River last November. It was apparent that early that word had been sent out from Madrid to all the commanders of Spanish settlements in the American continent. The papers which Keymis found in the Governor's chest at San Thomé have served to confirm the worst suspicions of every whey-faced coward that sailed with me.

They had one thought and one thought only – to be gone from Punto Gallo before this threatened Spanish armada descended upon us. I held a council of war. Captain after captain stood up and declared that we must fly away before the Spaniards came. My arguments concerning the location of the gold on Mount Iconuri – demonstrated first with a diagram, then on the actual map – cut no ice with them. Some of them drove me to fury by openly doubting the existence of any mine anywhere. They said that I was fevered. So I was. And am. (Though no longer, thank Christ, do I have to change my shirt three times a day as I did when the sweating sickness was at its worst.) In vain I argued that the fever would pass while the gold remained there for the taking. That while man is transitory, gold is eternal. Even Samuel King, the toughest and most loyal of my captains, gave it as his opinion that we should withdraw for a while from Trinidad and review our prospects from the Leeward Islands.

So the gold remains virgin. Intact. Like you, Elizabeth.

And I write these words at sea to the north of Grenada, southernmost of the Windward Islands, 140 miles or so south-west of Barbados, having sailed some eighty-five miles north by west of Trinidad, from Punto Gallo out of the Gulf of Paria and through the Dragon's Mouth. Our position being 13° north by 61° west.

Grenada: discovered in 1498 by Columbus who named it Conception.

Virgin gold.

Conception island.

But the worst is still to tell . . . For today, 6 March, while we were running with fair fat sails past this isle of Grenada, Captain Whitney and Captain Wollaston broke away with their ships. Deserted. Left my fleet. It is plain that they planned all along to turn pirate. I should have realized this from the moment I learned of their running their vessels aground on that sandbank.

It galls. It leaves a taste of wormwood in the mouth. Especially Whitney's defection. For when we were about to set forth in the first place from Plymouth he came to me saying that he lacked funds to man and victual his ship properly, and I valued him so much that *I sold my silver plate* for him, to meet his bills, and thus ensure his presence in our company.

I trusted Thomas Whitney.

I trusted Richard Wollaston.

And Whitney and Wollaston have spat in my trusting face by turning pirate.

The arithmetic of treachery.

I have only eight ships left.

When I was a boy I liked lists. My first piece of writing, at the age of six or so, was a list drawn up for my father, concerning the lease of tithes of fish and larks at Sidmouth. Later, I was fascinated by the lists of ships and cities that you find in Homer. By the lists of knights in Malory. By the lists of who begat who in the Old Testament of the Bible.

Here, then, I will set down the list of my remaining ships and their captains:

(1) The *Destiny*, 500 tons, captained by myself now Wat is dead.
(2) The *Thunder*, 150 tons, Captain Sir Warham St Leger.
(3) The *Jason*, 240 tons, Captain Charles Parker.
(4) The *Flying Joan*, 120 tons, Captain John Chudleigh.
(5) The *Encounter*, 160 tons, Captain Samuel King.
(6) The *Southampton*, 80 tons, Captain Roger North.
(7) The *Star*, 240 tons, Captain Sir John Ferne.
(8) The *Page*, a pinnace, 25 tons, Captain James Barker.

As for the crews of these vessels I have not the heart to bother counting or listing them. They are gallows-birds almost to a man. Those that sailed away with Whitney and Wollaston will no doubt end their days on the gibbet at Cartagena. Those that remain – both soldiers and sailors – are villains just waiting for the right moment to cut their captains' throats, unless their captains have made known to them their intention to turn corsair at the earliest opportunity.

I have command of a flotilla of turds.

Carew, I began this book by mocking Alexander. It is time to withdraw that mockery. It is time to attempt to express my own self-doubt.

If I do not leave giant chairs behind me wherever I go it is because in my most secret heart I have never been sure that I deserved any chair at all.

As a young man I wore silver armour. Why? Because I could never be certain that my spirit was not some base metal. I needed that silver, that splendour, that show. I used to have pearls loosely sewn on my cloak, so that when I strode through the crowd at Court some of the pearls would scatter. Then I could look over my shoulder with contempt for the small fry who stooped to collect them. But the best pearls were always double-stitched.

I am trying to say something of my own insecurity, my son. Never believe those who would speak of me only in laudatory terms, as some species of hero. If on occasion I have acted heroically – and I have – then it is because I was always afraid of my own capacity for fear. I have resolved my self-doubt in action. It has looked decisive. It was not. My spring was always the spur of the fear of confusion.

The fact of confusion made me determined to resolve my doubt in action.

One anecdote will give you the picture.

Very early in my acquaintance with the Queen I remember taking a diamond and scratching on a windowpane the words: 'Fain would I rise, yet fear I to fall . . .' It was winter. Through the window was a great garden full of snow and frozen fountains. And Elizabeth read the words, as I had intended that she would, and she took up the diamond from the velvet-covered windowseat where I had chucked it as casually as if it had been a stick of chalk, and she wrote underneath, capping my line: 'If thy heart fail thee, rise not at all!'

So I rose, you will say. Yes, I rose and fell, and rose and fell again. But I rose in the first place *because* I feared heights.

How many 'heroes' have there been like that?

More than you think, my son.

How I detest and despise and mistrust that crude concept 'hero' in any case!

Alexander was a fool. His big chairs.

And I am a bigger fool with nothing to sit on but a rotting ship on a stinking sea and no gold and my brains broken and my life in ruins.

5

We have dropped anchor in the Bay of Nevis, in the Leeward Islands, out of the prevailing north-easterly trade winds. Nevis is separated from the slightly larger island of St Kitts by a shallow channel only two miles wide at its narrowest point. In form the island is almost round, and from the sea has the appearance of a perfect cone. It reminds me, in fact, of that curious hat which the Indian Christoval Guayacunda always wears on his head.

I have found a medicinal spring which I bathe in regularly. It must come from deep down, a long dark way down, the water, from under the rock. It must start hot down there, sown hot and sulphurous down there under the black, but by the time it comes out in the bank here, in this place I have scooped clean and keep filled with white pebbles like pearls, it is cold and good. My leg likes it.

My son, I cannot begin to tell you of the beauty of these islands. This new world. New sky. New light like honey and new air like wine.

My old eyes can delight in it despite their tears.

These hellish tears that scald the page I write on.

What do I see but a vision of delight?

A Vision of Delight . . . Such power in words! And how strange are the twists and turns of memory! For the phrase written down had destroyed the earthly paradise I see. Instead of parrots and parrakeets I hear church bells. The blue sky above me becomes that midnight black over London when the firmament flared alive and was hung with sudden light. There were rockets and catherine wheels, incandescent squibs and illuminations by the sackful, whizzers and bangers, jumping jacks and little demons, spinning flowers and sparkling towers and sprinkling showers of green and gold stars by the thousand. The fireworks had been set off from long barges, a fleet of them, moored south across the Thames from the Palace of Whitehall where Ben Jonson's Twelfth Night masque had just finished to polite applause no doubt. *A Vision of Delight*, that's what he called it. But I'd lay all Lombard Street to a china orange that most of the audience found delight as usual only in Inigo Jones's glittering stage-effects and Nicholas Lanier's pounding music, both designed to display the talents of George Villiers as dancer.

Villiers, the King's catamite, stealing the show with his lovely ridiculous legs.

Unless it had been already stolen by Pocohontas, ill-fated princess of the Powhatan Indians, newly come to England from Virginia in company with her husband John Rolfe, and sitting as guest of honour on one side of King James on the royal dais.

Twelfth Night of a year ago, 1617. Now so far away and foreign to me that I could imagine I have been to the moon and back in the meantime.

Wat was there, that night. Wat always danced attendance on Ben Jonson. It was Wat who told me that King James was all eyes for the splendour of poor Pocohontas's medicine man, Uttamatamakin, bronzed and rancid with bear-oil in a scanty leather breech-clout. Wat who told me that Queen Anne danced drunkenly with Villiers, then recently created first Duke of Buckingham, down the gold and silver leaf interior of the Banqueting House, and who swore that he heard the Queen cry:

'My dear dog, you know that to be *amused* is all I ask of life.'

To which Villiers said nothing, just dancing. But Queen Anne went on:

'You must promise me that you'll do something about it. Why, in just a month that wretched ship of his has become the most fashionable lounge in London. More crowded than Paul's Walk. And I've begged on my bended knees, my dear, but the old sow positively refuses to let me visit. He won't even *name* him, or hear his name. He calls him *the man* all the time.'

The old sow being her husband James, by the grace of God the first King of England to bear that name, but the sixth of Scotland.

And *the man* being me.

Perhaps Wat invented the story? But it somehow rings true.

Villiers said nothing, Wat said, by way of direct reply. He just spun away from the Queen, his heavy gold cape swinging out like a wing, then bowed and came back to her, his right hand brushing the lace pompon roses that adorned his outstretched slipper.

Then Wat said he heard him say:

'His hatred for Ralegh is amazing. Do you think it can all be attributed to tobacco?'

While (Wat said) high above them on the dais, King James leered at Uttamatamakin, and the Indian glared back from under a coronet of stuffed snake and weasel skins, and Pocohontas coughed blood into her hand.

Wat liked to tell good stories. It may all have been untrue.

What I know for certain is that the set piece of that tomfoolery of profligate flame was gigantic: a fireworks lion rampant, in honour of James Stuart's fifty years as King of Scotland. (He inherited the Scottish throne at the age of one year and one month.) I can say this without fear of contradiction because it was still visible from London Bridge when two gentlemen strolling from different ends of that bridge met in the middle as if by accident and paused briefly to admire the show. I was one of the two gentlemen. The other was Sir Ralph Winwood, his Majesty's Secretary of State and my good friend; the prime mover, in fact, in the intricate business of obtaining my release from the Tower some ten months previous.

I said: 'The Scotsman's disbelief in the gold is what interests me. Why am I being allowed to sail if he thinks that it's all for nothing?'

'You have a certain standing,' Winwood said, 'a value in the public eye. He's using you in the game he plays with Spain.'

'Dangerous,' I said.

'Very dangerous,' Winwood said. 'For you.'

'For the country,' I said. 'It could lead in the end to war. And I can't believe that our fireworks lion wants that.'

Winwood said: 'You are right, of course. War – outright war – is the last thing he wants. But it suits him at the moment to flirt with the skirts of it. You're being used to snap the Spanish Match. The Scotsman was forced into a corner where that suddenly loomed very likely. It still does. But if you light a keg or two of powder under Spaniards in Guiana then the marriage of Prince Charles and the Infanta will be impossible.'

'That is his real policy?' I said. 'The Scotsman's?'

'Who knows what his *real* policy is?' Winwood muttered. 'Certainly not his Secretary of State. It is even quite probable that he doesn't know himself. He sees all sides of every question. He delights in debate. Coming up with an answer is a different matter. He detests decisions. They remind him of his mother on the block.'

I said: 'Which makes me no more than a pawn in his chess with the Spaniard . . .'

Winwood smiled. 'Hardly a pawn, sir. Your movements were always complicated, as much sideways as forwards. Shall we say that you must be a knight at the least?'

'Knight or pawn,' I said, 'you reckon I'm used by him?'

'Certainly,' Winwood agreed. 'But I think that you knew that. You must consider your position quite clearly. For the Scotsman there is everything to gain from your voyage. For you there is only everything to lose.'

'Except the gold,' I said.

'The gold makes little difference,' Winwood said. 'He doesn't believe in it.'

'Do you?' I said.

Winwood looked down at the dark Thames. 'I was waiting for that one,' he admitted. 'Well, to be plain with you, the gold isn't all that important to me either.'

'What is then?' I said.

'Empire,' Winwood said. 'Your name still lives on among the Indians. I hear every year of Dutch vessels that have been trading up the Orinoco. Everywhere they drop anchor the Indians come aboard hoping that non-Spanish white men means you. You need only inspire them and they will rise against Spain.'

I said: 'And then?'

'Then we will rule them,' Winwood said. 'Rather, we shall guide them. Be their partners in trade, and their educators. It means an honest profit to England, and a great loss to Spain. Even if there's no gold, there's still tobacco.'

I said: 'I agree about the Indians to some extent. The Spaniard rules the New World with a sword in one hand and a crucifix in the other. We could take the whole continent with a few fair words and a dozen kept promises.'

I watched a scatter of fireworks like diamonds over the Tower.

'All the same,' I went on, 'my voyage is more modest and specific.

50

The gold is there. And I aim no higher than to bring some of it back.'

Winwood said: 'Without fighting Spain?'

'I earnestly hope so,' I replied.

Winwood said: 'To be blunt again, sir, I have supported your venture from the start because I see war with Spain coming out of it, sooner or later, one way or another. Such a war is necessary if we are to keep a foothold on the South American continent. Such a war is also necessary to maintain the balance of power in Europe, and discourage any notion the Pope might have of ever getting England back into his fist. How can you believe that you will be able to avoid precipitating such a thing? The Spanish have been adamant on the point. They think they own the Orinoco. There are bound to be hostilities.'

'No doubt,' I said. 'But they will not spring from me. I shall be as peaceable as any Pocohontas. Just you see.'

Winwood took three sharp steps away. Looking over his shoulder, I observed my cousin Sir Lewis Stukeley emerge from the Southwark end of London Bridge. He was being escorted by Robin, my page, who was succeeding in distracting his attention with the aid of a billygoat on a lead.

'Money?' Winwood said.

'No more problems,' I said. 'I owe Pett. He will wait. But there's one important thing you might do for me.'

'Name it.'

'Convince the Scotsman I no longer need a keeper.'

'Your cousin is dangerous?' Winwood said.

I laughed. 'Not at all. The man is an idiot. But I have fish to fry which can't be fried with Stukeley in the kitchen all the time.'

'I'll do my best,' Ralph Winwood promised.

The city crier passed two distinguished gentlemen going their separate ways. 'And so goodnight,' he called, ringing his bell. 'And so goodnight.'

The stick of a final rocket fell on the Bridge at my feet.

Mr Secretary Winwood's best was always pretty damned good. By the end of that month of January last I was relieved of the need to be accompanied wherever I went by my cousin Sir Lewis Stukeley. By the end of February I had established via Captain Faige the connection with Montmorency, Grand Admiral of France, which gives me permission to seek refuge in any French port if I so choose.

And on **March the** 7th I entertained his Excellency the Count Des Maretz, the French Ambassador to London, on board the *Destiny* where she was lying in the Thames, and had his assurance that his patron Richelieu looked favourably upon my venture.

But the French contingent never turned up to join my fleet as promised. And neither was Queen Anne allowed to do the fashionable thing.

This evening I called my remaining captains together to dine on the *Destiny* in my cabin. I put it to them, over a well-grilled but still scarce congenial dolphin, that as I see the situation we have three possible courses of action left open to us.

'First,' I said, 'we could set sail either for Virginia or Newfoundland. In either place we could clean and revictual and trim our ships, before returning to Guiana to justify this voyage by getting the gold that Keymis missed.'

There was silence. It was plain that not one of them has any surviving confidence in the gold. Then John Chudleigh said: 'That would be suicide. We know now that the citizens of San Thomé were forewarned of our coming. The documents found in the Governor's house spoke also of troops from New Granada and the Main being sent to repel us. We should count ourselves lucky that the Spaniard is lazy. By now the whole Orinoco will be swarming with them.'

'Not to speak of the Spanish fleet ordered up from Brazil,' said Sir Warham St Leger.

The other captains concurred with these judgements. I considered them cowardly, but said nothing.

Instead, I went on: 'Very well then, how would it be if we pursued the same initial course – for Virginia or Newfoundland – but that then when our ships are refurbished we lie off about the Isles of the Azores.' I paused, enjoying the puzzlement on their faces. 'There,' I said, 'we could wait for Spanish plums to fall into our laps. I mean, gentlemen, say a straggler or two of the homeward-bound Plate Fleet.'

You could have cut the dolphin-odoured air with a knife.

At last, Charles Parker said: 'I can't believe this. I never thought I'd live to see the day Sir Walter Ralegh calmly announced his intention of turning pirate.'

The others kept their eyes down, looking at their dishes.

I took up an orange and began to peel it with my dagger. I said: 'Was Drake a pirate?'

No answer.

'Drake took the prime carrack of Spain,' I went on, 'the *Cacafuego*. She was laden with twenty-six tons of pure silver. Worth about half a million English pounds. Was this piracy?'

Sir John Ferne cleared his throat. 'No,' he said carefully. 'Privateering, rather.'

I nodded. I finished peeling the orange.

'Letters of marque,' Parker mumbled. 'To play the privateer one has to hold letters of marque. It's legitimate then.'

'Drake had no such letter from the Queen,' I pointed out. 'But he was never a pirate. He sailed under an English flag. He brought the silver back to England and the Queen took her share.' I split the orange into segments and popped two into my mouth. When I had finished eating them, and no one had disputed what I had said, I went on: 'The distinction between piracy and privateering is a fine one, but as I see it clear-cut. Piracy is theft for personal gain. Privateering is justifiable war at sea by a merchant ship against the trade of an enemy.'

'But England is not at war with Spain,' Captain North said.

I swallowed another segment of the orange. 'Spain is at war with us,' I replied. 'Spain has ignored the peace-treaty of 1604 as far as the New World is concerned. Spain has resisted peaceful Dutch and English vessels, traders and settlers alike, in these waters. Spain has deliberately and treacherously broken the peace with regard to our present voyage. Consider, gentlemen. Their spy Gondomar instructed his masters in Madrid regarding the very tonnage of our vessels. They were not men enough to send word back to England that if we sailed up the Orinoco they would fire on us. Instead, they planned – as Mr Chudleigh just now told us – to march troops overland to take us by surprise. And – as Sir Warham St Leger just reminded you – a fleet to cut off our retreat if they could. It is Spain that has broken the peace.'

'By killing three men?' James Barker burst out.

I turned to him, crushing the rest of the orange in my clenched fist.

'By killing two men and a boy,' I said. 'And the boy was a relative of mine.'

Barker blushed.

Then Samuel King said: 'The Admiral is right. It is the Spaniard who has broken the peace. We could go for the Plate Fleet under English flags and bear any spoil back to King James and no man would dare call us pirates.' He hesitated. When he continued his voice was almost apologetic. 'But the Plate Fleet never sails without a powerful escort. We have just seven ships and a pinnace. The odds against our success would be astronomical.'

I nodded.

'Quite so. We would have about as little chance as we had against the Spanish Armada.'

There was a shamed and embarrassed silence when I reminded them of that. But I could see that the prospect of attacking the Plate Fleet filled all of them with fear.

'You began by saying that we had *three* alternatives,' Chudleigh murmured at last. 'What is the third?'

'To go home,' I said.

'We could sail for a French port,' Sir John Ferne said. 'You have Montmorency's word —'

'To go home,' I said.

I stood up. I emptied my hands of the juice of the orange. It trickled on the crisp white cloth like blood.

'Think about it, gentlemen,' I said.

Carew, I am weary. But I want to set down here a word about Wat. To keep your brother's memory before you. To delineate his image. I would not idealize or idolize it. He would not have wanted that. Not your elder brother. Not my younger self.

Two stories.

The first you may know already? I will tell it here anyway. You will not have heard its aftermath, for Wat told me that only when we were moored at Kinsale last June, weather-bound by contrary winds.

But first the part you may already know. Five years ago, when I was still in the Tower, Wat journeyed to Paris in company with his tutor Ben Jonson. Jonson was always a great drinker. It was no difficult matter for Wat to get him so drunk that he neither knew nor cared what he was doing. Then, when your brother had made the poet ludicrous with wine, he had that corpulent body loaded on a cart, and he paid some labourers to draw the cart through the streets of Paris. Wat walked alongside it, making the labourers stop at every corner, and especially outside churches. Then he shouted: 'Roll up, roll up! Roll up and see the living image of the Crucifixion! Jonson as Jesus! The Poet Laureate in his best masque yet! Roll up! Roll up!'

He was fortunate that no officer of the law could understand his English. Such blasphemy may be a burnable offence in France for all I know. At all events, he carried this jape off without arrest. When the story got back to your mother she laughed it off, saying that I was much the same when young. It annoyed me when first I got wind of it in the Tower. Now it neither angers nor amuses me. It is Wat to the T. I beg leave to doubt that it was ever me, but then Bess may know me better than I know myself.

At any rate, the aftermath. And this is curious. Know then that on the day that I was released from the Tower – which was the 19th of March two years ago – Wat was not at your mother's house in Broad Street to welcome me home. When I asked Bess where he was, she whispered three words in my ear so that cousin Stukeley (my keeper) should not overhear them. *'Sowing wild oats.'* That was what she said.

I was furious at this. I was especially annoyed because again your mother saw fit to compare Wat's disgraceful absence with my own behaviour when I was young. However, I said nothing to him when he did at length come home that very evening. Indeed, the subject was never mentioned until he brought it up one afternoon at Kinsale.

We were sitting on top of the Old Head gazing out to sea. I was foolishly shading my eyes with my hand to scan the horizon for Faige and the promised French ships. Wat was blowing a dandelion clock. There was a something awkward and hangdog in his aspect. Suddenly he said:

'Surely you see why?'

'See why what?' I said.

'Why I was not there to greet you at the house in Broad Street,' he said.

His tone was most pathetic. It touched my heart. I could not bring myself to look at him, so I went on with the performance of examining the horizon.

'Tell me,' I said. 'I would like to understand.'

'I suppose I know him better than I know you,' Wat muttered.

'Know who?'

'Ben Jonson,' Wat said.

'You were with Ben Jonson that day?'

'All of it,' Wat said.

'Drinking?' I said. 'Whoring?'

Wat tossed away the dandelion stalk. 'I don't drink,' he said. 'Any more than you do.' There was a moment's silence, then he went on: 'As for the other item, I daresay I'm not so very unlike you in that regard either.'

I remember scowling at the light on the water and saying nothing.

Wat said: 'You are incalculable. He isn't. You are unfathomable. But I know how deep he is to the very pint!'

I said: 'Ben Jonson, rare as he may be, is not sailing to the New World to find gold. Let me hear no more about it.'

But Wat wanted to confess. I don't know why. He had to tell me how he had spent that bleak March day of my release from the Tower. And it was curious, what he told, because it was an almost exact repetition of the adventure in Paris which he knew had annoyed me.

They started drinking in the morning, Wat reported. He even took pleasure in remembering the names of the taverns where they had drunk. The Boar's Head, the Poultry, the Rose, the Three Cranes, the Mermaid, the Mitre which was next door to the Mermaid, the Nag's Head at the corner of Friday Street, the Razor and Hen, the Leg and Seven Stars, the Eagle and Child. He reeled off the names like a penitent listing his separate sins. Wat shared my liking for lists. The names of those taverns seemed burned on his memory. And now they are burned here on mine. As if I took his sins from him in that moment of confession in Ireland, and made them my own.

(Yet I make it sound too grim. There was relish in his recitation also. Just reeling off the tavern names seemed somehow to serve to raise his spirits.)

Jonson had drunk beer and wine and brandy. Wat drank only water. Jonson was dead drunk by late afternoon, and Wat was stone-cold sober. This, he assured me, was the usual pattern of their escapades.

Strange dissipation! But, yes, I can see myself in this. I did the same with Ben Jonson in my day. And, before him, with a better poet, a wilder spirit: Christopher Marlowe.

Anyway, Wat said, he eventually took a wheelbarrow from the yard of a tavern called the Goat in Boots. He needed it because poor Ben was no longer capable of walking. So his former tutor and surrogate father lay sprawled in the wheelbarrow while Wat pushed his way through Eastcheap. He kicked his mustard-coloured boots in the air, Wat said. He clasped a bottle of Canary wine in each fist, and there was another bottle of it plugged between his lips. Still staring out to sea, I could picture the scene vividly enough. Ben has a belly like a hill and a face like a map of the Indies, all boils for islands and pox-marks for sea-currents. His hair is red, his beard a rustier red.

I can picture Wat too, for you. He would no doubt have been wearing his favourite white cloak. He always looked every inch a brazen dandy. His beard turned up naturally, as mine did long ago. He wore one ear-ring dangling from his ear-lobe. His shoulders (remember, Carew, the day I caught you imitating this in the mirror?) – Wat's shoulders always looked as if he had just shrugged them and forgotten to bring them down.

He told me he pushed that wheelbarrow with its burden of potulent poetry down Milk Street, up Wood Street, along Hosier Lane. And (here is the curious thing) in his head, Wat told me, he stopped at every corner, cupped his hands to his mouth, and shouted the blasphemies he had shouted out loud in the streets of Paris. All that nonsense about Jonson being a better image of the Crucifixion than anything to be found in any Romish church.

Wat might have been a wag. But he was not a fool. He shouted the words in imagination only. London was different. In London, his sacrilege would be understood.

When they reached the churchyard of St Mary-le-Bow, Wat decided to rest. He trundled the wheelbarrow into the graveyard. Jonson had fallen asleep. The bottle had dropped out of his mouth. He was snoring, Wat said.

So Wat sat down between the shafts, and yawned, and leaned his cheek against his knuckles. Then he took a silver pipe from his pocket, filled it with tobacco from a pouch, set tinder to the tobacco and lit it. He sat smoking ambitiously, trying to blow rings.

(You catch the strangeness of this story, Carew? Here is Wat imitating me, his father, in dress and manner and habit, while having a sort of negative icon of me, drunk as I would never be, to hold up for mockery in a wheelbarrow. And the whole thing carried through on the one day of all days when you would have thought he might have met me honestly, and straightforwardly, with some kind of filial feeling. I catch the strangeness too. But I cannot claim to understand it.)

Well, Wat had hardly settled to enjoy his pipe, he told me, when he heard this shrill voice piping at his elbow. He looked up and he saw a small boy in a black velvet suit. And this boy was chanting:

'Tobacco is bad for you. Smoking is a noxious habit.'

Wat said that it now dawned on him that he had been vaguely conscious of this boy for some while – all the way from the scrivener's shop at the sign of the Spread Eagle in Bread Street. The boy had shoulder-length blond hair. Wat had first noticed him peering out of a lower window of the scrivener's shop, his nose pressed flat against the glass, his face like a white pastry. Ever since then the boy had been creeping along in their wake. And now he had dared to come right up to them. Wat judged him to be about eight or nine years old.

'Smoking is evil,' the boy said.

'Who says so?' Wat demanded.

'My father,' the boy said.

The boy stood squarely, little legs apart, his tiny feet encased in coal-black shoes with modest silver buckles.

He pointed. 'Is that *your* father in the barrow?'

'No,' Wat said. 'That's not my father. That's Ben Jonson. That's the Poet Laureate.'

'He can't really be a poet,' the boy said, dogmatically. 'He's intoxicated.'

'Poets are often drunk,' Wat said.

The boy stamped his foot. 'No, they're not,' he said. 'Poets are temperate persons.'

The boy had eyes like dried prunes, Wat told me.

At this point the Poet Laureate woke up in his wheelbarrow and immediately spilled out of it to show the boy the thumb on his left hand. That thumb has a brand on it.

Ben said: 'You know where I got that brand, boy?'

58

'In prison,' the boy said, without blinking.

'That's right,' Jonson roared. 'I was in prison for killing a man. How about that? I killed a man once in a duel.'

(Carew, this is true. The man he killed was one Gabriel Spenser, of Henslowe's company at the Fortune theatre in Cripplegate. They fought to the death one night in Hogsden Fields.)

'So what do you think of *that*?' Ben demanded.

'Duelling is unlawful,' the boy said. 'Why did you kill him?'

'He was an actor,' Jonson shouted.

'The stage is a breeding ground for many kinds of wickedness,' the boy said. 'But you still should not have killed him.'

'He was a *bad* actor,' Jonson explained. 'He was a *very* bad actor. He was *atrocious*. He ruined a play of mine. He couldn't remember his lines, and those he remembered he murdered. So I murdered him because he had already murdered me. Justifiable homicide for the sake of the nine Muses and in defence of their mother. You know who their mother was, lad?'

'Mnemosyne,' the boy said.

'Meaning?' Jonson demanded, a bit taken aback.

'Memory,' the boy said, shrugging, as if the question was too obvious to be bothered about.

Jonson turned to Wat. 'An excellent boy,' he cried, 'a most learned little lad. I could make a poet of him if he wasn't so constipated.'

The boy said: 'You're not a poet at all. You're a criminal.'

'I'm a poet *and* a criminal, of course,' Jonson replied, wiping his nose with his branded thumb. 'All real poets are criminals. Poetry itself is a crime.'

'That's not so,' the boy said. 'Poetry is a virtue. Poets have to know Greek and Latin and mathematics and music and cosmography. Poetry is truth. Poets are noble creatures.'

Jonson looked up at the sky in despair.

'My step-father was a bricklayer,' he said.

He smiled.

'My wife is a shrew, but honest,' he said.

Then he was sick and then he fell asleep again.

Wat said the boy stood staring at Ben Jonson.

'That man is damned,' the boy said. 'He will go to hell.'

Wat said lightly: 'If he's going to hell then I'll go along with him.'

Wat said the boy then turned and stared at him.

'Yes,' the boy said. 'I fully expect that you will. Blasphemers do.'

He walked off. Soon his neat black velvet suit was just a dot in the distance among the white gravestones.

Dusk came. Wat stood and pissed behind a tomb. 'Roll up!' he called softly to an early owl. 'Roll up and see the Prodigal Son about to go home! Roll up, roll up!'

It wasn't until that moment, Wat told me, that the full implications of what the boy had said sunk in. The boy had called him a blasphemer. But the actual spoken blasphemies had been long ago in Paris. Unless, of course, the boy had meant only that it was blasphemy for Wat to say that he would want to go to hell to keep Ben Jonson company. But Wat was sure the boy meant more than that.

The other story I must tell more briefly. (My eyes are raw with sleeplessness, and the night air is hot and bitter in this cabin where I sit writing by a single candle.)

It concerns the night before we dropped down the Thames on the ebb tide to rendezvous with the rest of our fleet at Plymouth. That would have been the 28th of March, last year. I had been invited, with Wat, and my other captains, to dine with Secretary Winwood at his house on Millbank. Winwood as you know had been a staunch supporter of my venture from the start. But I had been banned from Court since my release from the Tower, and Winwood for his part had needed to be discreet in his meetings with me. However, on this night before the voyage he dared to throw discretion to the winds, and kept open house for us.

I wanted to go alone. I had this premonition that Wat would disgrace me.

'You are a quarrelsome, affronting creature,' I told him. 'Sometimes I am ashamed to have such a bear in my company.'

But Wat stood his ground.

'I have been invited to Winwood's for my own sake,' he insisted. 'I have a right to go, along with your other captains.'

'You can be relieved of that duty,' I said. 'You can remain here in London while I sail without you.'

Wat was furious. 'You wouldn't!' he said.

It was true. I wouldn't. I couldn't. Whatever he said, whatever he did, he was always going to be my son, and I was always going to forgive him. Well, I had plenty to forgive him for that night.

Winwood had gone to considerable trouble to make the meal memorable. In the middle of the round table in the great dining-room was a likeness of the *Destiny*, made of paste-board, bran, saffron, and egg yolks, all well baked, then gilded with bay leaves, and set floating in a dish of claret wine.

The Secretary of State proposed the toast to our voyage, then we all sat down to dinner with our hats on. Wat sat next to me on my right, with Keymis next to me on the other side.

All went well until about halfway through the meal. Wat had been quiet and polite, on his best behaviour. Now, for some reason, a devil of maliciousness spurted up in him. He took advantage of a lull in the conversation. I heard his drawling voice say loud and clear:

'Gentlemen, I woke this morning without the fear of God before my eyes.'

He had got what he wanted. Every face was turned towards him. He had the complete attention of the table.

'So I went to this whore,' Wat continued, his voice sounding clear as a bell. 'She was the hottest whore in London, so I'd heard. I was eager, I can tell you. I kissed her. I embraced her. I put her down upon the bed. I was just about to mount her when she suddenly surprised me by asking me my name. She'd been looking at me strangely all the while, as if she thought she knew me. Well, I was burning for her, and considered this information little enough to give in view of what her naked body promised. So I told her who I was. Next thing, God damn it, what does she do but push me away and start reaching for her petticoats. "What's the matter?" I say. "I can't do it," says she, "it's not right, it's not natural." "What's not right and natural?" I say. She won't answer. She shakes her head. Every time I come at her she pushes me away. Every time I ask her why, she refuses me an explanation. At last, I've got her pinned down on the bed. She won't open her legs. I show her what she's missing. "No, no," says she, "I can't, you mustn't, it's not right, it's not natural." "Why?" I demanded, "why? why? why?" She covers her face with her hands. She's laughing. Then she's weeping. Then she whispers: "*Because your father had me just an hour ago!*"'

Stunned silence.

Then a gust of filthy laughter from Dick Wollaston. And others

61

join the laughing, nervously, and Wollaston's banging the table with his fists.

I turned to Wat and hit him in the face. I hit him hard. His hat went flying off.

They all stopped laughing. They all looked at Wat. They wanted to see him hit me back, of course.

Carew, he didn't.

You know what he did? He threw back his head, tossing his auburn hair. Then he laughed on his own. A brief laugh, a clever laugh. Then he turned to the man sitting next to him on his other side (it was Wollaston, that incipient pirate, I'm pleased to report) and he fetched him a blow just as hard as the one I'd fetched him.

'Pass it on round the table!' Wat cries. 'It will come back to my father in time!'

Wollaston didn't, of course. He just went to retrieve his crumpled hat.

I laughed then. They all laughed.

I laughed till the tears ran down my cheeks.

6

But Wat did not believe in my gold mine. Winwood's indifference and Bacon's scepticism do not matter. But the fact that Wat's dying words declared his disbelief in the gold – that rankles, that puzzles, that disturbs me. It might be taken to explain, of course, why he bullied poor Keymis and George Ralegh into travelling so far upriver. There was a something suicidal in him. He saw himself as my rival. He flung himself into death like a man making love for the first time.

Was Wat, in fact, a virgin? I should not be much surprised if he was, all his loud and vulgar boasting to the contrary. He wanted to be thought a man. But he bragged like a boy.

I say that he saw himself as my rival. It is all very strange. I can understand that he found it difficult to grow to manhood in the shadow of a father who had won some glory in the world's eyes. But Wat's sense of rivalry went deeper and darker than any mere wish to emulate my achievements as a soldier. It was much more personal; it made him match himself against my essence. That night on the way to Winwood's, for instance, he persisted in asking me a number of indelicate questions concerning my relations with the Queen. The subject appeared to obsess him. I had to parry one lewd suggestion after another, as if fighting a duel. At last he came right out with it. Ben Jonson had told him, he said, that Queen Elizabeth had this vaginal deformity, a membrane which made her private parts impenetrable, although Ben being Ben he had added that she tried many men for her delight.

Wat wanted to know: Was I one of them?

I told him I was not.

Which is true. And yet also a lie.

I have offered Keymis's cabin to the Indian. He has to sleep somewhere and I consider this a better solution than having him sling a hammock over the guns down below with the rest of the men. Truth to tell, most of my crew are more savage than this Christoval Guayacunda.

Yet it is doubtful if he appreciates the favour I have granted him. He says little even when directly addressed in the Spanish he can speak very well. His mood is withdrawn though not sullen or uneasy. He conducts himself with a degree of self-possession which both intrigues and repels me. I had anticipated that the further we sailed from his own land the more dependent on my authority he would become. This has not proved so. The more to my displeasure because I still entertain some hope of drawing him out on the matter of the gold.

But this evening, for instance, when I took a turn below decks in pursuit of him, with this end in mind, I found him crouched to examine the trunnions and axletrees of our guns, and before he would enter into any conversation to my liking I had to list for him the names of all our great ordnance and their appurtenances, because he kept silent, pointing to one piece after another, as it were demanding their names without uttering a word.

So I ran through them, for his useless instruction: the cannon royal, or double cannon; the cannon serpentine; the cannon petro; the bastard cannon; the demy cannon; the culverin and the basilisco; the saker, the minion, and the falcon; and so forth, and so forth. I should have left the task to our master gunner, William Gurden; but I was anxious to gain the Indian's confidence.

My effort was wasted. At the end of this inventory or anthology of guns, together with some tedious observations on my part concerning their shooting and other management, when I had by several stratagems steered the subject round to Guiana being like a magazine of all rich metals, the Indian merely grunted, squatting on his hunkers, and remarked:

'Guattaral has it wrong.'

'What do you mean? How have I got it wrong?'

The Indian flicked at the disc-shaped pendant which dangles from the septum of his nose.

'About the gold,' he said.

'But there *is* gold?'

64

'Perhaps. It is not important.'

I was angered by his indifference.

'It is very important,' I said. 'I staked my honour on there being gold in Guiana. I lost my son looking for it.'

He said nothing. He crouched, stroking the bastard cannon.

'Well,' I said. 'Where is the mine?'

'I don't know,' he said.

'You *must* know!'

'I don't know,' he said.

'Listen,' I told him. 'Did Palomeque not look for gold high in the mountain they call Iconuri?'

'Perhaps.'

'To hell with *perhaps*! What do you mean: *perhaps*?'

'I mean he may have looked. I don't know. He didn't find any.'

'Didn't find gold there? But he did somewhere else then?'

The Indian went on stroking the cannon. He offered no reply.

I lost my temper with him.

'Christ's blood, man!' I cried. 'I could have you hung overboard by the heels till you shout what you know or your brains are dashed out against the hull!'

The Indian smiled and shrugged. His eyes were unfathomable. 'Life is perfected by death,' he said levelly.

This answer shamed me.

I said: 'I have no intention of killing you, nor of torturing you either. But, in God's name, why did you come down the river with Keymis if not to lead me back to the bloody gold?'

The Indian took his time answering. At last he said:

'Because it was necessary.'

'Necessary to whom?'

'Necessary to me.'

'What was?'

'To keep Guattaral company,' the Indian said. 'To go with him where he goes. To see him live and die.'

I hit the bastard cannon with my cane. 'You talk like a fool!' I cried. 'I am not going to die!'

The Indian looked at me, his face a mask of wonder or astonished disbelief. (It was hard to tell which.)

'Then you will be the first man not to do so, won't you?' he said.

*

Captain Samuel King. Let me tell you a little about him. There is little enough, in all honesty, for me to tell. He is my one true friend, I think. He has served me well for nearly fifty years. A stubborn, scarred, and candid fellow, Carew. It is a relief to turn to Captain Sam King after talking about the Indian and his conundrums.

I first met King when I went to the Wars of Religion in France. My mother's cousin Henry Champernown got leave of Queen Elizabeth to take a troop of one hundred gentlemen volunteers to fight on the side of the Huguenots. The year was '69. And I must have been just a month or so short of my sixteenth birthday.

Our private company could expect no quarter from the Papists. England was not at war with France, of course, and those of us unfortunate enough to be captured during the Huguenot defeats at Jarnac and Montcontour were hanged on gallows with scrolls pinned to the corpses saying that we had died not as Englishmen but as damned Protestants opposing God's will in the destiny of France.

I suppose I suffered from the usual youthful fever for adventure. I thought it a splendid thing to ride armoured into battle, and to fight with sword and lance, a good horse under me.

Samuel King rode at my side, just one year older, but with a moustache that already compassed his mouth. At seventeen, Sam had already found his element. A born soldier, and he looked it. He even rode his horse with a kind of swagger, wide-footed in the stirrups, the tops of his boots turned down to meet his jingling spurs. No fool, no coward, he was my brother at arms, and we learned our lessons together in the art of war. Fearless himself, he taught me that the facing of fear can be less than the dread of it. Sam despised death. He said the dead looked ugly. He said he was ugly enough without adding worms to the picture. Yet he had his philosophy. A man can only die once, so let him die well. And at night, by the camp-fire, we talked, and I found there was more to him. We had different backgrounds, but many opinions in common. The callow opinions of youth, no doubt, and shallow, but some sense in them still, I believe. Sam reasoned that no man is born a hero, but if history gives him a chance then heroic times can raise a man up to their level. As to our present circumstances – Sam was no bigot, but he counted any man his friend who saw the need to fight for the right to worship God according to his own conscience. He was not one of those fanatics who equate the Pope with the Devil as the enemies, in this world and the next, of their immortal souls. But (like me) he had been brought up to detest the peculiar interpretation of the Roman Catholic faith which has led Spain to believe that she enjoys God's own permission to impose an iron yoke on the rest of the world.

Still, I make Sam and the others of our company sound too parsonical. The fighting in France was grim and bloody, but there were more times when we laughed than when we wept.

Ah, the smell of bacon sizzling in a pan in the dark that is just before dawn of a battle! And the rising sun seen through the pricked ears of a horse galloping full-tilt despite powder and shot into the thickest part of the fray! Drums! Trumpets! Pikes! Tented fields! Bare swords! Pistols and caliver!

But I romanticize. Both the abstraction and the actuality that is war. Mars is an ugly god. The wolf and the woodpecker are sacred to him. I have seen wolves dig up dead men to eat them. The woodpecker has a sly and spiteful laugh.

Fascination with war soon turns to disgust.

I was with Samuel King at Languedoc. The enemy had hidden themselves in the caves there. Those caves had only one entrance, and that very narrow, cut out in the midway of high rocks. We let down a chain with burning bundles of straw bound round a heavy stone. Most of the men down there in the caves were choked to death. The rest came scrambling forth like bees smoked out of a hive.

Alexander the Great once employed the same tactics in India. But I didn't know that then. I thought it original.

Our campaign, at all events, proved useless. We were fighting a losing battle right from the start. Word came from the Queen that we were to disband, disperse, and disappear. The Huguenot leader was captured, and beheaded on a scaffold. I remember his banner: It bore a severed head on a black ground, and the motto '*Finem det mihi Virtus*'. Just so, valour did end his days. And Sam, for once, was silent concerning death's uglinesss.

Not long after that, in the night of the 23rd of August, 1572, I was in Paris when Huguenot nobles were dragged from the Palace of the Louvre and slaughtered in the courtyard, while King Charles the Ninth of France leaned from his bedroom window wearing a nightcap and shouting out: 'Kill! Kill! Kill!'

The Massacre of St Bartholomew's Day. Ten thousand Protestants done to death. King Philip the Second of Spain was said to have smiled for the first and last time in his life.

Next morning I saw Gaspard de Coligny, that great Admiral, flung by a servant from an upper window of his house. Some Catholic Samaritan most charitably wiped the blood from his face, then kicked it in and rode away. Later, in the afternoon, some children came playing. They hacked off Coligny's head, and his hands, and his genitals. Then they sold them to souvenir hunters. What was left of his corpse was hung up by the feet on the public gibbet at Montfaucon.

All these things I witnessed in France with Samuel King. There are others of that company I remember: Philip Budockshide, who was always ready to wager on anything (two raindrops down a window it was once), and Francis Berkeley who could drink a pint of ale in a single swallow. But Budockshide and Berkeley were killed soon after, in the campaigns in Ireland. Only Sam King survives of that crew. My friend, my fellow, my oldest companion in arms. Trust him, my son.

And know that there are no such things as Wars of Religion. There are only Civil Wars. And by Civil War no nation is ever bettered.

So I have turned again to the past. Carew, to give you the past makes the present less intolerable for me here. We are still anchored in the shining Bay of Nevis. This morning I saw a turtle as big as a shield. The sea between here and St Kitts is as blue as your mother's right eye. Where it frets against the shore you can see swarm upon swarm of minute but bright-coloured fishes in it, striped and speckled, many with long fins that make them look like soldiers. I saw also a huge land crab whose popping eyes and fumbling oversized pincers put me in mind of King James.

As to the birds: This island is full of flamingoes. Tall, pink, stalk-legged, they remind me of those ephemeral lazy young dandies, all garters and lacework collars, who perfumed Elizabeth's Court before the rough wind of the Great Armada came to blow them away to some safer satin nest far deep in the heart of the country. But the species that interest me most are the boobies and the frigates or man-of-war birds. The booby, dusk-coloured, dives headlong down into the sea for its prey. The man-of-war bird is your perfect unconscionable pirate. Fork-tailed, with a seven-foot wing-span, it swoops down to make the booby vomit up what it has eaten, in order to eat it, and lives on nothing else.

To give you my past and my present makes some kind of future seem possible.

But where? When? And how?

To revictual and return to Guiana? To fall on the Plate Fleet? To go home?

I suggested this evening to Parker that my letter from Mont-morency could perhaps be construed as the letter of marque he thought necessary for any privateering venture. It speaks, after all, of the Grand Admiral's willingness to persuade Louis the Thir-teenth to admit me and my men to any French port upon our return *'avec tous ses ports, navires, équipages, et bien par lui traités ou conquis'*.

'"*Ou conquis*",' I said. 'Is that not a licence to privateer?'

Parker said: 'But last night you insisted we would not run for cover to France.'

'I meant not empty-handed,' I replied.

Parker smiled unpleasantly, and whistled one sour note through his teeth. 'I see,' he said. 'The prospect of selling the French a ship full of Spanish silver makes right what you thought to be wrong.'

I was silent. I thought of the frigate bird.

Parker said: 'And you'll hoist the French flag at your mast then?'

That stopped me.

This black *Destiny* may be my coffin and that blue sea my shroud, but Sir Walter Ralegh shall not die under false colours.

7

Chudleigh has gone. With the *Flying Joan*. John Chudleigh, of Devon, who was the first of my captains to look coldly on my proposal that we sail back to the Orinoco once our vessels are refurbished. Whether he elected to fly because he feared I would, after all, compel the fleet to return for the gold, I don't know. But this morning I woke to find one ship less in the Bay. Chudleigh had slipped away in the night, and all his crew with him, including William Thorne (a good and experienced master), twenty-five men, and fourteen fair pieces of ordnance.

It seems he gave no warning of his flight.

At least, none of the other captains will admit to knowing where he has gone.

My own guess is that Chudleigh and the *Flying Joan* are now heading for one of the pirate islands – Tortuga, most likely – there to rendezvous with Whitney and Wollaston and others already established in the dirty trade of piracy.

We are well rid of such vermin.

But their defection hardly simplifies my problem.

What to do next?

If I go for the Plate Fleet it means war with Spain. That much is obvious. And Winwood wants it. He got me out of the Tower to achieve that end. I remember the story he told me of Gondomar's fury when his spies brought him the news of my release. The Spanish Ambassador even attempted that most difficult of tasks: to speak to King James on one of his days spent out hunting.

You should know, Carew, that our King pursues the pleasures of the chase from dawn to twilight on four days in every week. Two other days he watches cock-fighting. Sundays are different, of course. Sundays he lies in bed, propped up against pillows and cushions, thin tapers burning in brass sockets on the headboard behind him, a seven-branched candlestick on the ebony-inlaid table by his bedside, the hanging tapestries drawn close around three sides of his giant four-poster, with (winter or summer) a massive log fire roaring in the grate. I have Winwood's word for these details. Sundays James meditates, by candlelight and firelight, upon key phrases in the Lord's Prayer; or else upon the Divine Right of Kings; or (but I flatter myself) upon the evils of smoking tobacco. Sundays, cosy and warm, with plenty of mattresses under him, he even denies himself his catamite Villiers.

I came out of the Tower on a Monday, however. And that particular Monday, the King was at Theobalds, in Hertfordshire, his favourite residence.

The hunting is good there. And always it ends the same way. King James plunges his naked feet into the slit-open belly of the stag. He wriggles his toes in the warm entrails. He paddles in the reeking bowels of the creature.

All day that Monday – so Ralph Winwood told me – he kept bringing up topics to keep the King's mind from the subject of my release. He was worried that James might renege, and then counter-mand it.

So now, standing up in his stirrups to relieve his heavy limbs from the ache of the long day's hunt, Winwood watched impassively as the King splashed up and down in the stag's insides, and remarked that it might be a good idea if James displayed his face a little more often in public.

Which stratagem drew the buffoonery he desired.

'My *face*?' James cried. 'Are you joking?'

'No, Sire,' Winwood said. 'I am serious. The people like to see their Sovereign now and then. They enjoy a show, you know, and it helps keep them loyal.'

James giggled. 'I'll give them a show!' he screeched. 'I'll pull down my breeches and they shall see my arse as well!'

(I am quoting Winwood's story word for word. You must learn, my son, what manner of man this King of ours is.)

James rolls his eyes a lot. He rolled them now. Then:

71

'Steenie!' he shouted.

This was the signal for George Villiers, Gentleman of the Bed-chamber and Master of the King's Horse, to spring from his saddle. A lithe springer, George Villiers. He knew what was required of him. Stooping, he scooped up two handfuls of blood from the dead stag. He began rubbing the King's naked legs with them. The King's mud-spattered boots and huge quilted daggerproof breeches lay in a heap by his horse. Villiers worked hard, an over-ripe smile on his heart-shaped face. Soon (Winwood said) the spindly regal shanks were criss-crossed with dripping gore.

'That's good,' James announced. (He would have pronounced it *guid*, but I'm damned if I'm going to sit here under a Caribbean sun trying to imitate a Scotch accent.) 'That's very good, Steenie,' James said. He fondled the young man's dark chestnut hair where he knelt to his task. 'Just the wee bit more? Just the finishing off now?'

Villiers finished his Majesty off. Winwood studied a hedge while he did.

Villiers winked at Winwood on the ride back to the hunting-lodge.

'It's good for his gout.'

'I don't doubt it,' Winwood said.

Supper was interrupted by the arrival of a messenger. The messenger being a tight-buttocked young man, the King did not immediately bawl him out. The messenger's scrap of paper torn from its envelope, however, Winwood told me that James turned irritably to confront him.

'Gondomar,' he said.

Winwood says he tried hard to look surprised.

'Requesting an audience,' James went on. 'Can it be that the Spanish Ambassador also requires a flash of the royal arse?'

Villiers laughed uneasily, then made a whistling mouth. 'Wants to lick it more likely,' he suggested.

Winwood winced.

(God knows if you will ever have the chance to peruse these pages, Carew. If you do, no doubt you will be old enough in the world's wickedness to read them without blinking. I am writing to you now not as my young son, but as the man you one day will be when I am no more. It is important that you understand this incredible clown

72

of a King who has done all he can to heap dirt on the throne of England.)

This King's hand played now in Villiers' short beard, tickling. 'Shall we tell him what he can go and do, sweetheart?' he said.

'He's a lecherous little prick,' his catamite replied. 'He's probably done it twice already on the way out here.'

Winwood got up to go. 'If your Majesty will excuse me,' he said.

'The devil I will,' James said. 'Sit yourself down, man.'

Winwood sat. He kept his gaze fixed on his plate.

James started sucking at a goblet of resinated Greek wine. That's his favourite drink, and I've seen him drinking it. (We have met only once, face to face. I'll be coming to that.) King James drinks as if eating. His tongue is too big for his mouth, and the wine invariably dribbles into his beard, which is wispy, square-trimmed.

When he had finished his drink and (according to Winwood) Villiers had leaned across the table to kiss his lips clean for him, his Majesty said: 'Some fun with Count Gondomar about Winwood's uncooked friend and his quest for El Dorado? Shall we, shan't we?'

(Winwood's 'uncooked friend' being me. James delights in puns. When we met he thought it the height of wit to declare that he'd heard of me *rawly*.)

Poor Ralph cleared his throat and gave it as his opinion that it was vital some pretence be kept up that my expedition was intended for Virginia.

'I wasn't asking *you*, sober-sides,' James gurgled. 'Steenie, my gorgeous Greek icon of St Stephen, what do you say, Steenikins?'

Villiers pursed his lips, clutching his head in his hands and going through a pantomime of considering the matter profoundly. Then he shrugged, took a gold coin from his pocket, tossed it, looked at the result and pronounced: 'St Stephen, who positively detests all stiffnecked men, says that little Spanish monkeys are no bloody good either. St Stephen says such monkeys should be taught their place. Say that you'll see Señora Gondomar – oh, next Friday. They're cooler on Fridays, these Catholics. On account of the fish.'

I was told that King James roared with laughter at this feeble witticism. He leaned across the table to caress his catamite's cheek. Then he turned an amiably contemptuous face back to Winwood. 'The difference between you and my Steenie,' he began, 'the difference between you and sweet Steenie is . . .'

73

Winwood says he had to bite his tongue and clench his fists. He's a solid man. I can imagine him sitting there, lowering his head like a bull about to be killed.

'Och the devil the difference,' James said, flopping back into his chair. 'It's what we men have in common that's so salient, after all.'

Winwood began to make a further noise about the advisability of not conceding an audience to the Spanish Ambassador.

James interrupted him. 'I never intended for a *second* to see Gondomar tonight,' he cackled. His watery blue eyes would be lukewarm with malice. (How well I remember that look, though I've seen it but once.) He addressed himself then to the messenger, who had watched this buffoonery without astonishment. He said: 'Tell our friend the Ambassador of our dear brother of Spain that we're feeling just a little *dreich* after a day when we had many momentous decisions to make. Tell him that we adore his company but couldn't possibly do it justice at this hour. But he can wait on us on Friday in our cockpit at Whitehall. At noon. On the stroke.'

The messenger bowed and departed.

'What's that *dreich*?' George Villiers asked idly.

'Fucked out and far from home,' replied King James.

I just discovered that the Indian will not sleep in Keymis's cabin. Robin, my page, told me that the sheets there have never been touched. I found the Indian on the quarter-deck and asked him why. He said nothing. He pointed to the bowsprit. It appears that he prefers to lie stretched on it at night. Of course, he won't be able to rest there once we sail. Unless he never sleeps, or wants to drown. I begin to wonder if this Christoval Guayacunda is a madman.

An interesting if depressing private conversation with Samuel King, who came aboard the flagship at seven bells especially to put it to me that even if we sail in boldly under our own colours and succeed against all the odds in picking off any of the stragglers from the Plate Fleet such action might entail the sacrifice of the security of our friends at home in England who have placed trust in us. My wife Bess, Mr Secretary Winwood, Lord Arundel, Lord Doncaster – *they* would suffer, *they* could be punished along with us.

I considered the point well taken, but argued that if such an act provoked outright war with Spain, which Winwood for one most certainly wants, then we would bring no discredit on ourselves or our friends at home.

Sam King said one word only in reply: 'Gondomar.'

I knew what he meant without any further need for discourse. Don Diego Sarmiento, Count Gondomar, Ambassador Ordinary in London of King Philip the Third of Spain, is a clever and complicated man. He runs rings round the English politicians, and – although the King may win the odd little battle as on that day of my release from the Tower when he refused him an audience – he has James in his pocket also.

Gondomar is dangerous. Gondomar is an enigma. He reads Winwood, for instance, like an open book. It might even be that his complaints about my voyage were so much bluster. That he *wanted* the fight at San Thomé – in fact, feels disappointed now, if word has already got back to him that the thing was no more than a skirmish. That he *expects* me to go for the Plate Fleet, the quest for the gold having failed. (I am not so unlearned in intrigue as to doubt that every word of my talk with viper Bacon that evening in Gray's Inn Fields went straight to the ears of the King, and from the King's lips to Gondomar.) It could be that Philip of Spain is looking for a righteous excuse to declare war on England, and with the Pope's blessing of course. And that Gondomar has been instructed all along to engineer an occasion for such war, behind his ceaseless pacific palaver about marrying the Infanta Maria to James's son and heir, 'Baby Charles' as he calls him, though the sad fellow is rising sixteen.

It looms large in my mind tonight that our English navy is rotten. I saw the shipyards at Deptford and Greenwich. Bad ships, old ships, corrupt officers, a navy stinking of bilge water and rotten meat. And the few new vessels that have been built since the death of the Queen are all too ornate and cumbersome to withstand another Armada. A clown for a King, and a few silly toys for a navy.

'You might be playing straight into Gondomar's hands,' my Captain King murmured.

Sam, I think you are right.

Gondomar is a Machiavel.

Carew, have you ever seen a cock-fight? The game-cocks come

75

at each other like miniature warriors, strutting and stabbing, with steel spurs sharp as razors on their heels. Each bird is well barbered and groomed beforehand – its wings trimmed so that they are like darts, its tail cut down by a third, its hackle and rump feathers shortened. Their combs are cut down close also, to make a good mark for each other's beaks.

Picture the scene for yourself. It is Friday the 23rd of March just two years ago. It is a battle royal in the cockpit which Henry the Eighth added to the Palace of Whitehall. In a battle royal, twelve cocks are set loose in the pit together. They fight until only one is left alive.

Five of the birds are dead already. A third is hopping about crazily with one eye missing. Most of the others spout fountains of blood as they come jabbing and spiking and scratching and cutting at each other, a raucous riot of feathers and spurs and claws.

(It occurs to me that my method in this writing is most curious, yet necessarily so. I am recreating past scenes for you, Carew, and to some extent for myself – the better to get to the bottom of them. Yet sometimes they are scenes in which as you perceive I play no part, not having been present to witness with my own eyes what things were done nor hear with my own ears what things were said. So do romancers write, who make up fictions for the entertainment of empty minds. My purpose is different. I am trying to get at the truth of certain past events that have bearing on my situation now. Truth needs no audience, but he who would tell it is helped to keep straight by a listener he loves. What better listener than a man's son? Especially a son whose father is almost a stranger to him. As you are, Carew, because of my long absence from you in the Tower. Be sure, however, that I am inventing nothing. I rely on Ralph Winwood's report in this instance, as in the scene set at Theobalds which I wrote earlier today. And, perhaps you will notice, I do not pretend to know what anyone was thinking or feeling, in other words, I refrain from indulgence in that trick of omniscience as played by our bold fictioneers. I tell you what Winwood told me. Where Winwood told me what *he* thought and *he* felt, I repeat that. For the rest, I report just the outward events and remarks to the best of my memory. There can be no steel glass in these passages.)

Now, where were we? Ah yes, the royal cockpit. With seven game-cocks left of the original twelve. And with four main persons present. Namely: King James, George Villiers, Ralph Winwood, and Count Gondomar.

James can never resist a little wager. So when Villiers remarked that he thought the Irish Gilder looked the gamest bird left in the fight, the King required him to put his money where his mouth was. Villiers did. To the tune of twenty-five triple sovereigns.

The King matched that, making his own bird the Dominique. Then he turned to Winwood. Ralph dislikes cock-fighting, but since he had to choose something, he went for the Shawlneck.

'"*Amor conciliatur auro*",' the Spanish Ambassador said.

James squealed, his eyes as keen as the fighting bird's he had selected to carry his wager. '"*Auro conciliatur amor*",' he said. 'That is, if you aspire to quote Ovid? You had it arsy-versy. "*Auro conciliatur amor*" . . . Love yields to gold.'

'I stand corrected,' the Spanish Ambassador said. Then he added: 'Your Majesty speaks Latin like a pedant. I fear I only speak it like a gentleman.'

Winwood has told me that this is an ancient routine. He cannot understand why King James has never yet learned to see through it. Count Gondomar will deliberately misquote one of the Latin poets, in order to flatter King James's vanity. For James will always leap in to correct him. The Spaniard then works some refinement on the fact that he has been corrected, so that he can insult our King in the next breath after the one which concedes that James is right. It happens every other time they meet, apparently. Yet his Majesty always rises to the bait.

That Friday, Count Gondomar was angling with a vengeance. 'Talking of gold,' he continued.

'Which cock?' James said.

'The Red Quill,' Gondomar said quickly, not even bothering to glance at the birds in the pit. 'Talking of gold, your Majesty will do me much kindness if we do not waste words and time pretending that the pirate Ralegh has any intention of voyaging to Virginia. His goal is Guiana, just as it was in '95. His object is gold.'

'Your Ovid is banal,' King James said, yawning. 'The power of hard cash is a truism known to every age. Philip of Macedon used to say that he could capture any town, just as long as he could drive to the gates of it an ass laden with silver – to bribe some of the defenders. Ah, the Shawlneck is done for!'

Winwood says he looked away, as much to avoid Gondomar's steely and ironical eye as to save himself from observing the doubtless bloody fate of the bird he had been obliged to choose for the wagering.

Gondomar's body is obese and his face lean. 'El Dorado,' he said. 'The golden city.' He laughed without amusement, Winwood said. 'Pah!' he went on. 'It is lunatic. This quest proposed by a ghost arisen panting from the bed of a dead Virgin Queen!'

Winwood told me that King James now launched into a longish speech, quite obviously got ready for the occasion. The gist of it was that he, too, disliked me. He referred to me never by name. Always as *the man*. *The man* might have been Elizabeth's favourite, James said, but he was certainly not his. *The man* had been released from the Tower, yes, but he was unpardoned and forbidden to show his face at Court; all he was permitted to do was to go about and make provision for his intended voyage – and that only in the company of a keeper. Further, *the man* was as it were *dead already*, a corpse, a person dead in law, convicted of high treason in 1603. 'The first year of our reign in England', as James reminded everyone present.

I can quote the rest of what his Majesty had to say verbatim. Word for word, you see, I once heard it before. Only before it had been from the lips of Sir John Popham, the Lord Chief Justice, wearing a black cap.

The King spoke with much relish, Winwood observed.

The King said: '*The man* was sentenced to be hanged and cut down alive, his body opened and his heart and bowels plucked out and his privy members cut off and thrown into the fire before his eyes, and then his head stricken from his body and his body divided into four quarters to be disposed of at our pleasure.'

The King was keeping his eyes on the game-cocks.

The King said: 'That sentence has never been revoked.'

There was a silence.

Then Gondomar said: 'More to the point – it has never been executed. And I never could understand why.'

'His Majesty's mercy,' Villiers purred. 'Infinite. Mysterious. And beyond any Spanish wit.'

James was cackling and pointing. 'Alas, poor Steenie,' he cried. 'So much for your Irish Gilder!'

Villiers' bird had gone down, hacked to pieces by the spurs of its few remaining rivals. The King's Cockmaster, who presides over the pit at Whitehall, leaned across the barrier to remove it from the matted stage with a net on a pole.

There was a lot more verbal fencing, Winwood told me. Gondomar made his usual speech regarding the many blessings which would flow from a marriage between Prince Charles and the Spanish Infanta. Such an alliance might in effect bring about a reconciliation of the English Church with Rome. He could imagine it leading (say) to a great Council of the Church, with his Majesty King James and his Holiness the Pope as joint presidents. There was also the little matter of the Infanta's dowry, et cetera.

King James countered this by mumbling something about negotiations for a possible *French* marriage for his 'Baby Charles' being somewhat well advanced, and before Gondomar could get another word in Villiers started complaining that they'd heard all this before.

'Whisht now,' James breathed. 'Look.'

They all turned their faces to the cockpit. Only two cocks were left – the Dominique (which the King had chosen for his wager) and Gondomar's own bird, the Red Quill. The Red Quill was down on its back. The Dominique was busy with beak and spurs, gouging and treading.

James gurgled with delight, so Winwood said.

Then, suddenly, the case was altered. The Red Quill rolled over in the pool of its own blood, scrambled and scratched through shed feathers and other dead birds, and came at the Dominique with a last and desperate vigour. Its fury, bred of hopelessness, made it invincible. Its spurs cut into the King's bird, its beak stabbed again and again into the Dominique's comb.

The Dominique went down. It was not dead, but it had no fight left in it. The Cockmaster used his long pole to get the bird on its feet again, prodding. But the Dominique was too exhausted to fight. It had lost too much blood. It stood, shivering, hot-eyed, resigned, in the middle of the pit. The Red Quill came at it and killed it.

'Birds and beasts are fortunate,' King James observed. 'They run no risk of going to hell.'

'They are there already,' Villiers suggested.

James does not favour remarks which substitute philosophy for

79

religion. 'We prate of hell like fools,' he said. 'Ask Count Gondomar about it. He ought to be well-informed upon such matters.'

'As a beast?' Villiers said, giggling.

The Spanish Ambassador bowed deep. 'As a devil,' he declared.

'Steenie,' James said, 'he is cleverer than us. Give him his winnings.'

My mind moves fast from one memory to another, but sorrow makes me slow in all their telling.

After the three years in France, where I learned the rudiments of war, I came back to spend three years at Oxford, learning nothing whatsoever.

Correction: I did learn how to borrow. The small spoils of war eventually ran out. I was too proud to go begging to my father. By the time of my last winter at Oriel College I was quite without money.

That winter was especially cold. I had to persuade a fellow student, a Mr Child of Worcester, to lend me a gown to walk out in.

When spring came, that is just what I did. Walked out of Oxford wearing Mr Child's gown and never came back. The direction I walked in was London.

8

London then. London in 1575. The grey Thames. The grey skies. The narrow streets so thick with folk that you could hardly walk from Drury Lane to Bridewell without getting a bruise. London: two hundred thousand people crammed and jammed together to make one monstrous dunghill with a few flowers growing on it. A breeding ground for pestilence and plague. A phoenix nest. A city much like hell, I think. Or heaven.

The city smelt. It smelt of beer and spices and money and muck. The Thames was a running latrine. Westminster was a sovereign cess-pool. Take sulphur and mix it with mud and you have something like the smell of the London to which I came in the seventeenth year of Elizabeth's rule.

The city sang. It sang of pedlars and poets and church bells and horses' hooves. Cheap-jacks would yell at you on every corner, trying to sell everything from odious eel-pies to almanacs that forecast the exact date of the end of the world. Coachmen would bawl and crack their whips at you to get out of the way of their iron-wheeled hell-carts. Every gentleman who rode or strode the streets went accompanied by his clutter of barging and bullying servants, brutes chosen as much for the size of their mouths as the strength of their muscles.

Beyond all and above all, though, the bells. From my first lodgings at Lyons Inn and then in the Middle Temple, I learned all their various chimes and tolls. St Paul's and Westminster Abbey, All Hallows Barking near the Tower, St Bartholomew's in Smithfield, the Dutch church of Austin Friars, St James's at Clerkenwell, St Giles in Cripplegate, Ely Chapel Holborn, St Dunstan's in Fleet Street (with its overhanging clock and two bells struck every quarter hour by wooden jacks armed with clubs), St Andrew Undershaft's (so called because the maypole was set up in the meadow in front of it each May Day), St Olave's in Hart Street, St Helen's Bishopsgate, St John of Jerusalem by Finsbury Fields, St Saviour's across the river in Southwark, and then of course the mighty booming bell of the Temple Church itself.

Such a blessing, such a scolding of bells!

On the morning of my twenty-first birthday (forgive an old man the recall of this small vanity) I stood wrapped in Mr Child's gown not far from the great flight of stairs leading up to the Queen's Palace of Whitehall, and I imagined that all London's bells rang just for me.

London smelt and London sang. But the city was really a hive. A vast hive of commerce and intrigue, of religion and politics, of froth and filth, pleasure, treasure, information, speculation, minds, bodies, dreams, rags and jewels, the teeming matter of life and of death. The people of the city were the bees: humble bees, bumble bees, soldier bees and social bees, mason bees and worker bees, with not a few drones. You could see them swarm at any time of pageant – a busy buzzing mass of gentlemen and hooligans, ladies and drabs, little Cockney shopkeepers and wealthy merchants from every part of the earth. The honey of the hive was not mere money. It was something altogether stranger, something common yet singular, durable yet elusive. It was there behind the dancing and the diplomacy, the plays and the processions, the bear-baiting in the Paris Garden on Bankside and the spiked skulls of traitors that grinned on London Bridge. This honey was dark and bright and hot and cold. It filled the whole honeycomb from the brothels of Cheapside to the chapels in Lambeth Palace. It intoxicated. It poisoned. It inspired. You could feel its excitement working in the crowds that gathered to greet ships returning to the Pool after great voyages of discovery, as well as in the crowds that flocked each morning to watch prostitutes stripped and whipped naked in public. It would like as not be the same crowd. It would assuredly be the same honey. No one could take it and break it or eat it or drink it wholly, yet everyone tasted it there on his tongue to a certain degree. No high foreign prince ever came with a glittering army to possess it for a lifetime, while the most beggarly knave in a ditch might dream through his shivers that he enjoyed it for a night. It made Shakespeare (but later, and distantly) its poet. It made me (and sooner, but all too closely) its slave. It was the sweetest honey that ever there was to flow into men's minds to gladden them, yet it was a honey which stung my heart nearly to death. It was cerebral and passionate and absolute and virginal. It had something to do with the queendom. It had everything to do with the Queen.

'Elizadeath,' the Indian says.

He came with me this morning to the spring. It is good there, before the sun makes the island too hot. I plunged my lame leg in the water. A most sufficient medicine, cold and sharp. I walk better for it, and my fever is nearly all gone.

This is the night of our fifth day here at Nevis. The mood that marks what is left of our fleet is one of the blackest misery and confusion. My captains avoid me. The men lie and cast dice in the shadows. Our morale has never been lower, nor discipline more difficult to maintain. Two sailors aboard Barker's pinnace, the *Page*, were found with their throats cut last night. It appears that they had been suspected of cheating at the dice. The state of our disorder can be measured by the fact that their murderer or murderers did not consider it necessary to conceal the crime by throwing the corpses over the side of the ship. Questioned about it, Barker himself just shrugged and turned away.

My own mood is one of despair and indecision.

A gnawing then numbing despair. An utter impotence of indecision.

What to do? Where to go? And why?

Why anything?

That is the basic and unanswerable question. My past, my present, and any imaginable future seem equal in their total lack of meaning.

The weather does not help. Hot days, parched nights, with never a whisper of wind. Nothing moves. Nothing, that is, save the birds which appear without fail over the *Destiny* at each dawn and each darkfall. Are they eagles? Or vultures? Probably neither, and I betray only my own state of mind in naming them so. Big birds, wide-winged, high up and indifferent, flying north, flying south, as many flying one way as the other, like the cripple-winged thoughts that fly through my head as I watch them.

Today, at any rate, there was the visit to the sulphur spring with the Indian. I never meant to take him. He just followed. No doubt he grew curious where I went each morning. Sam King followed also, suspicious that the savage meant me harm. Three men scrambling up a way of white rocks as the sun rose over a cone-shaped Carib island. The first man old and infirm, with a stick to lean on. The second man young and sure-footed, able to leap from outcrop to outcrop as nimble as any goat if he so wanted, but deliberately holding back, waiting for the first man to move on again ahead, keeping a respectful distance. The third man tough and burly, but also old like the first, his face like teak, his gaze never leaving the Indian. Sam never dropped far behind, though I noticed when the two of them caught up with me at the place where the spring issues forth from the ground that the effort had cost him much. His shirt was soaked with sweat, and his breathing sounded rasping like a bellows.

This cunning lovely water.

We are like kinds – the water and I.

I washed my lame leg in the spring. I watched the sun dry the sulphury water where it trickled down the lightning-marks of my scars. I got them at Cadiz, those jagged wounds. I suppose I was lucky to keep my leg. The ship's surgeon was all for sawing it off at the knee, and would have done the job no doubt if he hadn't been frightened off by the pestilential number of Spanish cannon-balls which came whizzing across the Bay to interrupt his carving. We won the day, of course, and my leg mended, but it has been my most imperfect part ever since, and the gross damp of the Tower of London didn't help matters.

The morning sun was soon so hot that it dried the water on my skin with a sort of hiss, even before I could feel the cold of the water doing me good.

The Indian and Sam King watched my ablutions without comment. The Indian squatted, chewing at a leaf. It is a habit of his which I have noted before, though not in these pages. He carries the leaves about with him in a pouch. They appear to be dried, uncurled, and are deep bright green on their flat upper surface and a softer grey-green underneath. He picks off the stalk quite fastidiously, then chews a whole leaf into a ball in his mouth. His cheek bulges with it. I notice he never spits when chewing these leaves. No doubt he swallows them eventually. That's what he seemed to do today at the mineral spring.

It was on the way back to the ship that the Indian started to shout. Some dark mischief, some nonsense possessed him. He cupped his hands to his mouth and made his voice echo and re-echo among the rocks. At first it was just sounds that he emitted, weird hoots, long trilling calls, some of them hunting cries perhaps in the dialect of his tribe. Then, quite clearly and suddenly emerging from this unintelligible hullaballoo:

'Elizadeath,' he cried. 'Elizadeath.'

Sam King, in a startled fury, would have struck him a blow with his fist, by the look of it. I stopped that. I sought to teach the man better:

'Elizabeth,' I said. 'The great Queen of the North was named Eliza*beth*.'

He tried hard. But the more muted consonant proved beyond his reach.

'Elizadeath! Elizadeath!'

The white rocks of the island rang with the word.

Elizadeath . . .

Perhaps, after all, this Indian has it right. He says by accident what I am still learning. He tells the truth of my life without knowing me.

I came, as I said, to London in '75, lodging first at Lyons Inn, then at the Middle Temple. I did not study law. I studied the hive. I determined how to make my own name buzz in it. I was a young male bee. I would court the Queen.

Understand, Carew, what I mean by this. Elizabeth was forty-two years old when I first saw her. That is, she was exactly twice my age.

What did I see?

A woman of middle height, whose upright bearing made her appear tall. A woman with thin reddish hair and short-sighted eyes the colour of gold, her eyelids heavy and hooded like a bird's. A woman with a high thin arched nose, prominent cheek-bones, a small unsmiling mouth, and a sallow complexion made artificially vivacious by rouge. A woman compact in body, strident in voice. A woman with lovely hands – Queen Elizabeth's long slender fingers were by far her most beautiful feature, and she made sure that men noticed them.

Yes, I saw that.

And I saw at the same time and in the same place a woman who wore a ring on one of those fingers, which ring – she had publicly declared it – was a token of her marriage to her kingdom. A woman who had said that to her it would be a full satisfaction, both for the memorial of her name, and for her glory also, if, when she had breathed her last breath, it was engraven upon her marble tomb: HERE LIES ELIZABETH, WHICH REIGNED A VIRGIN, AND DIED A VIRGIN. Yet a woman who kicked her legs high in the dance, and whose supposed love affairs were the scandal of Europe.

Yes, I saw that.

And I saw also something else. Something brighter and darker than the mortal habit. Something which made sense of every contradiction. Something beyond personality. Something beyond woman even. For I saw something that went riding like Alexander, hunting like Diana, walking like Venus, the gentle wind blowing the fair hair about her pure cheeks, like a nymph, by her gait, by her grace. Something sometimes sitting in the shade like a goddess. Something sometimes singing like an angel. 'All suddenly I saw the Faerie Queen . . .'

And she swore. As vividly and vehemently as her father in his prime. King Henry the Eighth. That minotaur. That magnifico. Defender of the Faith and murderer of his wives.

And in her everything there was a something more. A something witch-like. A something like that dancing slant-eyed never-to-be-mentioned Anne Boleyn, who had had one finger too many on her pinched left hand and who had had her lovely head cut off for going to bed with her own brother.

So. Quite so. And absurdly. But I feasted on that singular sexual honey even as I starved in my bare lodgings and borrowed maps from Richard Hakluyt, uncle of one of my friends at Oxford, himself a lawyer of the Middle Temple. I pored over the maps, dreaming of navigations, discoveries, battles and conquests, a life as a gentleman and a soldier. But I would also be a courtier. I would court the Queen. I would make myself her favourite.

How? You may well ask! I was unknown. I was alone. I was

twenty-one years old, and heir to no fortune, a penniless nobody from the West Country.

Did I imagine myself as some heroic figure in a folk story? The youngest son of a poor but honest man who would pass through trials and adventures and initiation tests before eventually marrying a princess and living happily ever after?

No. I was neither so ambitious nor so stupid.

I ask you merely to note that I saw Queen Elizabeth from a distance long before she ever noticed me. And that I saw that the Queen, the Virgin Queen, played a long-drawn-out and inconclusive game with princely suitors from foreign lands, while surrounding herself privately with a Court which was mostly male and wholly English. A Court of handsome young men and shrewd older ones. A Court which adored her, and which she adored to scorn. A Court which needed her, and which she needed to spurn.

It would take time. It would take pain. Being young, I was not altogether displeased by the thought that it might even cost me my life. But something in me made the Queen my destiny from that first time I saw her. I was standing on the riverside at Charing Cross. She passed in a gilded barge, Elizabeth, proceeding in state to visit her Archbishop at Lambeth. The Thames ran silver that day and the Queen rode like gold on it. As for me, I was no more than any other fame-hungry young man in a borrowed gown. I cried out: 'God save the Queen!' Her head did not turn.

Midnight. My nephew George has just come to me with a most extraordinary report about the Indian.

It seems that the morning after the taking of San Thomé, when Keymis started questioning him about the exact location of existing Spanish gold mines, this Christoval Guayacunda tried to get himself killed not just by refusing to co-operate but by deliberate and apparently pointless lying. He invited death by saying that he was a half-caste. The soldiers believed him, and were all for putting him to the sword, but a couple of black slaves who had served the Spaniards and now come over to our side declared that the man certainly was *not* a half-caste, that he was a pure-bred Indian, that he had been Palomeque the Governor's personal servant, and so forth. Keymis still threatened him with death by hanging if he would not reveal what he knew about the mines. He had the Indian mounted on a horse, with a rope about his neck, under a tree in the town square. When it at last became evident that nothing was going to make the man talk, Keymis gave the order (in English) to let him go. At this point the Indian appears to have made a definite attempt at suicide. He kicked his horse forward and was left hanging for a moment from the tree before Keymis cut him down. They thought his neck had been broken but it had not. He laughed at them when he opened his eyes and saw their astonishment that he was still alive.

My nephew had this tale tonight from one of the soldiers who was present.

After that, George says, the Indian kept himself very much to himself. He made no attempt to run away, but neither did he volunteer any information which might have helped Keymis. It came as a complete surprise when they were about to leave San Thomé and he appeared on the riverbank and asked to be taken with them. George says he was (and is) suspicious of the man's motives, and advised against his adoption, but Keymis just nodded nervelessly and the Indian leaped into the boat before another word could be said.

I asked my nephew what he made of all this.

'I don't know,' he said, 'but I don't like it. Why should a man try and get himself killed and then join the enemy who has failed to kill him?'

'Perhaps he is mad,' I suggested.

'And perhaps we are madder,' George said, 'to keep such a creature on board.'

9

Dawn. Dawn swift and tropical after a night without sleep. This is what happened –

When George had gone I sat brooding upon what he had told me. I smoked several pipes of tobacco. I wrote the account of it here to clarify my thoughts.

But that writing did nothing to cleanse my mind's eye of one bloody and terrible image. It was a mental picture drawn from my nephew's previous report on the events upriver, now curiously linked to what he had told me about the Indian. I kept coming back to it: The thought of the Spanish Governor's great fat body lying naked in the sand of the square at San Thomé, his skull smashed in, *and a hatchet in his back.*

At last I could stand it no longer. I abandoned any hope of a night's rest. I left this cabin and took a turn around the deck. I was looking for the Indian.

I found him where they say he usually is at night – stretched out flat on his back on the bowsprit, quite safe, between the fore-top-mast stays. He appeared to be sleeping. He looked like some weird figurehead in the moonlight, his pointed grey cap pulled down over his ears, his copper skin shining, his feet tucked into the shrouds.

I stood a long while watching him. I had made my approach without noise, and I said nothing now. I did not care to shake him from his slumbers.

Then, just as I turned aside, just as I determined to come back to the safety of my cabin with no word spoken, the Indian laughed. It was a long low laugh – mocking, sardonic, harsh. I realized that I had never heard him laugh before, and that the sound was carking and unwelcome: it thicked my blood with cold. I realized also that his laughter meant that he had not been asleep at all. His eyes had been shut, but he had been fully aware of my presence.

The Indian pulled himself up by the bowlines and nodded at me.

'Guattaral.'

He made the word a question. He wanted to know what I wanted. Well, I was willing enough to confront him.

I said: 'You told me once that Don Palomeque had many enemies in his own fort.'

'Yes,' he said.

'You told me also that he was not killed by my men,' I went on. 'You claimed that he was killed by one of his own.'

'That's right,' he said.

I looked him straight in the eyes.

'How can you be so sure?' I demanded.

He shrugged. He said nothing.

'Palomeque was killed by a hatchet thrown between his shoulder-blades,' I said. 'Whoever threw the hatchet presumably smashed in his skull as well. The same person took all his clothes off – the corpse was found naked.'

The Indian took a leaf from his pouch. He drew it gently through his fingers, as if savouring the texture. Then he picked off the stalk with an abrupt flick of forefinger and thumb.

'Who killed Don Palomeque?' I demanded.

The Indian was moistening the leaf with his lips. 'You know who,' he said.

I said: '*You* killed him!'

'You say so,' he said.

'You killed him,' I said. 'That's why you wanted to die, isn't it? That's why you lied and said you were a half-caste. You wanted Keymis to execute you for your master's murder!'

The Indian started chewing at his leaf. It went into his mouth like the tail of a mouse going into the gnawing jaws of a cat. He stared at me with jet-black cat's eyes in the moonlight.

'Why?' I said. 'Why did you kill him? And why strip him naked?'

The Indian said nothing.

'Honour,' I said. 'Was it to do with honour? But how can it be honourable to stab a man in the back, however much you hated him, however bad he was as a master?'

The Indian chewed in silence.

'Where are you really from?' I said angrily. 'Who are you? What are you? Why did you come back downriver with Keymis? Why are you here with me now? What do you want? Where do you think you are going?'

The Indian smiled without amusement.

'Guattaral asks many questions,' he observed.

'Damn you! Then give me a straight answer to just *one* of them!'

The Indian nodded, chewing.

'Very well,' he said. 'Where do I think I am going? I think I am going where Guattaral is going.'

'No you're not,' I cried. 'I'll have no murdering coward on my ship!'

The Indian rose from the bowsprit. He walked down it with great agility, placing one bare foot half-sideways behind another, his long toes gripping the round spar like an ape's, then came to a stand on the beakhead before me, taking a deep breath and drawing himself up to his full height. As I have remarked before, this is not tall. Yet the man gives an incontestable impression of power and authority.

'Christoval Guayacunda is not a coward,' he said in a soft voice.

I said: 'To stab a man in the back is cowardice.'

'What if the man is already running away?' he said.

'Was Palomeque running away?'

'Yes.'

'Why?'

'Because I turned to face him,' the Indian said. 'Listen well. Palomeque liked to inflict pain. That was his pleasure. Naked, he liked to flog me with the bull-whip. That night I turned to face him. I thought Guattaral was at the gates. I was wrong. It was only Guattaral's son and the man who looked sideways. But I thought if Guattaral came then Guattaral would surely set me free. So that night I had the hatchet. Palomeque was the coward. He ran.'

'From you?' I said.

The Indian shrugged. 'From me,' he said, 'or from those he saw over my shoulder.'

'You mean you had accomplices? Who?'

'My golden fathers.'

I must have frowned. Then I saw that the Indian spoke figuratively. He meant that the ghosts of his ancestors had risen up with him against the oppressor.

He went on quietly: 'I did not throw the hatchet. I went after him. I jumped on his back in the dark. I killed him with one blow on the side of the skull. He fell in the dust. It was then that I put the hatchet in his back.'

'Why did you do that?'

'To make sure he was dead. And to show contempt. I put the hatchet in his head for myself. I put the hatchet in his back for my golden fathers. My people are a proud and ancient people. We had our lands before the Incas came.'

'So you told me already,' I reminded him. 'Your Chibchas may indeed be the oldest tribe in the New World. And the Spaniards came here after the Incas, of course. And Don Palomeque could well have been a perfect monster of cruelty, for all I know. But can any of this justify the murder of a man who was when all is said and done your master?'

The Indian chewed in silence a long while.

Then he said, his voice a whisper: 'It is true that Palomeque was my master. He took me prisoner from the mountains with an iron collar round my neck. Three days and nights I had to run behind his horse on the way to San Thomé. If I had stumbled once, or fallen from weariness, I would have been dashed to death. I felt – I feel – no guilt in having killed him. If I did wrong it was in not having killed him sooner.'

I said: 'In God's name, man, then why did you wish to die?'

The Indian did not answer me directly. He looked at the moon where it was broken into silver on the sea. His jaws worked all the time, chewing at the leaf in a frenzy of what I took to be anguish.

Then, after much deliberation, he said:

'When I killed Don Palomeque I cried out. I stood over him and I shouted. I shouted the great shout which is the shout of the Golden Man. That shout is always answered. It makes whoever hears it run for blood.'

'I cannot understand you,' I said. 'You talk in riddles.'

'I will be plain,' the Indian said. 'I will be plain and you will understand. I stood over Palomeque's dead body and I shouted. The shout was answered. The shout made one come running in the night. It was my shout that killed Guattaral's son.'

I must be mad. My nephew George is right: I must be mad. To sit here writing this account of a meaningless conversation . . . To have spent half the night talking nonsense in Spanish with a crazy savage . . .

But:

Who else do I have to talk with?

George himself? – Quite inane.

Sam King? – Sam is my friend, and a good patient listener, but our acquaintance is of such long-standing that it is no longer much use for discourse. Besides, it was always a friendship based upon silence, upon a few important things mutually understood and held in trust, and Sam was hardly ever the world's greatest conversationalist.

The Reverend Mr Samuel Jones, our ship's chaplain? – Enough said!

The truth I admit is that I have no one else.

No one but ghosts from the past and you, Carew.

And sometimes that is too much like talking to myself.

I just passed a few hours in dreamless but unrefreshing sleep. The heat of noon woke me. This cabin is like an oven.

Summary of the remaining madness of last night:

The Indian fancies some kind of seemingly mystical connection between his killing of Palomeque and Wat's death. I cannot persuade him otherwise. He *will* have it so, and there is no arguing with the man. It was for this reason, apparently, that he more or less tried to commit suicide upriver, and then – when that failed – decided to come back with Keymis to Punto Gallo and put himself into my service. At the same time, he repeats his assertions that he voyages with me 'to see Guattaral die'. Not that he takes any manifest pleasure in the prospect. He seems to be convinced that there is some destiny which has linked his life to mine. Or, rather, which has linked his life to my death. It is all quite ridiculous.

Or is it?

I don't know.

I must be mad. Or very very tired.

IO

When I did at length achieve some proper sleep last night it was only to suffer a nightmare in which I dreamt that I was a stag being chased by the royal hunt of King James.

The King himself, trussed into his saddle with ropes, led the field on an iron-grey horse. Villiers and Winwood came behind him, keeping their mounts hard-held to maintain a respectable distance. Count Gondomar, accompanied by two Spanish cardinals and five Spanish priests, trailed in the rear.

Down the steep I ran, along the valley, and into a river. And down the steep, along the valley, and into the river, scattering shingle with their horses' hooves and throwing up the water in great glistening sheets, the royal hunt pursued me.

A bugle-note sounded from some distant forester, signalling that their game was 'at soil'.

And indeed I was.

Another brief gallop round that elbow of the river, and the cavalcade came upon me. I was standing knee-deep in a pool which was rapidly turning amber with blood from my wounds. Being a stag, I had antlers of course. I swung my head from side to side in a desperate last attempt to keep the King's hounds off. The dogs were struggling and swimming all around me, straining, with bloodshot eyes.

James turned to Villiers.

'You see, Steenie?' he said. 'I promised you that I would have more sport of the man than I ever had of the stags.'

There was a moment then when I realized that I *was* a man, that I was *the man*, the King's enemy, myself, and that I had no antlers. I was defenceless.

King James called out:

'Up, Jewel! Up, Bran! Up, Ringwood! Up, Buscar!'

The leaders of the pack went for my throat. Their teeth sank in. Sharp. Deep. As usual, it was the great hound Jewel, the King's favourite, which completed the kill. Blood and water gushed in all directions as I came crashing down.

In the dream, though dead, I retained a disgusting and pain-racked semblance of consciousness. So that I was aware of Villiers and Ralph Winwood dragging me from the river by my heels, and of Gondomar and his contingent of ecclesiastics ripping open my belly with daggers with crucifix handles.

Then the foresters unbonneted and wound the *mort* on their bugles, and King James was knee-deep in my slit-open corpse.

I must have screamed out in my sleep, for Robin my page came running to shake me awake.

We are, of course, at Nevis still. In fact, today it will have been one whole wasted week since we first dropped our anchors here.

I have to put it on record that I never intended to make such a stay. Indeed, when I called my captains together that first night we spent at this island, I was reasonably quick and lucid in my own mind as to what we might do. The alternatives looked quite clear-cut then, and the captains' lack of enthusiasm for any of them did not really daunt me. No doubt the same alternatives still obtain. And the near-mutinous silence of my captains does not matter. Yet something there is that prevents me from taking action. Something there is that makes for an agony of indecision.

What?

Wat . . . Yes, perhaps it has something to do with you. Something to do with the earth, red and virgin, beneath which you lie now, your young mouth stuffed full of it, with no prospect of whores or swords or wine, no jokes, no japes, no laughter, and no more chance of proving or measuring yourself against me, your prodigal father.

No, sir. Not so.

My son, forgive me.

It is of course not in you. It is not in the situation. It has little to do with the balance of probabilities. Nor is it in the too easily censurable stars.

It is wholly in me. It is my flaw which now appears, and hardly for the first time. Hullo, old unwelcome friend, old fault, old blot, old error.

Sir Walter Ralegh, that great adventurer, reluctant to venture forth. Sir Walter Ralegh, that prime mover of others, himself quite unable to move.

The Indian just came to me. I had discovered that the wine in our hold is no more than vinegar. So I was having the men wash the decks with it. The ship smells sharp as a consequence. Healthier.

The Indian watched the men scrubbing.

Then he said.

'Guattaral understands now.'

It was not a question. I did not reply.

'You prepare your ship,' the Indian went on, 'for the long voyage.'

His manner irritates me. It is so sententious.

'I have no particular voyage in mind,' I snapped. 'I make ready for nothing. The wine went sour. I use it to clean the decks.'

He turned away, smiling.

'Your ship smells of ashes,' he said.

I was weary of his company. I had no wish to continue another conversation compounded with riddles. But this evening, remembering my dream of last night, and turning over once more in my mind the courses of action which remain before me, it occurs to my fancy that his references to a long voyage and a smell of ashes must imply death.

In short, it becomes plain to me, after all, that I have only one choice to make:

Life or death.

It is that simple.

It would be life to sail back for gold from Guiana or even to attempt to take the Plate Fleet.

It is swift certain death to sail home to King James and the block.

Why, then, do I hesitate?

I had intended, today, to write down a few more brief particulars of my earliest existence in London. How I worshipped the Queen, as Gloriana, from afar. How my step-brother Humphrey Gilbert, patronized by Robert Dudley, Earl of Leicester, obtained a charter to explore the coast of North America and plant a colony if he could. How we sailed with seven ships in November, the winter of '78, and I had command of the *Falcon*, the Queen's ship, 100 leaking tons, old and under-masted but a start. How the others all turned back, and I got as far only as the islands of Cape de Verde on the coast of Africa. How when I returned I was still spoiling for action, and fought a foolish duel with Sir Thomas Perrot by the tennis court at Whitehall, and was committed to prison in the Fleet for a week. How I then attracted Leicester's patronage myself, and was commissioned to join Lord Grey of Wilton, in the long hot summer of 1580, and take a company of foot soldiers to help put down the rebellion in Ireland . . .

Well, none of that seems so important any more. I will pick up the threads of my young life where this drops them – in monstrous Munster, in Ireland, during the Desmond rebellion – but not this evening. My mood of self-divided indecision makes me indifferent to the past as to the present.

The Indian came knocking at the door of my cabin a moment ago, as I put down my pen and sat looking at the ink dry on the paper, detesting the shape of my own crabbed handwriting.

He made no reference to our earlier conversation during the scrubbing of the decks, nor to the fantastic story which he told me last night. He would not come in. But he brought me a gift.

It is one of his precious green leaves.

'Eat this,' he said. 'Chew it very slowly. Swallow the juice. Spit nothing out.'

I inspected the leaf which he had placed in the palm of my hand with a gesture approaching reverence. It looked innocent enough. Its only visual peculiarity, that I could see, was that it had in its centre the outline of another leaf just like itself. I sniffed at it. It had no recognizable smell.

I asked him: 'What do you call it?'

'*Khoka*,' he said. (I spell as he pronounced it.)

'Where does it come from?'

'The Valley of Sogamoso.'

'It grows wild there?'

'Yes.'

'And your tribe, the Chibcha, do they all eat it?'

The Indian nodded.

'They all eat it. And they eat it all.'

I turned the leaf over in the palm of my hand, thinking of the doubts and indecisions that beset me.

'Does it bring wisdom?' I asked.

The Indian shrugged his shoulders. He plainly found my question simple-minded.

'Wisdom is here,' he said, placing his hand on his heart, fingers splayed out wide.

'Not here?' I said, tapping my forehead.

The Indian said nothing. He kept his hand on his heart.

'Eat the leaf,' he said.

'I shall,' I promised. 'But what does it do?'

'That you must see for yourself. But eat it. It is good.'

'Better than tobacco?' I said.

'There can be no comparison with anything,' he said. 'The leaf is the food of the gods.'

All this he said with the uttermost seriousness. I asked him again to enter my cabin. I suggested that we might share a meal of the leaves. He refused. It was the custom, he said, for a man to eat first of the leaf on his own.

Then he gave me also a little flask made from a gourd. He called this an *iscupuru*, saying that (like *khoka* itself) he knew no word in Spanish which might be its equivalent. In the flask, he told me, is a lime-like substance made from ashes. He called this *llipta* or *llucta*. He instructed me to intermix it with the leaf when chewing by applying it to my tongue with a short stick which I have to dip into the gourd from time to time.

'But you do not do this,' I pointed out.

'No.'

'Why not?'

'I do not need to.'

'So why do I?'

The Indian shrugged. 'Perhaps you do not,' he said. 'But the leaf is strong. It is best not to eat it on its own until you have learned all its ways for yourself.'

He bade me goodnight then, with a curious abrupt lifting of his hands as if to bless or curse. I watched him walk away across the poop deck. At the door to Wat's cabin, he turned.

'Guattaral came for gold,' he called back softly. 'What I have given him now is more than gold. It is the food of the Golden Man himself.'

He was gone before I could think of a response.

So. I am chewing the *khoka* leaf as I write these words. It tastes pungent, bitter, faintly stale, but not so unpleasant when diluted with a smear of the *llipta* from the gourd. My mouth feels numb. My gums when I lick them are dry and give off a tang as if I had been eating salty meat or fish. Otherwise I cannot say that I notice anything special about it. If this is the food of the gods then it serves only to prove that I am very mortal. Which proof, I think, I did not really need.

One hour later.

I feel as though I shall not need to sleep tonight, that's all. I just took a turn around deck. All things past, present, and to come seemed to my eyes to be concentrated in the channel of the sea between here and the neighbouring isle of St Kitts. They met there and were consumed in its salt. That channel burnt like a cold blue fire, then a hot white frost, in the light of the withering moon.

To cross that night sea water – only a matter of a mile or two – seems quite beyond the *Destiny* or her master.

I I

And yet I have made that crossing. My *Destiny* is moored now at St Kitts.

Is this to be attributed to the leaf? I think not, though I ate it all, as the Indian had instructed me, and swallowed every last drop of its bitter juice.

There was *some* effect, but it is difficult to define it. Certainly I did not sleep for twenty-four hours. Certainly I experienced a sensation which I can only describe as like a gradual redeeming of the eyes – a feeling of the mind being clarified, the brain perhaps purified. And at the end of this I discovered in myself a power of action. But the leaf did not confer this. It was already there.

In short, the leaf inspired me to do nothing new. I would have done all the things which I have done in any event.

Also: I am unwilling to believe that the chemical powers of a mere plant could spur me on to action. On the other hand, it had no ill effects and I do not regret the ingestion of it.

I would be willing to experiment again with the eating of this *khoka*. But it has left me with no sense of urgency or need, and no excitement. I am content to wait until the Indian approaches me.

St Kitts. This island is in shape like a long loaf of bread. Mountains traverse the central part of it from north-west to south-east. The greatest height, my maps say, bears the name of Mount Misery!

Here are great trees that seem to touch the sky; pineapples with prickly tufted skins but sweet meat inside; iguanas which we roast between two pieces of wood for their good white flesh.

This island was discovered by Columbus on his second voyage, in

1493. Sad little Genoese, obsessed with sailing forever into the setting sun. You were once sent home in irons from these lands you found, kept sick and sweating below decks by order of the Spanish tyrants you served faithfully across 3000 miles of uncharted ocean. They say that you kept those irons by you to your dying day, as relics. Now they lie buried with you and your son in the cathedral of San Domingo in Hispaniola. No doubt they will prevail when your bones are clay.

This morning I wrote a long letter to the Secretary of State, my friend Ralph Winwood. Tomorrow I shall face the more difficult task of writing a letter to my wife. I intend to send these letters home to England by dispatching a flyboat, the *Page*, under command of Captain James Barker, with my nephew George on board to keep an eye on things. George is stupid (as I have before now remarked) but brave enough besides. He will need to be stupid to agree to go. He will need all his bravery to survive. The crew of the *Page* consists otherwise of a rabble of idle rascals, drunkards and blasphemers, the absolute dregs of those that remain of our never-exactly-glorious expedition. In the wake of the *Page*, I shall send home the *Thunder*. Her sick captain, Sir Warham St Leger, must carry and care for a cargo of others like himself. I have cleansed my fleet of the men worst affected by fever.

I gave Ralph Winwood a clear account of our passage and proceedings. I pointed out first that while the usual time spent in sailing from Cape de Verde to America is about fifteen or twenty days at the most, it was our misfortune to find winds so contrary, with violent storms and rains, when we found winds at all, that it took us six weeks. I told him of the great heat in which we had no water (our water-casks lost in a hurricane); how so many of our ablest men died on that long voyage out; how when we reached the Orinoco at last I was still myself in the hands of Death, unable to walk, and then carried about in a chair. I told him what seems to have happened upriver. How the Spanish were waiting for us, expecting our arrival. How they had lists in my own handwriting of the number of my men and the burden of my ships, together with details of what ordnance every ship carried. Which lists I had given to King James at his Majesty's express command. Who was pleased to value me so little that he passed them on to the Spanish Ambassa-

dor, who in turn dispatched them to the King of Spain. I enclosed
for Winwood's instruction the letter which the King of Spain then
sent to Don Diego de Palomeque, along with all my lists, which
letter was dated the 19th of March of last year, i.e. before my
departure out of the Thames even. I invited Ralph to draw his own
conclusions, and to extend to me whatever help he could. I told him
of Wat's death and Keymis's suicide. I apologized for the fact that I
am coming home without the promised gold.

Coming home.

Home does not necessarily mean death.

Even if it does, that's where I'm going, and that's what I'm going
to do.

And now – sitting in the shade of a palm tree, with my lame leg
plunged in a cool running brook of fresh water – I drink from a
coconut with one hand while with the other I write here to call back
with pleasure and affection our meetings in the early days, Ralph
Winwood and I, in the first weeks after my release (unpardoned,
with a keeper) from the Tower.

Ralph was always my friend, but he had to be circumspect. I
remember one meeting in particular. I was late. Stukeley dogged
me. I found Winwood kneeling in the Henry VII chapel of Westminster Abbey. How dank, how English, how far away! No bright
birds screaming there.

He was in front of the tomb where Queen Elizabeth now lies side
by side with her elder half-sister Queen Mary. The only bed they
ever shared, for sure. The one, a Protestant, remained a virgin all
her life and had Catholics stretched on the rack. The other, a
Catholic, married a Spanish prince and had Protestants burnt at the
stake.

Ralph was peeping through his big blunt fingers at that inscrip-
tion which announces that SHARERS OF KINGDOM AND TOMB
SLEEP HERE, ELIZABETH AND MARY, SISTERS, IN HOPE OF THE
RESURRECTION.

I said: 'No doubt they will be one dust before that day.'

Winwood hid his face in his hands, as if he was deep in prayer. I
knelt with difficulty beside him. To kneel hurts my leg.

I said: '*Our Father which art in heaven* . . . All goes well with Pett.
But I shall need more ships.'

He said: 'Naturally. How many?'

'A dozen,' I said.

'That will prove expensive,' he murmured.

'*Give us this day our daily bread*,' I said.

Always pray in a good round voice in public, my son. There's nothing like it for boring or embarrassing any eavesdroppers, and ensuring that only God and your best friends hear the things you say quietly.

Winwood whispered into his hands. 'Can you raise the money in the City?'

I said: 'The City prefers whales and spices.'

'Explain,' he said irritably. 'We have no time for riddles.'

I explained: 'The City prefers the Muscovy Company and the East India Company to an old ghost from the Court of the Faerie Queen. Anything that smacks of privateering is abhorrent to them. *For Thine is the kingdom* . . .'

'Privateering is out of date,' Winwood commented. 'So what will you do?'

'I have old-fashioned friends,' I said. '*Amen*,' I added.

'*Amen*,' Ralph said loudly. Then, very softly: 'How much will your friends be willing to invest?'

'The best I can hope for is £15,000,' I told him.

'And your Sherborne money?'

'That – plus money from Bess selling land – brings us up to about £25,000.'

'Not enough?'

'Not enough.'

Winwood bent further forwards and took a swift peep under his shoulder. I did likewise. We both saw the familiar shadow of Sir Lewis Stukeley stooping to read an inscription on the wall. Ralph must have judged that my cousinly keeper was just out of earshot. He said quickly: 'I'll do what I can. You understand that as Secretary I mustn't be *seen* to assist you.'

'Of course,' I said. Then: '*In the name of the Father and of the Son and of the Holy Ghost* –'

'*Amen*,' Winwood bellowed.

I stood, coughing, and limped off down the aisle without a backward glance.

*

I trust Ralph Winwood as I trust few politicians. Nine years my junior, a Northamptonshire man, once Queen Elizabeth's Ambassador to France, a lifelong enemy of all things Spanish, King James's Secretary of State for four years now, a bulky, bluff, barrel-shaped fellow, not glowing, not shining, but decent English oak through and through. Without Ralph Winwood I would still be locked up in the Tower of London working on my unfinished (and unfinishable) *History of the World*. No doubt about it. I picture Ralph in Whitehall, reading my letter when it arrives, pacing up and down like a bear in a cage, seeking to find some honest way to present my case to the King. A task I do not envy him. But if Ralph Winwood cannot do it, then nobody can. And if Ralph Winwood will not do it, then I'm done for.

Back aboard the *Destiny*.

Tonight I feel, at last, that my ten days of crippled and crippling indecision are at an end.

I have crossed the narrow channel to St Kitts. (The first step in the final direction I must take.)

I have written a clear and truthful account of all our misfortunes and made provision for it to be delivered to my only real friend at the Court of King James. (My nephew George has this minute taken that letter from me, under my seal, and sworn on his life's blood to see it safe into Ralph Winwood's hands.)

I have (privately) made up my mind what I must do: I shall sail first for Newfoundland, and then home.

I have (publicly) resolved to send the sick on ahead of me.

And tomorrow I shall write to Bess, my wife.

12

I told her I was loath to write, because I knew no way to comfort her. I said, God knows, I never knew what sorrow meant till now. 'Comfort your heart (dearest Bess),' I wrote. 'I shall sorrow for us both. And the Lord bless you and comfort you, that you may bear patiently the death of your valiant son.'

For the facts about Keymis and the gold I referred her to Secretary Winwood's letter, knowing that Ralph would give her a copy of it if she asked. 'My brains are broken,' I told her, 'and it is a torment for me to write, and especially of misery.' But I promised her that she should hear from me again, if I live, from Newfoundland.

It would not do.

The letter being sealed, I realized that it would not do.

Nothing would do. But this in particular would not do. Because I knew in my heart that I had to address Bess herself with the infernal facts of the story.

So I broke open the seals and added a postscript three times as long as the letter, telling her how they say that our poor Wat died, how Keymis had undone me in the matter of the gold and then tried to excuse it, how I rejected his reasons, how he shut himself up in his cabin, how Keymis killed himself. I told her also of the letters and lists discovered at San Thomé. How King James himself betrayed me into the hands of my enemies. How Whitney and Wollaston turned pirate. And all the weary unendurable rest of it.

Both letters are gone with George Ralegh. The *Page* has sailed, loaded to the gunnels with rats who will lose no chance to malign me as soon as they get back to England. But my friends can have the true story as I have told it to Bess and to Ralph. And for the rest I care not.

The *Thunder* weighs her anchor as I write. Storm clouds gather over the island. Mount Misery is dark with sudden rain.

This evening I called my remaining captains together again to dine on the *Destiny*. Only four faces now across the good white linen of my table: Samuel King, Roger North, Charles Parker, Sir John Ferne.

I told them of my decision: To sail first for Newfoundland, and then home. I explained that I favoured this route for several reasons. First, as I knew from the letters found at San Thomé, there must be a Spanish fleet somewhere in the offing, sent out to take me captive. If we sailed for Virginia, or even a straight course for England, we were likely to run into this, and we had neither the numbers nor the nerve for such an encounter. Second, a landfall at Newfoundland would enable us to clean our vessels thoroughly, and revictual. We had tobacco from Guiana to pay for it. Third, having rejected all idea of attacking the Plate Fleet, I was concerned to keep us well out of its route, so that no one could accuse us of trying. The Spanish treasure ships sail in spring from Havana through the channel between the Bahamas and Florida, then east to the Azores, and thence Cadiz. We would avoid them by making our way due north to Newfoundland, from which we could sail home to England across the narrower ocean.

When I had finished speaking there was silence.

Then Sam King said: 'That makes good sense to me.'

And then there was another silence. A long one. I imagined that I could hear the moonlight on the roof of my cabin. It was, of course, only the gentle dissonant sound of the rain. I listened to that because my other three captains said nothing.

Nothing.

Nothing.

Nothing at all.

I sat there watching the candlelight on their faces. Parker smiled unpleasantly. North smoothed his moustache with his thumbnail. Ferne fiddled all the while with a piece of broken bread.

'Well, gentlemen,' I said at last, 'what is your verdict?'

They would not look me in the eyes. Each one murmured a word or two of impeccable, curt and insincere approval. Then, one after another, they made their goodnights and went out.

'Now what do you make of that?' I asked Sam.

He shrugged.

'Trouble,' he said.

Trouble is too small a word, but then I like Sam's taste for understatement.

I lit my pipe and we talked of other things.

I keep coming back to the night before the *Destiny* left London. I dreamt a dream that night and Bess dreamt another. We were together in bed at her house in Broad Street.

In my dream it was the first voyage to Guiana all over again and I remember I was running to the top of a hill and when I reached the top I could see how the river forked three ways, about a mile off, and there were the twelve waterfalls, and every one of the waterfalls rose as high above the one in front of it as a church tower over a church, so that the side of the second hill was one giant cathedral staircase of water, water falling with such force that I felt the sting of the spray on my face, and higher up the second hill it looked like a city all turrets, and the waterfalls like a smoke that was rising from a burning city of salt.

In my dream I turned to Keymis and said that I could not go on. I was cold and sweating. It was 1595 but I had my Cadiz wound of '96. The ague was on me. My bad leg was giving me hell. But the Indian guide pointed. 'Beyond the cataracts the land is perfect.' Keymis went on immediately. So there was no turning back. I followed, Keymis climbing, the Indian beckoning, until we passed through the thunder and lightning of the falls and came at last into the promised place.

I had never seen a more beautiful country, nor more lively prospects. Hills raised here and there over the valleys, the river winding into divers branches, the plains adjoining without bush or stubble, all fair green grass, the ground of hard sand easy to march on, either for horse or foot, the deer crossing every path, the birds towards evening singing on every tree a thousand different tunes, cranes and herons of white and crimson and carnation perching on the river's side, the air fresh with a gentle easterly wind, and every stone that I stooped to pick up promised either gold or silver by its bright complexion.

But I had neither knife nor mattock to chip out the bits of the rock, and the rock was as hard as flint, and when I scrabbled at it with my fingers my nails cracked across and my hands came away bleeding. The men picked up bright stones and carried them, convinced that their glitter meant gold. And Whiddon and the surgeon brought me more stones like sapphires. But even in the dream I knew they were not sapphires.

The Indian guide, the son of Topiawari, pointed ahead to two mountain peaks. He said they were called Picatoa and Inatac. Each was about 7000 feet high. Beyond them, the Indian said, was the lake called Parima. And by the lake was the city. The city! Manoa! More rich and more beautiful, the Indian said, with more temples adorned with gold images and more sepulchres filled with treasure than either Cortés found in Mexico or Pizarro in Peru.

Then Keymis cried out. The Spaniard was coming, he said. We had only one line of retreat. But that was all right, for our line of retreat would take us within sight of Mount Iconuri, and now in the dream I remembered that Mount Iconuri was the site of Putijma's mine, and that there they said gold could be plucked up with the roots of the grass, gold lay all around on the ground, so that it didn't matter that we had no shovels or other implements with us.

But the rains came down, and the shirts were washed on our backs ten times in a day, and the river raged and overflowed. I was back with Topiawari himself, and Topiawari gave me another of his sons to take to England and I left Francis Sparrow, the servant of one of my captains, with Topiawari in return, and also Hugh Godwin, who was fifteen years old, to learn the language. We came back down the river in thunder and lightning and torrential rain, our hearts cold, stopping only to gaze at the faraway mountain like crystal. 'Putijma's mine,' Topiawari said, pointing. I was unable to walk all the way with Keymis and the others. I called on a chief who had promised to help me. I found the chief drunk, and his village all drunk, with the pots going from one to another without rest, and the rain lashing down, and all the drunkards lying in each other's arms in the mud in the rain. Then I feasted on armadillo meat, and went back to my ship, where –

I was woken by Bess screaming beside me. I got up and lit a candle and came back to bed. She was holding her hands to her lips.

I took her in my arms and she said: 'I wish you would not go.'

I said nothing. I caressed her hair. I could feel her tears on my neck. 'All our life has consisted of parting and meeting,' she said. 'All our life you've been going away, coming back. This time is the last time. I know. This time you will never come back.'

'Bess, Bess,' I said. 'Of course I shall come back. What's more I shall come back with gold. You will have pure gold to buckle your shoes and gold combs to wear in your hair.'

Bess turned away violently. 'I hate it,' she said. 'I detest it. Gold is like a maggot in your brain. Sometimes I think you went mad with it long long ago.'

I pulled the sheet down from her neck and started to fondle her breasts. 'You will feel differently in the morning,' I suggested.

Bess said: 'No, I won't. I shall see things just the same. To get gold for that sow of a king. Where's the honour in that? Where's the glory?'

I said: 'Would you rather I had rotted in the Tower?'

'Of course not,' she said quickly. 'But you're free now. You have your fine ship. Oh Wat, we could sail away.'

'And where would we go, Bess?' I asked.

'Anywhere. Everywhere. *Where* doesn't matter.'

'Guiana?' I said. 'Would you sail with me there then?'

Bess shivered. She brushed my fingers away from her nipples.

'Never,' she said. 'I abhor the very name. It's a hell. It's a false paradise waiting to sap and swamp what little is left of your wits.' She sat up in bed, her breasts heaving with a sudden sharp intake of breath. 'I remember the dream now.'

I said: 'It was nightmare that woke you?'

'I was at this lake in the mountains,' Bess said, 'and there was a person – some sort of emperor – who was rolling in gold dust, all covered with it, sticky. Then he was carried by his people on a litter and cast into the lake. Only then I saw that I'd been mistaken and it wasn't a man at all. It was Queen Elizabeth. She lay naked on her back in the lake and there was gold running out of her private parts, like blood, just as if she'd been ravished. And you were there, Wat. You were swimming towards her, and then you were licking the blood like a snake, you were drinking it where it stained the salt water. And I cried out: "Don't drink it! It's poison!" I woke up then, screaming . . .'

I was roused by Bess's dream, and we made love.

Afterwards, when I had huffed out the candle, and had lain for a long while searching the darkness with raw unsleeping eyes, I whispered: 'Bess, I will tell you something few ever knew. It's about the Queen. I never shared the secret with anyone before. But I know now that I must tell you.'

I stretched out my hand to her cheek. Bess snuggled against it. She kissed it, but she was kissing my fingers in her sleep. She was snoring softly. She had not heard a word that I had said.

I lay sleepless there beside her until dawn, when I heard the street door opening, and then Wat's tiptoed tread upon the stair.

It is a different kind of darkness here. The rain stopped round about midnight. The Carib night is vast and velvet. Lying in bed in London beside Bess was like lying in a brass-bound coffin box. The night about St Kitts is soft and tropical and malicious. The sea laps at the *Destiny*, dark and warm, teeming with silver sharks, a track of moonlight scratched across it as if by God's fingernail. If I opened one box in my mind that last night in London then there was a second smaller box inside it, and inside the second box a third, and so on, and so on. But sleep was not to be reached, there was never an infinitely small and perfectly empty box. Here, tonight, I have been equally sleepless, but that is to be attributed to an immensity of pitch-black space and shadow. I just took a turn around the deck. The night sky is enormous. Its stars are like explosions far away. The moon's full and needs a shave.

What was I going to say about Elizabeth?

Nothing. Not now.

I wish my bones could dream without my flesh.

13

I have been studying my charts and tables.

From St Kitts to Newfoundland is about 2500 miles. With reasonable winds, and allowing for good days and bad, it is clear that we need to average some eighty miles a day to complete the voyage north in thirty-one days.

Not impossible.

On a good day, before a fair wind, we might well sail 150 miles or more. A bad day would see us sailing anything less than fifty miles. Eighty miles a day is an average quite comfortably achieved in these latitudes and at this time of the year. If we maintain it then we should drop anchor in the harbour of St John in Newfoundland in about one month, give or take a day or two.

Besides, this direction I intend to pursue lies under the beneficent eye of the Pole Star. My sea quadrant is fitted with a mirror to permit star observations, and I have here on board the *Destiny* a nocturnal which gives the correction to be applied to the altitude of the Pole Star to obtain true latitude. Thus, when the need arises and the weather allows, we may sail at night as swift as we sail by day.

Newfoundland. The name begins to haunt me. The word gives new edge to old wits. I look forward to Newfoundland becoming actual. Cathedrals of ice and seas like diamonds. Their cold will cure my fevers finally.

Ireland in 1580 in the summer. I was twenty-six years old, I was a captain, and my pay was four shillings a day. I had a lieutenant, Michael Butler, and four junior officers under me. I had command of a company of one hundred men. Five of these men were dead. That was in accord with the usual practice. A captain could have a few dead men on his roll and pocket their pay without anyone complaining. No more than half a dozen, that was the only rule. My five dead men brought in a further three shillings and fourpence. Making a grand total of seven shillings and fourpence a day. After my years of borrowing and burrowing in the Inns of Court this was a princely wage I assure you, Carew. I didn't sniff at it.

Cork I did sniff at. Cork in that long hot summer of my first year in Ireland stank to high heaven. It consisted of one long street and a great number of middens. The Irish wore yellow shirts and were usually drunk. Irish horses were small in stature and the natives used to tie a plough to the tails of half a dozen of them to plough the fields.

In September word came into Cork that the Spaniard had landed on the west coast of Munster, and that there was a great fleet from Spain just offshore. We marched to meet the invader, found that he numbered about 600, and fought with him, capturing the Papal Nuncio's altar cloth. The enemy fell back and took possession of a fort at Smerwick. Lacking artillery, we withdrew to Rathkeale.

The invading army was small, but the whole country now rose to support the pugs of the Pope.

Grey himself, the Lord Deputy, arrived from Dublin with more troops. We heard that the Irish rampaged and burned their own villages behind his back as he came south. He took command of our English army and marched on the fort at Smerwick.

I tarried and stayed behind.

The Irish do most of their fighting in the manner of bandits. They like to sulk and skulk behind walls of stones, shooting the enemy in the back or waiting in ambush to fire darts at him. They have few soldiers as such. Most of the time in Ireland we found ourselves fighting an army of shadows, men who wore no uniform to declare their bloody trade, cowards who were peasants by day and cut-throats by night. The Irish have a special name or title for these secret killers. *Kerns* – that's what they call them.

Now I had noted that it was a custom among these Irish kerns to come creeping along out of the ditches whenever any English camp was struck. They would wait until our soldiers had departed. Then they came picking and plundering, taking whatever they found to be left behind.

So, when my Lord Grey hurried off with our main forces against

Smerwick fort, I elected to play the Irish at their own low game. I had my men conceal themselves about the remains of the camp at Rathkeale. We lay close in the darkness and we waited.

Soon enough a gang of these Irish kerns came slipping out of the night. We waited until they had made themselves comfortable and taken complete possession of our camp. Then I drew my sword, we leaped out from our hiding places, and we had the lot of them our prisoners in a matter of minutes.

One of the kerns was laden with loops of willow and osiers, bound and plaited together into withies, which they use instead of halters for their horses. I asked him what he intended to do with them.

'They are for hanging English churls,' he said.

'Is that so?' I said. 'Well, they'll serve just as well for hanging an Irish kern.'

I had the man hanged in one of his own withies. The rest I handled according to their deserts. Then I rode at the head of my company after Lord Grey.

I never saw a land so desolate. It was all wastes of bog and rocky outcrop, with ill-marked tracks, low hills, dwarf trees, and practically never a sign of human habitation.

When I arrived at the English camp below Smerwick fort I found Lord Grey in difficulties. His problem was that he could not attack the Spanish in their lair without proper artillery, and artillery is hard to transport in a land without roads. We had therefore to wait while messengers were dispatched to summon a handful of the Queen's ships to the coast of Munster. Each day that the ships never came we sat watching the woods to our rear, fearful that Desmond's rebel forces would come overland to join with the invader before we could blast him out.

Desmond never came. The ships did. Their ordnance once ashore, we had the fort at our mercy.

What's more, they soon knew it, those Spaniards. A single volley of cannon-balls and they desired a parley with the Lord Deputy. The Lord Deputy declined. A second volley and they requested that they might have liberty to depart with bag and baggage. Which was again declined. Then they sent out urgent word promising the surrender of the fort if only their leaders were permitted free passage to go home to Spain. But my Lord Grey refused this as quickly as all the rest. We required an absolute yielding or nothing.

Privately, I heard Grey remark that his outriders reported Desmond just four days' march away. If the rebels arrived before the fort fell then our only means of retreat would be cut off, and the ships could not save us or even hold their own against the combined might of Spain and Desmond's insurgents.

But it was at this point that any prospect of defeat became purely academic. The Spanish in the fort decided that there was no way they could escape. They hoisted a white flag, therefore, and with one voice they all cried out: 'Misericordia! Misericordia!' They sent messengers across to us offering to yield both themselves and their fort. Unconditional surrender.

My son, I am not proud of what happened next.

When the captain of the Spanish troops had yielded himself to Lord Grey, and the fort had surrendered, I was sent in together with another English soldier, Captain Mackworth, at the head of our two companies. To do Grey's dirty work. Which I didn't enjoy.

To be brief, we made a great slaughter. We put the most part of the Spaniards to the sword, killing 507 of them. We also hanged seventeen Irish and a few English who had turned traitor.

This action had been miscalled 'barbarous' and a 'massacre'. In fact, Captain Mackworth and I behaved exactly according to orders. Wholesale slaughter of enemy prisoners of war was orthodox military practice in Ireland at that time. (It might be regretted that we had been reduced to the level of what the Spanish or the Irish would have done to us, had the boot been on the other foot; but that is another matter.) If I have a criticism to make it is only the one that the Queen made, when she had Grey's report: namely, that he treated the leaders of the invading forces rather better than the rank and file, sparing some of them their lives for the sake of the ransom money. That was wrong. Those fat rats held no commission and should have been dispatched the same way as their mice. For the rest: Death is always a harsh sight, and it is true that the occupants of Smerwick fort died unarmed and in cold blood. But so does every murderer on the gallows. And these were mercenary murderers and papistical gallows-birds.

Lord Grey I did not like, and the dislike was mutual.

He had been a penny-pinching patron of my friend George Gascoigne, poet and soldier. Another good friend of mine, another poet, Edmund Spenser, became Grey's secretary in Ireland. Gascoigne was a boisterous ruffian, Spenser a gentle spirit; Grey treated both of them abominably, never recognizing their special qualities, using their need to further his own career. In which pursuit, I might add, he was not conspicuously successful.

He was a born complainer, a ruthless and insensitive boor, forever bemoaning his lot and asking the Queen to recall him from Ireland to the Court.

It was well known that he gave the confiscated lands of Anglo-Irish traitors to his own favourites. What was worse and less common than this was the way he infected those favourites with his private melancholy concerning that benighted country – so that the men despised their appointments, and abused them, and treated Ireland itself as a place irredeemably lost. Not a commonwealth, but a common woe.

When, later, I was asked by the Queen and the Council for my own reading of the Lord Deputy's character and policy, I pointed out a few of these shortcomings, and Grey got to hear of it. He went on record then to claim that his own experience and reason made him my superior in every respect.

'For my own part I must be plain,' he said, 'I like neither Captain Ralegh's carriage nor his company.'

I can return the compliment.

Grey stooped. He was companionable as the pox.

Queen Elizabeth's pedantic witty prattle. Sometimes that shrill Tudor voice reminded me of nothing so much as the monotonous sound made by the beak of a woodpecker when it is drumming, drumming, drumming against the bark of a tree.

'Stop your senseless chatter, spinster!' I'd mutter under my breath, exasperated beyond endurance.

What makes me remember this?

The *khoka* leaf perhaps. The Indian brought me another this afternoon and I am chewing it as I write. The herb has the power to sharpen the past, to make it like a thorn in the mind. It also heightens one's awareness of the present. A moment ago I cut myself a slice of bread. Cutting a slice of bread. What could be more everyday, more ordinary? Yet I found myself transfixed for a moment *in* the moment. The knife seemed to glow in my hand, the bread as it broke apart looked to me like a miracle, and I had all at once this sensation of being one with the knife and the bread and yet standing in the corner of my cabin and watching the whole transaction – bright blade cutting through brown crust – as if I were someone else, a spectator. I must question the Indian about the leaf's chemical properties. Also I must determine the limits of his harvest of them. The herb is without doubt a thousand times more potent than tobacco.

I remember Elizabeth's smell too. When she died they said that she had sat for many days and nights on a pile of cushions in the middle of her private chamber, refusing to go to bed. Then she danced. Then she fell down on the dancing floor. They had to strip layer after layer of cheesy petticoats from her. I remember –

What is it that says 'I' in *I remember*?

Memory has more to it than the first person singular. Memory's life is larger, deeper, darker, more abundant. Better to go along with these movements of remembrance than to get stranded in midstream on the mere stepping-stones of identity. What such movements amount to is not exactly a flowing river, either. Even less a long thread of moments passed through that eye of a needle which is the self.

But now I forget what I set out to say in the first place.

And where *was* the first place?

It was Windsor.

And Elizabeth never heard my complaint about her voice, I might add.

As antidote I call to mind what another man said of the Queen: 'When she smiled, it had a pure sunshine that every one did choose to bask in if they could; but anon came a sudden gathering of clouds, and the thunder fell in a wondrous manner on all.'

Thus Sir John Harrington, her godson, inventor of the water closet, and translator of Ariosto. (Whom he called Harry Osto.)

A fly is trying to get out of my cabin. It rages round the room: a meagre fury. And I have to get it right, of course. But what then is 'right'? My sea charts and tables, my almanacs? A very simpleminded sort of rightness. The smell of the dead men in Smerwick fort? More complicated that, if right at all. Yet I acted under orders, I did my duty. But there were flies on them, a passion of flies, and what if obedience can be a sin? God damn it, in Youghal, when they sacked the town, the Irish kerns were not content to slaughter all their brothers. They gouged out every woman's eyes, and slit every child's nose, besides. There is a long tally to count, and what I did that flyblown summer day with Captain Mackworth goes only a little way towards the reckoning.

Yet I mean there can be no escape. No escape from the past. No escape from the present. No escape for the fly from this room. No escape for your father, Carew, from this endless and pitiless remembering and repeating, always the same, always different, always the knife and always the spectator, always coming back to the present definition of events and then the sudden sharp despair of knowing that yet again the event has eluded me.

Elizabeth droned and Elizabeth stank.

Yet Elizabeth danced.

Yes. Elizabeth danced high and disposedly even on the edge of the grave. Elizabeth was nothing if not her father's daughter. I remember a story that she told me once. It concerned the day when she passed through London, one week before her coronation, in a procession of recognition. In Cheapside the young Elizabeth was seen to smile just once. An immeasurable smile, that pure sunshine. Many remarked on it, but few or none knew why she smiled. She told me why. It was because she had heard a voice in the crowd, the voice of an old man saying: 'I remember old King Harry the Eighth when I look at her.'

Note added later. What King Henry the Eighth has to do with anything is beyond credence. It seems to me now that the words I wrote under the influence of the eating of the leaf pass understanding. I let them remain here only as a warning to myself. For the rest: My talk about average speeds to Newfoundland and so forth strikes me as not allowing for the damnation that without doubt has gone with us on this voyage. Such estimates presume normality, and in the circumstances I must be a fool to presume anything of the kind. This infernal ship. This hellish voyage. How dare I imagine that we could ever enjoy fair winds in our sails?

As for the fly: I opened the door and it flew out to die in the larger cabin of the world.

14

So now we are down to two.

I must confess it: I am not much surprised. Overnight, the *Jason*, the *Southampton*, and the *Star* have fled. Parker, North, and Sir John Ferne, with their soldiers and their sailors, have deserted me.

Only the *Encounter* remains here beside my *Destiny* at St Kitts. The *Encounter*, of London, a ship of 160 tons, with seventeen pieces of ordnance. Thomas Pye is her master, and my old friend Samuel King her loyal captain.

The rumour runs among my own men that Parker, North, and Ferne have not gone to join the others who ran away before. Indeed, it is said that they have not turned pirate, but have sailed for home. Perhaps they have, perhaps they have not. They have elected to disobey their lawful Admiral, and to pursue their own ends upon the seven seas. Thus they are no better than mutineers. I shall say no more on the subject.

Their going makes me the firmer in my purpose.

We sail for Newfoundland, then sail for home.

'When?' Samuel King came aboard to ask me this morning.

'Tomorrow,' I told him.

And so tonight I choose to remember that moment just before dawn on the morning of Monday the 19th of March two years ago, when a black coach drawn by two black horses rattled across the bridge over the moat of the Tower of London, came to a brief halt while the great gates of the Middle Tower on the west wall swung open to allow it out, and then went hurtling north down Tower Hill. The coachman cracked his whip. One of the horses stumbled. The coach rocked from side to side, its iron wheels striking sparks from the frosty cobbles.

There were two men in the coach. One was Sir Lewis Stukeley, Vice Admiral of Devon. The other was Sir Lewis Stukeley's cousin.

'Damn this,' I said. 'Tell the coachman to stop. I want to go home with a few teeth as well as my head.'

'You will *walk*?' Stukeley asked. He seemed startled by the prospect.

'I always preferred it,' I said. 'That or horseback. These hell-carts are for women and invalids.'

Stukeley sighed. 'Very well then,' he said. 'I shall bear the responsibility.'

'You must,' I said. 'Don't forget. You're your cousin's keeper now.'

We were into Houndsditch Minories before the coachman could pull up his horses. I climbed down instantly and limped off up the street. Stukeley must have seized one of the flaring torches from the front of the coach before he came hurrying after me.

'Are you a bat or a devil?' he said, when he caught up. 'It seems you can see in the dark.'

I responded, I suppose, with a noise which was half grunt and half growl. I had come to a stop, leaning hard on my silver-topped stick. Stukeley stared at me. What must he have seen by the light of his torch? An old man's face, white, haggard, pinched with pain. Big beads of sweat on the high furrowed forehead, no doubt. And more sweat trickling down the hollowed-out cheeks.

'I remember my London,' I told him. 'And a man gets used to doing without daylight in the Tower.'

I moved off again, walking fast despite my limp. Stukeley kept up with me now. He snatched at my elbow.

'Sir Walter,' he said, 'this is dangerous. Let me go back for the carriage.'

'It's no more than a mile,' I said. 'Less, unless the streets have been stretched since the last time I walked them.'

I shivered, wiping froth from my mouth and from my beard. Then I stopped and considered my cousin in the torchlight. Stukeley looked little more than a boy. A plump, slightly petulant boy, fine-nostrilled, handsome, but with a weak chin and the merest scribble of hair on his upper lip. In fact, he must be about forty. His father died in '78. Thomas Stukeley. An adventurer, a malcontent. Killed by Moors at the Battle of Alcazar. In fair fight, apparently, though some say he was murdered *after* the battle by his own Italian soldiers. Peele wrote a play about him. A poor piece. No one is ever likely to write a play about his timorous son.

I said: 'What particular dangers do you have in mind, cousin Lewis?'

'I mean that this isn't the best of times to be out and about,' Stukeley said mildly. 'There are few honest men –'

'True, very true,' I snapped. 'Honesty never made a crowd even in my day. But I assure you that for an ancient prisoner any time is a more than good time to be "out and about", as you put it.' I chuckled. 'Besides, can you doubt that King James isn't taking care of us both every minute?'

Stukeley frowned. 'What do you mean?'

'I mean that you are inexperienced,' I told him. 'Too green and too close to me to be left to do a difficult job like this all on your own. I mean, sir, that you, my keeper, are yourself being kept. In other words, that the King's concern about his faithful subject Walter Ralegh is so great that if you were to turn around now and stroll back down the Minories you would have trouble not tripping over a few fine fellows in long black cloaks. No, don't look over your shoulder. Let us go on our way again.'

I set a slower pace then and the sun was just starting to come up over Aldgate when we met a man walking towards us. He was rough-looking, I remember, plainly an artisan of some kind, wearing a flat cap, coarse doublet, and trunk breeches. The man was carrying a small wooden box under his right arm. I nodded to him, and the man returned the greeting civilly, passed us, then turned on his heel and came back.

'If I'm wrong then I'm wrong,' he said. 'But you look like Sir Walter Ralegh.'

'Thank you,' I said.

'You *are* Walter Ralegh?'

'No less,' I admitted. 'And no more.'

The man set his box down on the pavement. He did this so carefully that it crossed my mind that it must contain eggs. The man bowed, removing his cap. 'So it's justice at last,' he said. 'King James has pardoned you. I give thanks to God, sir.'

'King James has not pardoned me,' I said. 'He has only let me out of my lodgings in the Tower to exercise my lame leg a little.'

The stranger looked confused. 'Do you joke with me, Sir Walter? I am only a simple man.'

I said: 'Then you are to be congratulated. Simplicity is the hardest thing of all, I think. What is your name?'

'Barnaby Adams, sir.'

'And what is your trade, Mr Adams?'

'I'm a bricklayer, sir. That is, when there's bricks to be laid. Times are bad. Times are very bad.'

'I am sorry to hear it,' I said.

'They've been worse for you,' the man replied generously. 'Locked up in the Tower all these years. But everybody knows you were never a traitor, sir, never a friend of the Spaniard like they said.'

'"An English face with a Spanish heart."'

'What's that, sir?'

'Something Mr Attorney Coke called me,' I explained. 'The words stuck in my head. What was the rest of it? Ah, yes. "Spider of hell." And "the greatest Lucifer that ever lived". Most picturesque.'

'Coke!' The bricklayer spat. 'They say that one can't even cope with his wife, sir. She's the biggest whore in London, if you'll pardon my Spanish!'

'Mr Adams,' I said, 'your simplicity is shrinking. You must not suppose that I hate Sir Edward Coke because he hated me. He is only a lawyer. As to my trial, it is my belief that he failed to do *himself* justice. As to his marital difficulties, one of the pleasures of imprisonment is that a man can concentrate his mind on other matters. Especially if, like me, that man is under a sentence of death which has never yet been revoked.'

The bricklayer, realizing that he was being scolded, I think, while perhaps not understanding how or why, covered his confusion by stooping to pick up his box again.

At the same time, Stukeley doused his torch by thrusting it into a puddle on the road. There was light enough now to be safe without it.

'Know the last time I saw you, Sir Walter?' the bricklayer said. 'It was when you marched through Westminster right alongside her coffin. The Queen's. Captain of the Guard you were then. Black plume on your helmet, black band on your arm. I remember the drums –'

I remembered them too. I did not want to indulge their memory further in a public street with a total stranger, however civil that stranger seemed. I coughed, therefore, and interrupted him.

'What's in your box, Mr Adams?' I asked, tapping at it lightly with the point of my cane.

The bricklayer stepped back as if wounded.

'My child, sir,' he said.

I stared at him.

'*Your child?*'

The man bit his lip. When he went on he sounded almost apologetic. 'My little son, sir,' he said. 'Dead of the fever. He was just the three weeks old, sir.'

I said: 'And you are carrying his body down the Minories in a box? I fail to understand . . .'

'Well, you see, sir, it's the parish dues,' the bricklayer said. 'It's the parish dues charged. I can't afford them. For a proper church burial and all.'

'So what do you intend to do?' I asked.

'What everyone does, sir,' he said. 'I mean – what everyone does who is poor. Take the morsel over London Bridge and dig a hole and bury him secret like, in St George's Fields or some other field south of Southwark.'

I shook my head. 'You say you are a bricklayer. What do you earn?'

'Varies, sir,' the man replied. 'Can be a shilling a day. That's six shilling a week and good enough when there's work to be had. But there's no work now.'

'How much are these parish dues for a burial?' I asked him.

'Nineteen and six, sir.'

I reached for my purse. Then I realized that I hadn't a purse. Sir William Wade, Lieutenant Governor of the Tower, had not supposed that his prisoner would need a few shillings. Not during a short coach ride from Tower Hill to his wife's house in Broad Street.

'Cousin Lewis –?' I said.

'Yes, yes, of course,' Stukeley said. He took coins from his purse and pressed them into the bricklayer's hand.

I had turned aside, my body racked by a bout of coughing.

Stukeley came and put his arm around my shoulders. I was shivering, I know, and my teeth were chattering. I must have made a rather alarming spectacle.

'I am not ague-proof,' I muttered. 'Don't be alarmed. It will pass.'

When it had, I drew myself up and nodded to the bricklayer.

'Good day, Mr Adams.'

I moved off to avoid the shower of blessings which the fellow started to invoke upon my head. I daresay I was limping badly by the time we passed through Bishopsgate and turned into Broad Street.

'That was horrible,' I said. 'Most horrible and pitiable.'

Stukeley said nothing. His face was angry and embarrassed. I asked him why. Then he pointed out to me that the bricklayer, after taking leave of us, had continued on his way towards Southwark and the open fields beyond it. I hadn't looked back, I hadn't noticed this as my cousin did. Nor was I in a position to know what Stukeley told me next. Namely, that there was currently a boom in the bricklaying trade, with houses going up everywhere in the open country north of the Strand, in Long Acre, all around St James's Park, in Tothill Fields, and even out as far as Islington.

'So we were cheated?' I said.

'I suspect as much,' said Stukeley.

I shrugged. It was no great matter. But I could see that my cousin pitied me for being taken in.

We came to the house on Broad Street.

Bess was waiting.

Carew, you will know that your mother was born Bess Throgmorton, daughter of Sir Nicholas Throgmorton, friend and familiar of the boy-King Edward the Sixth and that she is some twelve years younger than me. You should know also, truth to tell, that your mother was never a great beauty, but that her face was always fair to me, and well-beloved, as I am sure it is in proper part to you, for those qualities of sensitiveness, intelligence, and humour which makes it as rich and resourceful as her heart. She has a peculiarity, my dear Bess, less rare than it is believed. One of her eyes is blue and the other is black. I remind you of this, Carew, in order to draw out a moral lesson from the physical fact. Your mother's eyes were made for love and hate, for happiness and misery, for the mixing of joy and sorrow in equal measure. My dearest Bess has known all these things in the twenty-six years of our marriage – a marriage which cost her five months in the Tower at the outset, and thereafter banishment for life from Elizabeth's Court. For Bess Throgmorton was one of the Queen's Maids of Honour when I first loved her, and Elizabeth's sexual jealousy could be pitiless.

She was waiting for me there, as I said, at her house on Broad Street. We embraced and kissed without words. I stroked her grey hair, remembering its gold.

She said: 'You're shaking, husband. Here, drink this hot peppermint cordial I've kept ready for you.'

I took the cup and drained it.

She said: 'You walked?'

'Of course,' I said.

'Idiot!' she said. 'Dear idiot. Mad March hare on a cold March morning. Will you never learn sense?'

'I doubt it,' I told her. 'Too old for that now, Bess. But this ague is nothing. Nothing your kitchen comforts can't put right.'

I kissed her again as she helped me off with my gown. 'Where are our boys?' I asked.

Bess folded the gown and stood holding it clasped in her arms. 'Poor little Carew's fallen asleep,' she told me. 'Can you credit it? He was up most of the night, running upstairs and down, opening doors and pretending you were standing there, rehearsing all sorts of pretty speeches he would make to welcome you, then slamming the doors and worrying you'd never come. There was no way I could make him go to his bed. In the end he got so worn out with excitement that he fell asleep on the windowseat in the library. I tiptoed in and found him, and put a rug around him.'

God bless you, my son!

'And young Wat?' I said.

Bess shot a swift glance at Stukeley, then whispered three words softly in my ear. You know already what those three words were. '*Sowing wild oats.*'

I must have frowned, and drawn down the ends of my mouth, for Bess said, 'Now don't be angry, husband,' and touched my lips with her fingers, as if to make me smile.

'He's your spit and image, our wild wag,' she went on. 'You'd have been much the same at his age, and you can't deny it.'

I did not deny or affirm anything. But I think my eyes must have been cloudy and troubled as I watched Bess move matter-of-factly to put my gown away in a wardrobe.

'Come,' she said, turning. 'You go and wake Carew. Then we shall all have some breakfast. Cousin Lewis too.'

Every inch Lady Ralegh now, she held out her right hand to Stukeley, who bowed and kissed it.

'I apologize for being here,' he murmured.

'You are welcome,' Bess said. 'Someone had to do the job. It was kind of you to volunteer.'

'Thank you, cousin,' Stukeley said.

Bess turned back again to me. 'Breakfast,' she repeated. 'Oysters and anchovies, with warm white wheaten rolls. And afterwards you will smoke a pipe of tobacco. I've missed that more than anything in this house. The smell of your old Indian tobacco!'

'More than *anything*?' I quizzed her, shaking off my gloom.

We shared what should have been a private smile.

Sir Lewis Stukeley went awkwardly to the window. He told me later that he had intended only to turn his back on us out of politeness, but as he gazed down into Broad Street he saw two men slip out of an alleyway and take up positions opposite the house. They were not wearing long black cloaks, but then they didn't need to. Their trade was obvious.

That's how it began. This latest and last grand adventure. This damned pilgrimage. This quest for mere gold which has cost me the life of my son.

From the Tower I came forth, after thirteen years in the darkness. From London I sailed, one year later, full of hope, puffed with pride, at the head of a fleet of new ships.

Now it's over. All over. Now I go home to die.

'Guattaral,' the Indian says.

The Indian is right.

It is not Sir Walter Ralegh who writes this. It is a broken man, a wasted mind, a ghost, the senseless echo of a dying name.

Guattaral sails for Newfoundland, and then home.

15

We sailed out from St Kitts at six o'clock in the morning, with white birds all around us like a plume, having fair skies and seas sweet as new-mown hay and the wind in the south-east blowing strong yet not too strong. From six until ten at night we ran 100 miles north by north-west. Since ten o'clock we have had hardly a whisper of wind, and journeyed not much more than five miles due north. It is now approaching midnight, with a good round moon and a black sky packed with stars but no sign of the wind coming back to us.

All the same, a satisfactory first day.

I have given Wat's old cabin to the Indian. It was standing empty, and since the man refused to inhabit or employ Keymis's cabin this seemed the only sensible thing to do. He appears content with the honour, at all events, and has retired to rest in his new quarters now. So at least we should be spared the trouble of having him tumble overboard from his makeshift bed on the bowsprit in the middle of the night.

Why the Indian would never sleep in Keymis's cabin is not clear. I suspect that it had more than a little to do with the knowledge that Keymis killed himself in there. However, the man has said scarcely a word all day, being withdrawn and preoccupied, sometimes appearing silently on deck to watch us at work sailing the ship, occasionally following the progress of the *Encounter* in our wake, more often to be observed standing alone in the bows and staring out ahead across the sea.

What he might expect to meet there is beyond my imagination.

When I told him that I had decided that he should have my son's cabin, he bowed his head as though beginning a gesture of gratitude, but then raised it again abruptly and gave a mere nod as if this was no more than what he considered his due.

Enigmatic tropical night!

The stars are the only friendly things in all this friendless sea of warmth.

In such a night as this one should be able to forget and forgive much.

I can forget nothing.

And forgiveness was never my style.

I spent the winter and another year in Ireland. I did nothing much, but in that waste of desolation it was enough. At Christmas, 1581, I was called home. I stepped at once from a country as wild as the nether limits of Muscovy into the fantastic Yuletide festivities of the Queen's Court at Westminster.

I was twenty-seven years old. What had I achieved? I had held command of one of Elizabeth's ships, but on a voyage that met with no success. I had been captain of a band of volunteers in Elizabeth's army, but in a war which was getting nowhere. My coming out of Ireland to the English Court was scarcely to be welcomed by fireworks or announced with a roll of drums. Yet, at a stroke, I established myself in the Queen's eyes. How? I'll tell you how. By a piece of poetry.

This poetry was not written. It had nothing to do with words. To understand it you must rid your mind of the idea that poetry is always and of necessity limited to the world of language. Poetry can be in persons and their actions. A poem can come into being between a man and a woman. This concept of poetry has to do with an idea of absolute rightness. But while such rightness is commonly a matter of the best words in the best order, it can also be a matter of the best acts in the best order. Or, rather, the *only* acts in the *only* order. That's what I mean by absolute rightness, my son. Sometimes there is only one thing to do, the right thing, but you have to be inspired to do it.

Also you need luck.

I had luck.

On the opposite side of the road from the Banqueting Hall in the great honeycomb which was the Queen's Palace of Westminster there was an arena known as the Tiltyard. That Christmas of '81 they had bear-baiting in the Tiltyard, especially for the entertainment of the creature Elizabeth called her Frog Prince. This was the Duke of Anjou, brother of the King of France and heir to his throne, a pock-marked nonsense who for six years had been going through a pantomime of courtship with the Queen. Elizabeth had no intention of marrying the Frog, but it suited her to pretend that she might. It suited her also to make an elaborate but inexpensive fuss of amusing Anjou. Hence the bears brought across the Thames from their regular stadium in the Paris Garden and baited in the Tiltyard.

Now the Queen watched such shows from the Tiltyard Gallery, which she reached from her Privy Gallery in the Banqueting Hall by walking through the Holbein Gate and across the road. It was a narrow place, ill-paved, and on that Christmas Eve it was all plashy with half-melted ice and snow.

Bearing a dispatch from my Lord Grey to the Earl of Leicester, I came walking from the Tiltyard across to the Palace at precisely the moment when the Queen came walking in the opposite direction. Suddenly I found myself face to face with a proud fastidious woman in confusion, hesitating, seeming to scruple at the prospect of having to step out of the Gallery and into the plashy road. Around her, behind her, others, lords and ladies, also in momentary disarray.

I did not hesitate.

I performed the poetry.

I plucked my cloak from my shoulders and bowed and spread it out across the mire for the Queen to walk on.

Elizabeth clapped her hands together and laughed. Then she stepped on the cloak. Then she stopped and turned and asked me to tell her my name.

Understand, Carew, my clothes were then a considerable part of my estate. It was a new plush cloak, red as flame, which I had purchased just the day before, especially for my appearance at Court. The rest of my captain's wages had gone on other items of apparel. I was spreading out all that I had for the Queen to walk on. I was offering everything that I possessed in order to save her a moment's embarrassment. I was throwing my life and fortune at her feet.

There lies the poem.

For her part, Elizabeth trod gently on my cloak. And when she had crossed over she bade me take it up again. She understood my action perfectly. The ladies and gentlemen who were following her had to make the best way they could through the mud.

That was all, then. I delivered my dispatch to the Earl of Leicester, who was delighted to have the opportunity to remark that I looked for all the world as though I had just hopped straight out of an Irish bog. I didn't mind. I wore the mud on my cloak with as much pride as if it was blood won in a war.

The Queen, no doubt, had gone on to enjoy the bear-baiting. But she had not forgotten me. I had caught her eye and held it. Not just by my good looks or my youth or my wit either. By being in the right place at the right time and doing the right and only thing. Not easy, Carew. Not to be despised.

All the same, I must not make too much of this. Elizabeth made enough of it for two.

The next day, being Christmas, I was summoned to appear before her Majesty and give an account of my experiences in the wars in Ireland. Truth to tell, I got no further with this than the mere announcement of my name. She had smiled when I told it to her by the Holbein Gate. A quick, inward-turning, private smile which I had not understood. Now she threw back her head and laughed out loud and I was made to understand.

'*Water?*' she said. '*Water Rawly?*'

My Devon drawl served to intrigue and amuse her from the start. She inquired graciously after the cleaning arrangements for my cloak. After much verbal playing on *water* and *rawness*, in which I was encouraged by her to join, and during which her eyes never left my face, I was eventually dismissed with the instruction to present myself again before the Lord Chamberlain, the Earl of Sussex, at nine o'clock that evening.

When I did I was told that the Queen had been pleased to appoint me an Esquire of her Body. This meant that I joined the small company of young men who took charge of the Presence Chamber each night, and slept there. The Presence Chamber was that part of the Palace of Westminster where the Queen and her Councillors appeared usually in the afternoon, where most of the Court danced attendance, and where ambassadors and other official visitors were granted audience. Beyond the Presence Chamber was the Privy Chamber, where the Queen took her meals with her half-dozen Maids of Honour. Beyond the Privy Chamber were the Privy Lodgings, the Queen's private apartments, where she slept.

From being a rough soldier in a wretched war I had been transformed into a member of the Queen's personal bodyguard. All because of one moment, a single inspired gesture, in which I declared without words my longing to make her my life and my fate. You see, Carew, when I spread my cloak I spread my dreams at her feet, and Elizabeth was woman enough to know it.

Mr Child's gown would not have done.

Two o'clock after midnight, four bells of the middle watch, and the wind has begun to fresh. I shall leave Robert Burwick, a good master, to hold our course north until morning.

Sackerson and Harry Hunks.

Names of bears. Bears in the Tiltyard that Christmas I came first to Elizabeth's favour.

I remember Sackerson in particular, standing upright in the centre of the sanded circle, a huge brown bear, one hind leg chained to a stake, being attacked by some half a dozen mastiffs. The dogs snarling, the dogs worrying and snapping at their lumbering opponent, but the bear more than a match for them. One mastiff lying dead in the sand. Flash of the bear's teeth in the December sun as it bit off the ear of another dog. Sackerson clawing, roaring, tossing, tumbling, dealing such buffets that mastiffs went spinning through the air and out of the circle. The bear dancing then, shaking blood and slaver from its muzzle. Pink eyes, pink paws, and bad breath stinking up from the Tiltyard.

Anjou the Frog Prince applauding. His hands like pale gloves filled with wet sand. His face pitted with pock-marks. Especially his nose, like a great blunt strawberry.

Elizabeth watching her Frog Prince, smiling pleasantly with her mouth, her eyes not smiling. Long fingers playing with the little green-jewelled frog she wore in her bosom.

A new Esquire of the Body watching his Queen.

Due north, Mr Burwick. For Polaris, Stella Maris, best and brightest star in the constellation of Ursa Minor. Due north while I sleep. If I sleep.

16

Describe her now as she appeared to me.

I had seen her before, of course. But never close up.

I had seen Gloriana. Now I saw Elizabeth. There was not so much difference. The difference came later.

Elizabeth looked tall, but she was not. Her habit of holding herself erect and straight-backed accounted for that. Her neck was long, and smooth as ivory. She was pale, she was haughty. Well-favoured but high-nosed. The iron beak of her thin Plantagenet blood. Her eyes, which changed rapidly from gold to grey if you displeased her, had lost little of their original sceptical sharpness. For all that, she was short-sighted, and would blink, bewildered, lost, if emerging too fast into light from darkness or vice versa. The whole compass of her countenance somewhat long. Small sucking lips, often parched, visited now and again by that flickering ironic inward-referring smile I first noticed by the Holbein Gate. At forty-eight not the rouged waxen doll in a wirework ruff which she would become, but the ghost of a girl with red hair like wisps of fire, her hands (which she took care not to hide) of special beauty, her glance quick and sidelong, with always an air of complicity and radiant busyness about her.

She was divine.

She was devilish.

I do not speak lightly. There was an angel at work in the Queen, and there was a devil. She was very woman. The angel and the devil were at war. Not just for her soul. For her body. She was never at peace with herself save when she was dancing. Dancing she loved. To see her dance was to see her whole spirit at work.

An English Cleopatra.

Our Lady of Albion.

Something about her also of Diana. The moon goddess. Hecate. Hag and maid. Mistress and virgin.

> A knowledge pure it was – her worth to know.
> With Circe let them dwell that think not so.

I wrote that once, in a poem in praise of the Queen. My verdict on the purity or impurity of knowing her was to place me in Circe's company in the end.

I slept in the Presence Chamber every night. I observed the Queen's comings and her goings. I saw her flirt perversely with Anjou, then laugh behind his back that the stupid Frog could be so taken in. I watched her listening to her Councillors and yawning into her hand. I watched in particular the game she played with Sir Christoper Hatton, her Vice Chamberlain and the Captain of her Guard. She called him her 'Sheep', her 'Mutton', and her 'Ram'. I watched the teasing and teased looked which passed between them.

Hatton, dark, handsome, in his early forties, was her favourite dancing partner. Their dances were like no others that I had ever seen. Lutes and virginals playing in a candlelit room full of mirrors, with much leaping and turning and touching of hands, then standing and slapping and clapping. The Queen would dance always a little out of Hatton's reach, like a child twisting this way and that in a game of tag. But by the end of the dance she would be looking back over her shoulder at him, her pale face flushed, her gold eyes hot and bright, her parched lips slightly gasping and apart, in a fashion not like any child's in any child's game.

They would go dancing out of the Presence Chamber and into the Privy Chamber, Elizabeth leading, Hatton following, while the rest of us Gentlemen of the Body were required to stand and stamp to the long pounding music. Then the door of the Privy Chamber slammed shut behind them and that was that. The music stopped, the musicians put away their instruments, and we were left staring stupidly at one another, aroused, disappointed, but never saying a word about the arousal or its disappointment.

As for the closed door – who could think ill of it? The Privy Chamber was not empty. That was the perpetual province of the

Queen's Maids of Honour. Sometimes I caught a glimpse of her in there in the midst of her white-clad female attendants.

If Elizabeth chose to lead Hatton out of the Presence Chamber and into the Privy Chamber then that was her privilege. What happened next was anyone's guess. Not that anyone dared to speculate about it aloud. Not that anyone *would* have guessed, if my experience is anything to go by, and what happened to Hatton is what happened to me, as seems more than likely, though I never cared to ask her nor she to tell me. Not that anyone could give free rein to galloping licentious imagination about it, in any event, for wasn't the Queen protected from such slanderous and possibly treasonable fantasies by the fact that there were *always* those Maids of Honour in the Privy Chamber?

Very well. Very true. But this leaves two vital matters out of the account.

First, the arousal caused by the dance. And here I should say that these dances – while they could be demanded or called for only by the Queen, as the whim took her, at any time of the day or more usually the night – were attended only by men, only by the select band of the Esquires of the Body, arranged and aligned in good order around the mirrored walls of the Presence Chamber.

Second, not every dance would end with the door closed behind the two dancers. I should say that rather more than half the dances which Elizabeth danced with Hatton ended with the door closed behind Elizabeth alone. She would kick it with her foot, encased in a tiny gold shoe, as she went dancing through into the Privy Chamber. On these occasions, it was Hatton who was left in the palpable but indescribable state of arousal and disappointment. He never said a word. He would turn on his heel and stalk from the chamber, head down, fists clenched, breathing heavily, often with a foolish grin on his face as if it was no matter.

As to what determined his fate on each occasion – whether the capricious Queen would let him dance into the Privy Chamber at her heels, or whether he would find the connecting door slammed in his face – there seemed no telling.

Yet I felt that I was on the edge of some momentous secret, in the first avenues of a maze of great mystery, and that along with the other dozen or so Esquires of the Body I was being permitted, however ignorantly, however imperfectly, to participate in something that was essential to our mistress Elizabeth.

Perhaps I need hardly add that these strange and secret dances were never discussed at the Court, nor were they ever reported or referred to by anyone. The silence was so complete that one could have been forgiven for supposing the whole thing a dream. There seemed to be an unwritten rule on the subject. And an unstated knowledge besides that if that rule was broken then the breaker could expect the Queen's displeasure to amount to a demand for his death.

I said nothing.

I never even so much as wrote down a sketch of the matter until this present and private writing.

True, I did hint at it in certain verses – but that was later, and the poems were for the Queen's eyes only, and they are now no doubt destroyed.

I hinted also in those same verses at what happened (as it were) in the dance that followed the dance.

None ever spoke of that, nor even threatened to speak of that, and kept his head. (Witness the fate of my Lord Essex.)

But this was later also, when I was learning by experience, when I had taken Sir Christopher Hatton's place.

I'll come to it, if I dare, if I can, soon enough, when it is time in the story, although I am not yet clear in my mind how much of it I ought to tell at all, if anything.

Meanwhile, that first Christmas, that glittering New Year, that beginning spring, I watched.

I watched Queen Elizabeth and she watched me watching her.

And the music hammered and the dancers danced and the blood coursed hot and furious in my veins.

The winds have swung round to the south and west by south. Today we sailed another ninety miles, taking care to avoid the Spanish island of Puerto Rico, which Columbus christened San Juan, and the Indians call Borinquen. Our position is 18° 50′ north, in 66° west. I saw at evening a rainbow in a waterspout. Terrible beauty. The rainbow faded. The waterspout remained. It was huge, about a mile and a half ahead of the ship when I first saw it. Then it moved round rapidly to port until it was a bare half a mile from our side. I couldn't take my eyes off it. If we ran foul of something like that then I fear we would stand little chance of getting through. The *Encounter* managed to keep directly astern of us. For nearly fifteen minutes the whirling column of water twisted up to a low black cloud before I lost sight of it in the swiftly fading light.

17

Main sail, fore sail, main top-sail, fore top-sail, top-gallant sails, royal sails, studding sails – we are riding the sea under every bolt of canvas that will haul and hold wind.

Exhilaration of taking the wheel as we do!

I imagine I can feel all the timbers singing through my hands, from keel to cross-trees, and from stem to stern . . .

Steady, old fool that you are. Be quiet, my heart.

What a parcel of confusions and contradictions the flesh is, to be sure. Here I am, half-drunk with delight at taking a turn at the wheel of a ship which flies through the foam to speed me home to disaster and (probably) death. As soon see beauty in the way the vultures turn against the sun to spread their wings downwind in search of carrion to eat? Yes, and I do that too.

Details from the log.

27 March: From six in the morning till twelve at night we ran 140 miles. Wind strong from the south. Our course being north by north-west. Crossed latitude 20° north.

28 March: The wind failed in the night but continued well from nine in the morning until eleven this evening. We steered away north-west by north, running 120 miles.

29 March: From midnight to midnight our best day yet. Winds fair to strong, and constant from the south. 170 miles run. Course: north by north-west.

Now it is noon, 30 March, with the wind still following, making a generous shoulder of seas on which we sail. In the past twelve hours we have come another ninety miles. Since quitting St Kitts we have completed a total of 715 miles in five and a quarter days. This is the best time we have made on the whole voyage since leaving Plymouth last year. It amounts, by Mr Burwick's calculation, to an average rate of 136 miles a day, and he calculates also that during some of that time we have been sailing at speeds of twelve knots.

This is, of course, excellent. If it could be maintained we should reach Newfoundland in about thirteen days, making an overall time for the voyage of little more than eighteen days. It would be foolish to hope for that, perhaps. But it does begin to look as though my original allowance of one whole month for this stretch of the journey home might err on the side of pessimism. It is, all things considered, quite possible that we shall see the harbour of St John in Newfoundland three weeks after quitting St Kitts instead of four.

We are presently, whatever happens, and whether the future holds a bag of fair winds or ill for us, within about one day's sail of San Salvador, that little island where Columbus fell ashore in October 1492, believing that he had found his way to the Orient. The Indians call that island Guanahani.

At the same time, I must report that our ship's master, Robert Burwick, a most experienced mariner, has commented daily for the past three days on the fact that these strong southerly winds are uncommon in these latitudes at this time of the year. He refers me to the almanacs: about one half of the winds to be expected, on an annual basis, are from the east or north-east; in March and April this percentage rises to three quarters. Some of the crew are conversant with this figure. I have overheard idle talk of our progress being 'unnatural' and 'ill-omened'. Last night a meteor fell into the sea at four or five miles distance to the north. That will provide further fuel for their superstitious grumblings, no doubt.

We glide along and they have little enough to do. Our course determined, we square in the yards and keep the vessel before the breeze. The ship and the wind do the rest between them.

The sky presents an unbroken expanse of most delicate blue, except along the skirts of the horizon. There I can see a mass of milky-looking clouds in curious formation. In appearance it might be a forest of trees set on the silver shore of Valhalla. So mysterious and exquisite it seems.

As for the sea, its swell is long and measured, its surface broken only by shoals of flying fish, like showers of bright metal.

I note also how my mood has improved since we left the islands. Just to be moving is sufficient, just to be sailing along. My problems remain as they were. My life is in ruins. Yet not for the first time I observe how merely to take action provides me with relief from the tensions which tortured my mind. Past tense? Not quite. The rack travels with me, within me, but I am eased an inch or two by pursuing a definite course.

I eat better too. My appetite for everything is made keener. At dawn this morning I made my breakfast of yams as big as a man's arm.

As I told you, the Indian has been withdrawn and elusive ever since we weighed anchor from St Kitts.

At first, I ascribed his temper to the uncertainty which he must surely feel on account of being for the first time so far out of sight of land. But all the several attempts which I have made to reassure him on this subject have met with a blank response.

He stands for much of each day leaning up against the bulwarks, the skin of his face and arms and legs as dark as the timbers behind him, gazing out in a kind of trance of concentration across the sea. At night he employs Wat's cabin.

Notice that I avoid the term *sleeps in*.

I don't know if the Indian sleeps at night. I'm not at all sure that the Indian really wakes by day. Most of the time he seems to be suspended in some limbo between waking and sleeping.

This afternoon, during the first dog watch, I sought to rouse him from his torpor by referring to the death of Palomeque.

'What would you say,' I demanded, 'if I told you that I did not believe your story of having murdered your Spanish master?'

His eyes met mine. They did not flicker. His huge jaws worked methodically all the while. He was chewing one of his *khoka* leaves.

After a silence he shrugged his shoulders and said: 'What Guattaral believes is not important.'

This answer angered me.

I said: 'What *is* important then, in your estimation?'

'What I know,' he replied.

I thought of his life passed in obscurity in the dark hinterland of the southern American continent, comparing it with my own life, and I laughed.

'Your philosophy is arrogant,' I said.

'I think not.'

'What do you mean then?' I demanded.

'I say only that knowledge is the important thing,' he replied. 'What I know. What Guattaral knows. What men *know* is what is important. Not what they think they believe.'

'But there must be many things which belong to belief rather than to knowledge,' I complained.

'For instance?' he said.

'For instance, God,' I said.

The Indian said nothing.

He chewed. He stared at the horizon.

'Do you believe in God?' I said.

He spat. He shook his head.

'No?' I said.

The Indian shifted the bulge of the leaf from one cheek to the other. 'I do not believe in gods,' he said. 'I know.'

'Know?'

'*Know.*'

'Know what?' I said.

'Know gods,' the Indian replied.

His continual shift of emphasis is disconcerting. In this particular case it also served to make me feel ashamed. No more than Queen Elizabeth have I ever been possessed by a desire to make windows into men's souls, and to demand to see what secrets lie in them. The Indian's conception of the Deity is no doubt both strange and simple. His insistence that nevertheless he *knows* what he knows, rather than merely believing something which he has been told, impresses my conscience with its moral force.

Theology and science are one to him. His world and my world have different shapes.

'Very well,' I said. 'Let us leave that. But concerning things like the death of Palomeque. That is different. I can only believe or disbelieve what you tell me.'

'Not so,' he said. 'You know.'

'Know what?'

'You know the truth about that,' he said. 'I killed Palomeque. I also killed your son. And you have forgiven me. You gave me his cabin.

I looked at him for a long time. I said nothing. He did not look at me.

It may seem mad to say so, but I must say it: What he says is true. I *do* know. He did kill Palomeque. He did (in some sense) kill Wat.

I do not 'believe' it. I do not know how to believe such things.

But I know.

And I *have* forgiven him.

Myself, however, I have not forgiven. Which is perhaps another way of saying that while I know that what the Indian says is true, I do not understand how I know it, or why I know it, or what I should do with the knowledge. Nor do I know what it means.

Elizabeth got rid of her Frog Prince.

She went with him down the river to Gravesend. In Canterbury, at their parting, she contrived to cry. I suspect she used an onion in her handkerchief. Anjou set off on some fool's errand to the Netherlands, accompanied by Leicester and a hundred English gentlemen lent for the brief occasion by the Queen. I was one of the hundred.

In Antwerp, William the Silent lived up to his name. He saw through Anjou. Anjou drifted off to Paris in a huff. The Queen wrote to Leicester demanding our immediate return. We were spending too much money, so she said.

When I came back from Antwerp the Court was at Greenwich.

Ireland was talked about. I made several criticisms of current policy. Notably, I suggested that our soldiers there should not be kept waiting for their pay. English soldiers in Ireland without support were inclined to rob the native population. I spoke also of Grey's shortcomings. Lord Burghley made a note of all I said.

Elizabeth found my criticisms cogent.

I had gotten her ear in a trice. She began by being taken with my elocution. Soon she loved to hear my reasons to her demands. As Essex's protégé Sir Robert Naunton once said spitefully: The Queen took me for a kind of oracle, which nettled them all.

Sir Christopher Hatton – Elizabeth's 'Sheep', her 'Mutton', her 'Ram', her 'Bell-Wether', her '*Pecora Campi*' – was nettled the most.

The dances continued.

But the door to the Privy Chamber was kicked shut by the Queen's dancing feet more and more often.

I think Hatton guessed even before I did that his days in the dance were numbered, and that I was destined to replace him as the Queen's dear minion.

All that spring of the year 1582 I rose in favour.

It was Francis Bacon (who should have known) who said: 'All rising to great place is by a winding stair.'

My feet were on that stair. And I was rising.

'If thy heart fail thee . . .'

It didn't.

But what did I see from the windows of that winding stair? (Apart from my own diamond writing on the pane.)

I saw Elizabeth's golden idolatrous Court.

I saw the hierarchy of male merit.

I liked the prospect from the windows. I liked it a lot.

Summer came. Hatton absented himself. In October he sent his friend Sir Thomas Heneage to the Queen at Windsor. I was with her. She was mounted, in a green habit laced with gold, at dawn, and about to go riding to the hunt. Heneage bore gifts from the Mutton. Jewels in the shape of a book, a bodkin, and a miniature silver bucket.

'What does this mean?' asked the Queen.

I read the symbols for her.

'Sir Christopher swears (by the book) that he will kill himself (with a bare bodkin) if your Majesty does not see less of me.'

'Less of you? How so?'

'Not much *water* to be got in a dwarf-size bucket, a thimblekin.'

Elizabeth laughed.

'I shall send him back a bird,' she said.

'A bird?'

'Like the one sent back to the Ark to announce the covenant that there should be no more Flood. That is – not too much water.'

The meaning was perhaps obscure. And the bird was not a dove. And, besides, she could hardly send the poor fellow an explanatory rainbow to go with it.

Which accounts, in part, for the Ram's continuing sulks.

Two months later he sent the Queen a tiny fish-tank. No doubt he meant that water creatures, fishy types, should be kept in confinement.

'Ah,' said Elizabeth. 'A fish prison.'

She turned to me.

'What am I to make of this?'

'Are there fishes in it?'

'See.'

She held up the little bright bowl. There were several small fry swimming round.

'I don't know,' I said carefully. 'Unless we are meant to infer that mutton is preferable?'

Elizabeth smiled.

She sent Heneage back with the message that water and its various creatures contented her less than Sir Christopher evidently supposed. Her food, she said, had always been more of flesh than of fish. Her opinion, she said, was steadfast that flesh was more wholesome.

Hatton was mollified.

He came back to Court.

And they danced again.

But increasingly Elizabeth was watching me in the steps and turns and teasings of the dance. Her cool eyes watched, her long hands waved and fluttered. Her eyes pierced me. I longed to kiss that hand. I wrote a rather bad poem about this. It began: 'Those eyes that hold the hand of every heart, Those hands that hold the heart of every eye.' A pretty confusion. And my senses were pretty confused.

I waited.

Horizon. Nothing but horizon.

Dolphins and porpoises fool in the cut water, leaping here and darting there. It's difficult to follow any particular one for more than a few yards.

Wind whips the wave-crests into a fine mist, which catches and reflects the sun's rays in a barrage of rainbows. The sea is pure blue, with patches of gold and salmon reflected from the sky.

When I am at the wheel I have the whole ship before me. I hold her as I might hold an apple in my hand.

My flag as Admiral. It flows with the wind.

Five silver lozenges on a field of blue.

My coat of arms emblazoned up there, streaming from the top-mast.

Its motto: '*Amore et Virtute*'. By love and by courage.

I feel like a part of this ship now. I feel the strain upon the masts, within the sails, as if it were a strain on my own heart.

At the same time, in the same breath, I despise myself for these too simple feelings. Be sure, the sea is a pasture for fools. Myself among them.

18

The wind whirls us northwards. The wind is master of my *Destiny* now. The wind whirls us faster and faster.

In the week that is past we have sailed another 800 miles. Our position is on a parallel with Cape Hatteras and Roanoke Island. That is, in 33° of north latitude.

We stand about a thousand miles off Newfoundland.

And the seas for two days now have been stained with that swift-flowing weed which betokens the Gulf Stream. The weather is more mixed and the air has an edge to it presently.

Roanoke Island. I sent seven ships there in '85, under command of my cousin Sir Richard Grenville. He planted a colony and came home. This was the start of my disillusion with the New World. In no time at all those colonists succeeded in turning friendly Indians into enemies. They were fortunate to be picked up by Francis Drake at the end of one of his privateering voyages to the Caribbean, and ferried back to England for a fee.

I lost money but not all heart. No doubt it would have been better the other way round. Two years after that abortive attempt at a first colony in the land I named Virginia (in honour of the Queen), I dispatched 150 pioneers to the same place. There were seventeen women among them. A new fort was set up on the star-shaped ruin of the abandoned old one. John White was appointed Governor.

Briefly, for a cruel moment of kindness, it seemed as if this colony might survive and prosper. In the summer of '87 the first English child was born on the American continent, a daughter to Eleanor and Ananias Dare. They called her Virginia, of course. But then nerves began to falter. The settlers sent John White back to England for more spades, more seeds, more axes – all those small necessities of civilization which might serve to save them from extinction.

White took his time. He was not really a man of action, being more adept at painting water colour pictures of plants and animals. Bess still possesses some of his pictorial records of Indian life. You will have seen them on the walls of the house in Broad Street.

Anyway, when John White finally returned to Roanoke he found the tiny settlement deserted.

No one there.

Nothing.

There had been a prearranged signal in case of danger. A Maltese cross was to be cut in the wood of the stockade and a sign carved to indicate what had happened. No cross was ever discovered. All White could find was a tree with three letters cut into its bark.

The letters spelt:

CRO

What happened to that Roanoke colony? Had the settlers gone to live with the Croatoan Indians? Were they massacred by them? Or did something else happen?

White never found out. And I cannot presume to guess.

For years, though, I liked to believe that Virginia Dare was not dead. I dreamt that one day (maybe centuries hence) there would come reports of a breed of white-faced, blue-eyed Indians somewhere in the interior.

But this is romance.

The lesson to be learned is not romantic. The lesson is that all that may finally survive of us is a few enigmatic letters carved on a tree, letters without sure meaning to those who find and read them.

Like these words I write now?

Here's something definite, beyond ambiguity. All day yesterday I was seasick. Put it down to the force of these winds that pursue us. The ship rears and bucks and plunges in the water. My gut was racked. I could keep nothing down.

I remember Sam King's old joke on the subject.

'You know the best cure for it, Admiral?'

'Is there one?'

'Only one. But infallible.'

'A cure for seasickness? Quick! Tell me, man, tell me . . .'

'Sit under an elm tree,' Sam said.

'Keel haul that damned comedian!' I shouted. But the burst of laughter stopped my vomiting for a moment.

That was many long years ago, on the voyage to Cadiz.

I kept thinking of it yesterday, even as I lay retching into a bowl on my bed in this great cabin. Lord God, how I longed for a level English meadow beneath me and a sweet spiring elm tree above! I'd have traded all the gold of Guiana to be out of that agony, and safe and calm in one good green acre of Devon, with or without the tree, just so long as the spot was landlocked and my stomach still.

However, I have also to report that the Indian has proved not unhelpful.

Evidently he heard me being sick, or Robin my page may have told him. This morning at dawn he came to my cabin with a fresh supply of *khoka* leaves.

'Eat,' he said.

I was reluctant, but he persuaded me.

And now I must say that the drug has worked. I no longer vomit. My belly and bowels are calmed and my head feels as though a tight steel band has just been removed from round about my temples.

The leaf is remarkable.

I have always been fascinated by true medicines and elixirs. When Prince Henry's doctors despaired of his life – after they had tried letting his blood in the nose, and everything else they could think of – they consented to give him the quintessence of quinine which I had prepared for him, at Queen Anne's behest. (She sent her own messenger to me in the Tower to beg for it.) That quinine did not save Prince Henry's life. But it brought him to some show of sense and opening of his eyes. Too late, its administration.

And yet I know that it should certainly have cured him or any other of a fever.

Except in case of poison.

Was Prince Henry poisoned? And if he was – who would have killed him, and how? He was my hope, and the hope of all England, the noble son of an ignoble father, as unlike our miserable King James as it is possible to imagine. If he had lived, I should have been delivered out of the Tower before Christmas 1612. If he had lived, I would have completed my *History of the World*, which I undertook in the first place for his instruction.

But I speak out of turn.

I shall come in due course to the manner of Prince Henry's living – and his dying.

Meanwhile, suffice it to say that my *History of the World* must stand for generations to come as yet another monument to despair and disillusion. It gets only as far as the Romans in Macedonia.

Khoka. I have been questioning the Indian about it. This is indeed the one subject on which he can unfailingly be drawn to speak, even if what he then says is not always coherent or comprehensible.

'How did you know that this would cure my seasickness?' I asked, mindful that he claimed originally that he had never been to sea.

He shrugged.

'The leaf cures many sicknesses,' he said.

'You spoke of it once as the food of the Golden Man.'

'Yes.'

'What does that mean? Who is this Golden Man?'

He answered me in Spanish, of course, which is always the language of our discourse, although native to neither of us. 'El Dorado,' he said.

'You babble of fables,' I told him. 'El Dorado. It means only "the gilded one". It was a story which some of your people told the Spaniards, no doubt to beguile or bewilder them, or to satisfy fools looking for more riches like those found in Peru. This El Dorado was supposed to be an Indian chief who rolled once a year in turpentine, was covered with gold dust and then dived into a lake. Isn't that it?'

The Indian shrugged. (How his perpetual shrugging annoys me! As if his shoulders can dismiss my every word . . .) 'Something like that,' he said. 'The leaf is good.'

I found I could agree with this simple statement. 'Certainly,' I said. 'But the goodness or badness of the leaf has nothing to do with any El Dorado nonsense.'

'The leaf is good,' the Indian repeated. 'The leaf makes the head understand what the heart knows.'

'*Khoka*,' I pressed him. 'The word *khoka*. What does that mean?'

'The tree,' he said.

There was an unmistakably reverential inflection in the way he said this.

'Tree of what?' I demanded. 'Tree of Knowledge? Tree of Life?'

'No,' he said.

'Tree of the Golden Man?' I insisted. 'El Dorado tree, perhaps?'

The Indian shook his head.

'The tree,' he said.

So. The *khoka* leaves appear to constitute both the basis of the Indian's philosophy or faith and its means of expression. In a word, you might say that they fulfil for him a *sacramental* function.

Khoka is the divine plant of the Chibchas, he told me. It was also regarded as divine by the Incas.

I asked him several times what exactly he meant by this remark, but he seemed unable or unwilling to explain. I have the impression that here I am up against the edge of a mystery, something inexplicable except in terms of itself, a point where his world and mine are mutually exclusive, irreconcilable. However, I gather that one clear distinction is to be made: While his people reverence the *khoka* herb or tree, they do not worship it. It is employed as an offering to the sun, it is burnt in honour of idols, and it is used to produce smoke at his tribe's sacrifices. The priests of the tribe, he says, must chew it during the performance of their religious ceremonies, otherwise I gather they fear that their gods will not be propitiated. The places where the herb grows wild are considered holy places, sanctuaries.

In answer to further questions I learned that the plant is of very great antiquity, that the Chibchas believe that its ingestion before death assures them of entry into Paradise, that they apply it also to sores and broken bones and against malaria and other fevers, but that its chief use is as a spiritual stimulant. They regard it as incomparably potent in fortifying the user against despair, and sovereign against all manner of misery. It purifies the blood and cleanses the soul. Yet it is, he says, essentially a food, and when it is eaten regularly then a man has no hunger for other (lesser) foods. He claims indeed that it is possible, under its influence, to go for many days without other forms of nourishment. It enhances the mental power of its users to a marked degree, and their physical power is also materially increased. He spoke again of running behind Palomeque's horse. It was the leaf that gave him the strength, he says.

For my own part, I concede that the drug cured my wretched seasickness. Also, on reflection, it may have acted as some kind of spur in enabling me at last to overcome the torment of indecision that beset me all the time we lay at the anchor in the Bay of Nevis. That is sufficient to suggest that it is an elixir of a sort I can respect – not magical but conferring a power of human endurance. It confirms a man in what he is already.

At this moment, then, far from suffering from seasickness, my mouth is full of the aromatic taste of the *khoka* leaf, giving an increased flow of saliva, a feeling of comfort in the stomach, and a general sense as though a rich but frugal meal has just been eaten with good appetite. I notice also that my pulse is beating faster, and that my brain participates in the exaltation produced. I experience from time to time a peculiar ease as though isolated from the external world, accompanied by an irresistible inclination to exertion not readily satisfied by mere pacing about on deck. A while ago I felt moved to climb into the rigging – and did so, to the astonishment of Mr Burwick and some of the other ship's officers. Now, however, there follows a state of quietness accompanied by a sensation of intense content, consciousness being all the time perfectly clear, indeed refined.

In this mood I resume the wandering story of my days. During the period leading up to my being afflicted with seasickness I found within myself no impulse to do so. To sit and stare at my pen and my papers appeared to me then of more importance than to employ them in scribbling. Rather, writing and not-writing seemed equally *un*important. I was in some deep sense quite paralysed. It occurs to me that this state has been one to which I have been prone all my life. There is a sense in which the Tower suited me, being a perfect emblem of my self-imprisonment. No doubt that is why I hated it so much.

This evening, at any rate, I think I begin to see what the Indian means when he calls his leaf divine. It brings with its ingestion a peace and confidence and a heightened awareness of the present moment in which one is peaceful and confident, at the same time quickening memory and the desire to reach back into the past for its truth, cancelling also all idle or ambitious cares and fears concerning the unknowable future.

In such a temper a man is at one with whatever he understands by the word *God*.

In such a temper I turn again to examine my own mortality by autobiography.

Elizabeth was not mean or miserly. But she didn't spend much money on her favourites. She couldn't. Her income was perhaps a quarter of a million pounds a year, rarely more. This sum might seem large but it had to cover the expenses of government as well as her own personal expenses. I remember her delight when she made £250,000 from little Captain Drake's otherwise rather stupid voyage around the world.

However, if the Queen could not give money, she gave opportunity.

I always preferred opportunity.

Within that year following my quick thinking in the matter of the cloak I was rewarded first with the gift of many suits. It amused her Majesty to see me well dressed. Each set of clothes came with some remark concerning the cloak incident. For instance, I recall one suit of spotless white which was accompanied by her handwritten message referring to 'so fine and seasonable a tender of so fair a footcloth'.

She lost no chance either to keep showing me her little feet in the dance. She would kick off her gold satin dancing slippers and go barefoot up and down the Presence Chamber.

Her feet were exquisitely tiny.

She moved on them with the grace of a gazelle.

Elizabeth did not so much walk as dance, and not so much dance as glide across the floor.

I was becoming well bewitched, as you see.

Elizabeth's habit of coquetry was remarkable in a modern monarch.

I often saw her tickling the red beard of Robert Dudley, Earl of Leicester, my most important patron at that time. She had tickled his neck also when publicly investing him with the collar of an earl, to the reported disgust of the Scottish envoy. On another occasion, riding one early morning in the park past the Queen's apartments at Windsor, Leicester instructed his fool to make such a hullabaloo that the Queen came undressed to the window to see what the matter was. There was also the hot afternoon when he lay with his head in her lap in a barge on the Thames, and Quadra the Spanish bishop had to cover his embarrassment by offering to marry them on the spot.

Leicester fell somewhat from favour when he did actually marry – but then his wife, Amy Robsart, was found soon after with a broken neck at the foot of a staircase. It was said that the Earl had come to regret his imprudence in face of the Queen's displeasure. It was said that he had pushed Amy Robsart. Or had her pushed by his servants. Nothing could be proved.

Leicester was now married for a second time, and was even less in the Queen's favour than before. Yet now and again I heard her still addressing him softly as her 'sweet Robin'. Men claimed that if Elizabeth had ever really contemplated marriage, then it was Leicester that she would have married. I doubt this myself, and not just because Leicester was a torpid impotent creature who had to drink dissolved pearls and amber to excite his lust.

The truth is that however much the Queen loved any man, she loved England more. She held herself as wedded to her kingdom. She liked to flirt and promise and suggest – and to do more than that, in certain secret circumstances, as I must soon tell. But when it came to the ultimate gift of the person that is marriage then Elizabeth was queen first and a woman second. She regarded her coronation ring as her wedding ring. The realm could be her only lawful husband.

So Elizabeth was wise as well as flighty.

It was because she was wise that she could be flighty. It was because she belonged by choice to no man that she could choose to flirt with any who took her eye.

I took her eye in my new splendid suits.

That sounds somewhat less than honourable, yet it is the truth and I must admit it. The Queen was sufficiently a woman to be pleased by my body as well as my mind. I knew it, and I knew the sting of shame in appearing before her in clothes which she had given me, cut to declare my parts to the best advantage. There were plenty at Court who delighted to despise me because they were jealous. They saw me only as Elizabeth's pet or gallant, the coming man. I bore their contempt by lengthening my stride.

When I say that the Queen gave opportunity I mean that there were offices and properties of the State which it was of course in her power only to confer. It was well known which ones she liked to award to her favourites – licences, monopolies, houses taken from too worldly prelates of the Church, that sort of thing. She had given the freehold of Ely Place in Holborn to Sir Christopher Hatton; it had been the London residence of the Bishop of Ely before that.

That dank November of the beginning of winter of 1582 the Queen's once precious 'Mutton' spent much of his time in moping in that house. When he showed his face at Court he reserved his darkest looks for me. Poor Hatton! He grew so depressed that he even turned to literature. His ability was not large in this direction. He succeeded in perpetrating the fourth act of a tragedy, *Tancred and Gismund*. The Thames was not set on fire, nor the Queen impressed.

My own first token of the Queen's approval – apart, that is, from the wardrobe of extravagant cloaks and close-cut doublets – came when she appointed me commander of a large band of soldiers to be sent back to Ireland.

I thanked her for this indication that she had taken to heart my comments on English policy in that green wilderness, but in the same breath I announced my regret at having to leave her company.

'Then do not leave it,' she said, smiling.

'I do not understand your Majesty.'

'Appoint a substitute,' Elizabeth said.

I obeyed. In this way, I had some small wages from the art of war, while remaining at Court and keeping in reach of the Queen.

It was at one and the same time a definite sign of Elizabeth's intention to have me advance in the world while wanting me near.

Lord Grey, in Ireland, was much irritated, so I heard. So was Hatton, in London, as I saw.

I went privately to a dancing master in the Strand.

Elizabeth's nicknames were usually to the point. They might seem like mere verbal caresses, plays or puns upon the given names of her male companions, but there was often a deeper truth concealed in the joke. I *am* like water. There is something volatile in my temperament, unsteadily so. I need banks and limits to define my courses. I require some cause beyond myself to give my life direction. This I am finding again (at last) in the now reliable progress of the ship. They will say I am mad, for the ship bears me home to my death. Let them say what they please. I say that all voyages end in the same harbour.

Several times in the past week I have been disturbed in my own opinion of myself by some strange mistake on the part of the Indian. It is absurd – but his misunderstandings throw all my life momentarily into a cauldron of confusion. He can be obtuse when he speaks of things outside his own experience.

'Elizadeath,' he said once. 'She set Guattaral free.'

'What?'

'The Queen of the North. She set you free to die.'

I explained that he had it wrong. That it was King James.

'No, no,' he said. 'Your enemy. Elizadeath.'

It was useless trying to make him understand. Yet he seemed once before to have grasped this simple point.

The wind has dropped now, but the weed flows faster. I estimate that this Gulf Stream must itself flow north-east and then east at perhaps as much as seventy miles in a day. It is a phenomenon I have noted before in the wilderness of water which is the Atlantic Ocean.

So here I am. Locked in a current which runs on inexorably towards my death.

North.

Going north and then east.

Hard comfortable words!

We shall be sailing soon in colder sharper seas.

And something there is in me which likes the cold. Respects it. Which welcomes the prospect of ice.

Like a lodestone: the north, the cold, the finer definitions.

When I came full of fevers last November to the Guiana coast I sent at once to inquire for my old servant Leonard the Indian who had been with me in England in the Tower for three years.

I sent also to find out about my other Indian servant, Harry.

Harry sent back his brother and two chiefs.

I remember the letter I wrote to Bess the next morning, which letter I sent home by Captain Janson from Flushing who was trading on that coast.

'To tell you I might here be the King of the Indians were a vanity,' I wrote. 'But my name still lives among them. They feed me with fresh meat, and all that the country yields. All offer to obey me.'

My dearest Bess, forgive my lie which was only to comfort you. The truth is that I hadn't been able to eat any meat for a month. Leonard never came to me. And Harry, when he did, had almost forgotten his English.

19

At midnight, five days ago, on the 8th of April, every least breath of wind went out of our sails as suddenly as if a great giant had given up the ghost and stopped puffing into them. My flag hung straight down from the mainmast like a long wet rag. I found that a candle would burn on the poop deck with its flame bolt-upright.

Ordering all sails to be struck, I went below. I could not sleep. My spirit was possessed by the strongest sense of impending disaster and doom.

My forebodings proved true. The storm hit us just before dawn.

I never knew anything to exceed the sudden fury of that blast. Coming out of my cabin I found the whole ship shaking to her heart. In the next instant, to the accompaniment of an almighty crack of thunder, the sea swelled up to starboard and came rushing across our decks for all the world like a tower falling, a tall green tower of furious foaming ocean, sweeping sailors overboard in its roaring course, hurling us upon our beam-ends, smashing down below decks and tossing our great ordnance about like toys.

My *Destiny* spun round and round like a crazy cork in a cauldron. We could not hear each other's shouts and screams, for the force of the hurricane whipped all our words away the instant they were uttered.

Then a second wave hit us, crashing with shattering force across the full length of the ship, breaking high up almost to the main-yards. Stunned by the shock of the water, I found myself, when I recovered, jammed in between the stern-post and the rudder. I regained my feet with difficulty. Vast traceries of lightning lit the sky.

It was then that I saw the Indian.

My first thought was that he had taken leave of his wits. He was high up on the mainmast, lashed to it with a white rope tight about his waist. I imagined for a moment that this was an apparition.

We went plunging down in the trough of the boiling sea. My ears were full of the thunder, then the screaming of ropes torn loose and dashed through the pulley-blocks. Once more the before-dawn dark was split apart by lightning. I saw that the figure up there against the mast was no apparition. It was the Indian all right. His face was contorted in some cry which it was of course impossible to hear. Then his right arm shot out, finger stabbing. He was pointing down across our stern behind me.

A third wave hit us, less frightful than the former ones. The *Destiny* pitched and staggered, but rose, after a minute, from the blow. I felt driving rain on my cheeks. I cried out at this benison. Somehow I knew that the extreme fury of the first two blasts of the storm was not to be repeated, and that this rain would never have fallen if that was not so.

Confirming my conviction, the thunder now rolled away swiftly to starboard, the lightning ceased, and the sea swept over our bulwarks with less mountainous force than before. To be sure, the gale still made all our shrouds and ropes howl like devils in hell, but the vessel was holding her own, she was riding the storm, badly battered, but unbowed, undestroyed, perhaps inextinguishable.

I gave thanks to God as the good rain ran down my face. I never tasted any wine so sweet as those great gouts from heaven. Then the sun inched up over the horizon. It was yellow and sickly, swathed in black clouds, but *there*.

Remembering the Indian, I looked up.

He was still perched high above, lashed to the mainmast. As I made out his shape in the gloom of rain and misty light he pointed again behind me with outflung arm. He was shouting something. The wind wiped the sound away. He called once more, taking advantage of a flaw in the blast. I heard him.

'Your other ship!' he cried. 'Your other ship!'

I spun round, clutching at the splintered wood of the stern-post. My leg had been lacerated and my arm crushed with the impact of that first tumultuous wave. There was blood soaking my sleeve and spurting from a gash in my hand. I barely noticed it. I had eyes only for what the Indian was pointing at.

There, to our stern, about two hundred yards away through the hissing spray, the *Encounter*, her masts snapped, her framework shattered, was slowly tilting down into the sea. She looked like a great swan bending her neck to death. I saw men running this way and that way in panic, fighting to ascend to the poop deck which was still above water, some of them vaulting the bulwarks to take a last desperate chance in the sea.

It was the *Encounter*'s heavy ordnance which proved her undoing. These cannons, torn loose from their trunnions by the deluge of the three great waves which had smashed holes in her hull, must have rolled right across to her port side, wreaking new havoc there. She sank in a matter of seconds. I saw her go under, half-rising again like a bird with broken wings still determined to fly despite all. Then she keeled over finally and disappeared into the deep.

I scanned that treacherous sea. There were men down there in it. Mortal flotsam and jetsam flung this way and that by the waves.

'Mr Burwick!' I shouted. 'Ropes! Ropes!'

Buntlines and clewlines were snatched up and hurled overboard. They fell short, of course. In the gaps in the gale my ears were assailed by a torrent of demented shouting, imploring, and cursing from our men craning over the sides.

I saw two heads appear for a moment in a trough between the waves. They were shrieking and babbling, lashing about with their arms. In a moment the next wave was upon them, sweeping them from sight. When that wave had spent its force, I saw that only one man was left there in the ocean. He was utterly exhausted. He looked like a half-drowned rat. But the whirlpool of the current was kind to him, for it swept him now in a vast concentric circle until he floundered almost within reaching distance of the furthest outflung of our trailing lines. He clutched at it. Missed. Clutched again. Missed again. I saw his eyes were glazed. They were blind and red with salt water. Wild. Raw. Rolling up towards death in their sockets.

'Sam!' I shouted. 'Sam! For the love of God! Sam!'

My old friend Samuel King made one last despairing effort. He grabbed at the rope. He got it. He held on.

By noon on that same day the storm was gone. It had become but a distant smudge against the rim of the world where sea and sky meet.

The sun shone fair, the winds blew mockingly moderate. Mr Burwick reported that the damage to our stern-post was of no material consequence. To be sure, my *Destiny*'s rake in the water is now more like a Frenchman's, but this is no great matter for indeed it makes her give sharp way and keep a good wind and since she has a full bow she does not pitch her head to meet the waves. Apart from this, the breechings on six of our cannons are smashed, there are two gunner's quadrants lost, the chained pumps stand in need of repair, and some of the yards are spent. We lost four men overboard: Jan Suff, Thomas Burough, Davy Howell, Ned Anger. (May God have mercy on their souls. Not even cockroaches deserved such a death.) Of the crew of the ill-fated *Encounter*, we saved only Sam King.

I asked the Indian why he climbed the mast and tied himself to it when he saw the storm coming. He said he felt safer so.

'My people go into the trees when wild beasts come prowling or Spaniards come marching,' he told me.

Whether to believe this or not, I don't know.

He appears, at all events, unshaken by our narrow escape.

As for myself: my wounds proved superficial. Which is just as well, since we no longer have a ship's surgeon.

Since the night of the storm we have not been a day without wind, and only once have we experienced rain again. Then, thank God, it poured from the sky in such abundance that I was able to instruct the men to set every available empty cask about the decks, and especially under the dripping sails, with a result that we managed to fill twenty-five barrels with that precious liquid manna.

Our position now is in 43° latitude north, with a longitude reading of some 57° west.

The winds for the past twenty-four hours have been cutting through my ancient bones like sword-blades. I wear the chilly mists as another cloak. Elizabeth, you could not walk on this.

We run within two days' sail of Newfoundland. But whether I will ever safely reach the harbour of St John there, or perish here at sea, I do not know. For my crew are plotting secretly to follow the example of Wollaston, Whitney, and the rest. I discovered this just yesterday for certain, but the rumour of it has been rife ever since the storm.

My mind is like a vat of boiling wine.

To have come so far, to have risked so much, to have lost my son, to have saved my friend – and now to find such treachery in my crew!

A disaffected soldier, Richard Head, would seem to be the ringleader of the rebels. His followers desire him to take command of the ship and turn pirate with her. Their assessment of the situation rests on the fact that they reckon I am sailing to my death, and most of them believe that they will be condemned along with me.

Robin my page brought the first intimation of the plot. He burst into my cabin, poppy-cheeked, goggle-eyed, as if the Devil himself was at his heels.

'Master,' he cried, 'they mean to murder you!'

I confess that I paid him scant heed. He is a bright but idle boy, his head always full of imaginary adventures.

'Murder me? Who?'

'All of them! They say they'll put a dagger in your back!'

'The whole crew to wield one dagger? Why, how they must be weakened by the scurvy!'

Robin did not smile.

'Be wary, master. I overheard them scheming down below. One of them said you were mad. It was the soldier who wears the black patch on his forehead. He told the rest that their only hope was to be rid of you.'

'I'll bear it in mind,' I promised. 'Now, wash the curtains.'

The green silk curtains that hang about my carved oak bed in the great cabin had been badly stained with sea water during the storm. Mumbling and grumbling, Robin went off to scour them.

I know this soldier, Head, for a low-born scoundrel. The patch he wears is supposed to protect a wound got in Turkey. I doubt if the villain ever crossed swords with a Turk in his life. More likely, his patch hides a sore picked up in the greasy lists of lust.

I said nothing to anyone concerning what Robin had told me. To be honest, I thought little about it. I knew that the greater part of my company had been faithless to start with, mere mercenaries, brands plucked from the burning. Now they were weary, despondent, a rabble of disappointed rascals reluctant to sail home without any of the plunder they had come for, and with only the prospect of unwelcome justice ahead of them. But it is one thing to mope and to curse authority in such circumstances, quite another to murder your lawfully appointed leader. I kept a watchful eye on Head, but noticed nothing more than sullen ill-humour in the man. This was not new. I supposed that Robin had exaggerated, or even misheard or misunderstood a few empty expressions of discontent.

But then, last night, Sam King came to me bearing the same story.

'Head proposes piracy,' he said. 'He has at least three quarters of the crew behind him.'

'You heard this with your own ears?'

'Yes.'

'Then it's bad,' I conceded. 'Unless they mean business it would scarcely be such common knowledge that it could come to you. Of everyone on board, you are my man. Head must know that.'

Sam sucked at the moustache which hides his mouth. 'I suppose he could be playing clever,' he mused.

'You mean – deliberately making sure I have wind of the plot? Why should he do that?'

'To frighten you.'

I laughed. I shook my head. 'In that case we have nothing to worry about. I shall not be frightened by a shipful of Richard Heads. Does he imagine that I am going to hand over command to him? The idiot must be mad to dream it possible.'

Sam looked awkward. Then he went on: 'I believe he has two alternative ploys. The first is to seize command of the ship when we reach Newfoundland. His support is enough that he could steal away with her once she's been cleaned and revictualled.'

'Leaving me at St John?'

'Yes.'

'Dead or alive?'

Sam smiled bitterly. 'From Head's point of view that would be of no consequence. His only real difficulty would be Mr Burwick.'

'He remains loyal?'

'I think so. It's impossible to be sure.'

I nodded. I was not much surprised that even my own ship's master could possibly be bought or coerced to take part in this criminal enterprise. If we were sailing home to a monarch who had faith in us, then despite my own fate the ship's company might be reasonably confident of saving their skins. But by now the meanest swabbers of the decks of the *Destiny* must be only too aware that King James was desirous of our downfall from the start.

'You mentioned another ploy. What can that be?'

Sam sighed. He looked down, tracing a circle with his calloused right forefinger on the sea charts spread out upon my table.

'Laurence Keymis,' he muttered.

'Keymis? What about him?'

'Head hopes you'll join him,' Sam said.

I drew a sharp breath. 'Then he much underestimates me, this disgusting Mr Head. He fancies that I will kill myself because he lets it be whispered about that he intends to steal my ship and turn her pirate?'

'I heard him,' Sam said. 'He says you are committing suicide anyway. He cannot understand your present course.'

Something in Sam's voice made me silent then.

At length, I said softly:

'And nor can you.'

'Admiral?'

'You cannot understand it either. Sam, do you really know me? Do you really know me at all?'

My old friend closed his eyes. I saw tears on his face. 'I've known you since we first rode together to France. You're the best man I know. But I'll never understand you. No, sir, I admit it. I don't understand you, and I don't think you do either. You're sailing to your death. You're going home to certain execution.' His eyes snapped open. They were proud. 'I shall follow you. I'll be with you. Not just because you saved my life when the *Encounter* went down either. You know that well. You are my friend. I have no other choice. Your mind is made up and I accept what you are doing. But if I had a choice – if I could influence your decisions –'

'You would side with Mr Head?'

I regretted the stupid words before they had escaped from my mouth.

Sam did not flinch. He considered me levelly.

'I would save you from yourself,' he said, his voice a gruff whisper.

I could not meet those honest eyes of his. I sat staring at my sea charts. I drew my dagger and cut a line across the ocean.

'This is where we go,' I declared. 'Mr Head will not stop me. You will not stop me. And most certainly I shall never stop myself. I gave my word. I shall keep my word. Besides, you despair too fast. That alarms me. I never knew you for a quick despairer. Your escape from drowning must have left a certain dampness in your wits. Mr Secretary Winwood –'

'A forest of Winwoods cannot save you from King James! He means your destruction!'

'You think so, Captain?'

'I know so, Admiral. And so do you.'

I stuck the point of my dagger in the heart of England.

All day today I have brooded on what Sam said. To tell truth, his uncustomary eloquence dismays me more than these mutterings of piracy from the forecastle. Head would put a knife in my back while I slept, or have me put a knife in my own heart out of despair. Head would leave me stranded in the harbour of St John in Newfoundland, and take command of my ship and prostitute her. Sam King's counsel, however confused, is incomparably harder to stand up to. Head would keep me from England because he is my enemy and serves only himself. Sam has served me faithfully all his life, he is my friend, perhaps the only true friend I have had. He would keep me from England because he loves me, because he wants me to live, to survive, to escape the wrath of King James.

I am haunted by a single ridiculous image.

It concerns the death by drowning of my half-brother Humphrey Gilbert.

Humphrey was one of my mother's three sons by her first marriage, to Otho Gilbert. He was in Elizabeth's service even before she was crowned Queen. His great aunt, Kate Ashley, had been governess to the young Bess, and Humphrey himself was attached as a young man (being my senior by some fifteen years) to the Princess's household.

Poor ambitious Humphrey. His reach always exceeded his grasp. He grew to manhood with the one obsession: to prove himself in the colonization of the New World, to carve his name upon America. But he was obstinate, wilful, and cantankerous – altogether too rough and choleric a fellow to win the Queen's real favour.

Secretary Walsingham disliked him. He schemed to thwart all

Humphrey's enterprises. He called him 'a man noted of no good hap by sea'.

Well, it irks me to admit it, but Walsingham was right in this regard. Humphrey, scared of the sea, was a bad sailor. Yet what happened? What happened was that I was responsible for persuading the Queen to disregard her Secretary of State. I owed a debt to Humphrey for introducing me to Leicester at the start of my own career as courtier and seaman. That debt I unwisely discharged – at his insistence – by getting Elizabeth to agree to allow my brother to sail at the head of an expedition, ill-prepared, worse-fated, going this way, to Newfoundland. I even obtained for his good luck a token from her Majesty. It was an anchor guided by a lady's hand.

Humphrey Gilbert sailed these waters I sail into now. He never made landfall. Because men said that he feared death by drowning he determined on making the smallest vessel of his fleet the one in which he journeyed. Her name was the *Squirrel*, her draught was a mere eight tons.

In a furious storm she went down. The crew of her closest companion ship saw what happened.

Humphrey sat aloft through the storm with a book in his hand. While the wind raged about him, he pretended to be reading. Perhaps he *was* reading. He refused to transfer his person aboard the larger vessel. Every time they drew near him he waved them away again.

He kept shouting, they said.

What he shouted was this, they said:

'We are as near to heaven by sea as by land!'

Again and again he shouted it, till the wind got so overwhelming that his words were destroyed by it.

He drowned with his book, my brother Humphrey. The *Squirrel* was sunk, she was lost with all hands, and my brother went down with her, reading.

Was he mad?

Am I madder?

He died reading a book.

Must I die writing one?

We are as near to heaven by sea as by land . . .

20

At dawn this morning, the coast of Newfoundland off our port bow, I had the trumpet sound to call the whole ship's company together on the quarter-deck. Sam King, his hand on his sword hilt, stood on one side of me. Mr Burwick took up position on the other side. The air was chill. I had taken the precaution of having Robin lay out two shirts for my wearing, in case the cold made me shiver. I did not want the men to suppose I felt fear.

I wasted no time in coming to the point.

'Gentlemen,' I said, 'there has been a change of plan. I have decided to make directly for England and home without taking fresh provisions aboard or cleaning the ship in the harbour of St John.'

There was a general sharp intake of breath, some few rebellious murmurings, but then silence. Looking at the gang of ruffians clustered about Richard Head, I could see that my words had left them in no doubt that I was forewarned of their intention to turn pirate.

Head himself was lounging against a water-butt. He picked at his teeth with a small curved knife. The black patch on his forehead, catching the light off the water, winked as if he had a third malevolent eye.

'Are there any questions, gentlemen?' I inquired.

Most of the scoundrels looked sideways at their ringleader. Head said nothing. He went on picking at his teeth with the bright blade.

It was our master gunner, William Gurden, who broke the silence. He stood apart, arms folded across his broad chest. 'Admiral,' he said, 'I don't question your decision. But I'd like to know the reason for it. Why sail for England when you told us we'd rest at St John's?'

I nodded. 'I will tell you why, Mr Gurden, though it gives me no pleasure to do so. We have certain gentlemen aboard who care so much for my welfare and their own profit that they would prevent me from returning to England. There is a plot afoot to seize my ship if I once put her into harbour. I am to be left in Newfoundland, high and dry, while the new masters of the *Destiny* traffick as pirates. Well, sirs, it is my opinion that those who have flirted with this notion have not thought it through to its conclusion. I was let out of the Tower at the King's pleasure. I return to England to throw myself upon his mercy. Any man who acts to prevent this does more than turn pirate – he steps between me and the King. If I do not kill such a man, then King James most assuredly will.' I paused. I looked from one face to the next in the crowd about Richard Head. I could see that my words had struck home. 'But let us not put his Majesty to any trouble of blood-letting,' I went on calmly. 'As for me, I have nothing left but my honour, and I go to redeem it. If any of you is serious in this purpose to deprive me of the pleasure of a noble death let him step forward now and do his ignoble best.'

I drew my sword.

I waited two whole minutes.

No one moved.

Not one of them moved an inch.

They looked surly, they looked thwarted, they looked embarrassed. But they did not move. They did not move a muscle. Some of them stared at Head. But Head shut his eyes.

I noticed the Indian standing high in the rigging. He was gazing down impassively upon us. How much of this scene he could understand I don't know. I suppose in the end that it spoke well enough for itself. As the minutes ticked by, his face broke into a grin.

'Good,' I said. 'Very good. It seems, after all, that we have no real mutineers present. I am glad to learn it, gentlemen; glad for your sake, sirs, as well as mine. We are a small enough company to cross the Atlantic without wasting able-bodied fellows by having to hang them at the yardarm. You agree?'

Some nodded foolishly.

But I was asking only one of them.

'*Mr Head, you agree?*'

Head, scowling, considered the point of his knife. For a second, it looked as if he might hurl it at me. His lips were set hard. His face was as black as any thunder.

'Mr Head!'

The rogue looked up sharply.

'You agree, Mr Head? You agree that we have no mutiny at all?'

Head stared at me. It appeared he was choking.

'The correct answer,' I said quietly, 'is "Aye, sir".'

Head said nothing.

'"Aye, sir",' I repeated. 'Say "Aye, sir", if you please, Mr Head.'

Head spat on the blade of his dagger. Then:

'Aye, sir,' he muttered.

'Louder.'

'Aye, aye, sir!' shouted Head.

I nodded. I sheathed my sword.

'Mr Head, you will now throw that knife of yours into the sea.'

A small but necessary moment of truth, Carew. If it was correct – as Sam King had ascertained, and I saw no reason to doubt – that three quarters of my crew had been prepared to support this villain in his treachery, then here was his ultimate chance to declare himself. I was gambling everything on my reading of the man's character. If that black patch on his skull really signified a wound won in combat with the Turks, as Head claimed, then I might be done for.

My son, I am doubly sure tonight that Richard Head never dared cross swords with any Turk in his life. Nor even with an ancient English gentleman needing two shirts to keep his shrivelled body from the obvious effects of the ague at sea on a cold April morning.

Because.

Because Richard Head faltered, shifting from foot to foot, and then he said, mumbling:

'But this knife was a gift from my father.'

Sam King laughed first. Then Mr Burwick. Then Mr Jones, the clergyman, a nervous fellow who laughs like an ass when he can. The laughter spread like wildfire among the men. All the tension was dissipated from that ugly scene as swiftly and easily as the mist steaming from our frosty decks in the rays of the rising sun.

I did not laugh. I did not even smile.

'Overboard, Mr Head. Either you or your father's knife. It is no great matter which.'

Richard Head shut his eyes. I observed a nerve that twitched in his unwashed throat. His cronies were suddenly silent.

Then, with a grimace of cowardly resignation, the oaf drew back his arm and hurled his knife overboard. It flashed in an arc in the sun. And there was such quiet that I heard the little splash as it hit the water.

'Thank you,' I said.

Some of the swabbers clapped hands and stamped with their feet. Head turned aside, his chin in his chest, completely discredited. But there was more serious business to come.

Simon Taverner, our ship's cook, a squat weasel-faced runt of a man, was the first to give voice to it. He stepped forth uneasily from his companions.

'Admiral,' he said, 'you overlook one thing.'

'Hold your tongue,' my Captain King commanded, all confidence now.

I laid my hand gently on Sam's to restrain him. 'Let us hear from the kitchen. We shall need Mr Taverner's salt beef and pickled pork. Yes, and his dried peas and beans, and even the hard biscuit with the worms in it. We have another eighteen hundred miles of ocean to cross, and a ship is no better than her belly.'

The cook cleared his throat. 'Sir Walter, I'm your man. No mutineer. Never. But if I sail back to England then I hang.'

'How's that?' I asked.

'Murder, sir.'

'Then you deserve it, Mr Taverner, do you not?'

Taverner spat. 'I killed an innkeeper, that's all.'

'With your foul soup?'

'No, sir. He refused me my wages. There was a brawl. I never meant to kill the mean old bastard. I hit him with a ladle. How was I to know his heart was weak?'

I shook my head. 'A pitiable story, master cook. But while I can see why you sailed with us, I can only condemn you for your short sight. You must have known that there would be a coming back. You have delayed your appointment with the gallows, nothing more.'

Taverner stood his ground. There was a kind of candid despair in his gaze. 'I hoped for a pardon, sir,' he said. 'And I'm not the only one. Not by a long chalk. There's plenty of us who signed on to sail with you because you promised the King you'd bring back gold, and gold meant the King would be pleased, we reckoned, and his pleasure meant pardon for past offences. But now you're wanting us to go back to England without so much as a gilded button to buy his mercy. I tell you straight, Admiral, if we stopped off in Newfoundland I'd never turn pirate. But I'd disappear, sir, Christ's truth I would.'

'Desertion,' growled Sam King. 'He boasts of deserting.'

I held up my hand. Taverner's truthfulness had touched me. Abhor it as I might, I felt sufficient sympathy with his argument to wish to hear more.

'How many of the rest of you must hang if we go back to England?' I demanded.

More than a score of them stepped forward, eyes downcast, shuffling their feet. I questioned each one. For the most part, their offences were trivial. I condone no crimes, Carew. But I beg leave to doubt the wisdom of the severity of some of our English laws. Should a man deserve to lose his life for filching fifty shillings? For stealing three cows? For setting fire to his neighbour's hayrick? The Francis Bacons of this world would say that he should, because the law is the law and a felon tears a hole in the fabric of society. I say that it is a mere spiderweb society which demands the death of such insignificant flies. Punished they must be, but not by execution. For do not the spiders, the Bacons, go free though God knows they are guilty of much greater misdemeanours? I have seen for myself how the mighty have the power to twist any law they dislike to achieve their own ends.

Just as a moment before Richard Head had stood revealed as a coward and a laughing-stock, now this rebellious surly crew of mine, his erstwhile followers, all at once appeared to my eyes as no more than a pack of wretched fugitive dogs. I would kick a bad dog, I would deprive him of his supper, but I'm damned if I'd think it worth hanging him.

'Hear this,' I said. 'I propose that we return to England by the way we came. Our first landfall shall be Kinsale, in Ireland. Those among you who have reason to fear the gallows will be free to quit my company once we reach there. You understand? I demand your loyalty as far as Ireland only. Is that agreed?'

It was agreed. I think, with gratitude.

And so the ship sails on. Under a dead sky, close to the wind, cleansing foregone, the water in our casks fast turning foul. What bread we have is mouldy and as hard as stones. My bones creak with the cold. My heart is bare of any hope at all. Our backs to Newfoundland, we face the Atlantic crossing. The crew go about their tasks like men in a dream. I have promised to save their necks, but not my own. Eastward we go, with a veiled moon mocking us. That mockery of a mutiny seems over. Head picks his dirty teeth with his dirty fingernails. Tonight I believe I have only the prospect of my death to look forward to. It is enough. I was always in love with absolutes.

Yet today is your birthday, dear Bess, and that I love too.

Birth and death are the absolutes. A birthday is beloved details.

So you enter your fifty-third year. Where? At your own house in Broad Street, most probably. I think of you there, sitting perhaps alone in the dining-room now, your eyes in the candlelight dwelling upon those exquisite pintado hangings, printed cottons we purchased from the East Indian merchant. Will you eat a morsel of rich comfit cake? Do you wear your purple kirtle fringed with gold? (The one that's cut low on the shoulder; how I wish I might bend now to kiss the freckles there!)

Your servant Alice will have set the dish of gooseberry creams on the great oak table. There was never a birthday when you did not enjoy your gooseberry creams, even when I was imprisoned in the Tower, even when (as now) I was not there to share them with you, an expanse of salt water between us. Cinnamon, nutmeg, mace, sugar, rose-water, and eggs – you see, I remember the seasoning. Good cold gooseberries lying in rounds upon the thick cream. You pick each one daintily, using the pure silver pin. Such pleasure. Your lips have it first, then your tongue, then your teeth, then your throat. You remember how once we halved a dish of these same cream-enriched gooseberries in the Temple Fields at Warwick on your birthday? There was a pageant being performed for the Queen's delight – a sham battle between two bands of men in two mock castles, with much noise of mortar-pieces, calibers, and the odd harquebus. Fireworks, squibs, and balls of fire in the April evening. Her Majesty, in fact, was bored, and didn't bother to hide it. (She never much cared for the sound of shot from that day when she was sitting in the royal barge on the Thames in company with the French Ambassador, and a madman called Appletree fired at random upon her party, narrowly missing the Queen and hitting one of the watermen.) As for us – that birthday of yours we spent in the Temple Fields – the pageantry is not what I recall now. I recall how you fed me your gooseberries and I fed you mine. These parched lips ache for your touch then. If my eyes should go blind, my lips would always recognize your fingers.

You ascend the wooden staircase, your blue-veined hand rests lightly on the balustrade. There is a fire in the grate in our bedroom. You sit before the looking-glass, and you unbraid your hair.

Out of turn, out of time, but in tune, I remember our first meeting. It was at Christmas, 1584, just before the night when the Queen made it crystal-clear to Hatton that I had now supplanted him as favourite – which she did by the incident when she tried to wipe a smut of soot from my face with her own well-licked handkerchief (but I shall come to that soon enough). You were nineteen years old, an orphan, your father once Ambassador to France. You were newly sworn as Elizabeth's youngest Maid of Honour, elected to that high company of Vestal Virgins which waited on her Majesty in the Privy Chamber. As such, it was your business to bathe the Queen and to dress her, to play for her upon the dulcimer, the clavicytherium, the lute, the viol, the rebec. Then there would be the endless games of cards and the nightly chatter. You had to let the Queen win her hand of cards, but cleverly, for Elizabeth never liked to think she won anything by default. As for your conversation, it had to be witty and graceful, quick, full of verbal resource, never too serious yet certainly not vulgar or trivial either. The Queen demanded elegance in all things. The misshapen in body or mind, whether female or male, were the only ones unwelcome at her Court.

You were eating strawberries dipped in wine. The clock was tolling midnight. One, two, three, four . . . The great clock of Whitehall, with its groaning dying sound on the stroke of twelve. Outside, the streets white with snow, and more snow falling. I came into the Privy Chamber unannounced. I expected the Queen to be there, but as it turned out she was not. I should have guessed, perhaps, that she'd be at her devotions in her private chapel. Christmas, the dead season, always brought out what little religion Elizabeth allowed herself to possess. But I do her wrong. She was a

Christian monarch. No doubt she kept a tight rein on her impulse in that direction because she could never forget the example of her father. Henry the Eighth, Defender of the Faith, had been insatiably religious. Lust and superstition do not amount to morality.

It was a cold night. The draught puffed the wood-smoke down the chimneys and the tapestries flapped against the walls. You sat there surrounded by candles that seemed to bow their long flames to your beauty. Yes, Bess, you were beautiful to me then, in the candlelit Privy Chamber, glancing up startled and innocent, a strawberry between right thumb and forefinger, red wine trickling down to stain your white brocaded dress. Your beauty was not in your face or your posture or in anything of outward show. It was like a fire that burned in you yet consumed nothing. A durable fire. Your mortal aspect its shadow.

'She is not here, Captain Ralegh,' you said, smiling, and finishing the strawberry. 'She is not here, the one you come to seek.'

I bowed. I brushed the oak floor with my feathered hat.

'Oh but she is,' I told you. 'It is only that a moment ago I did not know that I was seeking her.'

You said nothing. You sat licking your wine-stained fingers, staring at me. It was then that I noticed the blue and the black of your eyes. Sweet bitter iridescence. Two colours in one look. I admit I was fascinated – and more. How curious our bodies are! I could feel the short hairs prickle in the nape of my neck. The chamber was not warm, but I swear that I was starting to sweat. It was not lust. Nor was it fear. You must know what it was. I have spent my whole life since then trying to be true to it.

There was a silver jug on the long low table. A silver goblet stood on a linen cloth beside it. You would have set them there for the Queen's last nourishment before retiring to bed. Elizabeth always liked to drink a goblet of warm milk before she slept.

I crossed to the table. I took up goblet, jug, and linen napkin in my hands. I knelt at your side. Before you had time to protest, I poured some of the milk from the jug into the goblet, and grasped your stained fingers, and dipped them into the milk.

I washed your hands in the milk.

You were frightened. You whispered: 'But what if her Majesty –?'

'You can fetch a fresh jug,' I assured you. 'Fresh milk, another cup, a clean napkin.' I was drying your fingers with the crisp white linen. When I finished they were as white as snow, as soft as silk to my touch. I did not let go of your hands. Your hair smelt like honeysuckle.

'There,' I said. 'Not a trace remains of your crime.'

'My crime, sir?'

'The Queen's strawberries.'

'Those were not the Queen's strawberries. They were mine.'

'I stand corrected, madam. But now the strawberries are you, and you are the Queen's.'

You stood up swiftly, withdrawing your hands from mine. 'I wait on her Majesty, yes. I belong to no one.' Your blue eye seemed to laugh at me, your black one was cool and sharp in its appraisal. 'What of you, Captain Ralegh? To whom do you belong?'

'To myself,' I said. 'So it seems we are well matched, madam.'

'You think so? It appears to me only that you make far too free with the Queen's milk and her Majesty's Maids of Honour.'

I placed my hand upon my heart. 'I swear by Our Lady of Strawberries,' I said solemnly, 'you are the very first Maid of Honour I ever did wash in the Queen's milk.'

'And the last?' you said, wantonly. 'Come, sir, I am sure that having performed the office once you will now grow quite addicted to the practice.'

I scratched my cheek, pretending to consider this suggestion. 'That could be pleasurable. It depends.'

'Depends on what?'

'Madam, on how the other Maids of Honour eat their strawberries.'

You blushed. In that moment you looked very young. Very young, very vulnerable, yet not innocent.

You whispered: 'I must go and change my dress.'

I nodded, considering the wine stains. 'I apologize. I did not mean to startle you at your secret feast. What is your name?'

'Elizabeth. Elizabeth Throgmorton.'

I must have frowned. I did not want you to have the same Christian name as the Queen.

'Do your friends call you Bess?' I inquired.

'I don't have any friends, Captain Ralegh.'

I smiled. 'Then goodnight, Bess,' I said.

You snatched up the silver goblet and jug, and the soiled linen napkin. You half ran from the chamber. You forgot in your embarrassment the nearly empty bowl of strawberries floating in wine.

When your little footfalls had ceased to sound in the corridor I fished one blood-red strawberry out of the bowl, held it up against a candleflame to enjoy its brightness as well as the texture of it rolled between my finger and thumb, then popped it in my mouth and ate it whole.

I did not sleep that night. Nor did I look any further for the Queen. I spent all the hours till dawn composing six lines of verse. When I had finished I knew that I had not finished. The poem was not complete. To complete the poem I would need to know you better. I knew that, my dearest Bess. And the knowledge did not displease me. By God, it did not. I never looked forward more to completing a poem.

Anyway, the six preliminary lines. They were these, and you will know how they transposed and translated those details of our first encounter:

> Nature, that washed her hands in milk
> And had forgot to dry them,
> Instead of earth took snow and silk
> At Love's request, to try them
> If she a mistress could compose
> To please Love's fancy out of those.

By 'Love's fancy' I meant of course my own. The poem is not very good, as it stands, and it was not much better by the time I had finished it. As if that matters.

How did we keep our love a secret from the Queen? The answer, of course, is that in the long run we did not. But from the night of the strawberries to the time when Elizabeth discovered that I had made you pregnant, and then secretly married you, is a period of some seven years. Seven hard years of passion and pretence, when in public we had to be distant and circumspect, each of us feigning indifference to the other, not so much as a lingering look or a smile permitted to be shared when anyone else was present.

What helped us, I suppose, more than anything, was the Queen's belief that I belonged only to her. When I met you that Christmas Eve of '84 I was already her man in the sense that I had taken Hatton's place and danced through the door. You knew this, Bess. You did not know what it meant. I never told you. I never told anyone. Well, Elizabeth is long dead now, and it seems sure that soon enough, when this voyage ends, I must join her, follow the Queen again, only this time in the dance of death, through the final door, and into that chamber where all dark secrets shall be known in the infinite light.

I have thought much on this matter: Whether or not it is best that I go to the grave with my lips sealed fast on the subject of what things passed between me and the Queen. Tonight I have reached a decision. It is right that you should know. The knowledge will hurt you, dear wife, but it is my belief that the ignorance has hurt you more. Not knowing, you must have imagined me never truly yours – not least in those seven years when we were compelled to conceal our love from the eyes of the world. The truth may be less than you think, in which case I rejoice. There again, it may shock you and cause you to revile my memory and also Elizabeth's. I must pray it will not. And I ask you to pray for me, when all this is made known to you. Pray for the soul of Walter Ralegh, a poor miserable sinner. Yes, and pray for the soul of that poor miserable Queen as well.

You may not read these words till I am dead. If so, forgive me that small cowardice as well. I did try once, in bed, to tell the truth to you. You will recall? That night of your dream, the night before I sailed. You had fallen asleep before the words were out of my mouth. Blessed sleep! But how do I know that your dreams concerning this are not blacker by far than the reality?

What I shall write is not for Carew. Not yet. Not ever, perhaps. I leave that to your own discretion. My own feeling is that it were better he should never be told. The true story is something I owe *you*. And if I loved you less, and your heart was not as great as it is, then I swear that I would withhold it even from you, Bess.

Your birthday, and I cannot offer you gifts . . . What would I give you, darling, if I could?

Strawberries, yes. Sweet strawberries out of season. The very strawberries of our first meeting soaked in the best wine of our days together. You told me true. They were always *your* strawberries,

Bess. Elizabeth Throgmorton's, Elizabeth Ralegh's. They were never the Queen's. They were never Elizabeth Tudor's.

'Idiot,' I hear you say. 'Would he give me only what's already mine then?'

My dear, what else is there?

I would give you myself. Once again. I would give you my heart.

As when we first made love. As when you stood against the tree in the dark of the garden. 'Sweet Sir Walter!' you cried. 'Sweet Sir Walter!' And when the danger and the pleasure grew their highest: 'Swisser Swatter Swisser Swatter!' Bless you, Bess.

21

Fog. For two days now the ship has been wrapped in a clinging grey shroud of it. We must have run some six hundred miles eastwards into the Atlantic, our position being 40° west wanting three minutes in a latitude of 51° north. This leaves a good twelve hundred miles of bad ocean between my *Destiny* and whatever other destiny awaits me at the end of the long voyage home. To be brief, this foul fog is most welcome. I could drift for all eternity cloaked in it.

The wind died six days from Newfoundland. We are all but becalmed, drifting along with the Gulf weed, soundlessly, drearily, the vessel no more than another rank piece of flotsam at the mercy of the currents. Everything about us seems possessed by this fog and at one with it. Fog above, fog below, fog ahead, fog astern, fog to starboard and port; our empty sails look fashioned of fog, the grey seas also. This singular dull diffidence of the elements suits my mood. If I go and stand on the poop deck, above the coach where Mr Burwick has his cabin, the front parts of my ship are quite invisible. Fog blots them out, I am absolved from their care. At the same time, I note that there is a quality of fog at sea which causes near objects to loom larger than in fact they are. Ropes look as thick as snakes, the water dripping from them appears to my eyes like great globules of poison. Black knot-holes and splinters in the deck on which I walk seem big as cinders from extinguished fires.

If the basest clods among my crew had ever truly intended to carry their mutinous ambitions to any end, then the past forty-eight hours would have brought them out into the open, that's for sure. A blind ship, half-asleep, fumbling along through pestilential obscure Atlantic vapours, could readily be overrun, and her commander disposed of. They could have cut my throat any night –

though it might have cost them a few throats of their own, since Sam King now stands guard at my cabin door. If they shrank from outright murder, then they could have cast me adrift in an open boat with just my remaining gentlemen for company. They have done neither, and all such danger seems out-moded, out-manoeuvred. The truth is that by open dealing I showed up their Richard Head as a common coward, one of those born to moan and scheme below decks but to run like a startled rat when confronted by his betters. I am an old hand at dealing with Mr Richard Heads of this sad world. Elizabeth had rats in the holes at Whitehall.

My promise that all felons can make themselves scarce once we drop anchor in Kinsale has struck a sort of bargain with the lot of them. They realize, I reckon, that I have promised no less than to save their wretched necks, on condition that they help me to risk mine. It is a just exchange. Its irony affords me bleak delight.

I sit writing by a candle in my cabin. I know that outside now, by night, the fog itself seems stained black, with not a solitary star to be seen in the sky, and the very lanterns at our mast-heads glinting like the eyes of vultures – pale blue in the film of fog which clouds them. All is still, all is calm, the only sound the occasional creak of a timber, the call of the men on the night watch or their coughing as the fog sticks in their throats, with here within the cabin the slow steady scratching of my pen across these sheets of virgin paper.

Virgin.

Virginity.

More absolutes.

But how strange are the human details which they may hide!

The Greeks believed that Astraea, the goddess of justice, was the last of the deities to quit our earth, and that when she returned to heaven she became the constellation which men still call Virgo. My *Destiny* is guided by no star tonight, either virgin or whore, while my hand must write a story more peculiar than any in the Greek mythologies.

I write for truth's sake, for my wife and myself. I tell of the Queen. Of the Queen and Walter Ralegh.

There was a comet that appeared over London in the course of that summer. I mean, the summer of 1583. I was twenty-nine years old. Queen Elizabeth was twenty years older. Things happened in the great world, to be sure. The Earl of Desmond was slain in a skirmish; that was the end of his rebellion, with Munster reduced to a desert and some 30,000 Irish perishing of starvation in the last six months of the war. Galileo, at Pisa, is supposed to have been discovering the parabolic nature of trajectories – which he did by dropping shot from the Leaning Tower. There was an English expedition set out overland for India; nine years passed before it ever came back. In that August John Whitgift was appointed Archbishop of Canterbury; he put down the Puritans, riding everywhere attended by great squadrons of horse, more like a general than a clergyman. This, I suppose, is what I would write about if this was a history book. But I'm not writing history. I speak of what happened to me.

The Queen was at Richmond when the comet came. She summoned her astrologer, John Dee. Dee I did not dislike; there was no harm in him. Tall and bony, wearing a gown like an artist's with hanging sleeves and a slit, he used to amuse her Majesty with his so-called magic glass, and indeed she had employed him when she was young to select a favourable date for her coronation. It did not rain on that day, so Dee was made.

That summer in Richmond was the first time I ever saw Dr John Dee in company with a somewhat more sinister creature. This was Edward Kelley, a man who invariably wore a tight black skull cap (it was said that both his ears had been cut off). The two necromancers appeared with their magic glass and the Queen was pleased to grant them a private audience.

Whatever they told her exactly she never told me. I know only that when she emerged from their consultation her face was radiant. She ordered a window of the chamber to be flung open, and she strode across arms-outstretched to contemplate the comet.

'*Jacta est alea*,' she declared.

Jacta est alea . . .

The dice are thrown.

From Richmond the Court moved on with the Queen to her castle at Windsor. There was nothing unusual in that. Elizabeth always preferred to absent herself from the crowds and smells of London during summer. And that summer of the comet was preternaturally hot.

At Windsor the Queen passed much of the time enjoying the cool green pleasantness of the river. It was often her whim to have me for her waterman, my office to pole the glittering gold punt in which she lay dreaming all the long afternoons. The one I now remember fell that Midsummer Eve.

Elizabeth reclined in the royal punt in a nest of little silver cushions encrusted with pearls, under a silken canopy that had bells no bigger than cockle-shells attached to its fringes. Those bells made fairy music to my every motion with the pole. They vexed me out of all proportion, and I think she knew it. She hummed tunelessly to herself, offering no idle conversation to break the monotony of our sleepy progress, trailing her slender white hands in the water, reaching up now and again only to caress the flowing fronds of some weeping willow that overhung the bank. Bees buzzed about us, drunk with pollen. They didn't seem to bother her. Nothing did. She was wearing a brilliant gown of cloth of gold, with a black mantle, a ruff at her neck like gossamer, and a broad white taffeta hat which had gillyflowers pinned with diamonds to its brim. In short, she was overdressed for such an excursion, and I wondered (without remarking so) that her Majesty could keep a cool countenance despite going bedecked in such a weight of finery. For myself, I was dripping with perspiration like one of the damned. My palms soon grew so greasy that I could barely keep a good grip on the pole. My hose stuck to my legs. My doublet felt like a sack. But then mine was all the labour. Elizabeth sat still as some Cleopatra carved of white sandalwood. Under her hooded eyelids her eyes were amused. She always liked, I believe, to see a man hot.

Not a word did she say to me until near the end of our journey. Then, as we drew back within sight of the steps of the royal landing stage, the sound of viols echoing across the Thames to welcome her return, the Queen leaned forward suddenly, holding up her hands, flicking bright water from them to sting my cheeks.

'Such a sweet pastime,' she said. 'An afternoon's fishing.'

I bowed. 'But your Majesty has no catch to show for it.'

Elizabeth laughed. Her laughter was light and ethereal, tinkling, teasing, like those wretched bells on the canopy.

'You think not, Captain Ralegh? Then you can't know what my Mutton says.'

I must have scowled at this reference to Hatton, for the Queen laughed again.

'Would you like to learn his pretty compliment? There is much truth in it, perhaps.'

I forced my parched lips into some smiling shape of politeness. 'If it pleases your Majesty, then I'm sure I'd delight in whatever it was that Sir Christopher had to say in praise of the Queen of England's propensities as a fisherwoman.'

It was Elizabeth's turn to frown. Then she shrugged her shoulders lightly, ignoring my gentle disparagement, pulling the edges of the sable mantle together across her breasts.

'He said that I fish for men's souls, Captain Ralegh. And he said that I have so sweet a bait that the man doesn't live who can escape my network.'

I nodded. I managed to manage another smile. Hatton's homage struck me as clever trivial stuff, more suited to a playhouse than real life, and I was in no matching temper to compete with it. I busied myself by drawing the pole without too much violence through the lily-pads and bringing the punt to rest at the foot of the steps.

As I handed the Queen ashore, I heard her murmur:

'Of course, it is no great magic to catch a man's soul.'

I said nothing. She had spoken as if to herself, with an air of requiring me to overhear her thoughts but to make no comment. I think I guessed the drift of what was coming. Yet I underestimated her pleasure in teasing, her wit, her elusiveness, if I expected anything as crude as some direct reference to a man's *body*.

'Water,' she said. 'Now that's the difficult catch. Water runs through the fingers. You can never be quite sure that you have got it.'

For the first time, her pun upon my Christian name served only to irritate me. I knelt down, leaning from the landing stage, making a cup of my hands. When I stood up again it was to offer her brimming disproof of what she had said.

Elizabeth shook her head slowly from side to side. 'A handful of Thames? You insult me. I require more than that.'

'More, Majesty?'

'All.'

'The whole Thames?' I cried foolishly. 'All the rivers? All the streams? Every brook and rill and rivulet?'

Elizabeth did not smile. Her eyes were as cold as gold coins dropped down a well. There was greed in her gaze: a crazy dispassionate lust. Her look made me shiver.

She said: 'I want every drop of water in the world. The tides themselves, the vasty deep, the floods. You understand, Captain Ralegh? For a Queen, nothing less than the ocean could ever be sufficient.'

We stood staring at each other in the bright light that quivered off the river. I let my inch of Thames run through my fingers.

'It's not impossible,' I said. 'Not for a Queen.'

Elizabeth smiled then, and gave me her hand to kiss. She turned and ascended the marble steps, calling out for her ladies, declaring her desire to feast in the gardens.

I was left to change my clothes and to ponder this mischief. It was easier to wring the sweat from my shirt than to get the Queen's words out of my head.

That was the night of the fire in Windsor's great park. The Midsummer Eve fire, lit in Elizabeth's honour. The Court dined at long tables set out in the cool of the rose gardens. Then, at darkfall, blazing torches were carried in procession to the oak tree which they call Herne the Hunter's. A huge bonfire had been prepared there, wood, furze, bracken, coals heaped high, casks of tar. The Queen, dressed in white, set the first taper to it. Then the Gentlemen of the Body hurled their torches. There was music. We danced in a ring round the fire.

She looked like a goddess that night.

Crowned with flames, red hair streaming, she leapt and she danced in the firelight. The moon made her young again. Her fingertips played in my palms.

There was fever in her fingers. Her nails scratched me. She would hurt me, then dance away laughing, then dance back to caress and soothe the wounds, then hurt me again.

How long the dance went on I can't remember. The fire died. The Queen danced in its ashes. The fiddlers sawed at their strings. The torches guttered. Elizabeth seemed rapt in a trance. She danced on her own now. I walked in the dark and licked the hot blood from my hands. ·

We came back to London. To the Palace of Westminster. The comet had passed. The Queen's dance with me went on. It was every other night now, there in the Presence Chamber, up and down, round about, in and out amongst the other Gentlemen of the Body, them standing stamping, the same pounding rhythms, each time seeming more savage, more breathless, more and more elemental, their hands clapping, the Queen's hands slapping, all that touching turning twisting, the whirling skirts, the flashing slipperless feet, her red hair tossed in my face, her nails at their sweet crucifixions in my palms.

The door to the Privy Chamber did not close. Each dance would end with Elizabeth passing through it, dancing on into the Privy Lodgings, but not looking back. That door was never kicked shut in my face, but somehow I knew that the unspoken order of the dance did not permit me to follow her until the Queen herself invited me. What form such invitation might take I could not guess. I danced. I waited. I stood on the brink, on the threshold.

When, finally, it came, the Queen's invitation was simplicity itself. She did not not let go of my hand. We danced through the door together, side by side, no one leading, no one following. Then she stopped and looked at me and by a swift nod told me that it was now up to me to close the door behind us. Which I did. Which I did with a mighty kick that made her laugh.

The Privy Chamber was empty. No Maids of Honour. Her hand still in mine, she danced into the Privy Lodgings. I shut that second door too. But gently, but softly. And the Queen took a golden key from a silver chain that hung about her neck, and turned it in the lock, and made the door fast.

I danced through the door with the Queen for that first time on the night of the 15th of August. Which is in the Romish Church known as the Feast of the Assumption of the Blessed Virgin Mary, when they celebrate their belief that Our Lady's dead body preserved of all fleshly corruption was taken up into heaven to be reunited with her soul. I have no doubt at all that Elizabeth was aware of the date. She always did enjoy her little jokes.

*

Ben Jonson got it wrong. The Queen had no membrane, no deformity, no corporal impediment to keep her from the usual ends of love. I saw her naked that night, and many nights after. Her body was too thin to be called truly beautiful, her breasts pear-shaped, her skin somewhat less than satin to the touch. I will not make an inventory of her parts. Say, if you like, that by the time I became her Endymion this mortal Moon had waned just a whit from the full, from the height of her magic, from the pitch of her perfection. Yet she still took my breath away, aroused my passion, inspired every nerve of my body to burn with desire.

The Queen's bedroom was dark and low-ceilinged. There was only a single tall candle that burned by the bed. The bed itself, white-silk-sheeted, its ermine-lined counterpane neatly rolled down in a scroll, was hung about with heavy embroidered green tapestries. Candlelight wove another intricate web of shadows over them, making it like some enchanted cavern in an Oriental fairy-tale.

Elizabeth had not undressed herself. From the start, she assumed complete command of our love-making. She held out her hands and she told me to take off her rings. I was impatient. I did it too fast for her liking. She reproved me by rapping my knuckles, her lips in a pout. I wanted to kiss her. The Queen turned her face away angrily.

I had to learn slowness, delay, the delights of long dalliance. That first night did not please Elizabeth as much as some later ones. I was raw. I was new to the game. The excitement of privacy, the fact that here I was locked in a small room with the Virgin Queen of England, that her own hand had led me there and then turned the key in the lock – all this, you will understand, was too much for me. All the teasings, all the dances, and now this. To be plain, I was rampant with desire. I wanted to strip her and enter her. If, as men said (and I had heard the Queen herself claim often enough) – if this woman was really still a virgin, her love-parts intact, pure, unopened, then I wanted to make an end of that. This is not necessarily brutish. I feel no great dishonour in confessing it. I longed to make a woman of the Queen.

The way she refused my kiss was the first instruction. The others followed at intervals, with no words said. Far from this intimacy of her bedroom conferring power on me, it soon became clear that she wanted her lover to behave as no less than a slave. Sidelong looks, flicking fingers, arched eyebrows and frowns when I displeased her, a little cold ghost of a smile when I did right – these were the silent signs of our intercourse. And her very refusal to utter a syllable – she who before and in public I had known for a quick-witted chatterbox – this only made more mysterious and compelling the long-drawn-out erotic ritual which her Majesty now required me to perform.

May the Devil excuse me, it was never my intention to set down on paper a crude record of all that took place that night between me and the Queen. There are details which should remain secret concerning the behaviour of any man and any woman when they are alone together in the modes and moods and luxuries of their love. Even more is this true, I believe, when one of those lovers is the monarch of the realm, the sovereign head of State, God's earthly regent, however vicious or imperfect. I was never much given to gossip. I maintain now a certain respectful reticence even in this memoir tortured out from the depths of my heart for veracity's sake.

Once, certainly, in the course of a poem which I composed during my first spell of imprisonment in the Tower, I sought to find metaphors to fit the perverse pattern of what passed for making love with Elizabeth Tudor. The poem was bitter and obscure, bred of too much frustrated passion recollected in despair. I wrote it for her eyes only, making sure that it found its way tight-sealed to Secretary Cecil for transmission to her Majesty. She had shut me in the Tower for faithlessness, for what she saw as my turning aside from devotion to her by my marriage to Bess. Whether the Queen ever read it, I never found out. Robert Cecil was never such a friend to me as it suited him then to pretend to be. I should not be surprised if he used my poor inflammatory verses for firelighters, or more likely hid them away in that rat's nest of files which he thought it his duty to keep as the master of Elizabeth's spies. 'The Ocean to Cynthia' – that's what I called the poem. Myself being the ocean, of course, and Elizabeth that Roman goddess of the moon. These conceits are not fanciful, but accurate. I was as water in our love-games, my function like that of the tides. As for Elizabeth, she was always the moon which controls the tides, holding absolute sway over them, ordaining their comings and their goings. She had floods of her lover, Walter Ralegh. I had to be content with a little moonlight.

It was a burning poem on a hell-fire of a theme. I made myself love's heretic by writing it. But there are shames and vices unmentionable in prose which can go cloaked in verse, where only the poet knows the naked truth he is at one and the same time revealing and concealing. Not that my cloak of a poem was so very thick. If Elizabeth did deign to walk on it, her feet must have burned. If she did read the poem, for instance, what did she make of my likening 'the careful charge' of her love to some 'stream by strong hand bounded in' from the usual course of nature? More pertinently, more impertinently, did my cry of complaint bewailing my own 'long erections' bring a blush of something better than anger to those viciously chaste royal cheeks? I do not know. And I can no longer care. Suffice it to say that I call up those wretched images tonight. I remember that which bred them, and could breed nothing else. I remember each trick, each cheat, each turn, each parry, each tease, every ugly and pretty perversity which served to keep Elizabeth a virgin that first night with me, every further night (and day) with me, and no doubt with all her other lovers both before my time and after.

I speak of our love-making as a ritual. So it was. But it was a black, a necromantic rite. A rite in which the Queen herself was the sacrament, and I was her foul priest, her poor adorer. It was all for her, that blasphemy against the name of Venus. She feasted on me. I got nothing back.

To confess this is to acknowledge that she could unman me. I do so acknowledge. While protesting that I had no proper choice. With any other woman, I would have fallen on her, forced her, made her mine. With Elizabeth – God help me, I was no madman who'd try to rape a Queen!

At the end of that night, still denied consummation, communion, yet exhausted by plentiful libations of my own manly essence upon the altar of the Queen's naked body, I crept away, used up, dismissed, dazed with shame, half-hoping perhaps that matters might be different the next time.

They were not. There was never any difference.

The dice were cast. They said the same thing every night and all. They said that Walter Ralegh was now Queen Elizabeth's lover. They said also that Elizabeth was never more the Queen than when busy in bed with this lover who was not permitted entrance to her cunt.

What twist or taint made it so? I cannot pretend understanding. I

185

may only declare what I know from experience: the truth about me and the Queen. There was no physical reason why Elizabeth remained always a virgin. She demanded it that way. She had what she wanted of me.

Sometimes, of course, I have wondered . . . There are deeper deformities.

Consider her bloody inheritance, the forces that shaped her. Her father, King Henry the Eighth, was self-murdered by lust. Her mother, Queen Anne Boleyn, lost her head on the block for it. Some say that Elizabeth's step-uncle, Lord Seymour, laid siege to her maidenhead when she was still a child, with rompings and spankings in the nursery, and sly wicked tricks played on her private parts which the twelve-year-old Princess found exciting but terrifying. She was threatened with the axe because of this. And had to live with the knowledge that Seymour himself had his head chopped off because of what it was alleged that he had done to her, this sin she was too young to understand. Did they tell her also that her first lover (if in fact he *was* guilty of molesting the child) did not go gentle to that execution. It took a dozen men to hold him down – Seymour got up from the block with his head half-off – There were three more blows of the axe before he was dead.

I never yet saw a ghost. Did Elizabeth Tudor? Did these blood-bedaubed victims of lust make her cling to her virginity as if it were life itself?

I don't know. I never dared ask her. And she never spoke of it.

The fog at the door of my cabin, this ship and my whole life suspended in some kind of limbo, my last word on the subject is just that Queen Elizabeth's vicious vaginal innocence had no visible or tangible cause.

But the mind and the heart may have membranes.

22

Still fog. Such fog! I have never known anything like it. A confusion of the elements, a convulsion of nature that makes midnight out of noon. And this fog has got into my spirit, inhabiting my judgement, eclipsing sense, so that it seems I grope about in an inward darkness, blind to circumstance, having to fight to distinguish the dream from the fact. Dream and reality, in any case, have come together in the last few hours in a manner that makes all a kind of nightmare.

God damn this fog! God save this fog of a world!

Amen. That will do. No more curses or prayers. Just tell the story.

I must use my pen as I just now used my sword. To establish some true order, to keep command.

It will help if I go back to the beginning. Relate the whole mad bad business just as it happened . . .

First, then, I fell asleep with my head on these pages. Heaven knows what the time was. But it can't have been far short of the start of the morning watch. About seven bells, perhaps – which is half-past three.

I was dog-tired, more dead than alive, my soul spent with that writing about Elizabeth. I snapped the book shut. I used it for my pillow. I collapsed.

I dreamt a dream in that deep and exhausted sleep. Now, dreams have never overmuch interested me: What are they but excretions passed from our waking minds? Other people, I concede, hold higher opinions – my wife Bess among them. She always adhered to that teaching of Dr John Dee's, that a dream may foretell actuality, or cast light upon the present fortunes of its dreamer if correctly interpreted. I consider such beliefs mere superstition, yet confess that this particular dream has given my scepticism a shaking.

In my dream I was standing in the square at San Thomé. The Indian was sitting bareback on a horse in front of me. His hands were tied together behind his back. He had a noose around his neck. The rope went up and over the branch of a tree. There were two black slaves who were holding the other end of this rope. Now and again in my dream one of these slaves would give a tug on the end of the rope and the Indian's head would jerk. But the Indian seemed indifferent to their antics. He took no notice of the slaves at all. Whenever they made his head jerk he made it look as if he had intended to nod or shake his head in any case. There were two of our English soldiers in my dream also. They stood holding the horse by its bridle, one on either side of it.

This dream scene was uncommonly vivid. Plainly it has features which derive from my memory of the story told to me by my nephew George, concerning what happened in San Thomé on the morning after our forces occupied it. But Keymis was not present. And I was. I was the white man standing under the burning hot sun interrogating the Indian.

'Gold,' I said, in the dream. 'You understand *gold*? You know what I'm talking about?'

I was wearing that cloak which Elizabeth once walked on. I had this baton of polished wood in my right hand. I kept cutting at the air with it. (Keymis carried a baton like that. I gave it to him when he departed upriver. It was his symbol of authority as my Commandant.)

The Indian said nothing. He stared at me.

I was sweating like a pig. Then I started weeping. The tears rolled down my cheeks. In my dream I could taste them. They had a vile sweet taste. Like the taste of blood.

'Christ! Christ!' I started shouting. 'I know there's a mine here. I know there is gold and I know that you know where it is. Are you going to show me the mine? If you don't, I shall hang you! Hang you, you fool. You understand? Hang you by the neck until you're dead!'

The Indian nodded. He didn't say anything. His face was expressionless. Its bright copper skin was a criss-cross of red and black painted patterns. In my dream I couldn't tell if he really understood what I was saying to him, or if he kept nodding like a puppet only because the slaves holding the rope kept making his head jerk.

I managed to check my tears. I gestured to the slaves to stop their game. The Indian gazed at the sky. I looked up also. The sky was gold. The sun was a ball of gold fire.

When I looked once again at the Indian he seemed likewise to have turned to solid gold. Yet the horse that he sat on was still real enough. It shivered in the sunlight, flicked its ears.

'Who are you?' I demanded, in the dream.

The Indian said nothing. He nodded his head. This time it wasn't because the slaves had made him nod. He was nodding his golden head at something behind me. Something or someone. I knew in the dream what it was.

I knew what it was, but I still turned to look where he was looking.

I saw the church on the other side of the square. The doors of the church were broken. They were hanging like black snapped wings on their broken hinges. Wat's body lay on a litter in the shadow of those doors. I saw the pearl ear-ring that dangled from his left ear-lobe. There was blood on the pearl. There was more blood all over his face. An English flag covered the rest of him.

I turned back to the Indian.

'You know who that is?' I said quietly.

The Indian nodded.

'Good,' I said. 'Excellent. So you *do* understand me.'

I rapped my own chest with the baton. 'Now then, who do you think *I* am?'

The Indian smiled, as if finding my question absurd. His eyes had not left poor Wat's young corpse.

A bird was shrieking somewhere in the jungle.

'Are you dumb, man?' I cried out. 'I asked a question. Do you want to end up like your master over there?'

I pointed with my baton. In the middle of the square there was another corpse. The corpse of Palomeque. Long. Fat. Enormous. Palomeque was stark naked, sallow-skinned. There was this great wound in the left-hand side of his skull. It extended right down to the gaping jaw. Flies were at work in the wound, busy and buzzing.

The Indian shrugged. He didn't even glance at the second corpse. Instead, he shut his eyes. Gold fell from his eyelids.

Then the Indian spoke in my dream.

'Hang me,' he said.

His voice was no more than a whisper.

'Hang me,' he said. 'I am a half-caste. Can't you see that I'm a half-caste? Why, look . . .'

His face was melting as I stared at it. The red and black paint came away, then the gold skin also. Great flakes and scabs of pure gold seemed to drop from it. I saw his cheek-bones, his jaw-bones, his skull. Soon he had no flesh left. But his bones were gold. His eyes were two orbs of quartz in a head like an ingot.

One of the slaves started giggling. He pulled on the rope. The Indian's golden head jerked. An eye fell out of its gold socket.

The other slave said: 'Take no notice. He's lying. He's a dirty liar. He's not any half-caste. He knows where the mine is.'

It was the Indian's eye that now held my attention. A sudden wind whirled sand across the square. The eye rolled with the sand. It came to a stop beside my feet. I knelt and picked it up. And then all at once, cupped in the palm of my hand, it was Keymis's eye! Poor Laurence Keymis's eye, pale, bloodshot, with the cast in it, there in the palm of my hand. The *feel* of that eye was horribly real in the dream. Indeed, all my senses were quickened. I could hear every insect in the undergrowth – their chirping chirping chirping hurt my eardrums. My nostrils stung with the smells that came to them on the breeze: smoke, pineapples, decaying flesh. I felt sick. I turned aside to vomit.

How to define the transitions that obtain only in dreams? If I say that I seemed to vomit up all my past life, my very identity, perhaps that makes some sense of what now happened. For as soon as I stood erect again, there in the sanded square of the Spanish outpost, I was not Walter Ralegh any more. My splendid cloak had gone. I was wearing some oat-coloured jacket and breeches. There were black boots on my feet. Mud and blood on the boots.

The Indian suddenly shouted:

'What of your son?'

The eye that had been in my hand was now in my head. Keymis's eye. When I looked at the Indian I was Keymis looking up at the Indian. All sense of my own true identity had been drained from my body. I knew that the Indian saw Keymis there standing in front of him. That the soldiers saw Keymis. And the slaves. That they'd *always* seen Keymis. I knew this for certain.

That horrible alchemy by which the Indian's face had been transmuted into a gold skull was now reversed. He had his natural features back again. The incalculable dark eyes. The black and red patterns streaking his cheeks and his forehead. The disc-shaped pendant dangling from his nose.

'Gold,' I said. *Keymis* said. I spoke as Keymis: that slow pedantic voice, the halting lisp. 'Gold,' my dream-self Keymis said once again. 'That's all I want, that's all I came here for. I'll set you free, do you hear me? You're free, you can go back home to your tribe. But I must know where the mine is!'

'Your son!' the Indian shouted. 'What of your son?'

Then I realized that while all the time in the dream I had been Laurence Keymis to the others, nevertheless the Indian must have believed from the start that this balding Commandant with the baton in his fist was Walter Ralegh. I hope I make it clear what I am saying. Dreams have no logic, but in any event if you try to imagine the real-life scene at San Thomé that morning of January 3rd in this very year, then no doubt the actual Christoval Guayacunda *did* make such an assumption. He had heard from his Spanish masters that Ralegh was coming. When the English appeared up the river, and took the town, it would be quite natural for him to believe that their leader was me.

I tapped at my chest with the baton, 'Listen,' I said. (Keymis said!) 'You have it wrong. I'm not who you think I am.'

The Indian was staring at me. For the first time, he appeared disconcerted.

'You are Guattaral.'

'No. I am not Guattaral. My name is Keymis. I am Guattaral's general. Do you understand? I am the friend of the man you call Guattaral.'

The Indian looked around.

He said: 'Guattaral is not here then?'

'That's right.'

'Where is Guattaral?'

'He is with his ship.'

'Where is this ship?'

'Downriver.'

'Far?'

'Yes. Very far.'

'But why did Guattaral not come himself?'

Keymis, myself-as-Keymis, hesitated. Then, in the dream, this answer from my lips, words cold and clear:

'*Because he is a coward. That is why.*'

The Indian's mouth curved down in disbelief.

'That's the truth,' I heard myself say. 'He has a fever. But the fever is just an excuse. If there had been no fever, then be sure Sir Walter Ralegh would have found some other reason for not coming. He's a coward. All his life he's been a coward. He doesn't know it. He'd never admit that to himself. But I know Sir Walter. I know Sir Walter's secret heart. That's his secret, that's the truth about him.'

All this, in the dream, I uttered with the strictest sobriety. There was no contempt in my voice, and neither passion nor compassion. I felt nothing. I spoke as an oracle might speak. These words came *through* my lips, rather than from them. Having spoken them, I turned and I looked at Wat.

There was a long silence. Then I heard the Indian say:

'But that *is* Guattaral's son.'

It was not a question. A mere statement with the emphasis on the *is*.

'Yes,' I said in my dream. 'That was Sir Walter Ralegh's son.'

Another silence. The sweet sickly smell of death. A drum that started beating in the jungle.

'Hang me,' the Indian said.

The drum getting louder. Drum, drum, drum. Like a heartbeat. Like the beating of my own heart as I looked at Wat.

'Hang me!' the Indian cried. 'Hang me! Hang me!'

I didn't turn round. I couldn't take my eyes off Wat's dead body. *Drum, drum, drum.*

'*Hang me!*'

'Let him go,' I said.

'Sir?' (One of the soldiers.)

'I said let him go,' I shouted out.

In my dream I spun around to make sure that my order was being obeyed. As I did, the Indian kicked hard with his heels and the horse started forwards. The soldiers let go of the bridle. The horse bolted. For a moment the Indian hung from the tree with the rope round his neck. I took four quick strides, slashing at the slaves with my baton. They howled, letting go of the rope. The Indian fell in the sand.

I, Keymis, stood over his body. The Indian lay still. I poked at him with my baton. He did not budge.

'The crazy bastard's dead,' said one of the soldiers. 'His neck broke. I heard it go snap.'

One of the black slaves kicked at the Indian's body.

The Indian opened his eyes.

He laughed.

Then he started to shout –

He shouted. The Indian shouted. I heard him. Not in the dream. He shouted.

I woke. His shouting woke me. It was real. The Indian was shouting and shouting. The shout was terrible. I never heard anything like it.

I was soaked in my own sweat. The drum of my dream was my heart. I was lying sprawled over the table. That barbarous shouting went on.

I leapt up, kicking over my chair. I ran to the door of my cabin. It was locked! It was locked from outside . . .

There is an axe I keep by me. In the sea-chest that's under my bed. Dragging out the sea-chest, I laid hold of the axe. I smashed down the door in a minute.

Sam King lay slumped outside the door. My first thought was that he was dead. He wasn't. He'd been clubbed into unconsciousness. He lay there in a pool of his own blood.

Day had dawned, but the fog still made it hard to see properly. I blundered forwards in the direction from which the shouting came. Our decks were slippery. I fell down the steps from the poop.

There was a sudden silence. All seemed ghostly. For a moment, dazed by my fall, I thought I might still be dreaming. Then, crisp through the curtain of fog, the crack of a pistol shot. And following it, piercing my skull with its loudness, the incredible blood-curdling power of that shout. The sound seemed more than human lungs could manage. Yet nor was it like the roar of a wounded animal. I knew who was shouting. I think that I also knew why.

They had strung that Indian up from the starboard yardarm. 'They' being Richard Head and some six of his cronies. Head, pistol in hand, had command of the lynching-party. Command? The word flatters the anarchy of the scene I now ran upon. It was a turmoil of would-be murder. Pure pandemonium.

Head's accomplices scuttled about with their hands to their ears. They'd succeeded in binding the Indian, getting the noose round his neck, and attaching the rope to the spar. He was hanging up there in the fog. But someone had underestimated the man's strength. He'd torn one arm free of its bondage, and was clutching at the rope above his head. He was spinning round and round, and he was shouting. Not gagging him was no doubt their biggest blunder.

The Indian had told me of that shout of his. The shout of the Golden Man – that's what he called it. He attributed some demoniacal power to the shout. He said it made men mad. I'd not believed him.

Do I believe him now? It's not important. I only know what I saw with my own eyes. What I saw, what I heard, what I witnessed.

Those wretches were racing about like Gadarene swine. Their faces were contorted, their eyes bulged. They looked like men on the rack. And the shout was their torture. They dared not take their hands from their ears when he shouted. Each time the Indian drew breath they ran towards him, swarming up the rigging, struggling to clutch at his legs and drag him down to death. Every fresh shout drove them back, knocked them down like rotten apples crashing from a tree in the blast of some great wind, set them whirling on the deck like dervishes or victims of an epileptic fit.

Head himself held something to one ear in an attempt to shut out the Indian's shouting. I recognized what he was holding. It was the Indian's cap, that curious conical bonnet woven of the grey fibres of the *cabuya* plant. With his free hand, Head fired off a flintlock pistol. His purpose may first have been to counteract the sound of the shout, or to spur on his henchmen. But now he was trying to shoot the Indian.

I have pictured this scene at some length because it was complicated. It took me small time, all the same, to resolve its complexities. Axe in hand, battering riff-raff to left and to right of me, I leapt into the rigging and swarmed up the lifts to the parrel. Using that iron collar for purchase, I hacked with the axe at the spar from which the Indian was hanging. It splintered, it smashed, he went hurtling down to the deck. I acted swiftly and instinctively, blind with rage. On reflection, I did the right thing. If I'd chopped at the rope I might have hit the Indian. To do it carefully would have taken too long. Besides which, my body supported by the parrel, I could bring all my weight and strength down with each blow of the axe. Of course, I was running the risk that the fall might kill the Indian. It didn't. He rolled over and over on the deck. Then he crouched like a cat, shaking himself, and sprang to his feet. One hand still bound behind him, the rope with its scrap of shattered spar flailing out from his neck as he shook his head, he raised his right hand high and he screamed at me. What he screamed I don't know – the words must have been in the language of his people. But I knew without words what it was he wanted. I tossed the axe. He caught it on the run.

All that followed is no less than bloody nightmare. I can pray to forget it, but I think that I never shall. I'll set down the barest details. The whole is too horrible.

Not shouting now, the Indian went after his enemies. He hacked and he cut. Some fought back. But they hadn't a chance. He was wielding the axe like that angel that's in the Book of Genesis. He came on; unkillable. His opponents went down; they were not.

I dropped to the deck, drew my sword, fought beside him. Head was firing his pistol at us. He hit nothing in the fog. He ran out of shot, hurled his gun away, seized a boathook. He waited for me. I didn't waste his time.

I remember the shrill wail of the boatswain's whistle. Then the call-to-arms of Mr Burwick's trumpet. But by the time our soldiers appeared on the scene the fight was over.

Fight? It wasn't a fight. It was straightforward massacre. I never saw so much blood spurt and fountain since that slaughter in the Irish fort at Smerwick. The deck was a slaughterhouse floor. The fog itself rained red.

I killed only two men. Head was one of them. His patch came off. There was some sort of pimple underneath.

The Indian took care of the other five. Five? Maybe five. Who knows? He slashed their miscreant heads from their broken shoulders. He made meat of their mangled tangled bodies, and carved up the bits most meticulously. When he'd finished there was nothing left that remotely resembled a man.

*

Here's blood still sticking thick between my fingers. Smutches and smudges of blood from my hand where it moves across the paper. A snail's bright wake streaked with blood trailing down the page . . .

I am stunned, I am brainsick, used up.

I can write no more now.

Tomorrow will be soon enough to make sense of it. Sense of the dream. Sense of the waking nightmare.

If there is sense to be made.

If there's tomorrow –

23

Sun like a lump of coughed-up blood in the sky. Rifts and shifts in this hell-born mist. The fog is lifting. Yet the ship hardly stirs. There's no relief of a wind from any quarter. We idle as though tethered, transfixed, weighed-down by a cargo of doom and unpardonable sin. The sea's like black milk. If I could spy but one bird in this wilderness of water and vapour it would raise my heart. There is none. Not even the boatswain bird that sleeps on the sea. (But then no doubt they don't venture this far north.) The only living creatures to witness our present involuntary vigil are a number of water-snakes, ringed yellow and black, which swim round and about my *Destiny* in great circles. Vile vassals! Odious attendants! What do they wait upon? If I were a superstitious man I could believe that their wrigglings obeyed the pattern of some enchanter's wand, his hand tracing a magical web in which we lie trapped, bewitching us where we stand, forbidding all further motion either forwards or back.

I am no novice of fate, servant of bad stars or omens, no rhapsodist. I reject all such fancies.

I wait for the sun to grow strong and the wind to come back.

This morning I authorized Mr Burwick to instruct Simon Taverner to issue each remaining loyal gentleman of my crew with half a gill of brandy diluted in three gills of water from the rain barrels, with a little juice of lemons and sugar added. (The presence of this brandy cask in my cabin has been my best-kept secret. Lord Boyle, the Earl of Cork, made me a gift of it, the night before we sailed from Kinsale, oh so long ago! He knows my own abstemiousness, but foresaw the benefits of such liquor in an emergency.)

I have not imbibed myself. I have not even succumbed to the

comfort I could find in eating another of the *khoka* leaves. A long pipe of tobacco is sufficient. That helps to clear the brains, to make a necessary distance between the whirlpool of my wits and the worse-than-any-whirlpool which was yesterday.

It is a precious jewel to be plain.

First, then, a few facts. Truths that stick in my throat. But I must spit them out. Forgive me, my son, if I dash this down like a herald arrived full of insults. You will see, in any case, that what I have to say insults *myself*.

I was wrong about Richard Head. Quite crazily wrong. I had him dismissed as a worm who would never dare take action. Worms turn. This one did. He waited his moment, the devil. I had humiliated him in the eyes of his fellow creatures. I should have foreseen that a man like that would seek some twisted way to get his revenge.

His gang overpowered Sam King at the door of my cabin. They left him for dead – but not before my gallant friend, half-conscious, bludgeoned to his knees, had managed to lock my door from outside and throw the key overboard. This much I learned from Sam himself, badly battered, his skull fractured, yet with a good chance (may it please God) that he will recover from his wounds.

Head might have sent for a battering-ram to smash my door down. If he did, he wasn't quick enough about it. For at this point – certainly before any of his mutineers had got down the steps from the poop deck – the Indian emerged from *his* cabin, Wat's old cabin, and the scene was transformed.

Why? How?

I have only Guayacunda's own account to go by. His version of what happened is bizarre to say the least of it. Yet I believe what he tells me. Why should he lie, after all?

Head seems for some reason to have panicked. The swine spoke little Spanish, but as he held the Indian at pistol-point, talking frantically all the while to his accomplices, the Indian heard him saying, over and over, the single word: *brujo*.

Now, *brujo* means, in the Spanish tongue, a witch or a sorcerer, someone believed to possess uncanny or supernatural powers.

I asked the Indian:

'You mean that he considered you a sorcerer?'

'Yes.'

'For God's sake, why?'

The Indian shrugged. 'Who knows? Perhaps he was mad. Perhaps he heard the talk in San Thomé.'

'What talk?'

'Some of the female slaves.'

'*They* called you a *brujo*?'

The Indian nodded. 'It means nothing,' he said. 'They called me that because they did not understand.'

I did not care to ask him what it was that these superstitious females had failed to understand. I was more interested in why Head had suddenly switched his murderous attentions to this fellow as a sort of surrogate for me. Did the Indian have any theories on that subject? I put it to him. His answer were startling.

'The man with the patch – he tried to hang me once before.'

'At the Spanish fort?'

'Yes. There were two soldiers. They held the horse. He was one of them.'

I found myself foolishly recalling my dream, trying to remember if this detail had been reflected in it. I am sure that it was not. But it doesn't matter. The Indian, after all, was talking about the *reality*.

'So Head tried to hang you once,' I said. 'That doesn't explain why he should try to hang you again . . .'

'He believed I was a *brujo*,' the Indian said. 'He believed I had power, that I was a man of power. Perhaps he thought that he must find out if I *could* be killed. Perhaps he thought that by killing me he could take power away from you.'

'But that is absurd!'

The Indian fingered his neck. The skin there was still raw with the mark made by the noose.

He said: 'Perhaps he thought that *I* made him throw his knife in the sea.'

'*What?*'

The Indian smiled. 'When the white men first came to my country, people thought that they were gods. Perhaps the fear can work the other way.'

The notion was ridiculous. I rejected it.

'I think Head was mad,' I said.

'Yes,' said the Indian.

'You agree then? That all this talk of sorcery and power is so much nonsense? Head was a madman! He had no motive at all for trying to hang you from the yardarm. You admit it? That Head was insane? That he didn't know what he was doing?'

'Yes,' said the Indian.

I questioned him further. I was driven by a need to know every detail of what had happened before I burst upon that horrifying scene. How had Head and his accomplices managed to force him down from the poop deck? By holding the pistol to his skull, the Indian said. How did they manage to bind him and string him up from the spar, when I had seen for myself the great strength he could exert when he chose to? Still by the threat of a pistol ball, the Indian said. His answers seemed rational enough. It was all quite reasonable, all understandable, even if the actual context – the horrendous pantomime of the attempted hanging – was insanity itself. But then I came to the shout.

'You shouted,' I said.

'Yes.'

'That was what woke me.'

The Indian said nothing.

'I never heard anything like that shout,' I said. 'You spoke once before of it. You said it drove men mad, that it made them kill. You said it was the shout of the Golden Man.'

The Indian's eyes gave nothing away.

'I told Guattaral the truth,' he said.

I picked my next words with much care. 'That shout. Is that sorcery?'

'No,' said the Indian.

'What is it then?'

'It is the shout of the Golden Man.'

'Meaning *what*?' I demanded. 'That *you* are this Golden Man?'

The Indian shuddered. He drew up his right hand to cover his eyes as if I had threatened to strike him.

'No!' he cried. 'No! No!'

I felt ashamed. I felt I was asking him questions that I had no right to ask. I felt like a trespasser. But I was in the grip of a compulsion. No idle itch of curiosity. A compulsion to know, to understand.

I had to go on with it.

I said: 'Is the Golden Man your god then? Does the voice of your god speak through you? Is that what the shout is? The voice of the god of the Chibchas?'

The Indian brought his hand down slowly from his face.

'I don't know,' he said.

I was astonished. He had tears in his eyes. This man who just yesterday had fought like Sackerson the bear in the Paris Garden, who had torn and rent his enemies limb from limb, broke down now in front of me and started weeping wildly like a child.

I could not continue with this interview. I was filled with too much pity, too much puzzlement. I never saw the Indian so reduced. It occurred to me that – in his primitive way – he was as *wounded* as I am by the events of yesterday. Which is to speak of inward wounds, wounds of the heart and the spirit, as terrible in their fashion as the splintered bone and flowing blood of poor Sam King's head.

All the same, the Indian had the last word.

'I told Guattaral the truth,' he said, between sobs. 'I told him what I know and what I do not know.' He drew himself up. He stared at me, his eyes blind with tears, more bright tears pouring ceaselessly down his face. 'But there's more truth to tell. What I know. What I don't know. We shall speak of this again. Perhaps – *tomorrow?*'

His tone was at once proud and yet beseeching. As though he begged for time for our mutual good. I do not understand this, but I accepted it. I nodded. He turned on his heel. He ran. He ran away.

The swabbers out there are cleaning our decks of the blood. I can hear the brutes singing. Singing! They like their work, evidently. (Better than I like mine. Who can clean these pages? Who can purge my memory of the bloody images that befoul it?) No doubt the prospect of a little sour beer and cheese hard as horn makes them go about their business with a will. Or perhaps I underestimate the clods? These are men, whatever else, who did not align themselves with the mucilaginous Head and his gang of homicides. Perhaps even this bankruptcy which is all I have left for a crew is capable of some feeling? Such as? Such as that we are cleansing the decks of the *Destiny* of the spoor of mad murdering spirits, evil ghosts, men so possessed by hate that they sought in an utterly meaningless manner to bring about my downfall. By hanging the Indian! Why; they might as well have hacked a great hole in our hull, and drowned every one of us, themselves included! We are rid of an insanity. Those singing fools must realize that now at least there's the chance that this voyage can have an end. A proper end. In port. In the harbour at Kinsale. Where they can draw their wages from me and then go. Scuttle away, the vermin, into whatever dark holes Ireland has always offered them and their like.

I can hear the sound of saw and hammer also. Nicholas Markham, our ship's carpenter, employed on a fresh spar for the starboard yardarm. No song from him. An honest silent workman. He knows his job. He does it. God be praised.

Some nonsense just now from the Reverend Mr Samuel Jones. Should he or should he not recite a few words of Cranmer's over the parcels of tangled flesh and bone the swabbers were busy slinging in the sea? I advised him to do whatever his conscience directed.

My own conscience makes me sit here writing.

I have tried to make some sense of the waking nightmare. But how, in God's name, can I make any sense of my dream?

I don't mean the fearful imagery – the Indian's skin peeling off, his skull being gold, that eye which I fitted in my socket . . . Such horrors are the common stuff of dreams. I count them as nothing.

When I speak of making sense of the dream I mean two things.

First: How to account for the fact that my dream, as it were, *came true*? I dreamt of an attempt to hang the Indian. And, at the very same time that I was dreaming it, the devil Richard Head and his loathsome disciples were actually out there in the fog with the rope round the Indian's neck. Prophecy? Coincidence? I dreamt that the Indian shouted. It was his real shout that woke me. But perhaps there is nothing so unusual in this? There is often a sort of hinge between the dream-world and the world of reality. The Queen told me once of a dream she had. Her half-sister Mary was burning her. Elizabeth dreamt that she had gone to join the ranks of the 300 Protestant 'heretics' done to death by fire in the filth that was Smithfield. Rogers, the Canon of St Paul's, whose crime was that he had translated the Bible (with Coverdale and Tyndall), stood close beside the Queen in her terrible dream. He was bathing his hands in the flame as if it were cold water. He was urging her to do the same.

That it would not hurt. Elizabeth woke. She found Mary Fitton at her bedside, throwing water on a bolster which had caught fire from the wick of a fallen watch-light. As fire and water at the point where the Queen's dream met her waking, so the vast shout of the Indian both in my dream and out of it yesterday. And who has not dreamt that he walked through some oven of a desert, only to wake and discover his feet on a warming-pan? These analogies are some comfort. They seem reasonable. But the fact remains that I woke from a horror not to the lessening of it; rather to the selfsame horror magnified, made worse, given substance and circumstance. I dreamt, in the essence of my dream, neither future nor past, but *what was actually happening in the present!* So that – So that now, for the first time in my life, I fear to sleep at all. The necessary border seems gone. Is there to be no more clear distinction between what I imagine, asleep, and what I do, waking? The thought is ridiculous. I despise myself even for framing it. I sound like some fantastic in a Shakespeare play – his 'Prince of Denmark' perhaps, poor work, dashed-out, confused, neither drama nor true history. Dearest Bess, how I need you now to share my bed! (And I never said *that* before. Me! Whose cabin was his sanctuary . . .)

Fear. There's the second crux of that abominable dream of mine.

'*Why did Guattaral not come himself?*'

'*Because he is a coward. That is why.*'

In the dream, when I said that, I was Keymis. Keymis's eye was in my head. I spoke with Keymis's voice. Yet it appeared to me also that I spoke like an oracle. (Sir Robert Naunton! He once called me the Queen's oracle!)

'*He has a fever. But the fever is just an excuse. If there had been no fever, then be sure Sir Walter Ralegh would have found some other reason for not coming. He's a coward. All his life he's been a coward. He doesn't know it. He'd never admit that to himself. But I know Sir Walter. I know Sir Walter's secret heart. That's his secret, that's the truth about him.*'

Would Laurence Keymis have said that?

No. He would not.

Did Laurence Keymis even *think* that?

No. I stake my life on it.

But *I* was Keymis in the dream. *I* said it. *I* must have thought it. And if I spoke like an oracle does that not mean I spoke true?

NO.

I reject the dream utterly.

Would any coward –

Too much introspection. It makes the heart sick. Literally. That must be it, for I broke off the self-tortured and self-torturing stuff above to blunder out of this cabin and to vomit. My arm about the swivel gun mounted on the rail of the poop deck, I leant over the ship's side, unseen (thank God) in the thin shroud of fog which still clings to us, and I spewed up – *what*?

God knows. And the sea.

My stomach was empty to start with. I have taken just the one pipe of tobacco all day.

Heartsick, was that it?

Heartsick or lifesick.

Certainly not my usual bout of ordinary ugly seasickness. For how or why should I be seasick on a ship which scarcely moves?

Sir Walter Ralegh threw up. I record the wretched fact in the third person because that is how it felt to me. As if I was momentarily outside this poor racked body, standing beside myself, watching it go through its pathetic little act of mortal vileness.

Sir Walter Ralegh, that great Lucifer, famous and proud, once the world's envy, courtier and soldier, explorer and founder of colonies, hero of Cadiz, Queen Elizabeth's lover, the glass of fashion and the mould of form . . .

The same Sir Walter Ralegh.

Throwing up.

I threw up every gobbet of my self-esteem, the bitter-as-wormwood dregs of my life and my hopes, whatever secretions remained of a long feast on nothing.

Nothing. Nothing. Nothing.

Nothing at all.

24

At midnight – can that only be an hour ago? – the first faint stirrings of a gentle wind. Now it fills our sails. The fog is dispersed. My *Destiny* runs on east beneath a black sky packed with stars. The complete absence of haze produces a phenomenon I have never seen before: Where sky meets sea the line is as clear and definite as the edge of a knife, so that when a star rides down low on the horizon it loses none of its brilliance and eventually the waterline seems simply to cut the star in two, the upper half of the star throwing a long shaft of fire along the sea to light us on our way.

In this last sixty minutes I have learned much. I spent that time together with the Indian, locked in earnest conversation on the quarter-deck. No one disturbed our colloquy. The night air was cold. We walked up and down as we talked.

What was said is of the uttermost importance. It is the key, I feel, to many locks. I must resist, for the moment, the temptation to apply that key to everything. Even – on second thoughts – I would do well to reject such facile images as 'keys' and 'locks'. They are alien to the spirit of what I have learned, what I am still learning, what I must go on learning if I am ever to bring this ship and my life safe home to any harbour of sense.

It will serve the truth best to set down our talk unadorned. Listen closely. I have every word of it by heart.

The Indian began: 'The first time that we met you asked me *what* I was. I told you I had been the servant of the Spanish Governor. That is true. Later, I told you that I killed him. That also is true. But I did not tell you everything. It was not time. I told you what I knew – but there are other things. I did not tell you what I do not know.'

He stopped. I did not interrupt his silence. It was plain that he spoke from the heart, choosing each word with care. I was prepared to let him have his say in his own way. There was that unmistakable air about him which a man has when he has wrestled long with some difficult truth, come to its conclusion, and elected to share what he has learned with another man. Silence is part of such speech. Only shallow rivers chatter all the while.

'I don't know *what* I am,' the Indian said. 'I know my name and the place where I was born. Christoval Guayacunda. A native of Sogamoso. Of the Chibcha tribe. So much I know, and so much have I told you. But what it *means* to be those things, I don't know.'

He paused briefly, flicking at the pendant which dangles from his nose, for all the world as though dismissing it as an emblem of mere savagery. When he went on his sentences came in a flood. The deliberate prologue spoken, I was now to be given his story in one headlong rush. He poured out the contents of his mind like a penitent self-lashed to confession.

'Guattaral, the truth is I am *nothing*. My people were conquered by the Incas a hundred years before the white men came. Our homes were burned, our lands were taken from us. I said we were proud. Our pride is the pride of the dead. We are ghosts, we are shades, we are what all our enemies have made of us. Why, even our very name – Chibcha – is not our real name. Some say that real name was Muisca, but none knows for certain. *Chibcha* was what others called us, since our god of all gods we called *Chibchachum*. Think of it! To be wiped out as men, to be known only by someone else's mockery of your god! We were persons no more. We were shadows. Then Cortés came, with his white men on white horses. He destroyed our own destroyers. We were dust of the dust his *conquistadores* trampled on. Shades of shades, ghosts of ghosts, a forgotten nation, phantoms in other people's dreams! You may say that a man can arise from such ashes? I say that a man has his own flame in the fire that is his family. I boasted to you once of my Golden Fathers . . . That was the boast of one who calls his ancestors "golden" because he cannot know them as flesh and blood. Oh, and more flows from this! From this endless empty talk of *gold* and *golden* . . . But I shall come to that before I've done. So much I owe you. And some sense about this matter of the gold perhaps most of all.'

He turned to face me, spreading wide his hands in a gesture of supplication. 'Do you understand? That what I am is this nothing? Even my name! *Christoval Guayacunda*. The Spaniards gave me that name. Their priests threw water over me. Water leaves no mark. When I look into the looking-glass what do I see? Only what *they* call "Christoval" and *you* call "the Indian". (I have heard you say it often, when you shout at your boy with the cock's feather in his cap.) This "Christoval", this "Indian" – *I don't know him!* Who is he? He is some made-up man, some shadow cast by his masters!'

I found myself deeply moved by what he said. I admit I was also astonished. Not so much by the intelligence evident in his self-insight – I never supposed him anything but intelligent, his primitive appearance to the contrary – but by the force and fluency with which he expressed himself. We always speak (please remember) in Spanish. Somewhere, sometime, this man has acquired a quite extraordinary command of that language. It occurs to me, now, that this fact only underlines the pathos of what he declared. He speaks Spanish like a Spaniard; but then not even his language is his own. I note also that his reference to Robin my page ('your boy with the cock's feather in his cap') betrays that he has mastered a little English since coming on board. In short, there's no denying that this Indian has a brain.

I addressed myself, however, to his heart. 'Listen,' I said. 'I understand you well. A man needs roots. It gives him strength if he knows what he has sprung from. But men are not trees. We can make ourselves. Do you think I was *born* just as you see me now? A leader of others? A great commander? I am no prince! My father and my mother –'

'I thought you were a god,' the Indian said.

A paroxysm of coughing shook me. It was as if my ague-ridden all-too-mortal body cried out in protest at this rank absurdity.

'A god?' I croaked. 'Look, man, here's blood in my hand! Blood that I cough up from lungs rotten with years of imprisonment for a crime that I never committed!' Another thought struck me. 'You speak of yourself as a ghost? Why, I'm less than a ghost! I was sentenced to death by my King. All those years in the Tower – I could have been dragged out to my death any morning when it pleased that King to be rid of me. A god? My friend, *I am a dead man!*'

I chopped at my neck with my hand. The Indian reached out swiftly, catching my wrist.

'He will cut off your head?'

'Probably.'

'Because you bring no gold?'

'That is one reason.'

'The other being the killing of Palomeque?'

I shrugged. 'I gave my word no Spanish blood would be spilt. It was an impossible condition. I accepted it. I shall accept the consequences.'

The Indian still had hold of my wrist. His grip tightened. His eyes blazed in the moonlight like a madman's. 'But *I* killed Palomeque. I shall tell your King!'

'Thank you,' I said. 'No doubt his Majesty would be graciously pleased to hang and disembowel you. A dead man and a ghost going hand-in-hand to enter their rightful estate. Very neat, very pretty. But, I fear, just a trifle unnecessary. You recall, I am sure, that other Spaniards besides your former master were killed by my soldiers at San Thomé? Oh, I know that you will now say again that it was that golden shout of yours which inspired my son to spring to the assault . . . And, having heard you shout, I could well believe it. But for a man who says he is nothing, you lay claim to too much power, sir! Dust of the dust? Since when has dust been able to assume such absolute responsibility over life and death?'

This speech, as you see, had grown more bitter and sarcastic the longer it went on. By the time that I had finished, I regretted having started. Yet now, on reflection, I am glad that I allowed myself the sudden sharp upflare of anger. For it drew forth a second outburst from the Indian.

Relinquishing his hold on my wrist, he turned aside to fix his attention on the sea. I knew that he did this to avoid my eyes. I knew also that there was no evasiveness in such action. He spoke with an intensity which eye-to-eye confrontation must have marred. Once more, the image which comes to me by way of comparison is that of a passionate penitent. There are some things which a soul must address to the crucifix, not to itself, and certainly not to the priest. The sea served the Indian for crucifix. God's sea, now anointed with moonlight, and crucified with stars.

'Guattaral, listen well. I am dust. I am nothing. But the dust that I come from is gold dust. And my nothing is your everything. When my people were extinguished by the Incas, we left them with a dream. Our lands were poor and bleak, cold, high in the mountains. Our houses were simple – walls of wood, roofs of twisted *ichu*-grass. I told you the Chibcha were proud. That is true. But their pride was the pride of men who made dirt their daily bread. We used fire-hardened sticks and stone axes to hack out a bad living from our land. A little maize, a few potatoes, some *quinoa*. Not enough. One yearly harvest. More wind than rain. So why did we remain there in the mountains? How did we survive before the Incas came? To answer that is to tell you *why* they came. After all, if our lands were so poor, why should *anyone* want them?

'I will tell you. There were two reasons. The first reason is real. You have eaten of it! Yes, the leaf, the food of the gods . . . For some reason, known only perhaps to those gods, that was the one thing we had in abundance. It grows wild round our five holy lakes. Especially all about Lake Guatavita. Some say the Sun God blessed us with it. Others that the first seeds were planted by Bochica. You know of Bochica? He is the one the Aztecs and the Toltecs called Quetzalcoatl. A very great god. His face is as white as your own!'

The Indian glanced at me sidelong, entreaty in his eyes, as if what he said had explained something. A grim smile shaped his lips when he realized I still had no notion of his meaning. He looked back at the sea. His discourse grew even more urgent.

'You know some of the power of the leaf. You do not know all. Men may live by that leaf, become more than men. It can make us like gods, so they say. I have told you it grants strength and endurance. That is true. It made the Chibcha strong, that god-food made a mighty nation of a poor mountain tribe. But, Guattaral, you have merely nibbled at it! There are visions in its root. Empires of sense. Whole kingdoms of the spirit. Deathless worlds.'

He shook his head suddenly, almost to deny the note of ecstasy which had transfigured his tone. 'But I speak like an Inca!' he shouted. 'You see how my voice is not my own? That's what *they* believed, that's why they came with their armies to destroy us. The Chibcha didn't "believe". The Chibcha *knew*. Our enemies wanted that knowledge. But they never got it. They slaughtered our men, raped our women, burned our dwellings. They stuffed their bellies with the leaf until their wits turned to dung and ran out of their arse-holes in rivers. Then their chieftains put our priests to the torture, believing there was some secret we withheld. The priests had no secret. There is none.'

'I do not understand this,' I admitted. 'Do you mean that the mystical properties you ascribe to your *khoka* leaf can only be appreciated by the Chibcha?'

'Perhaps. I don't know.'

'But why should that be? Because your people were eating it for many years? Generation after generation? Because it was like life's blood to them?'

'Possibly. But some of the priests said that it was because we had been given it in the first place. That we were the chosen nation of the Sun God.'

'Does the plant grow nowhere else?'

The Indian hesitated. Then he murmured: 'Yes. It does grow elsewhere. In fact, the Incas already had it, though not in such abundance. And certainly the power of our leaf was considered superior to any other.'

I shook my head, for I still could not grasp the significance of what he told me. 'Are you saying that your enemies did not appreciate the value of something they already had? That they came to conquer your tribe simply because you had a stronger species of this herb? Why, man, what you're saying is absurd!'

'Yes.'

'*You* think it is absurd?'

'It happened long ago,' the Indian said. 'All that I am now telling you does not come from my own experience. I have had to listen to lies and legends, stories spun by old men to explain what their grandfathers reckoned of all this when those very grandfathers were young. Who can say what the truth is? I thought I knew it once. Now I say only this: Men live by dreams. The Incas imagined that we were gods. We were their dream. They found we were only men.'

I said: 'And what was the dream of the Chibcha?'

The Indian sighed. 'A worse dream perhaps. That *we* were gods. A mountain people high above all others. Yes, I must face that too. Perhaps the gods let our enemies destroy us because of this great vanity.'

He fell silent.

I considered the perfect brilliance of the stars. They were clustered so thickly together that in places there seemed to be almost more dazzling points of light set in the blackness than background of sky itself.

I said quietly: 'The second reason.'

He said nothing.

'You spoke of *two* reasons why the Incas destroyed your people. The first reason you said was *real* –'

'The leaf exists.'

'I don't dispute it. I've eaten the damned thing!'

'Guattaral should not speak like that. The leaf is not accursed. The leaf is holy.'

'So you say. I won't dispute that either – though it seems to me you are in two minds about it.'

The Indian frowned. 'Two minds? How is that possible?'

'A figure of speech. Did you never encounter it from your Spanish masters? It means that you have doubts, that you are confused. You certainly appear so. In one breath, you speak of the food of the gods; in the next, you declare that the Incas –'

'The Incas wanted more than the leaf. They wanted what they thought the leaf gave us.'

'Divine power? Wisdom? But then you said that was illusion! Some crazy dream!'

'*They* suffered that illusion,' the Indian said. 'I know it was their dream. Our dream I don't know. That's what I'm trying to explain. I have come to the point where I can speak with some knowledge of these other dreams. It is other men's dreams that have made me the nothing I am. As to the dream of the Chibcha – I don't know it! It is gone, it is lost, it is less than the wind across the Andes. I don't have two minds. I have none! Sleep and waking are as one to me. Both mean oblivion. Do you understand now? I do not dream. I am *dreamt*. The Spaniards dreamt my father's father's father. The Incas dreamt my fathers before those. And who dreams *me*? Guattaral, do I have to tell you?'

I snatched at the ship's rail, but its cold was no comfort. Those blazing stars seemed to whirl in a wheel in the sky. I thought they'd come crashing down, and that one would annihilate me. Never before had the stars seemed so fatally near. The world . . . The very universe of sense . . . I fancied it could crack, burst apart at the straining seams, fall in meaningless pieces. And my fancy was correct. The world *was* about to break. *My* world.

I swear before God that some part of me knew this, intuited the worst, was darkly aware that the Indian now threatened to tell me some truth which would make madness of my life. I could have turned away, stopped up my ears, refused to listen. I didn't. I did none of those things. Why not, in Christ's name? Moral courage? No, no, my son. Quite the opposite. My spirit was broken. *I knew what he was going to tell me.* Not the substance, of course. But the essence. He told me what I knew I had to know.

'*You* dream me, Guattaral,' the Indian said. 'The Incas had your dream – the dream of gold. That was the second reason. Gold, gold, gold! They dreamt we were made of gold, that our rivers ran with it. Like you, they dreamt the dream of the Golden Man!'

I confess that just for a moment I thought him a devil. How else could he know of my dream? Of that terrible vision? My knuckle-bones cracked where my hands clutched the ship's icy rail. Bless all such small tokens of mortality! That cracking sound sobered me. When he went on, I was soon undeceived. He had spoken in metaphor.

'The Golden Man, El Dorado, the gilded one. It was a title we gave to our King, the King of the Chibcha, the Zipa. King? Casique? Ah, the dream now becomes magnificent? To the Incas, no doubt, an obsession. Like the Aztecs, like the Spaniards – nothing stirred their imaginations as much as the fever of gold. I have told you of Lake Guatavita, our most sacred place. When the Zipa was crowned he was carried there, borne high on a wooden litter. Our people walked backwards before him, sweeping the way where he would pass. It is dawn. It is high in the mountains. The lake holds the first light of the sun. The priests strip our King of his garments. They anoint him with *el varniz de Pasto*, sap tapped from a tree, simple resin. Then more priests step forward. They have hollow canes. In their left hands they bear bowls with gold dust. The priests blow this gold dust through their pipes. It sticks to the resin. They blow and they blow until the whole naked figure of the King is covered with the gold dust. Transfiguration! He is now the living image of the Sun God. The litter is borne out into the lake, with our gilded King riding high on the priests' shoulders. El Dorado! The Chibcha, rimming the lake, are hailing their Zipa. Each one holds a golden offering in his fist. The priests kneel. The litter floats out on the water. As the sun makes gold fire of Lake Guatavita, the Golden Man rises, he spreads wide his gold-encrusted arms, then he dives . . . Down, down, down into the lake. He must swim beneath its surface for many minutes. Until every golden particle is gone. Those depths are icy cold, but the King will stay there. He knows that if there is a single flake of gold left on his body when he emerges, then the priests will say the Sun God has rejected him. The penalty for that, of course, is death. No Golden Man, so they say, ever paid that penalty. We were a mountain people, our chests deep and our lungs large to cope with the thin air of the *cordillera*. At last, the King steps forth from the lake. Not a spot of gold on him. The priests bow their heads to the ground. The people run forward. Golden trinkets are hurled in the lake. It rains gold. Guatavita's a glory. Its waters flicker and glitter. A fit mirror for the Sun God. A lake of pure gold. Long live the Zipa! May the Zipa live for ever! A great shout goes up from the mountain tops. From the crowds round the rim of the lake. The Sun God's chosen one, King of the Chibcha, is carried aloft in triumph to his palace. He is the golden one! The Golden Man!'

The Indian's voice had risen to a high pitch of excitement, as if he was seeing the scene that he spoke of, as if it were being enacted even now before his eyes and mine. Suddenly he broke off. He pointed to the moonlight on the water.

'There is the truth.'

'I don't understand you.'

'What does the water show? The moon's shining reflected. What is the moonlight? The moon has no light of her own. Her face takes its light from the sun. So the Spanish priests taught me.'

'Then you learned your lesson well,' I said. 'These things are all true. But what do they have to do with your Golden Man?'

'They fit,' said the Indian, his voice sinking to a whisper. 'The Incas and then the Spaniards moved in darkness. They were like the moon. They had no light of their own. They came as thieves to plunder the light of the Sun God, the gold of the Chibcha, the glory of our Golden Man.'

He turned. He was looking straight at me.

'There are no gold mines in the lands that were once my people's.'

'But you spoke of gold dust –'

213

'If there was gold dust then it was purchased. If there were golden images then we must have had them from trade. It is possible that the Chibcha sometimes traded the leaf for gold. Possible but unlikely. The leaf of the tree is sacred to us. Gold is mere trash. Gold does not live.'

'*If* there were images? Then your tale of this Golden Man –?'

'It is just that. A tale. A tale told by the Incas. Told by them to the Aztecatl, the people you call the Aztecs. Told by them to the Spaniards. And so on, and so on.'

'But there must have been *something* –'

'You need to believe so?'

'Does the moon *invent* the sunlight?' I demanded, reverting desperately to his former image of the way this strange story had been passed on through time. 'Are you saying there is no sun?'

The Indian shook his head. 'The Sun God is not mocked. He laughs at us. I am telling you all that I know, and all that I don't know. I don't know why our enemies chose to inflict on my people this dream of the Golden Man. *Perhaps* the Zipa was anointed with a powder of gold dust obtained from trading. *Perhaps* what our priests blew through their pipes over his body was only the seed of the tree. *Perhaps* traders from other tribes watched some such scene of coronation from afar, took it to mean we were rich in gold, and the story spread that way. *Perhaps* it was all an illusion, bred in the minds of those traders by misuse of our leaf. *Perhaps there was nothing at all* . . .'

'*Nothing?* Man, there must have been *something*!'

The Indian smiled grimly. 'Because Guattaral says so?'

'Because Cortés found gold!'

'Of course. But in the empire of the Aztecatl, in the empire of the Incas.'

'Then there must be gold elsewhere.'

'I agree. But it is not important. I tell you what I know. There is no gold in the mountains of my people. Not a jot, not a speck, not a crumb. There is not and there was not. There never will be. It must please the Sun God so. No El Dorado.'

'I did not come in quest of El Dorado. I knew that story. I thought it fiction. But I had facts. I had evidence. I brought back specimens from Guiana. There was gold in them. God damn you, you and your Golden Man! *Where were the Spanish mines up the Orinoco?* There

214

was one near San Thomé, wasn't there? Another in Mount Iconuri?'

The Indian shook his head slowly. 'I know nothing of them.'

'You lie! Keymis brought back ingots.'

'The Spaniards got ingots by trading.'

'Keymis brought documents also. From the house of your damned master, Palomeque. There were references in those papers to gold prospecting. On the banks of the Caroni River, in some *barranca –*'

'I assure you,' the Indian said, 'Palomeque found nothing. His men tried in these places that you mention. And they tried many others. There was always a new drunkard who'd come out of the jungle to tell Don Palomeque, in return for *cassava* liquor, that he knew where the gold was. Off they'd go, the next morning. Over that hill there! Just at the end of this gorge – what a pity, night's falling! Always one day's march away. Always tomorrow. And then in the night before tomorrow the trickster, of course, would abandon them, melt away into the darkness, disappear. That is, if he was not too drunk on *cassava* or the wine of the Spaniards' *borracheras*. The drunkest were the unlucky ones. Palomeque had them crucified on the sites of their imaginary mines.'

'But before Palomeque. The Governor before him. Antonio de Berrio. I knew him. I talked with him. He believed there was gold in Guiana.'

The Indian shrugged. '*Believed*, yes. They all believed. I have heard of that Berrio. He went mad with belief. He marched his men everywhere, day and night, sun and storm, making them dig till they dropped. What did they find? Marcasite. Sand and marcasite. Never gold. In the end his own soldiers turned on him. They plotted to kill him. Berrio escaped. He died raving, they say. Hiding from his own men on an island in the middle of the Orinoco. Raving about gold that was not there!'

'I am sorry to hear it,' I said. 'I thought him an honest gentleman. But that is not my point. Berrio built the fort at San Thomé. He protected it with a palisade. He had ordnance installed there. Why choose that spot and go to all that trouble if it wasn't near a gold mine?'

'You know why,' said the Indian. 'You know why, but you don't want to admit it. San Thomé was built where it was because it was the outpost of this empty dream I tell you of. The south bank of the

Orinoco, three miles east of the mouth of the Caroni. The nearest point upriver to the lands which were once my people's!'

I remembered something I told Francis Bacon that evening in Gray's Inn Fields. That Berrio saw the Orinoco as the road to Manoa, El Dorado, the golden city. I had only the river wrong. It had been the Caroni. But if what the Indian said was true – *if*? Christ's sweat, I *know* it is true, in my heart of hearts, don't I? – then even the Caroni is wrong. A river-road leading to nowhere. To less than a nothing. To a fiction compounded of a fiction. To a lie. To a hell. To the void. To the ultimate zero. My own!

'Palomeque,' I said desperately. 'Did he know what he was doing?'

'Oh, yes. Palomeque was not mad. Unless evil is madness.'

'I didn't mean that. I meant his going up into the mountains of the Chibcha. I meant his looking for gold there. And finding nothing.'

'He found me,' the Indian said. 'Yes, he found nothing.'

I was silent. I watched the sails swell, the wind filling them. Then: 'Did you tell him?' I demanded. 'Did you tell him the truth?'

'No,' the Indian answered. 'I did not tell him.'

I thought of that bull-whip.

There was silence, broken only by the sound of the sails.

I knew that he knew what I thought of.

'I have told you,' the Indian said, as we paced the deck again. 'Guattaral is the only one I have ever told. Guattaral is the only one I shall ever tell.'

'Why?'

'I don't know. I thought I knew.'

'The death of my son?'

'Yes.'

'Your shout?'

The Indian hung his head. He nodded miserably.

I muttered: 'But now you don't know . . . I can make no sense of you!'

'You must make sense of yourself,' the Indian said. 'As for me – perhaps there's no sense to be made.'

He shivered. I do not think it was only the cold night air which caused him to shiver.

'You have changed,' I observed.

'Yes,' he said.

'You once seemed a man of much certainty.'

'The further I go,' he replied, 'the less I know.'

'Perhaps it is good to admit it?'

'Perhaps,' he said.

We walked up and down without words. Once, twice, three times. Then the Indian said:

'I was wrong. May the Sun God forgive me my pride. The shout – It was all that I had. All I could offer in answer to this world where others dream me. I knew the shout. I thought that I knew it. Its meaning. Its source. Its great power.'

'I heard your shout,' I reminded him. 'It was incredible. Terrifying. And it did seem to drive your enemies mad.'

'It did not drive *you* mad, Guattaral.'

I stared at him. 'Does that make me a god then?'

'No,' said the Indian, unsmiling. 'But it makes me a man.'

He turned aside. He took his leave of me. He bade me no goodnight. He stopped momentarily at the top of the flight of steep wooden steps which leads down from the quarter-deck.

'A man,' he repeated. 'Not the Golden Man.'

'But the voice of your god shouted through you?'

'I don't know. I think not. No. I'm sure not.'

I exclaimed: 'But a shout of such power!'

His broad back still turned to me, he shrugged. For the first time, that shrug did not annoy me.

'I shouted out of fear,' the Indian said.

Eight bells. The end of the middle watch. My candle withers and decays in its shroud of wax. This cabin is a spindrift of tobacco smoke. My hand hurts from so much writing. Heart and head –

Heart and head. They hurt more.

I can clear and ease my head by going out in a moment to stand at the bow and watch the sun rise in the east. To sail towards the sun at its rising. To run on into the dawn in the morning. Small comfortless comforts. Not to be despised.

But to clear and ease the heart?

A different matter.

My heart can never forget what it learned this night. It must welcome each new sunrise now as a token of nothingness. O heart, can you learn how to live with this knowledge? *That the sun is not*

217

there. That there never was and never shall be any sun, any gold in Guiana, any mine, any meaning. That the Indian spoke true. That the truth is the moonlight on the water. That I have wasted my life and sacrificed my eldest son in pursuit of this moonshine, this fiction cast into my mind out of other men's fictions, this dream that is not even my own.

Heart, go out and watch yourself break.

Greet your certain damnation.

25

The wind gives us no quarter.

I suspect it is from none.

So we run. We run on. East always. The right wrong direction. Always east. With the New World all over, put behind us, at our backs, rejected. And, ahead of this my *Destiny*, that my destiny. The Old World I must learn to accept again. The place of my beginning. Where I'll end.

It is the trivial things that keep me going. I live by *minutiae*, by attention to the thousand minor details of a ship's life at sea. This morning I spent with our carpenter, Mr Markham, making sure he used large-headed tacks to nail fresh leather to our worn pumps and scuppers. In the afternoon I went about with the cooper, to look to our casks, hoops, and barricos. I stand with the boatswain at the chest to oversee the boys when they box the compass. I go the rounds with the corporal at the setting and relieving of the watch. These matters do not need me, strictly speaking. *I* need *them*. They serve to hold me in my wits.

Shearwaters blown before us. Wings like black bent bars of iron.

We are making eight knots.

Some small rain this evening. Difficult to distinguish it from the incessant spray which the wind blows like smoke across the face of the waters.

I attend Robin where he attends poor Samuel King. The worst is undoubtedly passed. My old friend (please God) appears well on the way to recovery. Tonight he managed a dish of buttered rice with a little cinnamon; also a can of some of our precious fresh water brewed with sugar and a root of green ginger in it. Alas, as Sam grows stronger he wants only to engage me in conversation about the vile Head and his villains. The topic no longer interests me. I fear that in the end I was curt with him, said that the blow to his skull had left him obsessed with its perpetrators, and abandoned him to the company of my page.

Good kind complaisant Robin! He will listen to Sam's monologue all night if necessary, pinching his own leg to keep himself awake. For all his occasional faults of uncivility, how much finer a spirit than I was at his age! Sweet Robin. I am lucky to have him aboard with me. As honest a lad as ever lifted a ladle.

Putijma must have lied, all those years ago.

Lied to me. Lied to Keymis.

A casique? Was that Putijma even truly a casique? A prince? A chieftain? (And what does it matter if he was? Princes can lie. Princes lie better than commoners. I, of all men living, ought to know that!)

The point, in any case, is that Putijma with his tale of the gold in Mount Iconuri fits in only too well with that rabble of scoundrels described by the Indian – drunkards who would tell you that the gold was always just one day's march away, over the next hill, up that inaccessible cliff-face . . .

For I have to admit it: Putijma drank well and deep at my expense. I feasted him too. While he, the trickster, feasted on my folly.

Others, too. Plenty. All of them liars.

Damned liars.

Bloody damned liars to a man –

What use to write of this?

None.

What use even to recall my own fine discriminating distinctions drawn out for such as Francis Bacon? Spiderwebs spun to impress a king of spiders. That it was not El Dorado that I sought. That it was not Manoa I believed in any more. 'Real mines,' I said. 'In the foothills of Manoa,' I said. What self-deceiving sophistry! What art! What drivel! The wonder is I did not choke on my own innocence. The foothills of a madness are still madman's ground. I made my El Dorado 'real', my Manoa 'credible', by reducing the *size* of the lunatic dream, that's all. Not a city of gold. Just a few golden caves.

Open sesame! For Sir Walter Aladdin. That stupid Sindbad. This pathetic Old Man of the Sea.

I wanted and I didn't want to talk to Samuel King about some of the things the Indian has taught me. How my 'inland sea' called 'Parima' probably corresponds to his Lake Guatavita, for instance. (No reduction there! On the map of my folly it was *larger*!) Now I know I never can and never shall talk to Sam about any of this. The sting is too sharp. My shames! My stupidities!

Better not talk to anyone. Not even myself. (Least of all: myself.) Not even you, Carew, my perfect unanswering listener. Should a son look upon his father stripped naked?

Better destroy this book. Drown it in the sea. In the pasture for fools. Where it belongs. Let the crabs turn its pages. Reading matter for mermen and mermaids. I deserve deliquescence.

Dear Christ!

Enough.

So others made a fool of Sir Walter Ralegh. Is this to be taken for news? *How and why I made a fool of myself.* That's the bone I must gnaw on.

Not now. Not yet.

I comb salt from my hair and my beard. The whiteness prevails. Some salt you shall never comb out. Not now. Not ever.

The wind shifts. Still rising.

Better see Mr Burwick and his mates about getting the starboard tacks aboard and settling our main top-sail. Better instruct the younkers to smear a bucket of grease up under our parrels. Better sleep then, and pray Christ for something deeper than oblivion.

26

To accept my own incertitude. To make doubt my bread. No easy tasks for a man who once dined on his reason.

Yet the seas are uncertain. Only this wind is sure. And there's an albatross which wafts along with us to leeward, wide motionless wings the colour of pitch, as if fallen asleep in the air. The bird puts itself at the mercy of the wind, and so flies without effort. Lord, teach me just a modicum of such faith. Not to soar on my pride, not to plummet through despair. Just to dwell in Thy mercy. Not to fly.

Another conversation with the Indian. I found him helping our quartermaster down in the hold. As our stock of food is depleted it becomes necessary to fill the empty casks up with salt water, to maintain our ballast and give the ship good purchase in the sea. Once again I'm impressed by the strength of this Christoval Guayacunda. He tossed barrels as though they were bottles. He stacked the full casks as swiftly as he rolled out the empty ones. Watching, I remembered the way he'd killed those men.

When he'd finished, he came and sat beside me. I was resting on a bollard to ease my leg.

His right cheek bulged. He tapped it with his forefinger.

'Good for work,' he remarked laconically. 'You want one?'

I shook my head. Thanking him, I said something to the effect that I was trying to live without dreams.

His reaction was angry. 'The leaf clears the head, cleans the heart. As to dreams: it has nothing to do with them!' He frowned, snapping his fingers. 'I know what you're thinking. You can't get it out of your mind that I said that the dream of the Golden Man might have come from abuse of the leaf. Yes? Well, the Chibcha have

222

never abused it. Remember: that dream is not ours. We know the leaf. We respect it.'

I said: 'I have heard the same thing said about wine.'

'Wine makes a man less. The leaf makes more of him.'

'How can you be so sure?'

'You saw me work.'

I conceded that he had shown great strength in his handling of the barrels. But asked ironically if he attributed *all* of his strength to the *khoka*.

His answer surprised me. Once more it brought me up face-to-face with the unsophisticated streak in this Indian's nature. For he did no more than refer my attention to certain narrow woven bands which he wears to restrict the muscles above his biceps, and also on each of his legs just below the knee. These tight-twisted bonds, he assured me, were to keep his physical vigour in check just where he wanted it.

I said: 'And your shout? And your fighting? Will you tell me that they got their power from the rope you had tied round your neck?'

I spoke irritably. I suppose I had been infected first by his anger, then by his childishness. Also, no doubt, there is that in me which *resents* this Indian and all that he stands for. Without him, I might be a less broken man. Besides which, to descend to unimpeachable base banality, my bad leg was giving me hell. Lame excuse! Ha! It serves me right that I got back a most upright answer.

'I told you,' the Indian said. 'It was fear that made me shout. And fear is too small a word. It was terror. Guattaral does well to remind me of the rope. Yes, the rope inspired me. It struck terror into my soul, and my soul shouted.'

There was no shame in his voice. He spoke flatly, without a hint of emotion. Yet there was that in his aspect which made me regret my taunts, want to comfort him.

'Then you must have a great soul,' I said, 'for its shout was like thunder.'

The Indian rose to his feet. He looked down at me calmly. There was patience in his eyes. There was also pity.

He said: 'Just now, when I was working in the hold, I learned the lesson for a second time. It was the empty casks that made the most noise. Guattaral, you must understand me. It is the coward that shouts loudest. I am a coward! No god shouts through me, no power, no Golden Man. I, Christoval Guayacunda, shout out my cowardice. I shout like a coward, and I fight like a coward as well. Have you never seen the black rat fight when the snake has bitten it? The rat becomes a fury. Is this courage?'

'But Palomeque . . .' I protested. 'When you killed him –'

'I attacked him from the back,' the Indian said. 'The act of the coward. A coward who never dared turn to try to stop that monster's arm when he whipped me for his pleasure. A coward who waited for the dark, and for the coming of an army which he thought might be led by a god.'

'*Why* did you think I was a god?'

'Because of your name. Guattaral. Guatavita. You begin to see? I tried to make meaning out of nothing. There is not so great a difference between us as you suppose. I, too, have lived by follies. The matter of your godhead is a minor one. My thought that I *knew* my shout is far more foolish. I see now that when I shouted over Palomeque's corpse it was a shout of pure panic. The shout of an empty man. The shout of a coward.' He rapped with his knuckles against his breast. 'A great soul? Guattaral, I know nothing about the size of my soul. I come of a mountain people. We Chibcha are born with big lungs, deep chests – that's our stature. The natural shout of a coward, that's all I have!'

I said quietly: 'And the death of my son?'

The Indian did not answer.

He looked up at my ensign where it streamed in the wind.

'I climbed the mast one morning to read the words,' he said. 'I could not understand them. Not Spanish. Not English?'

'*Amore et Virtute*,' I said. 'Latin.'

He said nothing. He stood staring at the flag.

'They mean,' I said, 'By love and by courage.'

The Indian nodded slowly. He transferred his gaze back to my face.

'You live by these words?'

'Yes. I've tried to.'

The Indian said: 'Your son died by them.'

Not by an Indian's shout then.

By my *whisper*.

*

224

Love? Courage?

Wretched motto. Wretched knighthood. Wretched words.

Words less than what the gulls scream in the wind.

Have I ever known love? Have I ever shown courage?

My love for the Queen was a game, a long dangerous dance by candlelight, a way up the winding stair. 'If thy heart fail thee . . .' Elizabeth, chattering witty magpie, quick clucking hen, did it never once cross that virgin *mind* of yours (I swear now before God and the angels that are His Intelligence: you preserved it all your days and nights inviolate from a single real idea, an honest thought!) – Did it never occur to you, stupid Majesty, that I climbed so well because I had no heart at all? I could not fail. I had no heart to fail me. You played your game with me; I mine with you. They were different games. They only looked the same in the steps of the dance. Your game? Now known only to God, and I shall not presume . . . The antics which Eros inspires in us make us strangers to each other. Lady Pembroke, they say, had a secret chamber built onto the stables at Wilton House, from which she could watch my Lord Pembroke's stallions service his mares, while the servants of that happy household did the same for his wife. Is this comedy or tragedy? I say nothing. It is certainly not love. No more than what happened between us all those times when I danced through the door. And, in our case, how imperfect the lust! It was always the way that you liked it, the way of a bitch high on heat, not wanting the heat to be satisfied, getting pleasure from the howling of her dog, draining him to the dregs, giving nothing. That was your game, God knows why. I could play it. I played it till I bled. (How you laughed that night at Kenilworth when you had blood of me! Was that the ultimate of your desire, *King Harry's daughter*? Would you have liked me on the block – but not my *head* . . . ?) I go too far. Forgive me, sovereign mistress. I will speak harder of the game *I* played with you.

It was a common game. The game of power. I rose by your hand. I had what I wanted of you. My knighthood, my monopolies, Durham House. That great house, with its mighty turret, once Leicester's dwelling . . . The symbol of my ascendancy! A diamond to live in! More jewels, more jewels. The richest man in the world? Of course not, but the world thought so, or that world which is London. And I let them think, let them say, relished their envy, gloried in my game. They were right. I was proud. I took pride in my titles: Captain of your Guard, Lord Warden of the Stannaries, Lord Lieutenant of Cornwall, Vice Admiral of Devon, Governor of the Island of Jersey, all the rest of it. Not bad for a mere upstart. The crystal Thames at my door, swans like handfuls of pearls poured upon it, my white suit with its diamonds to the value of three score thousand pounds, my shoes so bedecked with gold that just one of them would have ransomed a prince. All this for a few dances. But I danced well. The galliard, the cinquepace, the coranto. The allemande, the volte or lavolta . . . None could leap higher than Sir Walter when they danced the lavolta. (Yes, I'm laughing as much as I weep just to write such a sentence!) And, all the while, of course, our secret dance. Your silk stockings, Elizabeth. Your dresses of dove-coloured satin. And the dancing which followed that dance. The dance for one dancer. I leapt high. I danced well in that too.

Humility was never much my style. I'm too old to start learning it now. Permit me the one final boast, then, bigger than those tracts of land (ten thousand acres) which you gave me in Ireland when the rebels were put down, taller than the tower of Durham House, more weighty than all the great ships I had built with the money which flowed from my monopolies in wine and in cloth and in mining. A boast which may seem like self-disgust, self-defence, self-abasement. But is none of these things.

This last boast is the truth.

I *disliked* you, Elizabeth.

You understand? There was never love. By the end, there was not even liking.

Worship, yes. Devotion, maybe. A little tumult now and then of infatuation. Those things come easy. Particularly to earthly divinities. I gave them to you as all England did. You were our substitute for the Virgin Queen of heaven. It was not so very difficult or unpleasant to kneel before your pedestal. To adore. To pray to you – especially when *my* prayers were answered . . . More titles! More power! A suit of silver armour! To represent my county in the Commons! An increase in my tax drawn from the vintners! Permission to found a colony! (And to call it Virginia, of course, all in your honour, my goddess.) More jewels! More estates to plant in Munster! 'See, the Knave commands the Queen!' as Tarleton said. And you: 'When, Sir Walter, will you cease to be a beggar?' To which I, with the deepest of bows: 'Why, when your gracious Majesty ceases to be a benefactor.' A few more ships now? A small pension for my friend, the poet Spenser? But your Majesty is too kind, too royal-hearted! Your Majesty would do well to beware of her own benevolence. There are those who lack grace to be grateful, young men of no experience, rash themselves, yet greedy for preferments, who mistake your many sweet favours shown towards me. No, no, it does not matter what they say! For myself, I care nothing if mad dogs snap at my heels where I walk in your service. Ah then, for your sake, since you command me, and it is my bounden duty to obey, only yesterday Secretary Cecil breathed it in my unwilling ear that one of his agents had overheard my Lord Leicester's step-son, that puppy, Essex –

Play-acting. Self-seeking romance.

Not love, not affection.

A game of chess in which I let you win. Losing, I won each time. And I think you knew it. I think you knew it and you did not care. How *could* you care? You, who had no heart to care with. Your father had cut out your heart when he cut off the head of your mother. As for me, I have no such excuse.

You knew that too, Elizabeth: my heartlessness. It pleased you. You relied on it, in fact. You could not have coped with true feeling. In public, the pantomime: the Queen and the courtier, *amour courtois*, Courtly Love. In private? Why, yet another pantomime, a pantomime of the pantomime, more comic, more tragic, a parody passion in which the unattainable nature of the Queen was perfected by the courtier's ejaculations. In public, sighs. In private, seed. Both wasted.

I never regretted the waste. Perhaps you guessed that? But over the years, I see now, the sick jest of your virginity made me sour. My fault. My most grievous fault. I got all I wanted from you. God knows, it was little enough! A brief space of bright glory, and then darkness. I do not blame you for the darkness. I blame only myself for glorying in the glory. I don't hate you. I have nothing to hate you with. I *dislike* you, Elizabeth Tudor. Dislike, dislike. Which is worse than love or hate. Your stupid puns, your vanity, your tantrums. The way you pupped with your lips if your will was opposed. Spoiled ancient child, you *bored* me. Your conceit turned my stomach. And you never guessed that, did you, Majesty? I know you didn't. How could you? I never knew myself until this minute.

Lovers do not dislike. We were not lovers.

Love sees –

Never mind what love sees. How should I know?

I know only what dislike sees clearly through its absent-hearted eyes. Trivial things, shabby details, the dust in the balance of our senses. Dislike is nice. It wears a turned-up nose. Dislike is hard to please. It can neither forget nor forgive the least speck of dandruff. A mean thing itself, it makes much out of others' imperfections. It leaves a sediment in the soul, a small poison which corrupts the disliker.

You remember the lines I wrote for you after that quarrel in the rose-garden at Nonsuch in Surrey?

> But when I found my self to you was true,
> I loved myself, because my self loved you.

You found the poem 'pretty'. So it was. A pretty lie, a lying piece of poetry. The truth is that I *wasn't* true to you then. The truth is I was *never* true to you. Not in any sense, and least of all in the obvious. In that same rose-garden, the night before, your maid Anne Vavasour gave me twice what her queenly mistress (and mine!) either would not or could not give just once to any man. And the night after, when you went off to Mitcham for the masque, it was my Lady Layton, niece of the Treasurer of your Household, who lay down on her back in a soft bed of rose petals to be pleasured by my eager sharpish thorn. There was no love in these acts. There was lust, and some liking. I call them now to mind without displeasure.

> But when I found my self to you untrue,
> I disliked my self, because my self disliked you.

Less pretty lines? Yes. Broken-backed with their burden of exactitude. I only just penned them, and I'm past licking honesty to make it smooth. We were liars, Elizabeth; we lived a lie. The truth about us will make no poetry.

The truth is I must have disliked you from the start. How else could I ever have started? And how else gone on? Dislike made it possible to use you, while you used me up.

228

From the start. From that first night in the Privy Lodgings. Dislike. Despair at my own duplicity. *Dislike*.

Those dainty feet that twinkled in the dance: there was a rank cheese of dirt between their toes.

Those hands you made so much of: milkmaid's fingers.

Those precious, oh so spotless and never-to-be-penetrated private parts –

Elizabeth, the worms have your maidenhead now.

I trust those worms enjoy what I never wanted.

Amore . . .
By love . . .
Bess, my wife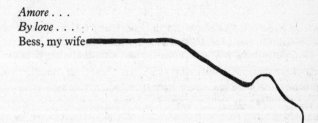

27

Position Report. Latitude: 50° north. Longitude: 18° west wanting four minutes. Distance travelled: 1500 miles from the coast of Newfoundland. Distance to go: 300 miles to Kinsale.

As these figures indicate, the winds have been inconstant when not unfavourable. True, there were spells when we dashed ahead, all canvas billowing, and it seemed the long voyage would soon be over. Our spirits rose with the wind, only to fall again. For then would follow days and nights of stillness, not a breath of air, while we drifted becalmed. At such times even the Gulf weed took on a sluggish look, as if it dragged at our keel, clawed us down. More like the Sargasso than the Atlantic. Then again, worst of all, about a week ago, a packet of storms from the north and east, which tossed us sideways and backwards, off course. In short, my *Destiny* goes by fits and starts. There is no sense or mercy to such weather.

Now we are back on course, but the breeze is feeble. We limp along. There's scurvy among the men.

The Indian has a fever. Refuses medicines.

Sam King is himself again. I thank God for that safe return to taciturnity.

Hemmed in by horizons. The sea slow and dark, vile and sickly. I'd trade all my tobacco for a grassblade. The sight of one green growing thing.

Even the albatross has abandoned us. Our progress too bewildered for his liking.

Crabb the trumpeter died yesterday. Black vomit. Bloody flux. I kept him alive for a week on an elixir of vitriol and vinegar, with salt water, and an electuary of garlic and mustard. No doubt he is better off dead. Mr Jones could scarce recite the words of the burial service for choking on the stink of the wretched corpse. Now I have no one left but Robin to attend me.

I have seen to it that fishing lines have been cast out from the stern, in the hope that we might replenish our dwindling stock of comestibles.

Bess! My wife! Bess . . .

I could not end that sentence I began two weeks ago. I do not know if I can end it now.

Amore et Virtute. The wind mocks my flag. One minute it flaps out, the next sees it hang down, limp, miserable, no more than a dishrag. The last time I looked it was wrapped round the flagpole, its colours no more than a blur of blue and silver, its motto tucked away and out of sight. An ill wind, but blowing some good to hide that boast away. The wind mocks my flag. My flag mocks me.

I wrote your name, Bess. I could not go on. I dug a line down the paper with my pen. That jagged savage mark says more than words can. Despairing new punctuation! A man biting his tongue off!

But I still have my tongue in my head, and my head on my shoulders. The tongue will not wag on this subject. It cleaves fast to the parched roof of my mouth. I write slowly and reluctantly, in other words. And yet I *must* write, shall say *something*. I owe it to you, to myself, to us, don't I? What I say, what I write, might well be wrong. If ever you read this, Bess, then remember that. I no longer speak of 'the truth'. I cannot believe in it. There is no 'the truth'. There are truths. I am trying to tell them.

This little, this much, I have learned by some study of my own confusion. During the fourteen days when I could not write, my spirit hanging skewered on that sentence which seemed unfinishable, I went back and read over all these pages. Having stopped myself from writing, I started reading. Incapable of speech, at last I listened. What I read, what I heard, I don't like. In fact, I detest it. Every word.

It is not just the contradictions that dismay me. God knows, these are bad enough, and anyone who came to this book looking for a narrative would have gone away long ago, convinced that its writer was mad. *Water* is right, they'd say. Queen Elizabeth was inspired to call him that. This man has no shape, no form, no meaning. He doesn't know his own mind from this day to that. In one breath he says he worshipped something (that same Queen, for instance); in another, he'll be telling you he noticed her feet stank in bed. Or, to take a plainer matter, consider these damned gold mines . . . He starts out all assurance that he *knows* of their existence; not belief, not supposition, he convinces me (though apparently not Francis Bacon) that he knows *exactly* where they are, that he can put his fingers on them on the map. He goes on and on about this. He damns and dismisses his companions as cowards and traitors because they fly from him, not sharing his faith in Guiana as a treasure-land of gold. But what happens eventually? Why, the old fool denies himself! He decides that there isn't any gold; worse, he declares that in his secret heart he always knew it! Drunken Indians misled him, he says. They played upon his need to believe in these mines. And how does he arrive at this mighty conclusion? By believing (so he tells us) every word that drops from the lips of another Indian! Not a drunken one, this time. No, sir. Much better. One addicted to the chewing of some drug!

Very well. Never mind this imagined reaction of some imaginary reader. What about Carew? My son, is all that I have written no more than solid proof that your father is a fool, self-deluded when not deceived by others, credulous, querulous, a blind idiot, quite possibly a lunatic? No giant, I told you. Unnecessary disclaimer! A mental and emotional *dwarf* . . . ?

Listen carefully. I was always my own cruellest critic. If this were some mere story-book, some adventure, some fiction, some romance, I could go back and make it consistent. I could cut out contradictions, confusions, especially those that shame *me*, its principal 'character'. But I let them all stand. I change nothing.

Not a sentence, not a word, not a comma.

Let it stand as it is. Right down to that long jagged line.

Neither pride nor humility dictates this. I detest what these pages reveal. I must learn to *accept* it.

Accept that in the attempt to make sense of my past and my present I've made a fool of myself. Not even that. Each lie, each stab at the truth, each contradiction, all and everything in this parcel of confusions, does not serve to 'make' me a fool. My book reveals me as *the fool I am*. This truth-besotted fool, this dunce of dreams (whose most self-deceiving dream was that he ever could play the rôle of a man of action), this senseless soul pouring himself out in one cancelling confession after another only to discover – What? That there was nothing to discover in the first place. Nothing in the first place. Nothing in the last place. No first place. No last place. No end and no beginning. Only the voyage. The voyage of the destiny.

And how much of what I have written about that voyage reads like a dream! The voyage of my *Destiny*, yes, and the voyage of my destiny. Other people mere ghosts. Only the voyager real. I have written about my life as if I have dreamt it. Is that how it was? Is that how I need it to be?

Some poet (it must have been Marlowe) once told me he wanted his life and his work to be one mighty music.

Well, this work of my life has no music. Even I can hear that. No music. Just notes struck at random. All jangling discordance. Mere noise. The sound of a spirit in torment.

My book is not a book. It is a bonfire of myself. I am consumed in it. Dear reader, my son, may you see something by the light cast from your father's burning bones. Something he cannot see. Something. Anything.

It is not the contradictions and confusions that appal me most. Oh no. Lord God, it is these wicked *certainties*. I can forgive myself my blunderings, my fumblings. Only You can forgive me this running of mine from one absolute illumination of 'the truth' to the next, and the next. Now I have it! *Now* I have it! *Now . . . Now . . . Never!*

Abandon this one-man ship of fools on its faithless quest for certitude. Its sail is the sin of pride. Its keel is despair.

My soul, you are water. Be thankful. You won't burn in hell.

So, Bess. Some small honesties. Not the Truth. Just a few home truths from abroad.

Do I love you? I don't know.

I miss you sorely. But that's a different matter. There is an element of enjoyment in this missing. My heart (if I have such an organ) needs a diet of absence. I never felt more tenderly regarding you than when debarred your company. Shut away in the Tower all those years – how I loved you! But when King James, in his infinite mercy, allowed you to come to me . . . Well, Carew was conceived there in my cell, but what happened afterwards? You took to driving

233

right into the Tower in your private carriage, as if you owned the place, as if you owned me. That made the King furious, of course. He soon put a stop to it. What you didn't know was that your visits often irritated *me*. I would long for them, wait for them, look forward to your arrivals with the keenest feelings of what I thought love and true expectation. But then, when you were with me, you were never quite the woman I'd been waiting for. I'd find myself bored by your prattle. I'd long to be alone again. You'll remember one particular occasion . . . You had Carew, still a baby, in your arms, Wat, a sullen embarrassed boy, tugging at your gown. (He knew! Wat always knew his unnatural father! Those quick eyes of his would catch me sneaking glances at the clock, while you noticed nothing.) You went on and on – about money, about Sherborne, about the loss of our lands, about estates. Carew wailing and puking, Wat all fidgets, my head ringing with your endless harangue of complaint. I think that was the only time I let you see my loss of temper. You wept. I had to comfort you. I felt ashamed. It ended with everyone in tears: cold father, bitter mother, screaming infant, and young son shouting that he wanted to go home. Poor Wat! He never *had* a home, and he knew it. Poor Bess! Neither did you, and you thought you had. You hated Durham House, you always said it was too draughty. (What you really resented, I suspect, was that the Queen had given it to me.) As for Sherborne – when I didn't busy myself with builders there, I absented myself in other ways, usually at sea. As for Broad Street – I daresay you will have noted that in these pages I never found the heart to refer to it as anything more than a house. Bess's house. My wife's house in Broad Street. I can't regard it as my home. Home, as they say, is where the heart is. Sir Walter Ralegh isn't sure he has a heart.

You, Bess, have a fine heart, a great heart, a splendid heart. 'Bear my destruction gently, and with a heart like yourself . . .' Yes, I recall those words I wrote to you, when I lay in prison at Winchester, betrayed by lying enemies into the hands of the King, convicted of treason, expecting my execution the next morning. 'Beg my dead body,' I wrote also, 'which living was denied you . . .'

O my dear Bess, who denied you that body?

Why, madam, *I did*!

I always loved you most when you were not there. I could write to you tenderly, beautifully, when I thought I'd never see you again. From the Tower, shut away from the world and your person. From Guiana. From the ends of the earth.

But when you were near, close at hand, within arms' reach – was I ever as loving? I doubt it. One eye on the clock in my quarters in the Tower, I longed most for solitude, my books, my papers, my little hut which was allowed me for the conducting of my chemical experiments. Imprisoned in myself, the Tower *suited* me. Oh, I complained, wrote petitions, begged this one and that one in high office to intercede with his Majesty and grant me my freedom. But I always enjoyed being able to complain, and freedom is probably not my element.

I suffer from this strange disease, you see. My attitude to you is a symptom of it. How to define that sickness? It has no name. It drives me always to reject the real, the immediate, unless my circumstances give me cause to bewail my lot. For more than half my life I have lived in such a way as to maintain a distance between myself and the objects or the persons of my love.

Consider this voyage: I have spent it most in talking to Carew. But when I *meet* Carew, when he stands there before me, grave-eyed, actual, will I spend all day talking to him? Unlikely. After an hour or two, the old itch of boredom will be on me. I shall wish myself a thousand miles away. And even in those first hours, I'll say little. Can I claim I love the real Carew Ralegh, with his cough and his stammer? I feel something, I feel much – but not enough to dignify with the name of love. I love the idea of my son. Not the same thing as loving him.

And poor Wat. *Dead* Wat. To be blunt: how intolerant I was of him when he was alive. His death made it easy for me. I felt then (at last) like a father. My son had to *die* to break through to me. I like the dead. I get on well with them.

Bess, my wife, you are married to a dead man. A man in whom the heart is atrophied. That's about the length and breadth and depth of it. Can you live with such knowledge? Will you bear this news of my self-destruction gently, and with a heart like yourself? I think you might. O my Penelope, you were always a match for this sick Ulysses. You are made of stronger stuff than snow or silk. If ever I had a heart, then it was you.

> But true Love is a durable fire
> In the mind ever burning;
> Never sick, never old, never dead,
> From itself never turning.

I wrote that once, long ago. Is it true, what it says? I don't know any more, but I doubt it. All I'd claim now is what I'd claim for the confusions and contradictions (and, yes, the certainties so uncertain) that have disfigured this, my present writing. That it was true to my own state of mind at the time when I wrote it. And perhaps that I spoke truer than I knew. One of your eyes will not weep, Bess, the one that sees *through* me. Sees that this 'durable fire', this proud obdurate thing 'from itself never turning', is nothing like an image of 'true Love'. It is your absent lover at his tricks, that's all. Making perfection of his own inadequacies, an ideal out of impotence, a burning lie.

I am sick. I am old. I shall soon be dead.

Would to God I could ever – just for a moment! – turn away from myself, and look at you.

Remember, if you can, our happiest days. Those years when our love was a secret we kept from the Queen. Surely, you'll say, he loved me then. Simply, whole-heartedly, with a love that had no need of this complicated diet of absence to feed it?

Bess, I can't answer.

I don't know.

I'm not sure about anything.

If I am to be honest, then I must say that for my part the shadow of the Queen fell over us. Danger lent spice to our dalliance. Each secret encounter was both sweetened and sharpened by risk. And the times in between *were* like absence. I could see you, you could see me, but there was this barrier between us. We had always to pretend, to dissimulate, for fear of Elizabeth's suspicion. I had to seem cold, you indifferent. Thus the normal flow of feeling was baulked from the start.

Understand: I'm not blaming the Queen for this. On the contrary, it suited me, that situation. Oh, it suited me very well; much better than marriage. Because (I suspect) it gave me excuse for a play-acting coldness which could express the real coldness I felt.

Not that I *knew* it was real. That's the point. At the time, all those years, I did blame the Queen. I could tell myself and you that I would love you utterly, if it were not for her. Now I have my doubts. Seven years! Would a man really in love have managed (as I did) to keep that love secret so long from Elizabeth? In her own household? Where she had eyes and spies everywhere?

But perhaps Elizabeth knew and didn't care? Didn't care because she knew me better than I knew myself? Knew about you, and Anne Vavasour, the others –? I cannot believe it. Sufficient to say that her fury only broke on our heads when she learned of the marriage . . . That I had married you because you were already pregnant by me . . . About your child, my son Damerei, who then died –

Enough. I can't write of this.

One confession, Bess.

In the very month that Damerei was born, I wrote a letter to Secretary Cecil. I denied that we were married at all! 'I protest before God,' I said (and may God and you forgive me, Bess), 'I protest before God there is none on the face of the earth that I would be fastened unto.'

But, again, did I write truer than I knew?

I lied to Robert Cecil, trusting the Queen would believe it.

Perhaps I did not lie to God or myself.

There *was* none on the face of the earth that I wanted to be fastened to in marriage. There *was* not. And there *is* not.

Bess, my wife.

A last word. Very brief. But I must say it.

The Queen's shadow came between us in another sense.

Christmas in her Palace at Greenwich, 1584. She dined in the Presence Chamber. My Lord Leicester there, the Earl of Oxford, Lord Charles Howard. Many others. I forget. But it was the night when she shamed Hatton. Shamed him by pointing at me, pointing with her finger at my face, and when he asked why she pointed, Elizabeth said (laughing) that it was only because I had a smut on my cheek, and licked her handkerchief, and beckoned me to kneel down at her feet that she might wipe it off –

But I wiped it off myself, which did not please her.

They laughed. Leicester, Cecil, Howard. They all laughed. So Elizabeth laughed too. All laughed save Hatton.

I laughed. Not at Hatton. Not at anything. Just because the others laughed. I compelled myself to laugh. I knew what they thought. I knew what one or two of them knew. That I was now her man. The Queen's lover. And knew that those one or two (Leicester certainly, and Hatton) knew what that meant. The service she now had of me. A service of smut and handkerchiefs. Or lickings. Wipings.

Which service the Queen had of me that night in the Privy Lodgings.

All as usual.

Only, afterwards, I left her, self-disgust was so great. I forget what excuse it was I offered. Most likely, none was needed. When Elizabeth had drunk wine and feasted well, *once* was enough. I gave her the single libation of myself. She slept. I went.

I went out. I walked down through the gardens. That dark night. No moon. Not a star in the sky. Frozen fountains. Snow hard as iron underfoot.

You remember the snow, Bess?

It came falling from the branches where you stood with your back to the tree. *Swisser Swatter Swisser Swatter!*

Forget me, Bess.

28

Et Virtute!

What courage?

Keymis called me, in my dream, an arrant coward.

I am not that. I fought well enough at Cadiz. But if I am not a coward, then what am I? Something worse, I fear. A man who has *acted* the hero. If despair begets courage, then I have been brave in my time. But there is a greater and more lively courage, which springs from nothing else but an assured confidence. That I have never had. I played as if I did. The play's nearly done.

I no longer count the miles.

I leave latitude and longitude to Mr Burwick.

The ship sails on.

We can't be far from Ireland. For some, journey's end.

> What is our life? A play of passion,
> Our mirth the music of division.
> Our mothers' wombs the tiring-houses be,
> Where we are dressed for this short comedy.
> Heaven the judicious sharp spectator is,
> That sits and marks still who doth act amiss.
> Our graves that hide us from the searching sun
> Are like drawn curtains when the play is done.
> Thus march we, playing, to our latest rest.
> Only we die in earnest, that's no jest.

I just watched the Indian catching a rat in a bottle. (His fever passed quickly. A deliverance he attributes to his leaf!) The rat must have been starving, there's so little left now in Mr Taverner's galley or our stinking ship's store. It ran out from the coils of the anchor

239

cable, down the foredeck, right across the main deck. The Indian was sitting in the ship's boat, lashed to port. He was drinking an inch or two of rainwater, collected in the bottle. The rat flashed past his foot, dodging round sweeps and spars, swerving first this way, now that, jumped into the firebox and out again, running fast, tail lashing, desperate to discover some new hiding place. It didn't. The Indian went after it. He ran faster. Leaping over the port cannon, he got ahead of the rat before it reached the binnacle. He scooped down with his bottle. The rat ran into it. He plugged a bung in the bottle-neck and brought me his prize. The younkers at the pumps applauded wildly. Or perhaps it was ironically. I don't know. The Indian moved fast. That much is certain. He moved fast and he thought fast. To catch the rat in the bottle was to catch it whole. He tossed the bottle up in the air and caught it again. Then he brandished it in the sun, his face triumphant. I observed that the rat was already at choking point, half-dead of its own foul breath in the prison of the bottle.

'What for?' I said.

'For you! For Guattaral!'

It crossed my mind that he mocked me. That he offered me this rat in its glass prison as a symbol of myself. Or perhaps of him.

Not so.

'What should I want with a rat?'

He rubbed his stomach.

'*Eat* it? Are you mad, man?'

'I can skin it and cook it for you. A good strong rat. For Guattaral's dinner.'

No jest. He was serious. He assured me that *he'd* dined on rat meat. That it tasted like –

But I didn't let him tell me what it tasted like. I thanked him. I said no. I said, if he wanted, *he* should eat it.

And now there is this smell of cooking from his cabin . . .

My stomach heaves.

I must add yet more bile to the sea.

Later. Yet now I am quite glad of this vile incident. It proves, if nothing else, that his world is not mine. Our destinies have crossed, mine and the Indian's. There have been times on the voyage when I thought him a sort of looking-glass in which I could see my own soul reflected, when his words seemed to speak for me, telling me what I must learn.

That was not *all* illusion. But here we part.

There is no way Sir Walter Ralegh must dine on a rat!

Bess dreamt of a golden man that night before I sailed for Guiana. But her emperor, all sticky with gold dust, turned into Queen Elizabeth! *Ergo*: There is no sense in dreams. Know this, then, Carew Ralegh. Keymis lied. Your father is a lame and hobbling hero. A bad actor in a part too grand for him. Not the same thing as a coward. Not at all. You are the son of a true man. A man who, in his own respect, despises death, and all his misshapen and ugly forms. I showed that at Cadiz. '*Intramus!*' I shouted to Essex. '*Intramus! Intramus!* In we go . . . !' And Essex flung his hat into the sea with joy, and we went in, and I led the attack. Two fleets in the narrow neck of the harbour. Pitched battle from dawn until dusk. And when I got past the Spanish galleys, answering their salvoes with blasts of a trumpet, I anchored right up against their galleons. Three hours they bombarded me. I did not flinch. I gave them as good as I got. I bestowed benedictions of fire upon them. And when they saw me coming to board them, those Spaniards slipped their anchors and ran themselves aground, tumbling into the sea heaps of soldiers, so thick, as if coals had been poured out of a sack. And two of their galleons fired themselves, and if any man had a desire to see hell itself, it was there most lively figured. Was Keymis at Cadiz? Keymis was not. Keymis did not know me. Keymis lied. I longed with all my heart to go with Wat. I could not go. My fever would not let me. *They* would not let me, Keymis and my squabbling captains. They trusted no one else to remain at Punto Gallo. To keep their rear from attack, to guard the river mouth. 'Run will I never,' I told them. '*Intramus!* In we go . . . !' Wat, Carew, my sons, I wish you had been with me. I wish you could have seen me at Cadiz. That was no dream. I did not act amiss.

The ship is still idling along, lolling listlessly in a breeze which one minute blows like a cracked bellows and the next minute doesn't blow at all.

Never have I seen anything more full of colour than when the North Atlantic sun stands on the rim of the world at daybreak.

Correction. Only one thing.

Essex's chopped-off head.

All that stuff about gold and the Indian. Was I mad? What the hell does it matter?

And what precisely did I think I was learning from him?

How to die.

That's all.

His shout, his tribe, his Golden Man, his ghostliness. His connection with Wat's death. It doesn't seem so important any more. Our destinies crossed. But they are not the same.

I made another son of him. He was someone to talk to. It helped the voyage pass. But now the voyage (almost) is done.

The voyage nearly over. Nothing more to say to you, Indian.

And I knew how to die. That's the one thing I knew all along.

Christoval Guayacunda: your simplicity awakened my complexity. Don't think me ungrateful. You were (almost) my friend. We are now (almost) strangers again.

Thank you, rat.

29

SIR WALTER RALEGH'S INSTRUCTIONS TO HIS SON, AND TO POSTERITY

CHAPTER I:
Virtuous persons to be made choice of for friends

There is nothing more becoming any wise man than to make choice of friends, for by them you shall be judged what you are. Let them therefore be wise and virtuous, and none of those that follow you for gain. But make election rather of your betters, than your inferiors, shunning always such as are poor and needy. For if you give twenty gifts, and refuse to do the like but once, all that you have done will be lost, and such men will become your mortal enemies. Take also special care that you never trust any friend or servant with any matter that may endanger your estate; for so shall you make yourself a bond slave to him that you trust, and leave yourself always to his mercy. And be sure of this, you shall never find a friend in your young years whose conditions and qualities will please you after you come to more discretion and judgement, and then all you give is lost, and all wherein you shall trust such a one will be discovered. Such therefore as are your inferiors will follow you but to eat you out, and when you cease to feed them they will hate you. And such kind of men, if you preserve your estate, will always be had. But if your friends be of better quality than yourself, you may be sure of two things. The first, that they will be more careful to keep your counsel, because they have more to lose than you have. The second, they will esteem you for yourself, and not for that which you possess. But if you be subject to any great vanity or ill (from which I hope God will bless you) then therein trust no man. For every man's folly ought to be his greatest secret. And although I persuade you to associate yourself with your betters, or at least with your peers, yet remember always that you venture not your estate with any of those great ones that shall attempt unlawful things, for such men labour for themselves and not for you. You shall be sure to part with them in the danger, but not in the honour. And to venture a sure estate in present, in hope of a better in future, is mere madness. And great men forget such as have done them service, when they have obtained what they would, and will rather hate you for saying you have been a means of their advancement, than acknowledge it.

I could give you a thousand examples, and I myself know it, and have tasted it in all the course of my life. When you come to read and observe the stories of all nations, you will find innumerable examples of the like. Let your love therefore be to the best, so long as they do well. But take heed that you love God, your country, your Prince, and your own estate, before all others. For the fancies of men change, and he that loves today, hates tomorrow. But let reason be your school-mistress, which shall ever guide you aright.

CHAPTER II:
Great care to be had in the choosing of a wife

The next and greatest care ought to be in the choice of a wife, and the only danger therein is beauty – by which all men in all ages, wise and foolish, have been betrayed. And though I know it vain to use reasons or arguments to dissuade you from being captivated therewith (there being few or none that ever resisted that witchery), yet I cannot omit to warn you, as of other things, which may be your ruin and destruction. For the present time it is true that every man prefers his fantasy in that appetite before all other worldly desires, leaving the care of honour, credit, and safety, in respect thereof. But remember: though these affections do not last, yet the bond of marriage endures to the end of your life; they are therefore better to be borne withal in a mistress than in a wife, for when your humour shall change you are yet free to choose again (if you give yourself that vain liberty). Remember, secondly: if you marry for beauty you bind yourself all your life for that which perhaps will never last nor please you one year. And when you have it, it will be to you of no price at all, for the degree dies when it is attained, and the affection perishes when it is satisfied. Remember, when you were a sucking child, that then you loved your nurse, and that you were fond of her. But after a while you loved your dry-nurse, and forgot the other . . . And did you not come in time to despise them *both*? So will it be with you in your liking in elder years. Therefore, though you cannot forbear to love, yet forbear to link. And after a while you shall find an alteration in yourself, and see another far more pleasing than the first, second, or third love. Yet I wish you above all the rest, have a care you do not marry an uncomely woman for any respect. For comeliness in children is riches, if nothing else be left them. And if you have care for your races of horses, and other beasts, value the shape and comeliness of your children before alliances or riches. Have care therefore of both together. For if you have a fair wife, and a poor one, if your own estate be not great, assure yourself that love abides not with want. For she is your companion of plenty and honour. For I never yet knew a poor woman exceeding fair that was not made dishonest by one or other in the end. This Bathsheba taught her son Solomon: 'Favour is deceitful, and Beauty is vanity.' She says further: 'That a wise woman oversees the ways of her household, and eats not the bread of idleness.'

Have therefore ever more care that you be beloved of your wife, rather than yourself besotted on her. And you shall judge of her love by these two observations. First, if you perceive she has a care of your estate, and exercises herself therein. The other, if she studies to please you and be sweet to you in conversation, without your instruction, for love needs no teaching nor precept. On the other side, be not sour or stern to your wife, for cruelty engenders no other thing than hatred. Let her have equal part of your estate while you live, if you find her sparing and honest. But what you give after your death, remember that you give it to a stranger, and most times to an enemy. For he that shall marry your wife will despise you, your memory, and all that was yours, and shall possess the quiet of your labours, the fruit which you have planted, enjoy your love, and spend with joy and ease what you have spared and gotten with care and travail. Yet always remember that you leave not your wife to be a shame unto you after you are dead, but that she may live according to your estate, especially if you have few children and them provided for. But howsoever it be, or whatsoever you find, leave your wife no more than of necessity you must. And only during her widowhood. For if she love again, let her not enjoy her second love in the same bed wherein she loved you, nor fly to future pleasures with those feathers which death has pulled from your wings. Thus, leave your last estate to your own lineage, in which you live upon earth while earth shall last.

To conclude. Wives were ordained to continue the generation of men, not to transfer them and diminish them either in continuance or ability. And therefore your house and estate which lives in your son, and not in your wife, is to be preferred. Let your time of marriage be in your young and strong years. For (believe it) ever the young wife betrays the old husband, and she that had you not in your flower will despise you in your fall, and you shall be unto her but a captivity and sorrow. Your best time will be towards thirty, for as the younger times are unfit either to choose or to govern a wife and family, so, if you stay long, you shall hardly see the education of your children, which being left to strangers are in effect lost, and better were it to be unborn than ill-bred; for thereby your posterity shall either perish, or remain a shame to your name and family. Furthermore, if it be late ere you take a wife, you shall spend your prime and summer of your life with harlots, destroy your health, impoverish your estate, and endanger your life. And (be sure of this) that how many mistresses soever you have, so many enemies you shall purchase to yourself. For there never was any such affection which ended not in hatred or disdain. Remember the saying of Solomon: 'There is a way which seems right to a man, but the issues thereof are the wages of death.' For howsoever a lewd woman please you for a time, you will hate her in the end, and she will study to destroy you. If you cannot abstain from them in your vain and unbridled times, yet remember that you sow on the sands, and do mingle the vital blood with corruption, and purchase diseases, repentance, and hatred only. Bestow therefore your youth so that you may have comfort to remember it when it has forsaken you, and not sigh and grieve at the account thereof. Whilst you are young you will think it will never have an end. But, behold, the longest day has his evening. And that you shall enjoy it but once, that it never turns again, use youth therefore as the springtime, which soon departs, and wherein you ought to plant and sow all provisions for a long and happy life.

CHAPTER III:
Wisest men have been abused by flatterers

Take care you be not made a fool by flatterers, for even the wisest men are abused by these. Know, therefore, that flatterers are the worst kind of traitors. For they will strengthen your imperfections, encourage you in all evils, correct you in nothing, but so shadow and paint all your vices and follies as you shall never (by their will) discern evil from good, or vice from virtue. And because all men are apt to flatter themselves, to entertain the additions of other men's praises is most perilous. Do not therefore praise yourself, unless you would be counted a vainglorious fool. Neither take delight in the praises of other men, unless you deserve it, and receive it from such as are worthy and honest, and will withal warn you of your faults. For flatterers have never any virtue. They are ever base, creeping, cowardly persons. A flatterer is a beast that bites by smiling. It is said by Isaiah in this manner: 'My people, they that praise thee, seduce thee, and disorder the paths of thy feet.' And David desired God to cut out the tongue of a flatterer. But it is hard to know them from friends. They are so obsequious, and full of protestations. For as a wolf resembles a dog, so does a flatterer a friend. A flatterer is well compared to an ape, who because he cannot defend the house like a dog, labour as an ox, or bear burdens as a horse, does therefore yet play tricks and provoke laughter. You may be sure that he that will in private tell you your faults is your friend, for he adventures your mislike and hazards your hatred. And there are few men that can endure it, every man for the most part delighting in self-praise, which is one of the most universal follies which bewitches mankind.

CHAPTER IV:
Private quarrels to be avoided

Be careful to avoid public disputations at feast, or at tables among choleric or quarrelsome persons. And eschew evermore to be acquainted or familiar with ruffians. For you shall be in as much danger in contending with a brawler in a private place as in a battle, wherein you may get honour to yourself and safety to your Prince and country. But if you be once engaged, carry yourself bravely, that they may fear you after. To shun therefore private fight, be well advised in your words and behaviour. For honour and shame is in the talk, and the tongue of a man causes him to fall.

Jest not openly at those that are simple, but remember how much you are bound to God, who has made you wiser. Defame not any woman publicly, though you know her to be evil. For those that are faulty cannot endure to be taxed, but will seek to be avenged of you; and those that are not guilty cannot endure unjust reproach. And as there is nothing more shameful and dishonest than to do wrong, so Truth herself cuts his throat that carries her publicly in every place. Remember the Divine saying: 'He that keeps his mouth, keeps his life.' Do therefore right to all men where it may profit them, and you shall thereby get much love. And forbear to speak evil things of men, though it be true (if you be not constrained), and thereby you shall avoid malice and revenge.

Do not accuse any man of any crime if it be not to save yourself, your Prince, or country. For there is nothing more dishonourable (next to treason itself) than to be an accuser. Notwithstanding, I would not have you for any respect lose your reputation or endure public disgrace. For better it were not to live, than to live a coward, if the offence proceed not from yourself. If it do, it shall be better to compound it upon good terms than to hazard yourself. For if you overcome, you are under the cruelty of the Law; if you are overcome, you are dead or dishonoured. If you therefore contend or discourse in argument, let it be with wise and sober men, of whom you must learn by reasoning, and not with ignorant persons, for you shall thereby instruct those that will not thank you, only utter what they have learned from you for their own. And if you know more than other men, utter it when it may do you honour, and not in assemblies of ignorant and common persons.

Speaking much, also, is a sign of vanity. For he that is lavish in words is a niggard in deeds. And as Solomon says: 'The mouth of a wise man is in his heart, the heart of a fool is in his mouth.' And by your words and discourses men will judge you. For as Socrates says: 'Such as your words are, such will your affections be esteemed; and such will your deeds as your affections; and such will your life as your deeds.' Therefore be advised what you do discourse of, what you maintain, especially touching religion, the State, or vanity. For if you err in the first, you shall be accounted profane. If in the second, dangerous. If in the third, indiscreet and foolish. He that cannot refrain from much speaking is like a city without walls. And less pains in the world a man cannot take than to hold his tongue. Therefore if you observe this rule in all assemblies you shall seldom err: Restrain your choler, hearken much, and speak little. For the tongue is the instrument of the greatest good and greatest evil that is done in the world.

Take heed also that you be not found a liar, for a lying spirit is hateful both to God and man. A liar is commonly a coward, for he dares not avow truth. A liar is trusted of no man, he can have no credit neither in public nor private. And if there were no more arguments than this, know that Our Lord in St John says: 'That it is a vice proper to Satan,' lying being opposite to the nature of God, which consists in truth. And the gain of lying is nothing else but not to be trusted of any, nor to be believed when we say the truth. It is said in the Proverbs, that 'God hates false lips, and he that speaks lies shall perish.' Thus you may see and find in all the Books of God how odious and contrary to God a liar is. And for the world, believe it, that it never did any man good (except in the extremity of saving life). For a liar is of a base, unworthy, and cowardly spirit.

CHAPTER V:
Three rules to be observed for the preservation of a man's estate

Amongst all other things of the world, take care of your estate – which you shall ever preserve if you observe three things. First, that you know what you have, what everything is worth that you have, and that you see that you are not wasted by your servants and officers. The second is that you never spend anything before you have it, for borrowing is the canker and death of every man's estate. The third is that you suffer not yourself to be wounded for other men's faults and scourged for other men's offences, i.e. by standing surety for another, whereby millions of men have been beggared and destroyed, paying the reckoning of other men's riot and the charge of other men's folly and prodigality. If you smart, smart for your own sins. And above all things be not made an ass to carry the burdens of other men.

If any friend desire you to be his surety, give him a part of what you have to spare. If he press you farther, he is not your friend at all – for friendship rather chooses harm to itself than offers it to another. If you be bound for a stranger, you are a fool. If for a merchant, you put your estate to learn to swim. If for a churchman, he has no inheritance. If for a lawyer, he will find an evasion by a word or a mere syllable to abuse you. If for a poor man, you must pay it yourself. If for a rich man, what need in the first place but to embarrass you? Therefore from surety-ship, as from a man-slayer, or enchanter, bless yourself. For the best profit and return will be this, that if you force him for whom you are bound to pay the debt himself then he will become your enemy, and if you use your estate to pay it yourself you will be a beggar. And believe your father in this, and print it in your thought, that what virtue soever you have, be it never so manifold, if you be poor withal you and your qualities shall be despised. Besides, poverty is oft times sent as a curse of God. It is a shame amongst men. An imprisonment of the mind. A vexation of every worthy spirit. You shall neither help yourself nor others by it. You shall drown yourself in all your virtues, having no means to show them. You shall be a burden and an eye-sore to your friends. Every man will fear your company. You shall be driven basely to beg, and depend on others. To flatter unworthy men. To make dishonest shifts. And to conclude: Poverty provokes a man to do infamous and detested deeds. Let no vanity therefore, or persuasion, draw you to that worst of worldly miseries.

If you be rich, it will give you pleasure in health, comfort in sickness, keep your mind and body free, save you from many perils, relieve you in your elder years, relieve the poor and your honest friends, and give means to your posterity to live, and defend themselves, and your own fame. See where it is said in the Proverbs, that 'He shall be sore vexed that is surety for a stranger, and he that hates surety-ship is sure.' It is further said: 'The poor is hated even of his own neighbour, but the rich have many friends.' Lend not to him that is mightier than yourself, for if you lend him, count it but lost. Be not surety above your power. For if you be surety, think to pay it.

CHAPTER VI:
What sort of servants are fittest to be entertained

Let your servants be such as you may command, and entertain none about you but yeomen to whom you give wages. For those that will serve you without your hire will cost you treble as much as they that know your fare. If you trust any servant with your purse, be sure you take his account ere you sleep. For if you put it off you will then afterwards, for tediousness, neglect it. I myself have thereby lost more than I am worth. And whatsoever your servant gains thereby, he will never thank you, but laugh your simplicity to scorn. And besides, 'tis the way to make your servants thieves, which else would be honest.

CHAPTER VII:
Brave rags wear soonest out of fashion

Exceed not in the humour of rags and bravery, for these will soon wear out of fashion. But money in your purse will ever be in fashion. And no man is esteemed for gay garments, but by fools and women.

CHAPTER VIII:
Riches not to be sought by evil means

On the other side, take heed that you seek not riches basely, nor attain them by evil means. Destroy no man for his wealth, nor take anything from the poor. For the cry and complaint thereof will pierce the heavens. And it is most detestable before God, and most dishonourable before worthy men, to wrest anything from the needy and labouring soul. God will never prosper you in aught, if you offend therein. But use your poor neighbours and tenants well, pine not them and their children to add superfluity and needless expenses to yourself. He that has pity on another man's sorrow shall be free from it himself. And he that delights in and scorns the misery of another shall one time or other fall into it himself. Remember this precept: 'He that has mercy on the poor lends unto the Lord, and the Lord will recompense him what he has given.' I do not understand those for poor which are vagabonds and beggars, but those that labour to live, such as are old and cannot travail, such poor widows and fatherless children as are ordered to be relieved, and the poor tenants that travail to pay their rents and are driven to poverty by mischance and not by riot or careless expenses. On such have you compassion, and God will bless you for it. Make not the hungry soul sorrowful. Defer not your gift to the needy. For if he curse you, in the bitterness of his soul, his prayer shall be heard of Him that made him.

CHAPTER IX:
What inconveniencies happen to such as delight in wine

Take especial care that you delight not in wine, for there never was any man that came to honour or preferment that loved it. For it transforms a man into a beast, decays health, poisons the breath, destroys natural heat, brings a man's stomach to an artificial heat, deforms the face, rots the teeth, and to conclude makes a man contemptible. Remember my words. It were better for a man to be subject to any vice than to this. For all other vanities and sins are recovered, but a drunkard will never shake off the delight of beastliness. For the longer it possesses a man, the more he will delight in it; and the older he grows, the more he shall be subject to it. For it dulls the spirit and destroys the body as ivy does the old tree, or as the worm that ingenders in the kernel of the nut.

Take heed therefore that such a cureless canker pass not your youth, nor such a beastly infection your old age. For then shall all your life be but as the life of a beast, and after your death you shall only leave a shameful infamy to your posterity, who shall study to forget that such a one was their father.

St Augustine describes drunkenness in this manner: 'Drunkenness is a flattering devil, a sweet poison, a pleasant sin; which whosoever has, has not himself; which whosoever does commit, does not commit sin, but he himself is wholly sin.'

When Diogenes saw a house to be sold, whereof the owner was given to drink, I thought at the last, quoth Diogenes, he would spew out a whole house. '*Sotebam, inquit, quod domum tandem evomeret.*'

252

CHAPTER X:
Let God be your protector and director in all your actions

Now, for the world, I know it too well to persuade you to dive into the practices thereof. Rather stand upon your own guard against all that tempt you thereunto, or may practice upon you in your conscience, your reputation, or your purse. Resolve that no man is wise or safe but he that is honest.

Serve God. Let Him be the author of all your actions. Commend all your endeavours to Him that must either wither or prosper them. Please Him with prayer, lest if He frown, He confound all your fortunes and labours, like the drops of rain on the sandy ground. Let my experienced advice and fatherly instructions sink deep into your heart. So God direct you in all His ways, and fill your heart with His grace.

FINIS

30

Not *finis*. Not all over. Not in the least. Not ended, not yet determined, barely begun . . .

This book, I see now, is the log of three voyages.

The first: The voyage of the *Destiny*. Set in the present time. Immediate. Actual. A day by day record of my long journey home to die.

The second: The voyage of my history. The tale of my life and fortunes. Descriptive. Expository. My confessions, if you like. Made for my son.

The third voyage is the most difficult to define. In setting out, at my beginning, I was not aware of it. I was merely a mariner on two seas, I thought. The sea of my past life and the sea of the present. My task, as I saw it originally, was simple enough: to relate the one voyage to the other, and make sense of both. But, increasingly, as I've gone on, this feeling, this knowledge of a *third* voyage has grown in me. By hints and glimpses, at first, by shapes looming out of the fog, by shouts in the storm. (And I mean the fog of memory, the storm brewed where past and present waters meet only to make a whirlpool in the mind.) Now the shapes come together, the shouts form a sort of a sentence. What sentence? *'The Voyage of the Destiny.'* That's my third voyage. The true task.

Not my ship. Not my life. Something *more* than either present or past, or both together. I sail on a sea without a name, an unfathomable ocean. There's no crew but myself. I can offer no 'position reports'. All I have is this sense that in seeking to go two ways at once I have lit (quite by chance) on a third way. Not backwards. Not forwards. Perhaps *inwards*? Yet the passage seems *out* –

Out! Out! And *beyond* –

254

Beyond all this babble?

(I should hope so! But I speak of something real . . . More real than that salt there on the rigging. More real than my own headful of times past.)

O for a dish of hot beef collops! With onions fried in butter! A slice of fresh bread!

My first voyage, at any rate, *is* all but ended. This morning I woke to see Mizen Head, the south-west extremity of Ireland. Now (midnight) we lie a mile off from Galley Head, so as to clear the Dhulic Rock. Miserable tides, rain falling, winds stammering and contrary. We have limped a mere thirty-four miles since that first sight of land. Our course must be from Galley Head to Seven Heads (9¼ miles), from Seven Heads to the Old Head of Kinsale (7 miles), from the Old Head into Kinsale Harbour (a further 6½ miles). My *Destiny* need only hold together for a final three leagues to make landfall at last at Kinsale . . .

If the men feel any excitement they do not show it. Most are sick, all are starving. Our crossing has taken its toll of every one. Truth to tell, none has energy left to feel *anything*, let alone express it. They go about their work like ghosts, sailing a phantom ship. Ghosts with lustreless eyes in sunken sockets. Spent men, hollow men, men too burnt-out and exhausted to shed even a few tears of *relief*.

The Indian betrays little emotion also. He kept to his cabin for three days and nights after eating his abominable dinner, yet seemed to have suffered no ill effects when emerging this morning to climb up to the crow's nest and get his first sight of what is (to him) a new world. When he came down his face was as impassive as ever.

'This land has no smell,' was all he said.

Since then he has passed the time staring at it, but politely, without much curiosity.

It is true. All day we have inched along under the cliffs and beside the rocky outcrops of a bleak, a barren, an inhospitable coast. For weeks my eyes have been sore for a prospect of trees, and my nostrils have itched for the kind comfortable scent of grass. The Irish shore does not just disappoint those desires. It mocks them. Even where there are trees they seem blasted or dwarfish. Even where there is grass, its green seems false, too green, a lush sentimental lie, more like a child's picture of grass than grass itself. And the land is quite odourless. Neither fragrance nor fetor wafts over the waters that separate us from this island. Schull, Toe Head, Dirk Bay – the very names sound outcast and accursed . . .

Of course (or so I tell myself) these are not the trees and the grass which I long for. This is not home. This is some other place.

But then darker thoughts come. Perhaps I have no home. And the whole world is now some other place.

Essex got most of the credit for Cadiz. And the booty from sacking the town. I lay on a litter and watched him. I was wounded. I was shot in the leg. Essex, Howard, and Vere – they did well that day. I did most of the fighting for them. They cleaned up. It's my opinion Essex went mad at Cadiz. He made sixty-six knights of his followers. What a joke! To be a 'Knight of Cadiz' was to be a laughing-stock. He was always a little mad, my sad friend Essex. Of course, by this time *he* was dancing the dance with the Queen. I was out in the cold. I was next to nobody. After Fayal, Essex tried to have me court-martialled. What for? For winning the battle before he turned up. I wore a white scarf and white breeches. They were riddled with bullet holes. Howard told me to apologize to the lunatic. I did. The court-martial was dropped. He was mad, but there was method in his madness. He got all the best ransoms at Cadiz. I got £1769 and a Spanish bishop's library. Essex danced high. She made him Earl Marshal. I got this wound in my leg.

I knew he was mad after that tournament. He found out the colours of my men. Then he swept onto the field in front of her ahead of a vast retinue – twice the size of my band – all dressed in the very same colours I had chosen! Right down to the orange-tawny feathers in the helmets! To swamp my show, to make *us* look *his* followers! She wasn't amused. The whole thing was a shambles. What did she expect? She was *thirty-four years* older than him! O glorious feather triumph.

She packed him off to Ireland. What did he do? Instead of fighting Tyrone he went and made friends with him. I played cards with Mr Secretary Cecil. Little Cecil in his paned black hose. The triple chain of gold about his neck. He trotted up and down. He always won. I never caught him cheating. Clever Cecil. He was the one who told me that Essex must die. His spies had provided him with copies of letters the madman had written from Ireland. I saw them. Essex was promising James the support of a huge private army! Why wait for the old woman to turn up her toes? he said. James could have England *now*!

But Scotch James was cannier. He bided his time. The Queen was a crab-apple. It would fall in his lap. He knew that. He waited. James didn't need mad dogs. Lap dogs were more his line. Still are, in fact. Good boy, Steenie.

Essex came back to London. Cecil had him arrested. The Queen set him free again. Why did she do that? Because he said that if he was brought to trial he'd teach his jury the Queen's dance, that's why. Elizabeth knew what that meant. Cecil was told to assassinate him. First-rate at assassination, Robert Cecil.

Before it could be decently done, my Lord Essex rode out. He rode out of his house and into the streets of London at the head of his men. It was a Sunday. His conspirators numbered 2000. My cousin was one of them, Sir Ferdinando Gorges. I tried to save the fat idiot. We met earlier that same Sunday. In boats on the river, by Milford Stairs. I came alone. Gorges had men with him. There was no persuading him. It was a trap, besides. Blount was hiding on the riverbank, Essex's step-father. He fired four shots at me. None of them connected.

Essex shouted in the streets. '*Say! Say! Sa! Sa!*' That's all he shouted. He'd gone completely mad. The crowds stood and stared at him. None rose to join him. '*Say! Say! Sa! Sa!*'

We shut the gates of the City. He rode back to his house. His men themselves were silent now. They saw the froth on his lips. They marched in silence through the streets of London. The crowds didn't even jeer. Essex House was soon surrounded. Howard turned our cannon on it. Essex surrendered.

That great boy died like a calf. He stood and bleated on the scaffold. He stamped. He cried. It was his mother's fault, he said. Then it was his sister's. Then it was his sister's lover. Then it was his step-father. Her Majesty played the virginals. She didn't stop playing. The Queen knew the stroke he died. She didn't stop playing. There were six executions. It was my duty to attend them. I was Captain of her Guard again. I got £14 a year. That was for the uniform. The tawny medley cost thirteen shillings and fourpence a yard, the fur of black budge came extra. I wore the uniform. I did my duty. But when it came to Essex's turn, I came down from the scaffold. I didn't think he'd want me there. I went up to a window. I couldn't believe he'd want me there. We'd danced the same strange dance. Later, they said he'd asked for me. By then it was too late.

Why go on? How go on? I mean: with this, the second voyage. This raking over the ashes of my past. Of my burning days, my burnt-out heart, the ashes.

It is too late.

It is all too late.

It's over.

Like the Spanish Armada? Like my part in the defeat of that great enterprise?

Carew, *I took no part*.

I wasn't there!

Drake – I have sneered at Drake, may God forgive me – Drake finished his game of bowls on Plymouth Hoe. You'll know the story. 'Gentlemen, there is time to finish our game and beat the Spaniards, too.' Drake knew what he was doing. He was only waiting for the tide to turn, you realize that? But at least he played bowls, then sailed out into Calais Roads to send a few fire-ships to worry and enliven King Philip's Pope-blessed argosy. The wind did the rest. The wind's a Protestant.

And what did your father do?

Your father did *nothing*.

Your father was safe on land. He didn't even play a game of bowls.

Not likely. I rode about. I 'organized' our land forces. We didn't need any land forces. I think I knew it all along.

But, later, I wrote about it. The defeat of the Armada. Wrote as if I *had* been there. One long and crowing sentence!

'Their navy', I wrote (and I'm copying now from my 'Report of the Truth of the Fight about the Isles of the Azores, 1591', which lies open on my cabin desk in front of me) –

Their navy, which they termed invincible, consisting of 240 sail of ships, not only of their own kingdom, but strengthened with the greatest argosies, Portugal carracks, Florentines and huge

258

hulks of other countries, were by thirty of her Majesty's own ships of war, and a few of our own merchants, by the wise, valiant and most advantageous conduction of the Lord Charles Howard, High Admiral of England, beaten and shuffled together, even from the Lizard in Cornwall, first to Portland – where they shamefully left Don Pedro de Valdes, with his mighty ship – from Portland to Calais, where they lost Hugo de Moncado with the galliasse of which he was captain – and from Calais, driven with squibs from their anchors: were chased out of sight of England, round about Scotland and Ireland,

where, for the sympathy of their barbarous religion, hoping to find succour and assistance, a great part of them were crushed against the rocks, and those other that landed, being very many in number, were notwithstanding broken, slain and taken, and so sent from village to village, coupled in halters to be shipped into England,

where her Majesty, of her princely and invincible disposition disdaining to put them to death, and scorning either to retain or entertain them, they were all sent back again to their countries, to witness and recount the worthy achievements of their invincible and dreadful navy,

of which the number of soldiers, the fearful burthen of their ships, the commanders' names of every squadron, with all their magazines of provisions, were put in print, as an army and navy unresistible and disdaining prevention:

with all which so great and terrible an ostentation, they did not in all their sailing round about England so much as sink or take one ship, bark, pinnace, or cockboat of ours, or ever burned so much as one sheepcote of this land.

I was proud of that sentence. Five paragraphs long! 312 words! Such verbal puissance, such rich irony. (You notice my artistry, Carew? The colons like cannon shot? The internal rhyming in the reference to the Queen: *disdain*ing, *retain*, *entertain* . . . ? An Armada of a sentence, eh? A literary trumpet blast?)

That sentence was my only active service.

At least I knew about the sheepcotes.

I commanded the sheep.

*

That sentence gives the game away. What game? Why, the game I have played all my life, and not unskilfully. A game of poses, disguises, masks, assumed identities. I have worn as many false faces as a whore of Turnbull Street. As an actor at the Globe or at the Fortune. I have always filled a part.

Take that serpent of a sentence. What is it, in fact? An exercise in style. A conceit. A soliloquy. No man of action wrote it. No hero. No protagonist. It is the speech of a poet desiring to be mistaken for a master of war. As usual, I overdid it. *Conduction*, indeed! (All I meant, I suspect, was that Howard employed my own vessel, the *Ark Ralegh*, as his flagship.) If I had fought the Armada, I could have said less. Because I didn't – Because I didn't, I took 312 words to sink 240 ships! Not warfare. Not literature. A grammar of self-deceit! An essay in folly!

I was trying on a voice in that stupid sentence. (Stupid because splendid, and the splendour quite foreign to me.) I did the same thing just two days ago, with those wretched *Instructions*. Great stuff! The accumulated wisdom of a Machiavel! Sir Walter Ralegh, a son unprodigalled, trying to play father . . .

Not satisfactory.

An old voice, a worn-out style, a deliberate attempt to sound like history.

To be blunt, I cannot bring myself to re-read such rot. Yet it works, and I know it works, and I shall use it. Here I am, a modern man, playing a rôle again. Who wrote that book-within-the-book? I did, my son. Sir Walter Ralegh. Mr Worldly Wise. A relic of Gloriana's glory. A ghost from the Golden Age. I wrote those ten chapters as much for myself as for you. To see if I could do it. To test out a style I might need.

It's a good style, a bad style, second nature to me. I shall use it to die in, that style. A good voice, a bad voice, second nature to me. The voice of the last Elizabethan.

Seven Heads. Robin just shouted it. I went out on deck. Filthy dawn. I could not see seven. I counted them. Tall black headlands of rock in sea-mist. Bad light and worse seas made it difficult. But there were not seven. I'd have staked my life on that. Not seven heads.

Mr Burwick guessed the source of my confusion.

'Seven castles,' he said.

'Where?' I asked.

'On the cliffs there.'

I thought I'd gone mad. I saw no castles. Only rock. Only spindrift. Desolation.

Mr Burwick explained then, tired, unsmiling. 'They say the Irish *once* had castles there. Seven of them. Hence the name: Seven Heads.'

I looked again. My head spun. I saw castles.

Incredible castles.

Castles of pure gold.

I shook my head. There was nothing. Then it rained like fury.

I let the rain soak my cloak. It was good on my face.

'Master,' a voice said. It was Robin. He tugged at my sleeve. 'Master, your ague! Come back to your cabin. You'll catch your death of this!'

The feather in his cap was half-snapped by that downpour.

I nodded. Robin offered his arm. I declined such assistance.

'How long, Mr Burwick?'

'With this head wind? Impossible to say!'

I struck at the main shrouds with my cane. *'How long, Mr Burwick?'* I repeated.

He shrugged. His eyes had no spirit.

'Seven hours, sir.'

Seven Heads. Seven castles. Seven hours.

The ship was spinning round me. I stood upright.

'Master, the rain!'

I had more than the rain to master. I did it. I mastered more than the rain.

I bowed to Mr Burwick.

He saluted.

I waved Robin aside. I walked back to my cabin.

I'm sure they didn't know, they couldn't tell . . .

I am *drunk*, Wat. Drunk on my Lord Boyle's brandy. Impeccably drunk, Wat. The first time for twenty-six years.

'Sotebam, inquit, quod domum tandem evomeret.'

Diogenes knew what he was talking about. Did he not sit blind drunk in his tub?

And Augustine, at Carthage. He knew too. Knew drunkenness. That devil. This sweet poison. 'Which whosoever has, has not himself.'

We drink in order to not have ourselves.

As a young man, when I drank, I drank to excess. My nature is always to do nothing save to excess. Including *restraint*. Hence those bitter, those exacting *Instructions*, that book-within-my-book, my Last Will and Testament.

I wrote '*finis*'.

Then I started on the brandy.

And for two days I've been drunk. Cold drunk. Dead drunk. Your cold dead drunken father. Drunk as Diogenes. Drunk as St Augustine.

O, I have a good head, a strong brain, inextinguished, inextinguishable. I used to dance drunk with Elizabeth, and she never knew. I came drunk to my wedding with your mother. She never guessed it. I stand straight. I don't babble. I carry my liquor well.

(To take pride in this! Twice-unforgiveable! But I must go on . . .)

Carew, your father is no cynic. I *mean* those *Instructions*. Every word. That's the hell of it. The way of saying may be false – but not what I say, what I said. You must read between the lines of what I wrote for you. Your poor father lies revealed there. His least mistake. I turned my misdirections to direct you. I damned no sin which I have not committed. I spoke of nothing that I do not know. Learn, by a father's ruin, a son's structure. By my rise and my downfall, save your life.

Drunk, boys, your father is damnation drunk. He is sailing in to Ireland in a freezing blaze of drunkenness, his mind benumbed with brandy, his heart made blunt.

O but it hurts, it hurts. My unfinishable heart.

The first time I've touched drink in twenty-six years –

Damerei – The first time I've been drunk since the day you died – The first time and the last, my long-lost son –

The cask is almost empty.

I shall finish it.

31

We dropped anchor at noon in the harbour of Kinsale, entering between Strookaun Point on the west side and Hangman Point on the east, keeping a midchannel course to avoid rocks and shoals, coming to rest in four fathoms a cable off the quay. It is necessary to lay out a kedge owing to the swirling of the tide here. That done, I took the longboat ashore, Sam King and the Indian attending me.

While they busied themselves fetching meat, oat-cakes, and beer to provide for the men, I limped off on my own to find solitude. I climbed up a hill called Rincurran that overlooks the bay. I drank from a spring of pure water. Then I slept, safe-cradled in the roots of an ancient oak.

When I woke it was evening and I was sober. I washed my face in the spring, combed my beard, and hobbled back down to the town.

Kinsale has one church, called St Multose. It stands right beside the quay. Its bell was tolling. I went in. I was in time for Evensong.

'*Almighty and most merciful Father: We have erred and strayed from thy ways like lost sheep. We have followed too much the devices and desires of our own hearts. We have offended against thy holy laws. We have left undone those things which we ought to have done; And there is no health in us. But thou, O Lord, have mercy upon us, miserable offenders. Spare thou them, O God, which confess their faults. Restore thou them that are penitent; According to thy promises declared unto mankind in Christ Jesu our Lord, And grant, O most merciful Father, for his sake; That we may hereafter live a godly, righteous, and sober life. To the glory of thy holy name. Amen.*'

Evensong was always my favourite service.

Some few of the crew had come ashore for it. Not many, and by no means the best. I was glad to be there in their company.

Mr Jones offered prayers of thanksgiving for our deliverance. I couldn't say '*Amen*' with such a will. The word stuck in my throat. Sam King shouted it. So did most of the others. May their enthusiasm atone for my reserve.

The last collect of Evensong remains with me:

'*Lighten our darkness, we beseech thee, O Lord; and by thy great mercy defend us from all perils and dangers of this night . . .*'

When I came out of the church I found the Indian lying on a tombstone.

'Guattaral thanked his god?'

I said I had.

32

They're leaving now. One by one, the exodus. They leave me. The quitters, the deserters, the wanted men.

Wanted? By whom? Not by me! By the common hangman.

I am better off without them.

I have kept my word.

I promised that once we made Ireland they were free to depart. No soldier or sailor of my company to be compelled into England. No man to be forced to face justice, whatever his crime.

For a moment, there, at Evensong, the day before yesterday, it did cross my mind that there might be a change of heart. Not a bit of it. The kneelers, the hymn-singers – they're the first to go! Should I be surprised by this? I suppose not. The worst sinners creep the fastest into churches. What else, after all, was I doing in there myself?

But how *many*. And how *soon*. That does surprise me.

I calculated there might be a score.

Already, *twice* that number have taken advantage of my promise. Drawn their wages from the purser, and departed. Mostly without a word, or a backward glance.

Not all of these fellows are criminals, I am sure. Some leave because they fear what will happen to me when I reach England. They presume my arrest and destruction. They have no wish to share in my fate.

Well, hard to blame them for that.

But just two days' rest here, safe in Kinsale's landlocked harbour, out of the muck and the waste of the sea, and I begin to find some small particle of hope still alive in me. Perhaps it is a hope against hope, a desperate and ill-founded fancy, a self-teasing delusion –

All the same, and with less than half my crew remaining, I remind myself that I have one friend left who could save me yet.

Ralph Winwood.

His Majesty's Secretary of State.

If anyone can save me, Winwood can.

A true friend, and a powerful one, and honest.

A hope with a very English sort of face.

The Indian just gave me a strange gift. It is a tiny idol, no more than an inch tall, a grinning devil *made of solid gold*.

'Where did you get this?' I demanded.

'I found it.'

'At San Thomé?'

'No. In the lake. Guatavita.'

'When?'

'Long ago. I was a boy. I went swimming.'

'So the tale is true!' I cried.

He shrugged his shoulders. 'I don't know. Does it matter? I only found *one*.'

'The Golden Man!'

'*A* golden man,' he said.

I questioned him further. Yes, he had gone back often to the lake, diving in search of other trinkets. He had found nothing else. In the end, he abandoned the search. No, he attached no particular significance to the idol. He thought it must be the image of a devil, not a god. Or if not a devil, then a man. 'Gods don't grin,' he explained.

I asked him why he had waited until now to show me this evidence that there was at least *something* behind his tale of El Dorado. He went over the old ground: it was not *his* tale, the legend had been imposed on his people, the Chibcha had perhaps been mere traders, they most certainly had no gold of their own . . . As to the delay, he claimed that he had not wanted to raise my hopes again at any point on the voyage. He was sure that my quest for gold was mistaken. Besides, he insisted, he had given me the *khoka* leaves. The leaf was worth more than any gold. And so on, and so on.

I grew tired. His conversation irked me. It was witless. It insulted my intelligence. Every word he said made it plain that to his eyes this idol was a toy, something childish, a half-forgotten relic of his boyhood.

He must have seen the impatience on my face. Abruptly, he broke off, reaching out to close my hand around the statue. 'Keep it,' he said. 'For you, it might be an antidote.'

'To what poison?' I demanded.

'Elizadeath,' he said.

The sea makes many false harmonies. The land allows for none. How could I ever have imagined that my destiny was linked with this Indian's? We have nothing in common but our failure to understand each other.

There is usquebaugh aboard. Most of the remaining men are drinking it. They have three barrels in the forecastle, Robin tells me.

The Reverend Mr Samuel Jones wants this forbidden. He approached me, quoting the seventeenth article of my own 'Orders to be observed by the Commanders of the Fleet': 'No man shall keep any feasting or drinking between meals, nor drink any healths on the ship's provision.'

I cannot summon up sufficient hypocrisy to act.

I know about usquebaugh. It is an Irish spirit, foul and fierce, raw alcohol with fennel-seed and raisins to disguise its fire. I drank it after that day in Smerwick fort. Its name, in the Irish tongue, means the water of life.

33

Winwood is dead.

Winwood was dead when I wrote that letter to him from St Kitts.

Winwood died more than seven months ago, suddenly, in London, on the 27th of October last year. (On which day I was still at sea, myself fevered, the ship horribly becalmed, with a fortnight left to go of that nightmare voyage out to America.)

I have pinned my last hopes on a corpse. I have counted for protection on a dead man.

O poisonous irony.

Gods don't grin.

Don't they?

I learned this news tonight from the Earl of Cork. He was startled by my ignorance of Ralph's death. I had gone to dine at his castle on the Blackwater. Over a capon, well-larded, he urged me to stay here in Ireland. The new Secretary of State is Robert Naunton. Naunton. No friend of mine, ever. The toad who once called me the Queen's oracle.

'Ireland is the answer,' Boyle said. 'You could stay here. Or go into France. King James will not welcome you. You embarrass him. The Spanish Ambassador wants your head.'

Then he told me the latest tales from London. (He keeps well-informed, my Lord of Cork. He's like an owl, and he feathers his nest with gossip.)

I shall cut this information to the bone. I have no more stomach for it than for that capon.

My letter to Ralph Winwood was intercepted. Naunton demanded it of my nephew, and George gave in. Next thing, of course, the

268

King was reading it. Then Parker and North came back – I thought they would. Having no guts to turn privateer, they turned private informers instead. They went straight to his Majesty, who was no doubt delighted to see them and even better pleased with what he heard. They went on oath to declare that the whole story of the Guiana mines was my invention. That there was no gold to be found, and I'd always known it. I'd pretended to be angry with Keymis, by their account. (And did Keymis *pretend* suicide? Damn both those fine liars to hell!) I'd cheated the King, they said. I'd tricked him to get out of the Tower. They'd heard me boast that I'd never return home to England, that it had always been my secret intent to seek sanctuary elsewhere. I was a traitor, they said. That's why they'd deserted me.

Simultaneously – evil strikes like lightning, all this happened in a space of about twenty-four hours, just at about the time the Lucifer of the piece was struggling towards Ireland in a blaze of my Lord Boyle's brandy (I didn't confess that; I didn't say very much at all) – simultaneously, Gondomar arrives white-faced and sweating at Whitehall. The Spanish Ambassador has his own gorgeous network of spies. He's already got a fistful of papers with 'details' of what they're calling 'the massacre at San Thomé'. Count Gondomar requests – no, *demands* – an immediate audience of his Majesty the King. James, guessing what this means, prevaricates. Gondomar sends in a message. He appreciates his Majesty's busyness. All the same, the matter is most urgent. Yet it need occupy less than a minute of his Majesty's precious time. He promises, in fact, that if admitted he will say *just a single word* to his Majesty.

James never could resist a ploy like that, and Gondomar knew it. Once into the King's company, the Spaniard shouted his single word:

'*Pirates!*'

He shouted it three times, with pauses for emphasis in between, and with each shout he shouted it louder. Then he bowed, turned, and raged out of the room.

Boyle says that I should stay in Ireland. Boyle says King James would be best pleased by that. Boyle says –

Damn Boyle and what he says!

*

Winwood is dead. Good Ralph, my friend. He died on my voyage out, and I never knew it. It's midnight. It's raining. I have lost my only advocate. He knelt with me at her tomb and promised money. He stood with me on London Bridge and spoke of empire. That barrel-like body. That face as honest as the skin between its brows. Dead. Gone. Deserted. I have no ally in high places any more.

They're singing in the forecastle.

I can hear them. I sit here staring at a golden grinning idol one inch high. I can hear every word of their song:

> I went to the tavern, and then,
> I went to the tavern, and then,
> I had good store of wine,
> And my cap full of coin
> And the world went well with me then, then,
> And the world went well with me then,

Idiot music! Deluded wretches! I sit here searching the pages of my own *History of the World* for some passage that will serve to give me comfort, blot out their song, make sense of my predicament, deny their mindless ditty. There is none.

> But when I was married, O then,
> But when I was married, O then,
> My horse and my saddle
> Were turned to a cradle,
> And the world went ill with me then, then,
> And the world went ill with me then.

The words of my own wisdom rise from the *History* to mock me, to pour scorn on my pursuit of gold and honour. I have made a fool of myself in that pursuit. And there's no fool like an old fool. Especially an old fool whose writings once declared that he knew better: 'When is it that we examine this great account? Never while we have one vanity left us to spend; we plead for titles till our breath fail us, dig for riches whiles our strength enableth us, exercise malice while we can revenge, and then, when Time hath beaten from us both youth, pleasure and health, and that nature itself hateth the house of old age, we remember with Job that we must go the way from whence we shall not return, and that our bed is made ready for us in the dark . . .'

> I took my wife home again,
> I took my wife home again,
> But I changed her note
> For I cut her throat,
> And the world went well with me then, then,
> And the world went well with me then.

Sam King is with them. Sam, my companion. A man to whom it has probably never occurred with any force: to be absent from himself, from what he is. An honest man, a loyal man, my friend. But a friend without power, with no influence. His voice is strong, but he'll never sing to the King. And here, in my *History*, my own voice raised in judgement of my follies: 'But what examples have ever moved us? What persuasions reformed us? Or what threatenings made us afraid? We behold other men's tragedies played before us; we hear what is promised and threatened; but the world's bright glory hath put out the eyes of our minds . . .'

> But when it was known, O then,
> But when it was known, O then,
> In a two wheeled chariot
> To Tyburn I was carried,
> And the world went ill with me then, then,
> And the world went ill with me then.

Winwood is dead. The men are drunk on usquebaugh. I sit here thinking of the water of life while others drink it. The worms will eat his cheeks and the maggots his brains. I don't have to search for his epitaph. I know the passage by heart. Ralph dead means my own death. There is none now to save me. It's my epitaph too: 'O eloquent, just and mighty death! whom none could advise, thou hast persuaded; what none hath dared, thou hast done; and whom all the world hath flattered, thou only hast cast out of the world and despised; thou hast drawn together all the far-stretched greatness, all the pride, cruelty and ambition of man, and covered it all over with these two narrow words: *Hic jacet* . . .'

> But when I came there, O then,
> But when I came there, O then,
> They forced me to swing
> To heaven on a string,

> And the world went well with me then, then,
> And the world went well with me then.

Dead. This grinning gold devil. Dead. That water of life. Dead. The words of my *History*. Dead. The words of their song. Dead. Dead. Dead. All dead. All over. All one. All the same. All nothing. *Hic jacet* . . .

   Here lies . . .

   Why not?

   Why not lie here?

   Why not take Lord Boyle's advice?

   I am a dead man whatever I do.

   Should I not dig my own grave then? Quietly. Privately. Here. Without pride. Without pomp. In dead Ireland. In this island of death.

   Perhaps.

   Too tired to write more.

   Not tired.

   Done. Spent. Dust. Ashes. Earth. Finished.

   Perhaps –

34

By The King
*A proclamation declaring his Majesty's
pleasure concerning Sir Walter Rawleigh,
and those who adventured with him*

Whereas We gave Licence to Sir Walter Rawleigh, Knight, and others of Our subjects with him, to undertake a Voyage to the Country of Guiana, where they pretended great hopes and probabilities to make discovery of certain Gold Mines for the lawful enriching of themselves, and these our Kingdoms: wherein We did by express limitation and caution refrain, and forbid them and every of them, from attempting any Act of hostility, wrong or violence whatsoever, upon any of the Territories, States, or Subjects of any foreign Princes, with whom We are in amity: And more peculiarly of those of our dear Brother the King of Spain, in respect of his Dominions and Interests in that Continent:

All which notwithstanding, We are since informed by a common fame, that they, or some of them, have by an hostile invasion of the Town of S. Thomé (being under the obedience of our said dear Brother the King of Spain) and by killing of divers of the inhabitants thereof, his subjects, and after by sacking and burning the said town (as much as in them for their own parts lay) maliciously broken and infringed the Peace and Amity, which has been so happily established, and so long inviolably continued between Us and the Subjects of both our Crowns.

We have therefore held it fit, as appertaining nearly to our Royal justice and Honour, eftsoons to make a public declaration of Our own utter mislike and detestation of the same insolences, and excesses, if any such have been by any of our Subjects committed: and for the better detection and clearing of the very truth of the said common fame: We do hereby straitly charge and require all Our Subjects whatsoever, that have any particular understanding and notice thereof, upon their duty and allegiance which they owe Us, immediately after publication of this Our pleasure, to repair unto some of Our Privy Council, and to discover and make known unto them their whole knowledge and understanding concerning the same, under pain of Our High displeasure and indignation: that We may thereupon proceed in Our princely justice to the exemplary punishment and coercion of all such as shall be convicted and found guilty of so scandalous and enormous outrages.

Given at our manor of Greenwich, the ninth day of June, in the sixteenth year of Our Reign of England and Ireland, and of Scotland the one and fiftieth.

God save the King.

Imprinted at London by Bonham Norton, and John Bill, deputy Printers for the King's most Excellent Majesty.
Anno M. DC. XVIII.

This proclamation came into my hands today, delivered at dawn by a horseman dispatched from Lord Boyle.

With it, a sealed envelope.

In the envelope, this scribble:

Sir Walter, be warned. *We* has promised Gondomar that *Our princely justice*, translated, means sending you in chains aboard yr own *Destiny* to be hung, drawn, and quartered by the noted *dear Brother of Spain*. France now yr only hope. Go to Richelieu at Avignon. He calls you *le grand marinier*. Why die like a dog when you could live like a lion? Set sail directly. For France! For new life!

Intramus.
Run will I never.
I set sail directly.
For England.

35

The voyage of the *Destiny* is done. Our anchor holds us fast in Plymouth Sound. I have sent my sails ashore. In a moment, when I have written here, I shall follow them.

Last entry in the ship's log.
These men, and these alone, sailed home with me:
Captain Samuel King, late of the *Encounter*;
Sir John Holmden, gentleman;
Mr Robert Burwick, master;
Robin Rogers, my page;
Christoval Guayacunda;
Rev. Mr Samuel Jones, chaplain;
William Gurden, master gunner;
George Inglesant, Peter Munday, Jack Savage, John Stowe, Saul Turpin, Francis Thackeray, Luke Grimes, soldiers;
Thomas Benbow, Robert Drury, Davy Flint, Matthew Pym, Mark Ratsey, Isaac Lampman, Ben Frost, Miles Standish, sailors.
That is all.
Twenty-two souls.

It is one year and nine days, exactly, since I sailed forth for Guiana from this same port of Plymouth.

Then, there were trumpets and drums. Farewell feasts for my captains, all paid for by the mayor and the townsfolk. Fireworks and bonfires on Rame Head. Church bells pealing. Clear call and echo of clarions across Sutton Pool, so loud the water seemed to ripple with their music. Salutes of cannon from every vessel anchored in the Sound.

The cannons stand dumb today. No church bells welcome us. No trumpets raised in fanfare. Sailors crowding the decks of the forest of tall-masted ships into which we have come stare at us in absolute silence as though we were ghosts. Cockboats and pinnaces scuttle out of our path as if we brought plague into Plymouth.

When I set forth it was at the head of a fleet which consisted of fourteen brave ships and one thousand men.

One ship and twenty-two brave men have returned.

I forced no man to come.

Our crossing from Kinsale to Plymouth took three days and ten hours. We had sweet seas and smooth, and a very fair following wind. The weather, you might say, was excellent.

36

THE LIE

Go, soul, the body's guest,
    Upon a thankless arrant;
Fear not to touch the best;
    The truth shall be thy warrant.
      Go, since I needs must die,
      And give the world the lie.

Say to the Court, it glows
    And shines like rotten wood;
Say to the Church, it shows
    What's good, and doth no good:
      If Church and Court reply,
      Then give them both the lie.

Tell Potentates, they live
    Acting by others' action,
Not loved unless they give,
    Not strong but by affection:
      If Potentates reply,
      Give Potentates the lie.

Tell men of high condition
    That manage the estate,
Their purpose is ambition,
    Their practice only hate:
      And if they once reply,
      Then give them all the lie.

Tell them that brave it most,
   They beg for more by spending,
Who, in their greatest cost,
   Seek nothing but commending:
     And if they make reply,
     Then give them all the lie.

Tell zeal it wants devotion;
   Tell love it is but lust;
Tell time it metes but motion;
   Tell flesh it is but dust:
     And wish them not reply,
     For thou must give the lie.

Tell age it daily wasteth;
   Tell honour how it alters;
Tell beauty how she blasteth;
   Tell favour how it falters:
     And as they shall reply,
     Give every one the lie.

Tell wit how much it wrangles
   In tickle points of niceness;
Tell wisdom she entangles
   Herself in over-wiseness:
     And when they do reply,
     Straight give them both the lie.

Tell physic of her boldness;
   Tell skill it is prevention;
Tell charity of coldness;
   Tell law it is contention:
     And as they do reply,
     So give them still the lie.

Tell fortune of her blindness;
   Tell nature of decay;
Tell friendship of unkindness;
   Tell justice of delay:
     And if they will reply,
     Then give them all the lie.

Tell arts they have no soundness,
  But vary by esteeming;
Tell schools they want profoundness,
  And stand too much on seeming:
    If arts and schools reply,
    Give arts and schools the lie.

Tell faith it's fled the city;
  Tell how the country erreth;
Tell, manhood shakes off pity;
  Tell, virtue least preferreth:
    And if they do reply,
    Spare not to give the lie.

So when thou hast, as I
  Commanded thee, done blabbing,
Although to give the lie
  Deserves no less than stabbing,
    Stab at thee he that will,
    No stab thy soul can kill.

These verses written this morning, between seven and eleven o'clock, in my lodgings at the Pope's Head in Looe Street, the product of a broken mind, a body racked by ague, but an unbent and unbending spirit.

Truth to tell, I have little else to do but turn my hand to verse-making. The voyage over, I am filled with a sense of futility. If only the King would arrest me, then at least I would know where I stood . . . But nine days have passed since my arrival, and no sign of a warrant. I spend my time in these rooms, their curtains drawn to shut out the sun's insult. England seems to be enjoying the hottest summer in living memory. Three times, at night, I have ventured out to walk upon the Hoe. I met no one. But I was followed. I never turned my head to flatter the King's agents with any advertisement of my knowing that they were there. Who they are and what they are supposed to be doing, I care not. Just paid informers keeping an eye on the old fox, I suppose.

I am worn out. I sleep a great deal, both by night and by day. No visitors come. I eat sparsely, and always in my chamber. Sam King pays the reckoning. Sam, Robin, the Indian, and the Reverend Mr

Samuel Jones – these are the only ones here at the inn with me. The rest of my last crew have gone their ways. I believe this to be sensible. Robin tells me that the whole of Plymouth, from St Nicholas Island to the Hoe, is plastered with copies of that proclamation. My men might be threatened with the rack, or worse, to make them testify against me at my trial. I have urged the remaining four to leave me also. Sam says he is too old, Robin too young! (Such jests are masks upon the face of courage.) Why our ship's chaplain stays close by me, I cannot say. There was never much love lost between us. I respect his cloth. It is possible that he respects my sash as Admiral. As for the Indian: I have offered on numerous occasions to let him go free, promising always that money could be drawn from my estate to pay for his passage to Spain, whence he could find some galleon bound for Guiana. He refuses these offers without reason. He seems determined to accompany me to the end. Perhaps he merely wants to see my head cut off?

The *Destiny* still lies in Plymouth Sound. Sam takes a cockboat daily to inspect her. He reports that no officials of the harbourmaster have been on board. Even more surprisingly, no thieves. That pathetic cargo of tobacco rests untouched in her hold. It is as though all Devon held its breath, frightened and indolent, sweating under the summer sun as if that sun were the eye of King James himself, waiting to see what I'll do next, or what will be done to me more likely.

I wait also, but with breath unbated.

I have written to George, Baron Clapton, repeating the facts of what transpired at San Thomé, together with some account of my difficulties in getting even one ship back to England. Clapton was Winwood's friend. He is of the Privy Council. However, I do not indulge myself with the vain hope that it lies within his power to save me, even should he want to. But a trial by my peers, is that too much to ask for? Not a *fair* trial, notice. I know the law too well to ask for that. But a trial in open court, that would be something. The verdict is a foregone conclusion. But at least I'd have the chance to put my case. Then let History be my judge, the only judge (in this world) worth his cap.

I have sent word also to Bess.

She should be here soon.

My Penelope.

Whose one eye will love and rejoice, while the other must weep for this Ulysses.

37

Bess came yesterday. She brought Carew. Also bad news from London. News which confirms my worst fears.

No trial is to be granted me. The King *has* promised Gondomar that, once taken, I shall be handed over to him instantly for public execution in Madrid.

So the Earl of Cork was right. He has long ears.

The Privy Council don't like it. They'd prefer my death here, upon English soil. Clapton spoke of a trial first. James just laughed at him. He's over-ruled his Council. All for Gondomar. No, all because he hates me. I'm *the man* . . .

A warrant is being issued for my arrest.

To be hanged in the square at Madrid! I cannot believe it. To die at the hands of King Philip! It's one of James's jokes. That twisted wit. That filthy slobbering humour. To select the very death that will most belittle me. Like a common pirate. In front of an audience of Spaniards. To be spat on by enemies. To be jeered at. To be cursed and execrated by Papist priests. My last agony to be witnessed by a mob of scoffing strangers. Under an alien sun in an alien place.

I thought my Lord Boyle was exaggerating. To make me run. He didn't exaggerate. He knows the King's mind to a turd. The only bit he got wrong was his guess that I'd be sent in chains to Spain aboard my own ship. I am to be spared that indignity. No doubt Count Gondomar will provide *a cage* for my safe custody and transport.

Is this, then, my destiny? A dirty dishonourable end? Neck snapped like a beggar's? *This* the end of my third voyage? *To die as Guattaral!*

Dear Christ, it is a torment to believe it, but believe it I must.

King James, in his apishness, would deny Sir Walter Ralegh his own death.

I am condemned to be snuffed out by Spaniards as this thing they call Guattaral.

Nightfall.

I can stand it no longer.

Bess begs me on her knees to run for France. All last night, all today, I've borne her weeping. I must fly before the warrant comes, she says. Not says. *Screams.* And Carew kneels there with her, tears pouring down his face, raising his piping voice whenever she stops to draw breath. O my son, my living son, must your father turn coward to please you?

I am too spent to think, to feel, to argue any more.

So be it.

I will go.

Sam King just brought to me a Frenchman, one Manourie, a doctor of physic. He is the ship's surgeon of a vessel now lying off the Sound. A merchant, the *Jeanne d'Arc*, she sails for Havre tomorrow. At midnight, on the ebb-tide, Manourie goes to join her. Bess has given Manourie her pearl necklace. So I go too.

Dawn, 4 July

We got within half a mile of the French vessel.

I couldn't do it.

I told Manourie to turn back.

I gave him my jacinth seal and my captain's gold whistle.

He cursed. He would miss his boat. He couldn't understand me.

I promised him a diamond.

He turned round. He brought me back here.

Sam King was with us. He said nothing. Sam knows me too well.

Bess was hysterical. She clawed at me. 'You're mad!' she kept shouting. Manourie fetched us a sleeping draught. We had to hold her, Sam and I, until Robin could coax her to drink it. Bess has peace now. She's asleep. I hear her snoring.

Carew stares at me. He's silent. He's stopped crying.

Boy, one day you will see through your father. You will understand this moment and all else. Know why his pride is broken finally. How he has *earned*, and now *deserves*, this death. It is all here. Even in those *Instructions*. Read hard. As I have written. Know your father.

The Indian just came. He asked me what poor Carew cannot ask. I gave him the answer. God knows if he understood it.

'Because I *am* Guattaral,' I said.

38

A week has passed. The longest week of my life. Bess will scarcely speak to me. She sits picking at a piece of embroidery, then unpicking all she has done. Carew is out of his depth. He plays with toy soldiers. My ague has been bad. Manourie brings me medicine. I have taught Sam King to play chess. He has no aptitude. He wins game after game. I sit waiting for knocks on the door. The Indian went for a walk. They threw stones at him, then ran away. Robin plays the gamba in the evenings. Bess weeps. I have to tell Robin to stop. The heat is intense. I can't sleep. My tobacco smoke makes the room foul. We are still here at Plymouth, but we shall be leaving tomorrow. I am going to London. I am going to give myself up.

No one comes. But one has gone. The preacher –
I'll write about that in a minute.

The King taunts me. How else to explain the non-appearance of his officers bearing the warrant for my arrest? This 'freedom' he consigns me to. Pure torture. Does he *want* me to run away? or try to? To prove to the world that I'm a coward? (I shall not, for my own reasons. That lesson's learned.) Or does he guess at the anguish of my waiting? Guess at it, savour it, enjoy it? Let it dribble in his beard like his Greek wine? By such torments of teasing James gets pleasure. I'd forgotten. But now remember well . . .

Remember in particular that day.
A Friday, it was. A rainy Friday.
Friday the 10th of December, 1603. Cobham, Grey, and Markham to be executed. My 'accomplices in treason', so they said.

James knew there was no treason. So did Coke. He never let me face my base accusers. Face them in open court. Deny their story. Force them to spout their damned lies *looking* at me. Of course not. Coke feared those liars would break down, that's why. My trial was a farce in consequence. It injured and degraded English justice. Judge Sir Francis Gawdy died confessing that with his last breath, five years later. No matter. That's not the point. What I witnessed that Friday –

Cobham, Grey, and Markham were the only traitors. Not traitors to King James. Traitors to me. They lied to save their skins. But they lied too well. They made the whole trumped-up 'plot' sound so plausible that the Judge found he had no choice but to condemn them to death along with me, the alleged arch-villain. James must have gnashed his teeth. Then he saw how he could have some sport from this turn of events . . .

I was led to a window, overlooking the execution yard. Markham came first. He lay down with his head on the block. The headsman raises the axe. But, suddenly, a shrill shout from the crowd. It's one of the King's catamites, Johnny Gibb, a pretty little page. He's waving a piece of rolled paper. The paper gets handed to the Sheriff. He reads it. He tells Markham he's been granted brief respite. Grey and Cobham to be executed *before* him, by order of the King!

Markham is marched away. Grey comes to the scaffold. It's pouring with rain now. His prayers and his confessions seem interminable. At last, he says he's ready for the headsman. But no sooner is *his* neck stretched on the block than Johnny Gibb pops up again, yet another sheet of paper is handed over, and the Sheriff announces that *Cobham* must die first, that this is his Majesty's pleasure!

His Majesty's pleasure indeed . . . I stood at the windowpane, the rain scalding down it. I had hammers working in my head to beat out the meaning of this stratagem.

Grey escorted from the scaffold. Here comes Cobham. He struts like an actor. He has a great grin on his face. His prayers and his confessions go on even longer than boring Grey's. The crowd get restive. 'For Sir Walter Ralegh,' cries Cobham, 'all I said of him was true! I swear it now, who am about to meet my Maker, upon my very soul, before God and His angels: that Ralegh is a traitor! He plotted with Spain . . .'

Et cetera, et cetera.

The hammers click home.

Cobham knows very damned fine he won't be meeting his Maker.

Not here. Not today. Not by execution, ever.

He's been promised a reprieve. The whole bloody (unbloody!) rain-soaked drama has been the King's pantomime.

As for Markham and Grey, I don't know if they knew. I don't care. Perhaps they were just better actors. In any case, those two vile canaries are brought back onto the scaffold to join Cobham. The Sheriff steps forward. He addresses the three of them:

'You are all agreed that you were justly tried and lawfully condemned to execution?'

They nod their heads. Such enthusiasm. Men glad that they have heads left to nod with.

A roll on the drums as the Sheriff prepares for the pay-off. He waves his papers aloft. They're sodden. The ink runs with the rain. It doesn't matter. The Sheriff knows his last crass lines by heart. He roars them out like Burbage in his prime:

'Then see the mercy of your Prince, who of himself has sent hither a countermand! Gentlemen, the King gives you back your lives!'

Applause (most probably paid-for) from the crowd. But not all have been delighted by these antics, I can see that. Some are disappointed. Others, being of better character, disguise their disgust. It was the first revelation in England of the Scotch King's perverse and pawky practical jokes.

As for me, I had to sweat it out for three more days, until the following Monday. Then I was told that James's mercy extended even to myself, the greatest 'traitor'. With the difference that I was to go to the Tower, and to stay there for good. No public announcement. No pantomime. At the same time, my death-sentence was never revoked, and I was warned that if at any point his Majesty felt less generous . . .

The truth was that King James *dared* not behead me. He knew all England knew I was never a traitor. What's more, he knew Spain knew I was never its friend. But James wanted me out of the way. I was just a dangerous ghost from a world beyond his ken. To let Ralegh rot in the Tower must have seemed like a reasonable act of exorcism.

*

I refused to rot. I read, I wrote, I kept a busy spirit. James put a woman with a running plague sore in the cell next to mine. I declined to die of the plague. I kept reading, I kept writing, I walked every day, miles and miles, by going up and down a thousand times on the terrace at the top of the inner wall. The years passed. The King forgot me, or seemed to. I was visited by my friends. I took an interest in expeditions, following their progress on a sea chart I had pinned above my bed. A new Governor came. I was allowed the use of a still-house in the garden. I cured my own tobacco. I made medicines. Keymis brought me ore from Guiana; I kept trying it, using cruset, coal, and bellows to melt it down. I found nothing. I kept trying, I worked day and night in that shed. I found nothing. Then Keymis took more ore to Gosson, that refiner in Goldsmiths' Row. He came back excited. Gosson reported that twelve grains of the ore, beaten with half an ounce of filed lead and a quarter of an ounce of sandiver, then put to the proper process under a muffle until all the lead was consumed, had produced of the twelve grains a quarter of a grain of pure gold. Did that refiner cheat us for the money? (I was foolish; I'd promised him £20 if he could find gold or silver in the ore.) Gosson must have cheated us. But it doesn't matter. I needed to believe in the gold. I could lie on my bed, then, and reach up with my fingers to my maps. The Caroni Falls. Putijma's Mountain. I could *feel* the gold there with my fingertips. The dream kept me going. If it hadn't been gold, it would have been some other folly. I *needed* to believe in the gold. So I cheated myself. That's all. That's the point. No matter.

Then *real* gold! But in the shape of a person. Such a person. Prince Henry, James's elder son, started visiting me. He was thirteen, the same age as my Wat. He came first in the company of his mother, Queen Anne. Anne was drunk. She drank like a fish. Anne was flighty and stupid. She came to collect a phial of my Great Cordial. The French Ambassador's wife had told her it was good for the nerves. So it was, so it should have been. The ingredients were as follows: mint, borage, gentian, a compound of pearl, musk, and hart's horn, bezoar stone, mace, aloes, with sugar and sassafras, all mixed in with powerful spirits of wine. Anne kept coming back for more. The Prince started coming on his own.

He was in all things the opposite of his father. He studied

deliberately to set himself apart from the Court. James doted on hunting; Henry hated it. James pawed at his catamites; his son scorned them. James was foul in his speech; the young Prince had boxes in his apartments, if his servants swore they were told to pay fines into those boxes for punishment. James was timorous; Prince Henry fought in the tournaments. The father was despised by the son.

Prince Henry was my pupil in the Tower for the last five years of his glorious but all-too-brief life. I wrote essays for the boy. I instructed him in foreign policy, the need to keep England from the clutches of Spain and the Pope. He was quick, he was able, he was witty. (Not his father's low wit; something lovely and lively sparked in him.) Queen Anne encouraged his visits. I designed a ship for him: the *Prince Royal*.

Henry would have made a splendid King. He was worthy of all England's glory. (A glory now gone, but I must not suppose it lost for ever.) His friendship gave me hope in my captivity. I began my *History of the World* for his instruction. I dropped it, dispirited, the day he died. The hope of all England, and my hope . . . But he died. I couldn't save him. Typhoid, they said. But the Queen said poison.

I'd refused to die. I'd survived. But I'd done worse. In James's eyes, that is. *I'd adopted his son.*

Fathers and sons.

How madly the world wags!

I have thought of it often this last week, sitting here smoking my long silver pipe, staring down at poor Carew.

While I was playing father to Prince Henry (his own father being less than a man), my imprisonment left Wat fatherless. Or something worse than fatherless. For he turned to Ben Jonson for father – of which the less said, God knows, the better. And James himself, unable to inspire his true son's love, had his male lovers fawn on him and call him their 'Dear Dad' . . . As for Carew, playing clumsily over there with his toy soldiers, my death will leave him more fatherless than Wat was.

Fathers and sons. Sons and fathers.

James hates me the more for being a father to his son.

I hate myself the more for failing to be a father to my real sons. You will say I had no choice. But I had a choice. If my climbing to power by the winding stair had not led me to seem like a threat to James, I would never have been in the Tower all those years. The choice was made long ago, and I'm the one who made it. *Fain would I rise . . .* I could have been a decent country gentleman, looking after my wife and my estate, my own garden, in the company of my sons. I chose otherwise. I have no one to blame but myself. My pride, my ambition, my self-insulting pursuit of Elizabeth's favour –

O antic father! I am as bad as King James. Whether he had his son poisoned, I know not. I know only that I have been the murderer of my own.

The King was wrong about one thing. I never said a word against him to Prince Henry. James supposed that I did, but I always avoided the subject.

As for the Prince, only once did he make any comment that could be construed as criticism of James. He was leaving. He stood at the door of my cell with his back turned to me. He spoke softly, addressing the shafts of sunlight which fell through the barred window. He said: 'Who but my father would keep such a bird in a cage!' It was the end of his last visit to the Tower. I said nothing. I never saw him again.

The preacher has gone. He fled in the night, last night, without paying his bill. I had wondered why he stayed with me here at the Pope's Head. He kept himself always to his own chamber, with hardly a word spoken to any of us. I had to summon him into my presence each day for evening prayers. He prayed in a most perfunctory manner – I might almost say with reluctance. Once he objected irritably to the Indian being with us in the room. 'This heathen,' he said. The Indian laughed and went out. I was angry. I am angrier now.

Sam King found a nest of half-burnt papers in the grate in the clergyman's room. Drafts of a letter he'd been working on all the time since coming ashore with me. We have pieced them together. Parts are evidently missing. There are many corrections, where the religious rogue laboured over his prose to get the best effect. The result is, as I say, fragmentary. But the drift is clear as day. I attach the wretched document here intact. I have no heart or stomach to copy it out.

To the Right Honourable the Lords of His Majesty's
most Honourable Privy Council. A true and brief Relation
of Sir Walter Rawley his late voyage to Guiana.
By the Reverend Mr Samuel Jones (M.A. 1604; B.D. 1611),
Chaplain in one of his ships called the Destiny

Right Honourable –

A common report of his Majesty's large commission to Sir Walter Rawley, the great expectation of success, the importunity of many worthy gentlemen, the good report I heard of Mr Robert Burwick, joined with the consideration of my want of employment at that time in the Church (under which misery I still suffer, despite my academic attainments noted above), were the inducements that prevailed with me to undertake so dangerous a voyage.

To which we set sail from Plymouth the 12th of June Anno 1617. We put in again at Falmouth in Cornwall, after at Kinsale in Ireland, where we arrived the 25th of June, and remained till the 19th of August. These delays, however occasioned, forced divers young gentlemen and others to sell their private provisions both of apparel and diet, to the untimely death of many of them . . .

The first ship we gave chase unto at sea . . . * * * * * * * * * * * The next day other four ships we took; and found to be Frenchmen * * * * * * * * * * At Lancerok, one of the Canary islands, we put in, desiring only water and some other provisions * * * * * * * . . . basely murdered, but at Gomera, after some intercourse of messages, they (seeing our force) gave us free leave to water, for at first they withstood us.

These passages I the rather relate because they put not only myself but many other gentlemen in some small hope that Sir W. R. had a certainty of his project, whereof by his many former delays we made great doubt * * * * * * * * * * * * * * * * * But at the Grand Canaries a Spanish carvel was taken, her men . . . * * * * * * * * * * Then from these islands we made to the Isles of Cape de Verde, in most of the seamen's judgements very impertinently: I am sure to the danger of all, and the loss of many men. For by steering such uncertain and unnecessary courses we were so becalmed that above a hundred persons, gentlemen most of them, died between those islands and the continent of Guiana.

In which great mortality I, visiting as many of the sick men in the duty of my ministry as the occasions of the sea would give me leave, heard sad complaints from many sick and dying gentlemen of Sir Walter's hard usage of them, in denying even those that were large adventurers with him such things upon necessity, of which there was at that time sufficient store. Others of great worth, either by birth or place of employment, of being neglected if not condemned and despised by Sir W. R.: of which number was Captain John Pigott, then our Lieutenant General, who complained to me thereof on his death bed . . .

During this time Sir Walter himself, taking a fall in our ship, being bruised, fell into a dangerous fever . . . He desired me to pray for him, spake religiously, and among other things told me that it grieved him more for the gentlemen than for himself, whose estates would be hazarded by his death, yet that he would leave such notes of direction behind him as should be sufficient for them. Which notes, however, I never saw, nor for aught I know any man else in the fleet ever saw.

At Cayenne, in November last, Sir Walter being somewhat recovered, he opened his project for the Mine, which upon the map he demonstrated to be within three or four miles of the town of Sancti Thomae. His conversation at this time made it clear to me that he knew the aforesaid town to be inhabited by the Spaniards, and he remarked oftentimes in my hearing that he cared not whether it had been reinforced or no.

Sir Warham St Leger was now made Lieutenant General. Yet had he gone up to the town, as I heard himself often say, he had not been given any particular directions concerning the Mine . . . But God suddenly visiting him with a violent sickness, George Rawley, then being Sergeant Major, went up Commander-in-chief . . . Captain Keymis as director for the Mine * * * * * Sir W. R. with four other ships remaining at Trinidado near the main mouth of the Oronoque * * * * * . . . reason for this remaining I never heard; he spoke much of his fever, but the surgeon made little of it in my company.

We parted with those forces that went in discovery of the Mine about the midst of December, and heard not of them again until the 13th of February following: during which time I very seldom heard Sir Walter speak of any Mine: and when he did, it was with far less confidence than formerly, intermixing new projects, propounding

292

often the taking of St Joseph's in Trinidado, expressing the great conceit of wealth that might be there among the Spaniards, and the undoubted great quantity of tobacco * * * * * . . . by this, and by many other things I heard, his contempt for the lawful Subjects of the King of Spain was made apparent. As for those . 10 were performing his adventure up the river, they were so slightly respected, especially the landmen, that he would often say for the most of them it was no matter whether ever they returned or no, they were good for nothing but to eat his victuals, and were sent to sea on purpose that their friends might be rid of them. And divers times did Sir W. R. propound to go away and leave them, but to which villainous course none other of his Captains remaining would ever agree.

Our companies that went up the river, as by the chief gentlemen at their return I was given to understand, arrived near the town of Sancti Thomae the second day of January, where the Captains desired Captain Keymis first to shew them the Mine, which Sir Walter had formerly said to be three or four miles nearer than the town, and that then if the Spaniard withstood them they would *vim vi repellere*.

This Keymis would by no means yield to, but alleged divers reasons to the contrary; as that if the town were reinforced, he should open then a mine in behalf of the King of Spain, and the like, which not on any terms would he be pleased to do. * . . . and in which conflict four or thereabouts of either side were slain, the rest of the Spaniards being forced to quit the town and flee for their lives.

The town being next day their own, and the place as it were in their possession, every man's expectation looked hourly for the discovery of the Mine. But Captain Keymis minded rather the tobacco, apparel, household stuff, and other pillage; often saying these would help if all else failed. Then one night, so I was told, Keymis himself, accompanied only with his own men, went out privately and brought in some mineral ore which he claimed to have cut. This was shown cheerfully by him to Captain Thornhurst. But being tried by a refiner, it proved worth nothing, and was no more spoken of. Hence it was reliably considered that Keymis himself might be deluded, even by Sir Walter Rawley, both in the ore and the place, and indeed in the very existence of any Mine at all . . .

For whereas the Mine was described to be three miles short of the town, they went not three miles but three score leagues beyond it, till at last they were forced to return. And all now doubted the story which Sir W. R. had told them, and cursed Keymis, who, for his part, fell into a sort of stupor of despair, from which nothing * * * * * * * * . . . . and had he really intended a Mine they must have carried spades, pickaxes, and taken refiners, surely? But none of these carried they with them.

The 13th of February we at Trinidado received news from them in the river, of the taking of the town and the missing of the Mine.

Sir Walter then protested to the Captains (as most of them told me) his own innocency, which to approve he would call Keymis to a public account in their presence before he spake with him privately. Which promise he never performed.

At their coming to us, which was the 2nd of March, Sir Walter made a motion of going back again, and he would bring them to the Mine; the performance of which at that time was altogether improbable, if not impossible. Our men weary, our boats split, our ships foul, and our victuals well-nigh spent. Then again he cried for the taking of St Joseph's. But no man would go with him, and the morning after that we disembogued.

From thence we fell down to the Caribee Islands till we came to Nevis: there we put into the bay the 12th of March. In which time Sir Walter promised to propound unto the Captains very often, as I heard, yet another project. He spoke now of a French Commission. Yet I never saw it, nor any man I know of ever did.

He now likewise freely gave leave to any of the Captains to leave him if they pleased, or thought they could better themselves in their own intendments. Whereupon Captain Whitney and Captain Wollaston, with their ships, left him the 6th of March.

Sir Warham St Leger (as I often heard him confidently report) one day in private desired to know of Sir Walter, whether he intended to come to England or no? To which he answered (with reverence to God and your Lordships be it spoken) that by God he would never come there, for if they got him there, they would surely hang him.

Being desired then by Sir Warham to tell him what course he would take, he said he would go to Newfoundland, victual and trim his ships, and then lie off about the Isles of the Azores, to wait for

some of the homeward-bound treasure ships of the King of Spain; that he might get something to bid himself welcome into France or elsewhere. As to the Mine, he never spoke more of it, so that no man doubted but that no Mine had ever existed * * * * * . . . the Captains presumed severally that they had been much abused in this project both by Keymis and Sir W. R. * * * * * * * * * * Sir Walter's uncertainty and many delays, his duplicity, the several changes of plan, resolved all to leave him, and consort no longer with him * * *
* * * * * * *

As for Sir Walter's return, whether it were willing or constrained, I give it as my opinion that a so-called mutiny amongst the men of his ship was arranged by him and those close to him, to make his return first to Ireland and thence into England appear in a more favourable light, and thus to avert the righteous and lawful displeasure of His Majesty. He made long delay at the harbour of Kinsale in Munster, so that many worthy men left him, being sure in their hearts (as was told to me) that he purposed presently to fly into France. * * * * * his crew so evanished and depleted, he came into Plymouth the 21st of June. I have ever considered it my duty (both to God and your Lordships) to lie close by him. From his lodgings here at the Pope's Head he has made already one attempt to join with a French vessel, in which cowardice his prevention was not clear, yet I suspect that the Frenchman would not have him, knowing His Majesty's anger and also the lawful displeasure of King Philip of Spain.

In conclusion, I give it as my considered belief, having regard to all the matters whereof I have written, that this voyage to the continent of Guiana was a mere stratagem whereby Sir Walter hoped to have respite from his imprisonment in the Tower; that there never was a Mine, and that his man Keymis knew this from the start; finally, that Sir W. R. undertook this illusory pursuit, at the cost of the lives and souls of many honest gentlemen, the better to slight the King's Majesty and his authority, and to stir up great trouble against the King's brother of Spain.

Of his inward thoughts and reasonings I cannot further speak, being never altogether in the confidence of so troublous and irregular a man. His ascendancy over others is most terrible. The only gentlemen that were near inward with him, as I hear and think, were Captain Samuel King, Sir John Holmden, his nephew Captain

George Rawley, the master of our ship, Mr Robert Burwick, and some of the chief seamen, but of them but few. * * * * * * * * * * * * . . . his strange dispositions most apparent in this choosing to consort with a heathen savage, to whom (I have heard it said) he poured out the darknesses of his secret soul as never to me, God's humble representative, yet a man of much Christian education. Touching this Indian, also, I with my own ears heard him once declare to Sir W. R. that there never had been gold in his land of Guiana. Whereupon, Sir Walter seemed not to evince surprise, but rather to the contrary.

Thus, Right Honourable Lords, in the simplicity of truth, free from all sinister affection, I have endeavoured to perform what by His Majesty's proclamations I am bidden to make known, though labouring with much weakness, which I refer to Your Lordships' views and favourable censure. My pen has never before been used to so high employment, but my prayers shall never cease to mount to the throne of Grace, that God will be pleased to make you all glorious in Heaven whom he hath made so gracious and honourable on earth.

Your honoured Lordships' ever to be commanded,

SAMUEL JONES

With clergymen like this, what need of the Devil?

'Tell friendship of unkindness; Tell justice of delay . . .'
I shall set forth tomorrow for London.

39

The comedy continues. I am its clown. Does King James plot the action and write every line of the speeches? He must do. Each scene-shift and stage-direction bears the indelible mark of that cunning cruel wit. What a loss to the theatre that this mighty genius has to play King in real life! How he must roll about giggling with Villiers in his cups at Whitehall! For if it's not James who is master-minding each crazy twist and mocking turn of my fate, then I must consider that God himself has a mind not unlike our queer King's – and that is no thought for a man to bear who must accept a near appointment with Him . . .

We journeyed, by carriage, a meagre twenty miles towards London. Then, at Ashburton, the carriage was stopped, and a most familiar face peers in the window. A nervous, handsome face, weak-chinned, pig-eyed, with the faintest fuzz of hair on its upper lip. A friendly face, at last. With a diffident smile. Sir Lewis Stukeley's face! My kinsman. My cousin.

'Sir Walter,' says he. 'I am very glad to meet you, Sir Walter.'

'Cousin Lewis,' I reply. 'Uncommonly good weather, don't you think?'

'Too hot for my liking,' grumbles Stukeley, wiping sweat from his brow with kid gloves. 'Too hot to be travelling, and that's a fact. But, then, it's even hotter in London.'

'Ah, you have ridden from London. How strange that we should meet. That's where I am going.'

'You? *Going*? To *London*?' (His voice breaks like a boy's, with incredulity.)

'To London,' I repeat. 'I have business there.'

'It's very hot in London,' Stukeley stammers.

'So you said, my dear cousin, so you said.' I nod to him politely. 'Well, I must press on, however hot the day. You will give my best regards to your lady mother?'

He grabs at the door.

'But, Sir Walter –'

'Yes, cousin?'

'Sir Walter, I don't know how to put this . . .' He starts biting his nails. I wait patiently. He stops biting his nails. Then he says: 'Sir Walter, this meeting of ours –'

'Most extraordinary. Quite a coincidence.'

He's blushing. 'Yes. No! That's the point. It's not exactly a coincidence, you see. I mean, I'm very glad I met you –'

'So you said.'

'Did I? Well, I meant it. You know that.' He sees Bess sitting in the corner of the carriage. Off comes his feathered hat with a wide flourish. 'Lady Ralegh! You too! *To London?*'

Bess stares at him, face as white as her dress.

'Cousin Lewis,' she snaps. 'You will excuse me. I have heard quite enough of these pleasantries. My husband travels to London. To the furnace! Are you really not aware of what is happening?'

Poor Stukeley hangs his head. He looks away.

'Forgive me,' he mutters. 'I thought it better –'

'There is a warrant out for his arrest!'

Then Stukeley smiled. He smiled with pride. He beamed at us.

'I have no warrant.'

'You?'

'I volunteered.'

'You *volunteered*! To come and arrest my husband!'

He bit his lip. 'Lady Ralegh, you do me wrong. I come to assist Sir Walter in this time of difficulty. I am his friend and his kinsman. My wish is to *help*.'

'Then knock him unconscious!' cried Bess. 'Knock him unconscious and carry him aboard any boat bound for France!'

'Peace, wife,' I said.

'He's mad, cousin Lewis! He cares nothing for me or our child! He knows what the King intends. He knows how they'll kill him in Spain. But he's out of his wits. He won't help himself. If you really want to help him then you must –'

298

I clapped my hand over Bess's mouth.

'Sir Lewis is Vice Admiral of Devon,' I said. 'He serves our gracious Sovereign Lord, King James.'

'As you do,' Stukeley said.

'As I do, yes. I am his faithful subject. That's why I journey to London. To save him the labour of arresting me. To give myself up.'

Stukeley smiled his approval. Then he said: 'Sir Walter, I have long admired your courage. Lady Ralegh is distraught, and I understand. Be sure of it, I shall forget what she said.'

'You are kind, cousin Lewis.'

'Think no more of it. This business is most disagreeable, yet it seems to me that all may not be lost. My purpose, in any case, is to make everything as easy as I can for you. When I heard the bad news I –'

Bess bit my hand.

'Bad news!' she shrieked. 'The King sells him to Spain to be butchered and you call it *bad news*! Dear God, are you lunatic too?'

Carew, clutching his mother's skirts, started crying.

I had had enough of all this.

'You will let cousin Lewis explain his errand,' I commanded. 'Sir, I take it that you bear the King's authority?'

'I do.'

'But no warrant for my arrest?'

'I went to the Lord Admiral. I told him no more than what he knew already. That you are a man of high honour. That I am your kinsman. In the circumstances, he agreed that no formal warrant would be necessary.'

Stukeley spoke simply and with dignity. What he said rang true – up to a point. Charles Howard, Earl of Nottingham, Lord Admiral of all England, was never a good friend to me. He's too much a Howard for that – his family close ranks when it suits them; they've held positions of power for centuries; and old Charles, now a venerable foul-tempered octogenarian, is one of the few men in England who've succeeded in prospering under King James with their titles granted by Queen Elizabeth still intact. Yet the Howards know somewhat of honour. A different breed from those who came south with King James. It crosses my mind, also, that this ancient

Lord Admiral might just have remembered the praise I heaped upon him in that salvo of a sentence about the Armada. Then again, his generosity in waiving the need for a warrant could well have been prompted by guilt. He took my share of the booty at Cadiz. He lost no time in making profit by my fall. The minute I was safely in the Tower, this same honourable Howard seized my wine licences. He got more than £9000 from that. How sweet are the quirks of human nature!

Stukeley said: 'I shall tell him you were on your way to London. It proves that our confidence was not misplaced.'

I said nothing. I got down from the carriage. I handed Stukeley my sword and my sash.

'I am yours to command,' I told my cousin.

He grinned nervously, swatting at flies. 'If it wasn't so damned hot,' he muttered. 'I never knew a summer like it. England's an oven. Men are dying of this, I've heard tell.'

I had a fit of coughing.

Bess had hysterics.

And at this point the second carriage of our entourage pulled up beside us. It contained Sam King, Robin, the Indian, and Manourie. The little Frenchman tumbled out and gave me a phial of physic for my fever. He was wearing a long russet gown with hanging sleeves, and on his head a filthy greasy hat with what looked like a rat-hole eaten in it. The Indian climbed down too. He has refused to adopt any English apparel. He stood there, arms folded, jaws chewing, skin glistening in the pitiless sunlight.

An incongruous scene.

As bizarre as any I ever saw on the Devonshire highway.

Stukeley's face was a study in stupefaction. He gazed from the Indian to me, from me to Manourie, then back to the Indian again. I began to feel sorry for my kinsman. Bess wasn't helping much by shouting at the lot of us.

'These are my friends,' I explained, effecting introductions most formally, once the physic had done its trick. 'Each one of them is what you call a man of high honour. For they have chosen of their own free will to travel with me to London. If I may presume to speak for them, then I give my word that they will accept your authority as whole-heartedly as I do.'

I offered Stukeley my hand. He seized hold of it like a conspirator. Not letting go, he drew me aside and into the shade of the hedgerow.

'Sir Walter,' he said quickly in a low voice, so that no one else could hear him, 'there is no need at present for you to give yourself up to his Majesty. Indeed, sir, there are many good reasons why you should not. The Lord Admiral trusts me. I have his ear on the Council. It will be sufficient that I send word to him that you are now in my custody. Cousin, I recommend delay! Let us return to Plymouth. Treat my house there as your own.' His voice sunk to a whisper. 'I will explain all to you in private. Believe me, I have only your best interests at heart, and I have thought long and deeply in this matter. Another week in Plymouth could be *vital*.'

A further bout of coughing shook my frame. Without relinquishing his fervent grip of my hand, Sir Lewis placed his free arm about my shoulders.

'Plymouth!' he breathed in my ear. 'I know what I'm talking about!'

I was past caring if he knew his jerkin from his hose.

'I gave you my sword,' I said. 'There is no need to cajole me. I shall do whatever you say.'

'Excellent,' cried Stukeley, slapping me on the back like some idiot schoolboy, so that I coughed again and had to spit blood in the dust. 'You will see, my dear cousin. One week could make all the difference.'

'With luck,' I remarked, 'it might rain.'

He looked blank.

'You complained of the heat,' I reminded him. 'You have galloped – doubtless, post-haste – all the way from London. I can quite appreciate *your* need for rest and refreshment. And – who knows? – in a week it might turn cooler. A little comfort of cloud for my funeral procession.'

Sir Lewis did not smile. 'You jest, Sir Walter.'

'My weakness,' I said. 'One problem: You intend to provide for my friends?'

Stukeley looked again, bemusedly, at Manourie and the Indian. He tried hard not to shudder. Then he nodded.

'Cousin, your friends are mine also. I am honoured to have them as my guests. Naturally, Lady Ralegh and your son –'

'They carry on to London,' I announced. 'That is, if my kind keeper will permit it . . .'

'A wise decision, cousin,' Stukeley agreed. 'But, now, I beg you, let us have no more of this talk of arrests and keepers. I am your brother, your kinsman. I am your friend.'

'I hear you,' I said.

I sit here writing in a pleasant garden. I have a footstool for my wounded leg. The bees are busy in the rosemary. Robin comes now and again to replenish my water jug. In the wide fields beyond the river, they harvest the hay. Red currants hang down the stone wall like drops of carnelian. The sun throws his golden net across the green wood.

Pretty stuff.

Pretty damned stuff and nonsense.

Just like Christopher Marlowe's stupid poem:

> Come live with me and be my love,
> And we will all the pleasures prove,
> That hills and valleys, dales and fields,
> And all the craggy mountains yields . . .

Thank God, I've forgotten the rest of it. Silver drivel. Something about gowns made of the finest wool, which from our pretty lambs we pull, wasn't it? And beds of roses to rhyme with fragrant posies; that sort of thing. 'The Passionate Shepherd to his Love'. He knew it was pure rubbish, the crafty little son of a shoemaker. He could cobble better verses than that. 'They that love not tobacco and boys are fools.' He said that to me once. I agreed about the tobacco. Kit was all right, though Cecil said he made a lousy spy. My poem tossed off as an antidote to his praise of bumpkins and pumpkins made him laugh. 'The Nymph's Reply to the Shepherd', I told him:

> If all the world and love were young,
> And truth in every shepherd's tongue,
> These pretty pleasures might me move
> To live with thee and be thy love . . .
> Thy gowns, thy shoes, thy beds of roses,
> Thy cap, thy kirtle, and thy posies
> Soon break, soon wither, soon forgotten,
> In folly ripe, in reason rotten.

I'd sooner hear Kit's laugh than these damned bees. Stabbed to death through both eyes in a Deptford tavern brawl, they said. Over some squabble about a game of backgammon, they said. That the knife was stuck in by one Ingram, a hired assassin, because poor Kit Marlowe could never keep his mouth shut concerning Mr Secretary Cecil's business – they never said that.

They never do. They never say things like that. Not the Cecils and the Howards of this world. How long, I wonder, before my loving cousin comes down the garden path, plump, bandy, diffident, tiptoeing oh ever so carefully between those delightful beds of strawberries like little robin-redbreasts flirting under furred green leaves, with a hero-worshipping smile on his foolish face and a backgammon board tucked under his left arm?

Of course, I don't trust Stukeley. Not an inch. The man is a fool in himself, but who may be using him? Howard? King James? King James using Howard to use Stukeley? The ramifications are endless. But of one thing I am sure: That there is a plot.

Perhaps I did wrong to send Bess and Carew on to London. Yet Bess didn't demur. She wanted it. And if I am to be assassinated, then they are better by far out of the way.

Four nights now I've slept in Stukeley's house. Sam King and the Indian take turns to guard my door.

I leave nothing to chance. I never go out. Robin spends much of the day with his eye on the cook. The little Frenchman tastes my meat before I eat it. A careless quack of a doctor, but not without pluck. I pay him well for his service. He seems to respect me.

Four nights and five days . . .

My dear cousin has still not 'explained all to me in private'. I have learned not a single one of his 'good reasons' for this further delay. He absents himself, for the most part, from our company. He goes down into Plymouth. It seems he has important duties there.

Midnight.
Cousin Lewis just came to my chamber.

(The Indian didn't want to admit him. I called out my permission. But Christoval came in as well.)

Stukeley looked very pleased with himself. Not so pleased with the Indian.

'Sir Walter,' he said, 'I have news for you.'

'Midnight news,' I observed, 'is in my experience bad.'

'This is neither good news nor bad. But it's definitely *hopeful*.'

Stukeley rubbed his hands together. He has most dainty fingers, like tassels. His nails, as I notice, are bitten right down to the quick.

I said nothing. I was weary. I stifled a yawn.

Stukeley glanced sideways at the Indian. 'Does this fellow speak English?'

'A little.'

'Enough to understand what we say?'

'Perhaps. I don't know. You can trust him, if that's what you mean.'

My keeper stood there a moment, hesitating, his face petulant in the candlelight. Then he gave a broad wink. 'I will tell you tomorrow,' he said.

'As you wish.'

'Let us meet by the sundial. In private.'

'By all means, if it pleases you.'

'At noon,' Stukeley whispered. 'We shall meet by the sundial at noon.'

'I'll be there.'

'Sundials don't speak English,' Stukeley told me.

'They don't even speak Spanish,' I said.

'Exactly. Nor do they have ears, my dear cousin.'

He chuckled to himself, quite delighted by this observation. I managed a smile. Then he left me. The Indian left too, without a sign one way or the other to indicate if this asinine exchange had been understood by him.

Till tomorrow, then. Till noon. By the deaf-and-dumb sundial.

'In folly ripe, in reason rotten . . .'

40

Woke late from a mad dream.

I dreamt I was in the Tower, but the Tower was a ship. I sailed in the Tower to Guiana, in a stone ship of death. When I got there, Guiana was a woman. This woman was half Elizabeth and half Bess. She had the eyes of my wife, one blue, one black, but those eyes were set in the white ageing face of the Queen in the year of my fall. She stood on a globe of the world. There was a storm on her left hand, the sun was shining on her right. I was struck down by the thunderbolt over her left shoulder. 'Why did you send me to London?' she said. 'You have condemned me now. My father will cut off my head!' She kicked me. She was wearing golden slippers. 'Get up,' she said. 'Get up and dance with me.' I got up. Her head was gone. There was blood on her dress. I danced with the headless woman. She had long jewelled hands, like the Queen's. She tore off her gown: Bess's body. 'Now, Sir Water,' she said. 'We make love!' She called me Sir Water, not Sir Walter. Her voice seemed to come from her privy parts. When I looked at them, they looked like the Orinoco – the shape of that river on my sea charts, but with a membrane of thick gold that linked their lips. I was naked. She took my member in her fingers. She played with it. My old rod would not rise. She drew back from me then. Her vulva seemed to laugh at me. 'Sir Water!' it screamed (Bess's scream). 'O Sir Water indeed! You are impotent! Swisser Swatter! You were never the Golden Man! Husband, you condemned me! You condemned me to my virginity! You condemned me to death!' Then the Indian came. He made love to her. His phallus was gold. I watched them. His great member pierced her membrane. Her legs danced with delight, she was down in the dirt on her back. 'This is the cannon royal,' said the Indian.

'This is the bastard cannon. This is the petro.' He thrust in and out, as if naming the pleasures he gave her. I watched, weeping, yet unable to move from the scene. When the woman was satisfied, he sprang from her. I saw that his gold phallus was still erect. King James was now at my elbow. He started pawing the Indian. 'You are very well hung, man,' his Majesty said. Then he pointed at me. 'We command you to graciously bugger him!' The Indian shrugged, then stepped forwards. 'Not here!' screeched King James. 'On the scaffold! In our brother's public square in Madrid!' The Indian shouted. A great golden shout of approval. Then he danced with the King and the woman, a slow, stately pavane, all three mocking me.

I woke then, my pillow stained with tears. There was blood on the sheet. I must have been coughing.

Mem.: I shall ask Monsieur Manourie for a different sleeping draught.

Stukeley was leaning on the sundial. He looked like some gross parody of my youth. That is to say, he was got up for some reason in garments which were all the rage some half a century since. His rich red velvet doublet was peascod-bellied, with winking buttons down the front, and silver thread points. Its collar, lace-edged and turned-over, met his weak double chins. He had leg-o'-mutton sleeves and pickadils. The pickadils were dark with perspiration. Skin-tight Venetian breeches completed the costume.

He consulted a gold-cased pocket-watch.

'You are six minutes late.'

I offered my apologies. He waved them away with a gesture no doubt intended to be magnanimous.

'It is no matter. But I like to be punctual myself.'

'Time has bald followers,' I remarked.

My cousin blinked like an owl. He's got fatter since those days when he was first my keeper. Also his hair, never plentiful, is now fast receding from his forehead.

'Do you laugh at me, Sir Walter?'

'No, Sir Lewis. I quote Shakespeare. One of the little errors in his comedy of them.'

Stukeley mopped at his brow with a fringed silk handkerchief. 'I never could understand Shakespeare. He was very obscure.'

'He didn't waste time,' I observed. 'He went bald before thirty.'

'Did he?'

'I think so.'

'You knew him?'

'Not well. He was never one for company. He'd say he was in pain. He didn't go out.'

'That's interesting.'

'Isn't it?'

'What do you think he was doing?'

'He could have been busy writing,' I suggested.

Stukeley snorted. 'Counting his money, more likely. He liked money. I've heard that. He made quite a pile from his stuff.'

I nodded absent-mindedly, coughing, and turning aside. This gave me the chance to be sure that Sam King had taken up position in the orchard. He was well-hidden in a pear tree. I caught the sun's glint on the barrel of his harquebus.

'Cousin,' Stukeley said, snapping out of his daydream concerning the playwriting profits made by the burgher from Stratford. 'Why don't you trust me, cousin?'

'I gave you my sword.'

'That is not what I mean. And you know it.'

I consulted the sundial. '*Tempus fugit*,' I said. 'Are you going to tell me this news of yours?'

'Of course. But your attitude dismays me. I am your kinsman. Sir Richard Grenville was my uncle. I know how close you were to him. Well, he's my hero too.'

'He died bravely,' I said.

'And you have *lived* bravely, Sir Walter. Can you not see? To my eyes, you are as great a hero as Grenville ever was. Drake, Frobisher, Hawkins. England had heroes once. You're the only one left. I would like to be your friend. It means the world to me.'

I studied him. 'Is that why you're wearing fancy dress?'

Stukeley blushed. 'You are shrewd, sir. Yes. I know it's absurd. But my boyhood was fed on such noble dreams. Of all the great heroes. Of England's glory in the golden days.'

'It was perhaps not quite as glorious as you imagine,' I said mildly. 'As for heroes – they are out of date, I think.'

My cousin sighed. 'You will not take me seriously!'

'I take you very seriously. Come, this news! Why have you brought me here? What reason do you have for our delay? For one

307

who watches the clock so attentively, it appears to me that you waste a deal of time.'

Stukeley walked twice round the sundial, hands clasped in a knot behind his back, his head bowed as if deliberating some weighty matter of state. Then he came to a halt, arms akimbo.

'I have sold all your tobacco,' he announced.

'You have *what*?'

'Sold the cargo of your *Destiny*,' Stukeley said with pride. 'There was twenty-five hundredweight. The merchant offered £100 a hundredweight. I beat him up to £112. A pound a pound, I told him; Sir Walter Ralegh is not a man to be cheated. You realize what that means? £2800!'

I sat down on the stone steps and busied myself lighting my pipe.

'Of course, he'll get more for it in London, I know that,' Stukeley prattled on. 'Good Spanish tobacco fetches anything up to £2 a pound in Gracechurch Street. But one has to allow these fellows their margin of profit.' He chuckled. 'Besides, the fool thought he was getting such a good bargain that he didn't inspect all the bales with the proper thoroughness. Some of them are soaking wet! I expect you knew that?'

'I didn't,' I said.

'You must have had a rough crossing?'

'I did,' I said.

'Well, that would account for it.'

Stukeley came and stood between me and the sun. He looked like a bandy blackbird. 'Have I not done well, Sir Walter?'

I puffed a cloud of smoke to blot him out.

I said: 'Sir Lewis, you have done splendidly. For yourself!'

He took two swift steps backwards. I must say I prefer him at a distance.

'Cousin, you wrong me once more! I acted on your behalf, as your humble *agent*. The money is yours, just as soon as I have it to hand.'

'No percentage for your trouble?'

'Not a penny.'

'I see.'

I saw Sam also, peering from the tree. I was comforted by the fact that he had his gun levelled on a bough, its muzzle pointed straight at Stukeley's back.

'One fifth must go to his Majesty', my cousin said.

'Of course. That was stated in my Commission.'

'A fifth is only £560. Leaving £2240 for your use.'

'You are excellent at arithmetic, Sir Lewis.'

He stamped his foot. 'And you are excellent at arrogance, Sir Walter.'

'So I have often been told.' I sent another puff of sweet tobacco in his direction. 'Cousin, perhaps you will pardon an old man his stupidity. I fail to understand how your sale of my cargo will help me one whit. Is it my wife and heir that you seek to benefit? Where I am going, they don't accept payments in pounds sterling.'

'You mean in Spain? But –'

'I mean in heaven, man!'

Stukeley sat down beside me. He had trouble with his sword. It was a large black-hilted affair, some species of antique. In the end, he had to unstrap it. The weapon lay on the flagstone between us.

'Listen carefully,' Stukeley said in a whisper. 'The Lord Admiral is your friend, and so am I. I told you when we met that there were sound reasons for returning here. The sale of the *Destiny*'s cargo is but one of them. I deliberately forbore from giving you the rest of it immediately. I did not want to seem to *buy* your trust. But now I see that nothing will satisfy you short of the whole truth. I regret that. God knows, I have given no cause for you to hate me –'

'*Hate* you?' I said. 'Are you crazy? I am old, I am sick, I must die. I assure you, I am past hating anybody.'

'Not even the King?' Stukeley hissed.

His breath smelt foul. He stuffs himself with sweetmeats. His teeth are rotten. Ulcerated gums.

I said: 'As Jesus is my judge, I hate no man.'

'King James is not a man,' my cousin snickered. 'You know the latest gossip? He made Buckingham –'

'This noonday heat is intolerable,' I cried, interrupting him. 'It's making my head ache. Will you please kindly come to the point?'

'Very well,' Stukeley murmured. 'I will come to the point. It is this. His Majesty is a weakling. He's been forced into a corner again by the Spanish Ambassador over this business of the Prince of Wales having to marry the Infanta. James does not want it. Prince Charles does not want it. No Spanish marriage will ever go through. Count Gondomar must know that himself. Talk of the Spanish Match has dragged on for years now, James always finding excuses to postpone it. But Gondomar has got him where he wants him. And, in return for not demanding the marriage, he's demanding your head! The King has little choice. You are being sacrificed to Spain to get James off the hook another time.'

'Cousin Lewis,' I said, 'you are no politician. His Majesty has cause enough in himself to be rid of me.'

'Perhaps so. But not by having you dispatched like a common pick-purse in Spain. That's an insult to England. My Lord Admiral himself says so. The whole Council are up in arms. But King James is powerless. He has to please Gondomar. And Gondomar hates you. He's obsessed with the need for revenge. It's a personal thing. Count Gondomar – there's your real enemy.'

'I never met this man,' I pointed out. 'Why should he flatter me with so much hatred? What have I done that makes him want revenge?'

'You murdered his kinsman,' said Stukeley.

'I beg your pardon?'

'Count Gondomar was born Don Diego Sarmiento de Acuña. He had a cousin, Don Diego Palomeque de Acuña. This Palomeque was the Governor at San Thomé!'

Here was news. I sucked hard at my pipe. I said nothing.

Stukeley hugged his knees, delighted that at last he had won my complete attention. 'All this is true,' he went on in a rush. 'My Lord Admiral Howard knows it. He has told the King. His Majesty expresses much distaste for being employed in a personal vendetta. All London knows also that Count Gondomar is sick. He suffers from a cancer in his gut. They say that he has the pox also. I can well believe it! He sleeps with Coke's wife, Lady Hatton. He cannot be long for this world, eh? With a mistress like that! In any event, I have it on good authority that he will soon be withdrawn as Ambassador. Meanwhile, our best policy is to wait. Every day that passes improves your chances. Do you see? King Philip of Spain may very well *decline* this petition to have you dispatched in Madrid. Why should he dirty his hands to satisfy Gondomar's lust for blood? His minister, the Duke of Lerma, will never agree to it. The Lord Admiral says so.'

I stared up at the pear tree. Sam must be getting tired . . . To tell truth, I was weary myself.

'We have two alternatives,' Stukeley said, counting them out on his fingertips. 'If, as I hope and pray, Spain refuses to go along with Gondomar, then the Council will press for your trial. That would give you the chance to redeem yourself. If not, and the worst comes to the worst, then you could use the tobacco money . . .'

He left the sentence unfinished. It hung on the summer air like the mouthful of smoke I blew between us.

'To do what?' I inquired.

'To do what your wife wished,' said Stukeley.

I have set down this curious conversation to the best of my remembrance, and in so doing to come at any sense there might be in it. Since doing that, I have also discussed with Sam King every material point which may be extracted from my cousin's rigmarole, and sought to relate these to his behaviour towards me, both now and in those far-off days when he was first my keeper. We are agreed that Stukeley is not to be trusted. If nothing else, his many fulsome protestations of allegiance serve to put me on my guard. It could well be, as Sam suggests, that the man is plain mad. There *is* a streak of insanity in all the Stukeleys. My cousin's father, Captain Thomas Stukeley, killed at the Battle of Alcazar in '78 when fighting for the Pope, was a villainous eccentric fellow, a traitor, a soldier of fortune, who dubbed himself 'Duke of Ireland' – I've said this before. What I didn't say was that, amongst other lunacies, this clown once declared himself Henry the Eighth's bastard son! No, cousin Lewis is definitely to be treated with very great caution. My own view, for what it is worth (and I confess myself exhausted and confused by the mental wilderness through which Stukeley leads me) – my private suspicion is that all this talk of Gondomar lusting for my blood, of our delay here being occasioned by the possibility that King Philip may decline the offer of the privilege of hanging me in Madrid, et cetera, et cetera, could be part of a well-laid plot in which my kinsman acts directly for King James. How do I know that he does not detain me here in his house simply to trick me into uttering incautious remarks which he passes on verbatim to his Majesty? As for the selling of my cargo, and his assurance that he will hand this money over to me to assist my escape into France – why, the whole wretched business stinks of James! What better proof could he have to demonstrate to the world that I am indeed a despicable villain?

The plot thickens, as they say. And King James is the hideous playwright. 'Thus march we, playing, to our latest rest.' I was always in some part the actor. I have more than once admitted it. But here I am trapped and enmeshed in a tragi-comedy not of my own making, no longer master even of a simulated destiny I can choose, the King's plaything, his victim, his Touchstone, his fool. My only hope is that, somehow, in the last act, at the play's end, I might have a chance to speak out loud and clear in my own voice. If not, if the King brings the curtain down while I am still dumb and in darkness, then let what I write here do service as my testament. I only wish I had more energy for elquence, a clearer head, a less depleted spirit.

Fathers and sons.

Kinsmen and cousins.

Is the world just a stage-set for a blood-bath of blood-relations?

My brain needs no maggots to consume it.

The Frenchman is my friend. He brings me physic.

The Indian stands close guard outside my door. Thank his golden gods for the leaf that keeps him from sleeping!

Bess, I do wish you were here. I miss even your scolding, your shrewishness, your voice raised in anger against me. I'm sorry I sent you to London. The same old story. Whatever I have for a heart needs absence to sting it awake.

But Carew is well out of this madhouse.

There's thunder in the air tonight. Cousin Lewis is practising scales on his violin. He saws at it, up and down, like a coffin-maker. He must be tone deaf, or blind drunk. The strings keep breaking.

41

A Warrant to Sir Lewis Stukeley, Knight,
Vice Admiral of Devon (23 July, 1618)

You have under your charge the person of Sir Walter Rawleigh, knight, touching whom and his safe bringing hither before us of his Majesty's Privy Council you have received sundry directions signifying his Majesty's pleasure and commandment.

Notwithstanding, we find no execution thereof, as had become you, but vain excuses unworthy to be offered unto his Majesty or to those of his Council from whom you received his pleasure.

We therefore now dispatch this Warrant unto you, and hereby do will and command you in his Majesty's name and upon your allegiance, that all delays and excuses set apart (of which we will hear no more) you do safely and speedily convey hither the person of the said Sir Walter Rawleigh, to answer before us such matters as shall be objected against him on his Majesty's behalf.

And of this you are to be careful as you will answer the contrary at your peril.

Signed with their seals:

The *Lord Archbishop of Canterbury*, the *Lord Chancellor*, the *Lord Privy Seal*, the *Lord Chamberlain*, the *Earl of Arundel*, the *Baron Clapton*, *Mr Treasurer*, *Mr Vice Chamberlain*, *Mr Secretary Naunton*.

Sent post by James Tailor, messenger, the same day at ten o'clock afore noon.

Good news, says Stukeley!

The Privy Council's messenger delivered this warrant into his hands at breakfast this morning, Saturday, the 25th of July. As a token of unswerving friendship (says Stukeley) he allowed me to peruse it later at my leisure, and even to make a copy of it, now inserted here.

'How can you call this good news?' I asked my cousin.

'It's a matter of interpretation,' he explained.

Then he gleefully pointed out to me that the Lord Admiral Charles Howard's seal is *missing* from the document. This, he would have me believe, is a very good sign.

'You mean Howard does not want you to act on this warrant?'

Stukeley was startled. He swallowed a great gob of bacon in one go.

'Not exactly,' he said, when his digestive tract had recovered. 'My Lord Admiral has withheld his seal as a cipher meant for me.'

'Signifying what?'

'That the omens are favourable. That in all probability Spain is saying no.' My cousin forked more bacon into his mouth. He chewed contemplatively. A straggle of rind hung down, dripping grease on his hairless chins. He looked like a neutered tomcat munching a mouse, with its victim's tail hanging out. He seemed pleased with himself, and impatient that I was not sharing in his pleasure.

'You'll see,' he murmured, smacking his lips with satisfaction. 'I know the Lord Admiral. He's as clever as a fox.'

'More clever than Count Gondomar?'

'No comparison. Gondomar's wits are poxed out!' His eyes roved greedily over my platter. 'Cousin, you have not touched your breakfast! I can tell you, this bacon is delicious . . .'

I offered him my helping.

'Are you sure . . . ?'

I nodded. 'I find I have no appetite,' I said.

'But breakfast sets a man up for the day. You should eat it, Sir Walter. You will need sustenance for the journey.'

'We set forth today then?'

'Immediately,' he said. 'They call us now to London. We go to London. The letter of the law must be observed.'

He took my plate.

He said: 'Cousin, your hand is shaking.'

'My ague,' I answered. 'It always comes worst in the mornings.'

314

'Of course. I do sympathize. But you appreciate at last what I have done for you?' He flicked at the warrant with his fingers. 'Not a word about sending you to Spain. And the mere fact that this warrant is to bring you before the Council. That can mean only one thing. A proper trial. A fair hearing. Here. In England.'

'Will his Majesty want that?'

Stukeley winked.

'His Majesty will do what Buckingham wants.'

'Buckingham?' I said wearily.

'Villiers. *Steenie*.'

'But he's not my friend.'

'Ah! You'd be surprised!'

Stukeley would say no more. He ate all my bacon.

Does cousin Lewis know?

About that *bribe*?

It pains me to confess this, but now I have no choice. His mention of George Villiers, Duke of Buckingham, makes me wonder . . .

Ralph Winwood advised it. I had put all my plans and promises concerning Guiana into his hands. Ralph placed them most persuasively before King James. For more than a year he worked on it, while I was still sweating in the Tower. At last Ralph came to me. The King was *almost* willing. But he needed just the final word to decide him. Only one man could provide that word, Ralph said. George Villiers, the ludicrous Steenie, James's favourite, the lover with the legs.

Villiers would not take a bribe directly, Winwood warned me. That would be tantamount to touching me – me and my cause. So I arranged for the money to be paid to Villiers' brother. It seemed little enough (£2000), but at the same time too much. Villiers' brother passed on my bounty to Villiers. Villiers had a whisper with his master. That was enough.

None of this makes James's catamite my friend. More likely, the opposite.

Can Stukeley mean that the tobacco money – gifted deviously to this toad Steenie, Duke of Buckingham – might purchase for me a trial in London?

If so, he's even madder than Sam thinks.

Buckingham must be one of the richest and most powerful knaves in the kingdom by now. He's unlikely to need the proceeds from my cousin's sale of twenty-five hundredweight of tobacco!

Stukeley is running about like a rat in a granary. Haste, haste, he says. He must perform his duty for the Council. Horses? A closed carriage? Which would I prefer? All shall be just as I wish. But – I *do* understand, don't I? – it is incumbent upon him that we set forth for London without delay. He trots up and down stairs, reciting all the great ones' names like a Papist going over his rosary: The Lord Archbishop of Canterbury, the Lord Chancellor, the Lord Privy Seal, the Lord Chamberlain, the Earl of Arundel, the Baron Clapton, Mr Treasurer, Mr Vice Chamberlain, Mr Secretary Naunton, the Lord Archbishop of Canterbury, the Lord Chancellor, the Lord –

The Lord help us. Amen.

I just interrupted his devotions to tell him that I elect for two closed carriages. Which surprised my dear cousin.

'You once told me you thought they were hell-carts!'

'That was before I sailed half the world over and back. I am an invalid, Sir Lewis. You don't require a corpse to deliver to their Lordships?'

'No, no! Of course not! Two carriages . . .'

I travel in the first with my keeper and Captain Sam King.

Manourie, Robin, and the Indian in the second.

My cousin's outriders, naturally, in close attendance.

But I have my own plan now.

An alternative plot.

And there are somewhat larger surprises in store for Sir Lewis Stukeley.

42

I made sure we didn't travel far on Saturday. All afternoon, I complained that I felt cold. Since the weather was exceedingly hot, and our carriage airless, cousin Lewis was soon regarding me with considerable consternation. We spent the Saturday night at a Mr Drake's. I demanded a fire in my chamber, warming pans for my bed.

On the Sunday we passed on to Sherborne. I sat huddled in a corner of the carriage, rugs muffled right up to my ears. Stukeley sought to enliven me with conversation. The idiot has about as much tact as a Spanish man-o'-war. Didn't I feel some twinge of *regret*, says he, to be so near to the great house which was once my own? Didn't I wish to look out and across the River Yeo? To see those tall towers, three storeys high, and the fine corner turrets I had built with stone transported from the old castle? I shook my head. My teeth chattered. I conveyed to him that I could scarcely see his face where he sat opposite. (In fact, Sam distracting the fool's attention with much detail on the subject of tropical diseases, I did manage to sneak one glance through half-closed eyelids, looking down over the parklands to the Lodge. The cedars I planted a quarter of a century ago have grown quite tall. I brought those young trees home with me from Virginia. When my cousin looked back at me again, it was not hard to be found weeping. Sam told him: 'Another symptom of malaria.')

The Sunday night was spent at the Sign of the George.

Today, Monday, Sir Lewis instructed the coachman to go faster. I protested that each rut and bump in the highway drove hot pokers through my bones. At the same time, I asked for Sam's cloak. I was freezing, I said. Sweat poured down my face, of course. I compelled

317

my teeth to chatter. Stukeley leaned forwards once or twice as if to touch my forehead, then thought better of it. 'These tropical chills and fevers, are they infectious?' he asked nervously. I pretended that I could not hear him. That I had gone deaf. 'Infection?' Sam growled. 'Infection's not in it. *Contagious!* That's the word. I've seen men rot alive who've just knocked on the door where such plagues have a household in thrall.' My cousin stuffed his kerchief in his mouth. Later, Sam put his hand gingerly to my thick-beaded brow. 'Sweet Jesu!' he remarked. 'As cold as death!'

Torn between fear of disease and fear of the wrath of the Privy Council, Sir Lewis passed a most miserable day, one eye on me and the other on his pocket-watch. He managed to keep the coachman up to his work. We journeyed thirty-five miles. We are now at the White Hart in Salisbury.

Stukeley plans to leave here tomorrow. We shall do no such thing. I intend to stay here until Saturday. Here is my reason:

Before we left Plymouth I took the trouble to send Sam in search of news concerning the King's summer progress. For it appears that he took poor dead Winwood's advice in this matter. Like Queen Elizabeth, he now shows himself to his people. Not anything like as liberally, of course. But, in summer, James flaunts about England from city to city, waving his dirty hands a little to encourage the mob, then retreating for some sport with his hawks and his hounds and his Villiers.

And this Saturday his Majesty comes to Salisbury.

I shall confront him, if I can. I shall beg for an audience of the King. A single opportunity to speak to him, face to face.

God knows, I have no hopes that anything will come of it.

I remember the first (and last) time I met him, in 1603. He was journeying slowly south from Edinburgh to London, in the direction of his coronation, but in no haste to arrive in time for Elizabeth's funeral. I took horse to pay court to him. We met at Northampton. I saw that he detested me from the start. 'Sir Walter Ralegh,' the herald announced. To which James of Scotland responded: 'Rawley? Aye, Rawley indeed! True enough! On my soul, I think *rawly* of you, mon!' Perhaps I should have laughed. Or smiled. I didn't. Within four months, he had me locked in the Tower.

But I want to see my destroyer before I die.

And I want to see him seeing me.

He'll have my head soon enough.

I want only his face.

The King's eyes. The King's ears. That's what I require. I'm not going to waste my time these next few days. I propose to pen some brief *Apology* for my voyage to Guiana. If his Majesty will not take notice, then the Privy Council may. And if not the Privy Council, then posterity. If I am allowed a trial, I shall use what I write as my defence. If no trial is permitted me, I might still find I can publish it from the scaffold. If that scaffold is in Spain –? Then no one will understand a word I say! (I refuse to quit this world spouting in the tongue of my enemies . . .) Yet, even then, though I am choked to death in Madrid, my written words will stand, they shall speak for me in London, my voice will be heard. At all events, I must seize this final chance to set the record straight, to present my own case clearly before history, to die upright in the truth like a downright man.

Hence all this counterfeit of sickness. My shammed fevers and chills in the coach were merely the prelude.

As soon as we arrived here at Salisbury, I lay down on my bed. I groaned. I moaned. I coughed up blebs of blood (never difficult).

Stukeley hovered anxiously in the doorway. I complained with bitterness of the day's long journey. He offered to bring me broth. I said I could not possibly sup it. I turned my face to the wall. I pretended to sleep. After a while, I heard him go tiptoe down the stair. I had banked on his stomach calling him to supper.

Manourie came immediately to my chamber. (Sam had instructed him.) I told the little Frenchman I wanted no more sleeping draughts. I asked if his knowledge of medicine extended to emetics. Something to make me vomit, that's what I needed. He recommended a certain root, *euphorbia corollata*. He promised he could procure this for me by tomorrow morning. I thanked him, swore him to secrecy, and gave him three gold sovereigns.

No sooner had Manourie gone, than Stukeley came back. He was

319

gnawing pigeon pies. He had a tray of them. He set his tray down in the doorway, covering the pies with a cloth, to avoid infection.

'Are you feeling any better, cousin?' he whispered.

By way of answer, I gave him a fright. I lurched up from the bed, drumming with my clenched fists against my skull. Then I staggered across the room, fell down, got up again, blundered towards the door as if half-blind, hands groping for him. Sir Lewis Stukeley retreated in alarm. I managed to stamp on his pigeon pies before falling once more, most violently, so that my head struck a post of the gallery which runs past my chamber.

Stukeley fled, shouting.

He fetched the Indian to get me back to bed. I heard him explaining to Sam King and Robin that it was better this way. No Christian soul should run the risk of such plague.

I have told the Indian my plan. For the first time in our acquaintance, he seems amused. Sam King will have told Robin what to do.

I shall snatch a few hours' sleep now.

These have been dress rehearsals.

Tomorrow I must launch on the great performance.

43

Perfect.

I rose early this morning, stripped naked to my shirt, then got down on all fours like Nebuchadnezzar, crawling about the bedroom, scratching the rushes strewn upon the planks, stuffing them into my mouth, pretending to eat them.

The Indian went running for Robin. Robin came, saw, gave an excellent scream, and ran to Stukeley's room. My cousin, still in nightcap and nightgown, took one peep around my door, then sent for Manourie. Manourie brought me the emetic. I swallowed it down in one gulp. I allowed Sam and the Indian to carry me back to my bed.

I lay as if dead for some minutes. Then I yelled out, and drew up my arms and legs in a knot, as if having a fit of convulsions.

'Contractions of the sinews,' Sam King said. 'That's always the next stage. I've seen it often.'

'He'll strangle to death!' Stukeley cried. 'He'll swallow his tongue! You must do something!'

'I don't care to *touch* him,' Sam remarked. 'The Admiral is too far gone. At this point, the contagion –'

'Gloves!' Stukeley shouted. 'Boy, you'll find gloves on my dresser!'

Robin raced off obediently, flicking the feather in his cap.

'Not the kid gloves!' cousin Lewis screeched down the gallery, as an afterthought. 'Not my *best* gloves . . . The ones to the left of the ewer . . .'

Robin came panting back. He delivered a great pair of padded buff gloves to Stukeley. Stukeley thrust them at Sam King. Sam put them on. They came up to his elbows. He looked like a lobster.

Sam caught my right leg in his lobster claws. I let him straighten it. But as soon as he caught at my left leg, I bent up the right one again. He tried seizing both legs at once. I threshed out with my arms. Sam went reeling.

'You, fellow, help the man!' cousin Lewis shouted at the Indian.

I was jerking about in all directions. I was coughing and choking.

The Indian stood stock-still. He stared at me impassively, jaws chewing.

'In the name of King James!' Stukeley roared. 'I command you to assist him!'

The Indian turned his head. He assumed a most innocent frown.

'Master,' piped Robin. 'The gentleman from Guiana can't understand you. He doesn't know English, you see. Can you tell him in Spanish?'

Stukeley snorted. Then he tried a few phrases in execrable *French*. Manourie blinked at him. My cousin blushed purple. The Indian didn't budge.

Stukeley grabbed at the Indian's arm. He propelled him in the direction of the bed, where Sam was now once again wrestling to fasten my feet to the trestle. Stukeley performed antics with his hands, to demonstrate to the Indian what he wanted done. The Indian gave a deep grunt, as of sudden comprehension. He nodded eagerly. Then thumped Stukeley on the back. My dear cousin went down like a ninepin.

'But, master,' shrilled Robin, 'the gentleman from Guiana has no gloves! Shall I go for them? The kid pair on your dresser?'

'*Gloves?*' Stukeley shouted. '*Gloves for a savage!* Why should he need gloves, you idiot, you nincompoop? He's a heathen! It's not as if he has a *soul* to lose!'

Grinning happily, my 'soulless' friend Christoval Guayacunda helped my other friend Sam to straighten out my limbs. When they'd finished, I was spreadeagled on the bed like poor St Andrew. They used cords for my ankles and wrists. Sam fixed a spoon in my mouth.

'That's better,' said Stukeley. 'At least, he can't swallow his tongue now.'

I kept very still, but made my eyes roll.

Masking his mouth with his nightcap, my cousin reviewed the situation. 'We shall carry him into the carriage,' he decided. 'It's the only solution. We *must* continue our journey to London. Their honourable Lordships –'

'What?' growled Sam. 'Bed and all?'

Stukeley drew himself erect. 'I have my duty.'

'But the bed will not fit in the carriage . . .'

'I shall consult with mine host. I am sure a *larger* carriage can be found. Of course, no one must be in it, save Sir Walter. And this Indian. It doesn't matter about him. I can ride alongside. That's the answer!'

He scuttled to the door. He checked. Two afterthoughts.

'Prepare your strongest sleeping draught,' he told Manourie.

'And burn those gloves outdoors,' he told Sam King.

I pride myself: I had foreseen this possibility.

As soon as Stukeley was gone, Manourie hurried off too. The little Frenchman came back swiftly, not with a sleeping draught, but with a composition of his own, which I had required of him. God knows what the stuff was. It tasted worse than bilge water. But it worked within the hour. Its effect was to make me look horrible and loathsome outwardly, without offending my principal parts, or leaving me inwardly sick. He painted my face with more of this odious physic. By the time that Sir Lewis returned, I was all pimpled and blistered. Robin held up a glass to my visage. I never saw anything so awesome! Each pimple and blister was black, having in the middle a tiny pustule of foul yellow, with a purple rash radiating about it. The rest of my skin looked inflamed with a terrible heat.

Robin hid the glass when he heard my cousin's footfalls approaching.

I lay back on the bed. I panted heavily.

'This afternoon,' Stukeley announced, coming into the chamber. 'The carriage will be ready by –'

The words died in his throat. He stared down at me.

'Christ have mercy!' he gurgled. 'What is this?'

'*Soit*,' murmured Manourie. '*Ainsi soit-il.*' He crossed himself. '*Gardez bien, Milord, gardez bien!*' He pointed at me. '*C'en est fait . . . La lèpre!*'

'*Leprosy!*'

'Looks like it,' grunted Sam. 'Shall we pray?'

323

If my dear cousin prayed for me, then he did it running. I doubt if he prayed much. He ran like hell.

I left nothing to chance. I did not rest on my leprous laurels.

I guessed Stukeley might well seek a second medical opinion. He did. He went further. He sought a second, and a third, and then a fourth . . .

By late afternoon, two doctors from Salisbury had visited my sick room. They examined me, confessed themselves baffled, but advised against moving me. In a tumult of fear of the Council, Sir Lewis then sent one of his men to Winchester. This man returned here this evening, bringing with him the Bishop of Winchester's personal physician. (May God preserve my Lord Bishop in good health – that quack certainly can't!)

Mind you, I pulled out all the stops for this last fellow, having been warned by Sam that the man was a Bachelor of Physic, no less. I got Manourie to give me a urinal in my bed, which urinal's glass he had rubbed inside with some chemical. I made water in the presence of the Bishop's quack. When he held it up to the light it was bible-black in colour, and gave off a stench like a charnel. He turned as white as chalk, and dropped the lot. At the same time, by a stroke of good fortune, Manourie's emetic worked its trick. I couldn't stop the vomits. My bowels opened. The Bachelor of Physic didn't tarry.

Later, Robin reported to me that he had eavesdropped behind a curtain and heard the final diagnosis delivered to Stukeley. My disease was undoubtedly mortal, the Bachelor said. He would ask the Lord Bishop to pray for me. Only heaven might know of a remedy. Robin says my cousin begged the Bachelor to petition the Bishop for prayers for him too. 'To save me from this leprosy!' he begged. 'And then to preserve me from the Privy Council and his Majesty's fury!' The Bachelor promised he would. He advised cousin Lewis to enter into my room no more than he was bound to by the demands of love and friendship.

And so I have been left to die in peace.

I have everything a dying man requires. A ream of paper. Pen and ink. A leg of mutton and three loaves (smuggled in by Manourie just now). A pitcher of good cold water. Four *khoka* leaves.

I asked the Indian for the leaves, and he gave them gladly. I shall use them to keep myself awake.

It is now one o'clock in the morning of Wednesday, the 29th of July. I can hear the hours as they sound on the clock of the Cathedral Church of St Mary. That cathedral has the tallest spire in England. May its shadow *in*spire me, by moonlight, by sunlight, in the task that lies ahead!

I have only three days.

Three days to justify myself before God and the King.

On Saturday, James comes.

May God not come before him!

I turn to my virgin paper. I begin –

44

I am finished.

It's no good. It won't do. I know it's no good. It's worse than useless. It will have to serve. It cannot serve. I've done it. I'm done for.

Forty pages.

Some 12,000 words.

Working non-stop for three nights without sleep. Sustained and kept awake by the *khoka* leaves. By day, lying moaning and groaning on my bed for the benefit of cousin Lewis or his spies sent to my keyhole. Refusing food. Acting mad as the prophet David when in company. Scribbling furiously by candlelight when they've all gone away for their hours of sleeping.

Forty pages, I've written.

12,000 words – I've just read them over, every one.

And it's hopeless. It's confused. It's worse than confused.

Stuttering, hectic, rambling, disordered, deranged.

O, it's all there. Long descriptions of the ends and events of my voyage. All about Keymis and the mine and the death of my son. How Guiana was rightly Elizabeth's and now must be James's. What my captains did. What I did. With reasons for everything.

Why, then, do those reasons seem reasonless? Why's the thing such a jumble?

For it sounds like the ravings of a madman. Nothing more. Nothing less.

Am I like Shakespeare's Prince of Denmark? (I hated that play when Ben Jonson brought me the quarto to read in the Tower. But perhaps we most hate what reminds us of ourselves in other men's thoughts and behaviour?) Hamlet counterfeited madness to escape all suspicion that he might threaten danger to the king. Then he became what he pretended. Is that my fate? And everyman's? We *are* what we pretend to be. There is no difference. Distinction breaks down. No gap between the soul and the soul's acts.

Forty pages of insensate histrionics!

Couched in a style like a leper's sores! Pure pus!

Carew, read only its beginning.

How I laboured at this beginning –

It's better (perhaps) than the rest . . .

Sir Walter Ralegh's Large Apology for the ill success of his Enterprise to Guiana

If the ill success of this enterprise of mine had been without example, I should have needed a large discourse, and many arguments for my justification. But if the vain attempts of the greatest Princes of Europe (both amongst themselves and against the Turk, and in all modern histories left to every eye to peruse) have miscarried, then it is not so strange that myself, being but a private man, and drawing after me the chains and fetters wherewith I had been thirteen years tied in the Tower, being unpardoned and in disgrace with my Sovereign King, have by other men's errors failed in the attempt I undertook.

For if that Charles the Fifth returned with unexampled losses (I will not say dishonour) from Algier in Africa –

If King Sebastian lost himself and his army in Barbary –

If the invincible fleet and force of Spain in '88 were beaten home by the Lord Charles Howard, Admiral of England –

If Monseigneur Strozzi and the Count Brissac, and others, with a fleet of fifty-eight sail and 6000 soldiers encountered against far less numbers could not defend the Terceres –

And, leaving to speak of a world of other attempts furnished by kings and princes, if Sir Francis Drake, Sir John Hawkins, and Sir Thomas Baskerville (men for their experience and valour as eminent as England had any), strengthened with divers of her Majesty's ships, and those filled with soldiers at will, could not possess themselves of the treasure they sought for, which in their view was embarked in certain frigates at Puerto Rico –

If afterwards they were repulsed by fifty negroes upon the mountain of Vasques Numius, or Sierra de Capra, and failed in all their passages towards Panama –

If Sir John Norris, although not by any fault of his, in the attempt on Lisbon returned (by sickness and other casualties) with the loss of 8000 men –

What wonder is it but that mine is the least? – Being followed with a company of voluntaries, who for the most part had neither seen the sea nor the wars, who (some forty gentlemen excepted) had with me the very scum of the world, drunkards, blasphemers, and suchlike, as their fathers, brothers, and friends thought it an exceeding good gain to be discharged of, with the hazard of some thirty, forty, or fifty pounds, knowing they could not live one whole year so good cheap at home –

I say: What wonder is it that I have failed? – Where I could neither be present myself, nor had any of the Commanders whom I might trust living, or in state to supply my place . . .

That will do. That will do to show you that it *won't* do. Notice the careful sly praise of my Lord Admiral Howard (as if the old walrus had defeated the Armada by himself!). And the sickly excuses for Norris, that porcine incompetent (but he's still alive, you see – unlike his 8000 men – still grunting and grouting around in the foul sty of his Majesty's favour).

It's rotten. It stinks. I despise my own right hand for writing it. I should do what Cranmer did. He thrust his right hand first into the flames, when Queen Mary had him martyred, because that hand was the one that had signed certain 'recantations' of his 'heresies' when he trembled in fear of the stake.

I have written no lies. But neither have I written the whole truth. How could I? How put into words – for instance – what I have learned (and not learned) from the Indian? The truth is: The truth is somehow knowable, but untellable. Or, if unknowable, only to be approached by the cancelling out of one ignorance after another. Or, if tellable, only to be related in some attempt to do justice to various momentary patterns made by the wind of the mind in those shifting desert sands which constitute the heart.

The truth is: I don't know what I'm talking about!

Too burnt-out to know. Too cracked and breathless to tell.

328

Must sleep now.

Dreams, mend my broken brain! My wasted spirit!

Can't sleep. Oblivion is denied me. My pulse races. My eyes in the mirror are red and raw. It must be because of those damned *khoka* leaves. I shall never consume them again. Well, there's no need now. There is nothing left for me to stay awake for.

The clock of the cathedral is striking three. It will be light soon enough. His Majesty will come. God save the King! God save Sir Walter Ralegh!

This book, with all its confusions, its doubts, its perplexities, its tracking back and forth in a trackless waste – this book makes a more honest shape of the truth than my accursed *Apology*. I can still perceive that, just about. What a joke. What magnificent irony. For King James and the Privy Council would have me crucified upside-down on a Spanish sheepcote if certain pages of it fell into their hands. And Carew (for whom it was started)? And Bess (for whom I must finish it)? I could understand and forgive them for desiring me some fate far worse than that.

'Simplicity is the hardest thing.' I said it. I said it to a bricklayer burying his son like a dog. He cheated me. Keymis cheated me. Wollaston, Whitney, Gondomar, Head, my cousin. Essex and Cecil. Parker and North and old Berrio. Elizabeth, James, that refiner. Coke. Cobham. The preacher – O but the line of them is like Macbeth's, it could stretch out to the crack of doom . . . All cheats, all liars, all hypocrites, from prince to poor, from high estate to low. And myself? I am the biggest cheat, the most self-deceiving liar, the whitest of whited sepulchres. I am the man who didn't even dig a dog's grave for his son. 'Simplicity is the hardest thing.' I said it. And I should know. Because I haven't got it. I never had it. The voyage of my destiny was always in the deep, the cunning, the complicated waters. I have not lived simply. How can I dare to presume that I deserve to die the death of a simple man? To die well one must have loved well. I do not think that I have ever loved at all.

Neither King James nor the Privy Council will pay heed to my

Apology. The futility, the humiliation of it! Of defending oneself before men who are bent on one's utter destruction!

I must snatch some sleep. My brains are bled.

Here's one sentence in my scribble that makes sense:

'As good success admits of no examination of errors, so the contrary allows of no excuse.'

I can see Francis Bacon drawing a fine spidery line under that for his Majesty.

And King James will be graciously grateful.

It means he does not need to read the rest.

45

Stukeley just sent word that we move on *instantly*.

He still hasn't seen through my ruse. Sam and the Indian are to bear me out on my mattress and deposit the 'leper' in a vast black hearse of a carriage specially prepared.

Will Sir Lewis ride in front and ring a bell?

No time for witticisms. The bare facts.

We shall progress towards London at a snail's pace. I have my kinsman's promise. Every care and comfort to be afforded me. *By order of his Majesty the King!*

Amen.

Just so.

In other words: Cousin Lewis has been in contact with King James. And King James has commanded him to remove me from Salisbury before the royal entourage arrives here.

His Majesty won't meet me.

His Majesty is determined never again to set eyes on me.

Perhaps I should feel flattered?

It cannot be merely my 'sickness' which strikes fear in that little sovereign heart.

Twenty crowns.

I just handed Doctor Manourie twenty crowns in pistolets, for his physical receipts, and in payment for the victuals he bought me.

More. He has smuggled out my *Apology* in his bag. He undertakes to put that desperate document into the hands of Sir Edward Pelham, my Lord Leicester's old attendant, now resident here close by the banqueting hall.

I knew Pelham in Ireland. I saved his life once, when we were attacked at a ford by a pack of Irish kerns.

He will get those ravelled writings delivered to the King.

For all the good they will do . . .

Manourie has proved himself a godsend. What with his vomits and his powders. God knows what I'd have done without the aid of this weird chemical fellow, this obliging little Frenchman with big ears and the bony beak from which stiff red hairs sprout down like wires.

For his part he seems to have formed quite an attachment to me. Our jape at the expense of my cousin delights him. He can't stop chuckling when we're on our own.

Of course, I am paying him well for his devotion. That helps. He is poor. He looks starving. He tells terrible tales of conditions endured on the French merchant ships. I must seem like a saviour to him. And there's nothing like hard cash for making good cement in the mortar of friendship.

The Frenchman asked me what I'd do if my *Apology* fails – which it will – to save me my life.

I told him the truth: *I don't know.*

Stukeley's trotting hoof-falls in the gallery!

Must stop now –

All writ in greatest haste –

46

At Andover.

We have rested here two nights.

This morning we move on to Hertfordbridge.

My cousin (whatever his reasons) is keeping his promise. We travel by easy stages. The Indian sits by my bed in the carriage.

I am still undecided what to do.

Last night Sam said to me: 'I wish you had boarded the French vessel.'

'To live in dishonour?' I snapped.

'Better that than to *die* in dishonour,' Sam said.

Then I told him what Stukeley had told me. That I might not be sent to Spain for execution. That I might even be granted some sort of hearing in London. That Howard and Buckingham could help. Every word that I uttered rang hollow.

'Stukeley's mad,' Sam said. 'Admiral, I wish you'd gone to France.'

And, at dawn this Monday morning, Manourie.

The same sentiments more volubly expressed.

He felt sure that my Sovereign Lord misprized me. He could not comprehend why I was treated so. Worse, in his eyes, that I allowed myself to be ruined. Especially when *his* Sovereign Lord would make me welcome. He rattled off some French proverb: '*Il vaut mieux plier que rompre.*' Better to bend than to break, that's what it meant.

'Milord Ralegh, why should you be broken in Spain when you could live out your last days in glory in France?'

I disliked this talk of bending, but let it go.

333

I asked him for mandragora. That I might sleep in the coach. Also to blunt my own anguish (though I didn't tell him this).

For the fact is – my *Apology* being worthless – there's a voice in some part of me whispering that Sam and Dr Manourie are right.

An old friend and a new friend, unknown to each other, each urging the same course.

The coward's course?

Or the course of a man brave enough to spurn fear of his own cowardice, be master not victim of his destiny, and accept that he might still have some duty: *To live?*

Mist steaming off the rooftops I can see from my window. The sky is a lake of pure cool blue. Robin just brought me a fistful of flowers plucked from the banks of the River Anton. The morning dew has given them new hearts.

Monday night.

I did not drink that drowsy syrup.

My mind was made up for good by the afternoon.

Sir Walter Ralegh refuses to die as Guattaral. He condemns himself to life as Guattaral instead.

I shall take Sam's advice, and the Frenchman's.

Give Stukeley the slip.

Escape to France!

We are put up at the inn in Hertfordbridge. I just called my friends to my room. The Indian guarded the door. I told them my decision. Robin clapped his hands with joy. I bade him to be silent. Then I addressed myself in a whisper, first to Manourie, then to Sam, saying that what I now proposed was quite impossible without their help. Being once more assured that each was only too eager to offer it, I outlined my plan.

To Manourie I said: 'Give me more of your abominable physic. I must keep up this pretence that I am a leper. I intend to petition my cousin to advise the Council that it would be best, in these circumstances, to grant me leave to go to my wife's house in Broad Street. They will insist, of course, that he stays with me as my keeper. But if he thinks me very feeble, and full up to the eyebrows with infection, then his guard won't be too close, with any luck. I shall escape out of the hands of this Sir Lewis Stukeley by a back-door!'

Manourie nodded. 'May I attend you in your flight? If I remain in England, they might hang me!'

'Of course.' I paused, having no wish to insult him. But I know he is poor, and in need of employment, so I went on. 'I would be gratified if you would continue in my service once we are safe in France. I can promise you £50 a year for the rest of your life.'

He grasped my hand.

I cut short his stutterings of gratitude.

Then I turned to Sam King.

'Sam, I shall get Stukeley's permission for you to go on ahead of us to Broad Street. I will say that Bess needs warning before she sees me in my leprous state.'

'And if Stukeley does not grant it?'

'Then just ride! Either way, with or without my cousin's consent. Ride like the wind! And not to Broad Street! Ride first to Gravesend. Hire a vessel. Swear her master to secrecy. Instruct him to have her prepared to sail for France on the morning tide next Monday.'

Sam grinned. He clasped my hand. He nodded his approval.

'Take money from my red leathern coffer in the corner,' I instructed. 'Help yourself. Take plenty. Choose your captain with care.'

'Jack Leigh,' Sam said thoughtfully. 'Once your boatswain.'

'Excellent. You know he is still at Gravesend?'

'By Windmill Hill.'

'And his vessel?'

'The *Greyhound*. A ketch.'

'Very well. But take no chances. Charter her in your own name. You can say that you want to avoid partaking in my punishment.'

Sam shook his head. 'Old Jack will see straight through that.'

I hesitated. 'But he will not betray us?'

'Never. He's straight as a die. All the same, I shan't mention your name. I'll tell him only that certain other gentlemen of the *Destiny* intend to fly. Men who have reason to believe that King James wants their blood. Men who distinguished themselves by their loyalty to you.'

'And if he requires a list of these fine fellows?'

Sam stroked his great moustaches where they compassed his mouth. Then his lips turned up. 'I shall put you down as a Mr Richard Head!'

I was grateful to my old companion for making me laugh. I gave him further instructions to hurry back to Broad Street from Gravesend, in order to inform Bess of my coming, to forewarn her indeed that my leper's appearance is no cause for alarm, and to assure her that within a few days all shall be just as she wishes and her husband safe in France.

Robin fretted. 'What do *I* do?'

'Ah,' I said. 'Yours is the most subtle part! On the night of our escape you go to Stukeley. You take your gamba with you. You praise his musicianship. You ask for a lengthy lesson. You make certain he gets drunk.'

Robin liked this. He thought of clapping his hands again, then thought better of it.

Manourie said: 'I shall prepare a strong sleeping draught you can put in his wine.'

The four of us shared a laugh that was pure satisfaction.

I believe I'll sleep well tonight.

And no need for mandragora.

47

Yesterday morning, well-pimpled, thick-blistered, and having tied a silk ribbon about my arms to distemper my pulse, I sent word down by Robin to Stukeley, requesting that for pity and kinship's sake he allowed me one more day and night to rest at Hertford-bridge, and that he might while we were there ask licence from the Privy Council to let him deliver me to Broad Street until such time as I was claimed by Gondomar.

A few minutes later, my cousin appeared in plump person at my chamber door.

He was sucking an oyster.

'Sir Walter,' he declared. 'Consider it done!'

'My weary bones –'

'Yes, yes. You must rest them.'

'And the other matter? The Council? You think they will permit it?'

Stukeley raised the first two fingers of his left hand, crossed together. 'The Lord Admiral and myself . . . We are like that.'

'You are kind to me, cousin.'

'I am your friend. If only you would see! But I allow for your present sickness distorting your judgement.'

I nodded my head weakly. 'Sir Lewis, a further boon. Lady Ralegh – she will not be prepared for the hideous sight I must present. Also, as an invalid, I shall require a room in the house where there's no risk of infecting her. May I send my man King on to London ahead of us? To forewarn her? And to break the news gently?'

Stukeley spread his hands wide in a gesture that aped huge benevolence.

'Why not?' he said.

'I thank you, cousin.'

Stukeley guzzled the oyster.

'Do not despair,' he advised me cheerfully. 'Your sickness makes you look on the black side.'

'What is the white side, Sir Lewis?'

'That Gondomar's demand will be rejected by his Spanish masters. If I was a betting man, I'd be wagering heavily on it.'

'And the odds against my having a trial?'

Stukeley was peering about for somewhere to dispose of his oyster shell. I pointed at my chamber pot. He took careful aim. He missed.

Then he said: 'I'll be honest with you, as always. The Council may want a trial, but the King will not. He'll be remembering your eloquence at Winchester. There was one of his Scotch friends who heard you then. He said that before the trial he would have gone a hundred miles to see you hanged. But, after, he would have gone a thousand to save your life. Of course, his Majesty is very unpredictable. But I must say I reckon it's odds on – he's frightened of your tongue; he won't permit you to use it in public at a trial.'

I indulged myself in a furious bout of coughing.

My cousin stepped back into the gallery. He covered his mouth with his sleeve.

I croaked after him: 'I *am* a betting man, Sir Lewis, and I think your reading of the probabilities is exact. I'd wager all that tobacco money on it!'

'Then you would win your wager, but lose your life.' Stukeley took a quick nervous glance up and down the gallery. There was evidently no one in sight save the Indian, for he added in a piercing whisper: 'There's a better thing to do with the tobacco money, and you know it.'

He waited, shifting from one foot to the other.

I said nothing.

Stukeley shrugged his padded shoulders. Then he went.

Sam was gone on his errand by yesterday noon.

This morning, Wednesday, we resumed our funereal progress. In the carriage, I told the Indian of my plan. I spoke low, and in Spanish. Stukeley, riding at the window, could not even have

338

known I was talking. I am sure of it. There was wind, and some driving rain to chasten at last this intolerable summer. I was pleased to see my dear cousin getting soaked to the skin.

The Indian expressed no surprise at my change of heart. If he felt disapproval, he did not show it. He sat hunched in silence for a long while. Then he said: 'Will Guattaral take me with him?'

I said I would.

I was feeling quite satisfied with myself by the time that we got here to Staines. The hostelry is clean. I had taken action. Once more I observe how simply to take any action, however desperate or risky, can serve to lift my spirits. As if I am a clock. I need to strike! It is the slow descent of the weight of my thoughts which depresses me. Then I swing to and fro like a pendulum locked in a case. And the winding up is hard, and the decision to apply the key harder. But once I have done it – and the chimes come – what relief!

Just now I asked Robin to fetch me some cold turkey to my chamber. I was eating it, when Stukeley came to the door. He didn't knock. The Indian followed him in.

'So your appetite has returned,' my cousin remarked.

I gave a long sigh of fatigue. I handed my plate back to Robin. Only half the cold turkey was gone. I could have done with the rest of it.

'The worst must be passed,' Stukeley said.

'I hope so. Dr Manourie does his best.'

'Yes, indeed,' said my cousin. 'An excellent type – for a Frenchman. I never trust froggies myself, but that one seems decent enough. His appearance, of course, is disgusting. What on earth ate that hole in his hat?'

'I never judge my doctors by their hats.'

Stukeley chuckled. He seemed in uncommonly good humour. His fat boyish cheeks were flushed pink. I guessed that he'd warmed himself well with ale or wine, the better to forget his ride in the rain.

'I trust you sleep soundly, Sir Walter.'

'And you, cousin Lewis, and you.'

'Me?' He slapped his thick sides. 'Oh, I always sleep as sound as any log. I have a little recipe. Infallible. I play my violin. That sends me off.'

'Heaven is music,' I observed.

He beamed. 'Just so. You have such a way with words. I envy you. "Heaven is music." God, I wish I could come out with things like that . . .'

'Sir Lewis, it was only a quotation.'

He scowled. 'Shakespeare again, eh?'

'No. Thomas Campion.'

He brightened up. 'Ah, Campion. Campion is a doctor, is he not?'

'I believe he is. But I have not seen his hat.'

Stukeley emitted a high-pitched screech of laughter. 'Your wit has returned too,' he cried. 'Why, you'll soon be yourself again, Sir Walter.' He turned to go. 'All the same, we shall rest here two nights.'

This suits me fine. I murmured gratitude.

'Think nothing of it,' my cousin said.

I think plenty of it, and not all good. Stukeley's excess of joviality is somehow disturbing. I even wonder if my meat was poisoned . . .

48

My meat wasn't poisoned.

But I was right to feel misgivings.

Things have changed.

When I woke this morning there were four figures seated around my bed. Two were familiar: Robin and the Indian. The other two were a couple of Stukeley's men.

Robin said: 'Master, we could not prevent this. Your cousin insisted –'

I waved my hand, cautioning silence.

I addressed the Indian in Spanish. 'What does this mean?'

'I don't know,' he replied. 'Nor do I know if either of these watchdogs can bark in this tongue.'

My eyes flickered over the intruders. They sat with stony expressions, their hands on their knees. But one had a faint spot of anger staining his forehead. I guessed that he spoke Spanish, and had not much cared for this reference to him as a watchdog.

I lay silent for a while. Then I told Robin I'd like some breakfast. He brought it. My cousin came close on his heels.

'You slept well, Sir Walter?'

'I slept better than I woke. These fellows of yours, they take my air. Why are they here? Why all this extra diligence?'

Stukeley was biting his fingernails. He seemed embarrassed. 'To make sure you don't escape me, you traitor!' he cried in a loud voice. Then he turned to his minions. 'I relieve you of your duty,' he said. 'Go and get something to eat. The rogue can't run while I am here to watch him.'

He ordered Robin and the Indian to leave also.

341

When he had checked that no one remained in the gallery, he approached my bed, smiling. 'Cousin Walter,' he said, 'I apologize.'

'For calling me names?'

Stukeley winked. 'That was for their benefit. You understand? Listen, I beg you, listen carefully. I swear as I hope to see God that what I say is true. I have no choice in this matter of guards being posted in your chamber. Word was sent in the night. From the King!'

'Not from the Privy Council?'

'From King James himself! From Salisbury! By personal messenger. Express orders. I am not to let you out of my surveillance night or day.'

'His Majesty is most solicitous,' I murmured.

'Cousin, forgo this sarcasm. We have no time for it.'

'What *do* we have time for, Sir Lewis?'

'For France,' Stukeley hissed. 'For France! For freedom!'

'You would go to the Tower,' I said softly.

'No,' Stukeley said. 'I'd go with you.'

He was smiling and smiling, like a madman.

I said nothing. I watched his lips twitching in that smile.

'My God!' Stukeley cried. 'What do I have to do to prove my love for you? You realize just what going with you means? I am Vice Admiral of Devon. That's worth £600 a year in itself. You have held such high positions in the kingdom. You know how other money tends to flow from them . . .' He sniffed. 'Of course, I'm sure you wouldn't care to see your kinsman starve.'

I thought for a while. At last, I said:

'So you are still willing to assist me? To fool your own men? Disobey the King?'

'Yes!'

'Willing even to share my life in France?'

He nodded vigorously. He smiled. His eyes were wild.

'Sir Lewis,' I said, 'would you be willing to share my *death* with me?'

I held out my right hand. It was mottled with Dr Manourie's foul pustules.

'Cousin,' I warned him, 'there could be death in that hand. The infection –'

Stukeley did not hesitate.

He grasped my one hand tight between his two.

I asked for a little more time to think things over. Cousin Lewis withdrew. My two guards and the Indian came back. I told Robin, when he came, to fetch pipe and tobacco to my bedside.

I lay smoking.

I sought to reduce my thoughts to some shape of sense.

Several long pipes later, I sent Robin to ask my cousin if Dr Manourie could come and dress my sores. And if the guards could be withdrawn to the door while this necessary office was performed. They might stand just ouside, I suggested. And I wrote on a piece of paper: 'Grant this, and the Frenchman will be sent to you with my answer.'

Stukeley must have gone through an agony of wondering over the matter. It was almost an hour before Robin returned. But, when he did, my cousin was with him. He dismissed the guards to the gallery. He insisted that the Indian and Robin go out too. Then he sent word for Manourie to come. When the Frenchman came, my cousin left us alone. 'But only for ten minutes,' he added suspiciously.

I told Manourie all that had happened. He paced up and down. He looked worried.

'*Il ne faut jamais défier un fou,*' he muttered. 'Never bid defiance to a fool.'

'My cousin is not just a fool. He is mad. And it's not just a question of defying him. I have to *trust* him now. I have no choice!'

'But once we reach your wife's house –'

I shook my head impatiently. 'With two of his men in attendance on me night and day? No. This changes everything. There is only one way I can get to Gravesend. By taking my wretched kinsman at his word.'

'You will tell him everything?'

'I will tell him enough.'

'He might kill me!'

'Don't worry. I'll say nothing about your helping me to counterfeit this sickness. In fact, he can go on believing I'm a leper. Imagine! He shook my hand!'

343

Manourie rubbed at his nose. 'You are right. He is certainly mad.'

'That was the final proof,' I said. 'My cousin is a crazy, greedy pig. But now, to be sure of escape, we have to cast pearls before him.'

The little Frenchman sighed. '*Milord, vous avez raison.* I don't like it. What do you want me to do?'

I pointed to my leathern coffer. 'There is a jewel in there. It is made in the fashion of hail, powdered with diamonds, with a ruby in the midst. Take it to him. It is worth £150. Tell him that besides that jewel, he shall have £50 in money.'

'I need say nothing else?'

'Not a word. Such things speak direct to my cousin's heart.'

Manourie bowed, and departed.

No agony for my kinsman this time. He appeared beside my bed within five minutes.

'Cousin Walter,' he said, 'you have made the right decision. I thank you for the gift. It is very fine. As for the £50, though . . .'

'That is merely a token,' I said wearily.

'Ah. I knew it!'

'As soon as you have seen me safely into France, my wife will send a further £1000.'

Stukeley smiled. 'Cousin Bess is generous. But —'

'And you may keep the tobacco money.'

Stukeley whistled. 'That's more like it! Naturally, I'm not doing this for the profit, cousin. But a man must live, eh?'

In his case, I did not perceive the necessity.

I bit my tongue.

Stukeley breathed on the jewel, then polished it busily on his doublet. 'Now, cousin,' he said proudly, 'I shall tell you how you may escape. I know a certain Frenchman call La Chesnay —'

I cut him short.

I told him I had made my own arrangements. All that was required of him was that he would not interfere. That he relaxed his close surveillance once we got to London. That he kept his mouth shut tight. That he obeyed my every order. As to the actual plan, I was selective in what I said, but I told him sufficient to make him feel confident that it had a fair chance of working. I implicated no one save Sam King. That was unavoidable.

When I had finished speaking, Stukeley nodded.

'Sir Walter, it shall all be as you wish.'

'I hope so, cousin.'

'You trust me now? At last! I am deeply honoured.'

'Well, honour is the subject of my story.'

'That sounds like another quotation, cousin.'

'Cousin, it is.'

'Dr Campion, cousin?'

'No, cousin. Mr Shakespeare.'

Stukeley kept smiling. 'I am glad to hear of something in
Shakespeare that a plain man like myself can understand. Most apt.
And it fits your great destiny, Sir Walter.' He got up to go. 'My
guards must remain with you for the present. I regret it. But we
must keep up the show. Once we reach Broad Street . . . Well, you
shall see. You can trust me, cousin.'

I could do with some usquebaugh.

I could do with some hemlock.

Honour?

Honour's a word.

And that is Shakespeare too.

I shall trust Sir Lewis Stukeley when I see the coast of France.

49

We reached Broad Street this afternoon.

Bess is here. And Carew.

Also Sam. All has gone to plan. The ketch lies off Tilbury, just twenty-five miles downriver from London Bridge.

I can hardly believe it.

One last voyage. Short and sweet.

Short follies are best.

Sweet folly of freedom.

Bess is pleased with me at last. She goes about singing. She gives it as her opinion that cousin Lewis was to be trusted from the start. Needless to say, Stukeley is much flattered. They get on handsomely together. This evening she supped with him. Partridge.

(I ate apart. I still keep up this pretence of a foul sickness, though Bess can't see why. How can I tell her that I don't share her confidence in our crazy kinsman? It would cause only disquietude. God knows I have given her enough.)

Bess says she will join me in Paris, bringing Carew, and that my nephew George has promised to assist her once they have word that I am there. I say we should lie low in some smaller place. She says anywhere they speak French and don't hang husbands!

Sam's not so pleased that Stukeley is now involved. But when Robin and Manourie told him of the watchdogs he became convinced, albeit grudgingly – as I am – that we really have no other choice at all.

That guard *has* been relaxed. The Devil only knows what Stukeley told them. I don't care. He's kept his word. He's mad. But he's kept his word.

I write this in a room by myself.

That's something.

Robin says Dr Manourie appeared at supper wearing a new hat! He's also bought himself a suit of embroidered taffeta, in the latest fashion of the Court of the King of France. He fluttered like a maypole each time he bowed to Bess (which was often, Robin says), with knots of silk ribbon whirling in all directions.

Some light relief for them, and not unwelcome.

Robin grieves and peeves. Because he now has no part to play in getting Stukeley drunk over a viol da gamba lesson. I said he could still do that in France. Only *he* should give the lesson.

The Indian is scared out of his wits by London.

The shouts in the streets. The traffic of coaches and carts. The crowds of people bustling. The taverns and shops. Spires, palaces, bells. It is all too much for him. He wept when our carriage passed through Ludgate.

This house alarms him also. So many rooms. So many corridors. So many nooks and crannies. He got lost in it. Carew heard him crying in an attic. My son took his hand and showed him the way back down the stairs.

He came in here just a moment ago, the Indian. He stalked round and round the walls, running his hands in bewilderment down the leather-bound spines of my books.

'Guattaral is a poet,' he said. 'To think that I once thought he was a pirate!'

Then he stood a long while at the window, staring down to watch the lighting of the lamps.

'Do you wish you hadn't come?' I asked him gently. 'Would you rather be at home in Sogamoso?'

He shrugged, without turning. (It's strange, how I have come to like that shrug now.) 'I was homeless at home,' he answered. 'Your London just serves to remind me this whole world is a place apart.'

He went then.

He said he would pray to his gods to attend us tomorrow.

It has to be tomorrow.

Sam King urged me to fly this very night. Jack Leigh would be prepared, he said, no trouble. Doubtless his ship, the *Greyhound*, is straining at her leash . . .

But I am too used up to escape tonight.

And tomorrow is Sunday. Sunday night the Thames will be quieter and safer.

Besides, I wanted things to work out the way they have. I need this night with Bess. I need it badly.

50

The third voyage is all over, bar the shouting.
   My destiny has come full circle.
   In my heart, did I ever expect otherwise?
   No. I didn't.
   It is exactly as I expected, to the last rank Judas kiss.

> O had Truth power, the guiltless could not fall,
> Malice, vainglory, and revenge triumph;
> But Truth alone cannot encounter all . . .

And so Sir Walter Ralegh is at home again.
At home.
In the Tower of London.
Where he belongs.

> Cold walls to you I speak, but you are senseless.

The dog returns to his vomit.
Here's what happened –

We left my wife's house in Broad Street at a minute before midnight. Conditions were perfect for escape. No moon. A thick summer fog steaming up from the river. The streets deserted. The night as black as the inside of a wolf's mouth.

We went slowly and by side ways, avoiding the great houses of Westminster. The coachman knew his London. He needed no torches. The horses' hooves were muffled. You could hardly hear the creak of a piece of harness. Perhaps he'd padded that. Or the fog served to mute it.

There were five of us crammed in that carriage: myself, the Indian, Robin, Manourie, and Stukeley. The Frenchman was wearing his absurd Parisian finery. My cousin, as usual, had dressed himself up in the sort of plumage fashionable about fifty years ago. He looked like a pregnant whore in his peascod doublet. High-heeled velvet slippers, peach-coloured. Puffed sleeves. Red garters. Slashed hose. A white wheel of a ruff round his neck. I noted that huge hideous antique sword again. He held it between his legs, his fingers playing nervously with the black hilt. I wondered aloud at the fact that, knowing my disease, he did not mind sitting opposite me. Responding, my kinsman waxed most eloquent in protestations of loyalty and love. He was only too willing, he said, to share whatever fate befell me. I had other things to worry about, so let the matter drop.

Manourie said nothing. The whole journey, he stared at the bright buckles on his shoes.

The Indian, arms folded, seemed wrapt in his own thoughts to an equal degree. Maybe more. His jaws moved all the time as he chewed on a leaf. It was so quiet you could hear when he swallowed his saliva.

Not far from my old residence, Durham House, Robin broke the silence by tugging at my sleeve and whispering that he had an urgent need to pass water. Stukeley swore. He did not want us to stop. 'Let the page piss in his breeches,' he suggested. 'We have no time to waste, sir, for such nonsense.' I reminded my cousin civilly that I was the one who was giving the orders now. Robin got down from the carriage and relieved himself while we all waited. It took a long time. Well, it seemed to. Two minutes which felt like two hours. Stukeley kept consulting his pocket-watch. I heard him pray under his breath. 'God damn that boy's kidneys,' he prayed. When poor Robin clambered back in beside me, his face was as white as any ghost's. 'I'm not frightened,' he said loudly; 'don't think that.' I assured him we had none of us supposed it. We continued on our way, a little faster.

The fog had thinned when we passed round Temple Gardens. But as soon as we began to descend the lane from Middle Temple and entered the maze of cobbled alleys which wind down to the water-front it came swirling back with a vengeance. Mist swelled up from the Thames in a pestilent cloud. It penetrated the carriage. It made me cough. Stukeley clapped a kerchief to his mouth. I smelt its perfume. An odour of pomander and pomade.

'We must be there,' my cousin spluttered, choking. 'I can tell it is Alsatia by the stink.'

I said nothing. The carriage moved on inch by inch. The horses were walking now. It was pitch dark.

'Sir Walter,' Stukeley begged, 'for Christ's sweet sake will you tell the man to stop? We'll go headlong down Whitefriars Stairs! We'll drown in the river . . .'

I leaned out of the window. I could not see the Thames. But I heard it lapping.

Then the carriage jerked to a halt at a single low word of command barked out of the fog right ahead of us.

I waited.

I heard footsteps hurrying.

One man.

The door was wrenched open from outside.

Two hands reached in to greet me.

It was Sam.

Good Sam. Faithful Sam. He had two wherries waiting. He took my arm. He guided me down Whitefriars Stairs. In fact, I could probably see a little better than the others. My eyes have still not quite forgotten the dark of the Tower. All the same, I was glad of Sam's grip. It was brotherly.

Manourie tripped and fell on a broken step. The Indian caught him. I heard my cousin ask for Robin's hand. Then, halfway down, Stukeley screeched. A rat had run over his peach slippers. We froze. But the night was as quiet as a tomb. My own feet got soaked. The water was flooding the landing stage.

Two wherries. Their watermen waiting.

Sam handed me into the first. Then he got in himself. Stukeley scrambled to take his place beside us. 'Gentlemen should go together,' he explained.

So the Indian and Robin took the second boat. The Indian had to carry Manourie in his arms. The doctor was moaning and groaning. He had twisted his ankle, he complained.

'Row,' said Sam.

The watermen rowed.

The fog began to lift as we went downriver. I sat in the stern of our wherry. I could not see the other, but I knew by the splash of its oars that it followed close behind. Sam was perched in our bows, peering forwards. My cousin had plumped himself next to me. A cork popped. He had opened a bottle of wine.

'Celebration,' I murmured, 'seems somewhat premature.'

'You think so? Well, *bon voyage*, as friend Manourie would say.' Stukeley drank.

Then he offered me the bottle.

'Thank you, no.'

'You will wait till we reach Gravesend?'

'I will wait till I reach the end of all Gravesends.'

Stukeley grunted. 'I forgot. You never drink.' He took another swig. He was guzzling greedily. 'It gives a man heart,' he declared. 'Tell me, cousin, have you never been tempted?'

'Bedlam,' I said.

'What?'

I pointed to the left bank. 'Little Bedlam. The Bridewell. The prison for madmen.'

Stukeley whistled softly through his teeth. 'You *can* see in the dark! You *are* a bat!'

'Bats go by ears and noses and sensitive wings. I can't see a thing, I assure you. I just know we must be passing by the Bridewell. You can tell by the swerve in the Thames.'

'Fancy!' My kinsman belched. 'Of course it was Bridewell *Palace* once. In King Harry's day.'

This statement seemed addressed to himself. I felt no comment was necessary. Truth to tell, I had no wish to talk with him. Sam was glancing back over his shoulder. Utter silence was best.

By the time we reached Blackfriars the fog lay in patches on the sluggish water. Our watermen kept close to the nearside bank. I could just make out the one wall still left standing of the monastery.

Stukeley drank some more wine. I was glad he had his bottle. It kept him quiet.

I looked back. The second wherry was right behind us. The night was still dark. But I made out the shape of the Indian.

Baynard's Castle has three towers. I hoped that I'd see none of

352

them. But I saw two. A wind was getting up. The fog was lifting. Those towers loomed murky against a sky now less than sable.

Puddle Wharf.

Paul's Wharf.

Queenhithe.

More wharves. More quays.

Dowgate.

Sam told the men to row faster. Their oars rose and dipped, pulled, rose again, dipped again. Bankside, and the fog was suddenly gone. Now there was a faint gleam of starlight on the drops of dripping water as the watermen feathered. By the Bear Garden, past the Rose and the Globe theatres. By Southwark, with its whorehouses and its jails.

Faster. Sam urged the men on. *Faster*.

But the men could not row any faster.

One of them blasphemed inventively. My cousin professed himself shocked. There was no need for this haste, he said. He drank some more wine. Smacked his lips.

The darkness seemed to be melting by the minute. Of course, it was not. It was night yet. But I could see the lanterns twinkling on Ebbgate. Could see. And did not want to see at all.

At least the Thames herself ran quicker now.

Ran down towards the twenty narrow arches of London Bridge.

Going under London Bridge is like shooting a rapid. The piers of the great arches are protected by timber frameworks called starlings, and these jut so closely together that the current creates its own force to rush and tumble between them in spate. You must fall all of six feet. Even by daylight, it's dangerous. At night, you need very skilful watermen.

We had them.

We shot under the Bridge without mishap.

I looked back.

The second wherry plunged after us, spinning sideways as one of its watermen had to fend with his oar to avoid direct collision with a starling.

I thought they were going to sink.

They did not.

Their oars pulled long, deep, and regularly again. They took up their position right astern of us.

I saw the Indian stand. He was raising his arms high in triumph.

'That's that,' Stukeley said. 'The worst's over.'

I suppose it was.

For him.

For me, the worst was just about to begin.

Cousin Lewis had finished his wine. He tossed the empty bottle overboard. He grabbed me by the sleeve. His face pressed close.

'Sir Walter,' he said. 'I expect you wonder why I wear these excellent clothes?'

Nothing was further from my mind. I stared at him, stupefied.

'Well, I'll tell you,' he confided. 'They're not mine, you know. At least, they are *now*. But they were not made for me.'

I could believe it. His plumpness made that doublet like a corset. The codpiece looked as tight as a chastity belt. He was like a toad about to come bursting out of its skin. All save his legs. His hose were wrinkled and baggy; he hadn't the calves for them.

'Cut by the best tailor in Cornhill,' Stukeley said proudly. 'Cost a packet, I can assure you. And that was when money *was* money. In your own dandy day.'

'Whose are they?' I asked, being curious now.

'Mine,' said Stukeley.

'Yes, yes, but you said –'

'Do you reckon me a second-hand man?' My cousin's voice, for a moment, touched hysteria. Then he calmed down. Mopped his brow with his silk handkerchief. 'Forgive me. But these clothes – they are an emblem of my honour. I did not purchase them. This suite is my *inheritance*, you see.'

'I see,' I said.

'My patrimony.'

'Yes,' I said.

Stukeley twanged the rose-red garter against his thigh. 'King Harry wore that once!'

'And the rest?' I said.

Stukeley scowled. Then he smiled. He kept on smiling. 'This garter was a gift. A token. A blessing. King Harry himself bestowed

354

it on my father. He wore it always. It was a sign, you understand. You know who my father was?'

'Captain Thomas Stukeley,' I said politely.

My cousin kept on smiling. 'Stukeley Baron Ross,' he said. 'Viscount Murrough. Earl of Wexford. Marquis of Leinster. The Duke of Ireland. My father.'

'Quite so,' I said.

There was a pause. I had to look away from my kinsman's smile. There were great vessels looming in the darkness at anchor all around us now as we made our way ever eastward through the Pool. Sam had no need to urge on the watermen. They were rowing flat out. I saw the white face of the Tower up ahead.

'These were once my father's clothes,' said Stukeley.

I said nothing.

'My father was King Harry's son,' said Stukeley.

I looked back at him. His eyes were cold and blazing, his lips still twisting in that crazy smile.

'My father was Prince Thomas,' Stukeley said.

I never met this madman, Thomas Stukeley. He ruffled it at Elizabeth's Court before my time, when I was still a penniless youth just up from the West Country. Later, I heard that his inordinate pride, his vanity, and his ambition were considered an amusement, rather than an insult to the Court. As for his titles – none of them was real. They were all of them self-assumed, or showered on him by England's enemies after he turned traitor. The Queen herself referred to him only once in my hearing, and that with laughter. Stukeley told her, she said, that in quitting England, he was determined to be recognized as a prince before he died. 'I hope,' said Elizabeth ironically, 'that you will let us hear from you, when you are settled in your own principality.' 'I will write unto your Majesty,' Stukeley said. 'And how will you address me?' asked Elizabeth. 'Oh! in the proper style,' Thomas Stukeley said, solemnly. '"To our dear sister . . ."'

'So there's royal blood in these veins,' my cousin cried, biting his fingernails.

'Blood will out,' I said.

Stukeley clawed at my cloak.

'You believe it then, Sir Walter? That my father was *Prince* Thomas? That my father was great King Harry's bastard son?'

We slipped past the Tower.

We pressed on fast downriver towards Wapping.

'I believe he was a bastard, sir,' I said.

I should note that Sir Lewis Stukeley's knighthood is real enough. He got himself beknighted by being one of the first to rush north to kiss King Jamie's arse as the Scotch king made his way down to England while Elizabeth's corpse was still warm. James scattered titles like confetti in the course of that progress.

The boat that pursued us must have come from the Tower. It would have been waiting there, lying close to the wharf by St Thomas Tower inlet. I never noticed it. Such a crowd of tall ships in the dark. Besides, Sir Lewis Stukeley did his work so well. He diverted my attention. He engaged me all the way to Shadwell Stairs with his boasts and his nonsense about his father. I insulted his family, he said. I was a sneerer, a scoffer, an atheist. Yet, in his magnanimity, he forgave me. He found it possible, having a quarter-royal heart, to forgive me all. He was my cousin, my true friend. Had he not endured much uncalled-for contempt and suspicion at my hands? He had suffered all silently, and with patience. I had tricked him. I had basely counterfeited sickness. He, great Harry's grandson, could pardon me even that. And now I knew his true worth, the depth of his love and compassion. He had proved himself to me as an honest man. More even than kinsmen, we were brothers. He embraced me. He kissed me on the cheek.

I said: 'What makes you think I counterfeited sickness?'

Stukeley chuckled. 'The little Frenchman told me.'

'*What?*'

'Dr Manourie. He told me the whole thing.'

The ague seized me. And something worse than ague I can't name. I was shaking all over. My hands gripped the sides of the wherry with such fierceness that I heard my knuckles crack.

'When?' I cried. 'When did the Frenchman tell you "the whole thing"?'

'At Hertfordbridge,' my cousin answered amiably.

My head swam. Then all clicked suddenly into place. Why

Stukeley had made no protest when I asked him to let Sam ride on ahead to London. Why he had consequently come to me in such high spirits. Why the guard had been tightened at Staines. Why he had even been prepared to shake my hand. By then he had *known* there was no death in it. How he must have laughed at me with Manourie! There had been no extra orders from the King. The watchdogs in my room, no doubt, their joint idea . . . My cousin and the Frenchman, hand-in-glove. To make sure that Stukeley stayed by me on the way downriver. To what end?

The answer was both obvious and horrible.

To discredit me. To have me caught in the very act of running away. To make perfect my ruin.

I pushed my cousin from me. I turned and looked back. We were passing the Isle of Dogs. The second wherry was following us. And behind the second wherry I saw the third.

I knew that I was done for. The Indian was shouting to me through the murk. He was pointing behind him. He had noticed the pursuing vessel also. He was spurring his watermen on. But the third vessel was bigger and stronger than either of our two. It was plain she could overtake us whenever she liked.

'How much did you pay the Frenchman?' I demanded.

My cousin looked shocked.

'Sir Walter, you *still* do not trust me?'

If I had been carrying a sword, I swear (God forgive me) that I would have run him through the heart. But I had no sword. And Stukeley's heart . . . I would not have found it, anyway.

'I didn't pay him anything,' he said. 'Dr Manourie is an honourable gentleman. He volunteered the information he gave me. He could see how you needed my assistance to escape.'

I knew he was lying. I recalled the rewards that the honourable gentleman had already had from me. Once more I had trusted a cheat, a liar, a serpent. Perhaps if I had offered that foul Manourie something larger than a £50 pension? But the thought is worse than futile. Traitors take pleasure from their treasons. Some are born to betray, others to be betrayed left, right, and centre. I am of the latter company, and there's an end to it.

'Shall I kill him?' Sam said.

He had overheard what Stukeley had told me, of course.

He had made his way between the watermen, still pulling valiantly for all they were worth.

He was standing behind my cousin.

His bare hands were extended.

'I would like your permission to strangle him, Admiral,' Sam said.

Stukeley was struggling to unsheathe the black-hilted sword.

'Cousin, your fellow does me wrong! You see this sword? This was my father's sword – I assure you that I know well how to use it! But you still don't understand . . . . I am with you now because I am your friend! I protest before God and His angels –'

'Don't,' I said.

'What?' Sam and Stukeley said the word in unison.

'Don't touch him,' I told Sam.

'Don't presume to tell God the same lies you are telling to me,' I snapped at Stukeley.

'But, cousin –'

'You are my friend, cousin Lewis,' I said. 'And I see with my own eyes those other friends of mine you have brought along to see me safely off to France.'

I pointed to the third boat. She was maintaining her distance behind the wherry that held the Indian and my page and the odious Dr Manourie.

'Good Christ!' Stukeley blustered. 'What a coward you are turning out to be! You imagine that vessel is following us?'

'I *know* it is following us, cousin Lewis.'

Stukeley's face set in a pout of pretended disdain. 'Then I am ashamed, Sir Walter. Ashamed to have risked my life, my name, my fortune, to assist a man who shakes at shadows. I assure you we shall reach Gravesend. We shall board the ketch all ready waiting. We shall –'

'*We shall turn back now*,' I said.

I ordered the watermen to stop rowing. I made them turn about. We rowed back upriver. Sam said nothing. There was nothing left to say.

When we got to the second wherry I explained all in few words.

The Indian wanted to dash Manourie's brains out with an oar. I told him I did not need this. Robin was weeping. The Frenchman crouched, staring at his shoes. I only looked at him once.

The third boat had come to a halt.

I ordered the watermen to row up to her.

We effected that passage in five minutes. Our two wherries moving up Thames side by side.

Stukeley tried to stand beside me in the bow of our wherry. Sam pushed him so that he went sprawling.

'You'll regret that,' Stukeley promised.

Then he started giggling.

'You fool,' my cousin cried. 'Fool! Fool! I fooled you!'

He lay on his back in the wherry. He was kicking his legs in the air. He was consumed with his own merriment.

'Do you think I did all this just for money? Of course not! Though the money is good, all the same. But I am a gentleman, Sir Walter. I mean: a real gentleman. A man of honour! A man with King Harry's blood in him! And you!' Stukeley spat at me. 'You, Sir Walter Ralegh, you are *nobody*! What are you? Muck and common clay, a pocky peasant! A brute bumpkin shit whose only claim to glory came from bedding my grandfather's daughter! I hate you. I despise you. I always hated and despised you, all my life. What got you to the top? Your *prick*! That's all. My aunt Elizabeth's little carnal weakness! Bloody Walter Ralegh and his proud prick! I shall be seeing it in Madrid, don't worry, cousin! When they hang you naked and you get your last erection!'

Sam begged me to let him kick Stukeley. I told him not to soil his muddy boots.

There was dim light beginning as the King's men leaped down with drawn swords and lanterns from the third vessel.

I looked at them. Hats with high crowns and wide brims. The Yeomen of the Guard. I was once their Captain. I recognized none of them. But they stood aside. They saluted. They sheathed their swords.

They let me climb the ladder unaccompanied.

Stukeley scrambled up after me.

'Sir Walter Ralegh,' he shouted, 'I arrest you in the name of King James!'

I looked at him.

'Sir Lewis Stukeley,' I said, 'these actions will not turn out to your credit.'

So they brought me here to the Tower, coming in through the Traitor's Gate which lies open to the Thames. I was searched and an inventory was made of my possessions.

£50 in coin.

A spleen stone.

One ring with a diamond which I wear on my finger. Queen Elizabeth's gift. The Tower Lieutenant allows me to keep it.

A map of the Orinoco.

The little grinning gold devil the Indian gave me.

An ounce of ambergris.

A lodestone in a scarlet purse.

One lump of Guiana ore with no gold in it.

A miniature of Bess.

That was it. That's all.

51

A month has passed. A month in the ultimate prison. I don't mean the Tower. I am locked in the prison of myself.

As to the Tower . . . Mr Lieutenant has treated me with kindness. First I was permitted to share his own lodgings. Bess, granted one visit, took away in her petticoats that last chapter describing my arrest. I shall not write down the present provenance of all that I had written formerly. (Because I know that whatever I write now can be spied upon at ease.) Sufficient to say that those papers were safely secreted *before* I left Broad Street on my way to be betrayed by Sir Lewis Stukeley. And that any wretch who, reading this, tears my wife's house apart in searching for them is wasting quite good granite and his time. One day Carew may read them. That's enough.

Sam King, Robin, and the Indian were arrested with me. Sam and Robin were released a week ago, after every attempt to persuade them to testify against me had failed. It was a sad parting. I know I shall not see them again in this world.

By order of the King, I was then moved to a cell in the Wardrobe Tower. The Indian was kept in the cell next to me. Yesterday, a third move. I am back in the Brick Tower, where I began. I mean: so many years ago, after my marriage. The selfsame room. With the Indian again next door. I do not know the purpose of these removals. Nor why the innocent Christoval is being kept. The Lieutenant (who seems honest) says that it may be to satisfy the Spanish Ambassador. Gondomar must intend that Christoval will be dispatched along with me to Madrid, and then perhaps returned to Guiana to bear witness that I was indeed executed with the appropriate ignominy.

Sometimes he is allowed into my cell to talk with me. Of course, these conversations are overheard by well-trained ears in the walls. I am a fool, but I have not spent so many years of my life in this Tower without learning something of its ways. Everything I say will be listened to. Everything I write here will be read. The fact holds no fears for me. I have nothing to hide. I am no traitor.

Nor is Christoval.

His company is some comfort.

We can talk freely, because we have nothing to hide.

King James has once more proved himself the most generous and thoughtful of monarchs. This very night – realizing my loneliness, no doubt, and my lack of opportunity for discourse with honourable men of my own high rank and station – he has sent no less a personage than Sir Thomas Wilson, Keeper of the State Papers, to occupy the cell on my other side. Not as a prisoner, of course. Just to provide me with a little fellowship. An amiable, intelligent man. A man of the most acute intelligence. His wit and his bearing afford me the keenest delight.

We were able to swap news for many hours. He was kind enough to tell me that much evidence has been collected already by their Lordships of his Majesty's Privy Council – enough to hang me *twice*, as he wittily remarked – but that despite all this, his most Excellent Majesty might still be prepared to grant me some partial pardon in return for a full confession of my crimes.

The King's munificent goodness touched me to the quick.

I was quite overcome with emotion.

It pained me to have to tell Sir Thomas Wilson that I could never repay his most Excellent Majesty's generosity, being poor, being wretched, being miserable, *and having nothing whatsoever to 'confess'*.

Sir Thomas Wilson tells me that my wife has been confined to Broad Street. I am grateful indeed that King James takes such kind thought for her safety. God knows, King James has no more loyal subjects than Bess and myself. It pleases me to learn that his Majesty knows what God knows. (I am not surprised by their affinity, of course.)

God save the King!

God save England from England's enemies!

God save Sir Walter Ralegh, Englishman!

52

Yesterday, Sir Thomas Wilson, Keeper of the State Papers, good companion to me here in my misery in the Tower, took pity on my several earnest entreaties and most graciously permitted me to scribble a few lines to be delivered to Bess.

It was raining.

But he bore the note to Broad Street himself.

O damp compassionate knight!

I wrote as follows:

> Dear Wife –
>
> I am sick and weak. This honest gentleman Sir Thomas Wilson is my keeper and takes much pain with me. My swollen side keeps me in perpetual pain and unrest. God comfort us.
>
> > Yours,
> >
> > W.R.

This morning the same kind attentive Sir Thomas has brought me back her letter in reply.

That letter reads:

> Dear Hosban –
>
> I am sorry to hear amongst many discomforts that your health is so ill. It is meerly sorrow and greaf that with wind has gathered into yor side. I hope yor health and comforts will mend and mend us for God. I am gladd to heer you have the company and comfort of so good a Keeper. I was something dismayed at the first that you had no servant of yor own left you, but I hear this honest

Knight is very necessary. God requite his courtesies and God in mercy look on us.

Yours,
E. Ralegh

This is absolute Bess. One cold eye, one warm. And she never could spell. And she never would take my pains seriously. I swear my swollen liver is real enough. Why, I have not been able to open my bowels for twenty-two days without benefit of clysters . . . Yet here is my dear wife dismissing my ailment as imaginary, saying that it can all be put down to 'wind' and mere 'sorrow and grief' . . .

I revere her for her coolness.

At the same time, she infuriates me.

I wept when I read what Bess had written.

Then I said to Wilson:

'My wife sent me no medicines?'

He shook his head.

Then he said:

'To be honest, if she had, I could not have permitted you to drink them.'

'Why ever not?'

'Sir Walter, in case Lady Ralegh sent you something to poison yourself!'

I smiled.

'Sir Thomas, if I wished to kill myself I would not need poisons. If I had a mind to commit suicide, I should dash my head a dozen times against that wall over there, until I stood and watched my brains run down! Do you think I couldn't do it?'

The Keeper of the State Papers (and me) began to look frightened.

'Don't worry,' I said. 'I trust in God's mercy. And the King's.'

He nodded with relief.

'Suicide is a very great sin,' he said piously. 'A mortal sin against the fifth commandment.'

I remembered poor Keymis. I said nothing.

Wilson was clearing his throat. 'Sir Walter, your lady wife *did* send something else by me. I suppose I can give it to you. To be honest –'

'Yes, yes, you are invariably honest –'

'Thank you. Well, I have had an apothecary test the substance. It seems harmless enough.'

He held out a plain box.

I opened it.

The box contained a little dish filled to the brim with fresh green gooseberry creams.

I dip in my fingers and pick out a gooseberry to savour as I write.

God bless you, Bess Throgmorton.

God keep you, Elizabeth Ralegh.

Forgive your hosban. Pardon that pathetic Swisser Swatter, pitiable only for his appalling and most ugly self-pity. This fool in the Tower who could write only about the pain in his guts when he should rightly have sent you whatever remains of his heart.

53

The spy has been called off.

I mean, of course, Sir Thomas Wilson, Keeper of the State Papers.

Jacta est alea.

I can write freely now. I care not who reads this.

For more than a month I had to bear with his company, knowing that every idle word I uttered was being written down and sent to their Lordships. He had nothing from me. There was nothing to have. If Mr Lieutenant considers it his duty to copy this present scribble and send it to the Privy Council then let me put it down now on record that I crave their Lordships' indulgence for such a waste of time and expense. The truth is that poor Wilson did his job well. He tried every trick in the book. A most experienced and sympathetic Government agent. I recommend him for their future use. He has failed to find out evidence against me for the very simple reason that there is no evidence to be had. No doubt when there are traitors to be persuaded to incriminate themselves out of their own mouths, this same Wilson will prove valuable. I place my trust in English justice. I am sure the sad wretch will not be punished by your Lordships if, due to a decent lack of imagination, he has not even managed to invent a few lies once he realized that he dealt with a passing honest man.

One small note of criticism, however.

In Secretary Cecil's day you could always tell a first-class spy by his clean teeth. (Even Kit Marlowe – by no means a first-class spy, being only a poet – used to make efforts now and again with a quart of honey, as much vinegar, and half as much white wine, all boiled together by the way of a mouth-wash.)

Now – your Lordships may welcome my advising you? – this otherwise admirable and most thorough Sir Thomas Wilson lacks somewhat in that important small department. If I had possessed any secrets I would have been unlikely to whisper them into his ear. It would take a stronger stomach than mine to delight in his close company. These cells are not well-ventilated, and when a man seeks day and night for more than a month to persuade you to confide in him there is a distinct reluctance which builds up if he does so with breath like a Chick Lane dunghill.

I prescribe for Sir Thomas Wilson a visit to some barber who will scale his teeth with Aqua Fortis.

Two items of news.

(I had these from Wilson, in amongst much other chatter designed to make me see him as something other than a wolf in sheep's clothing.)

First, Sir Lewis Stukeley has put in a claim for expenses incurred in the exercise of his vocation.

To wit:

'£965 6s. 3d. for bringing up out of Devonshire the person of Sir Walter Ralegh, Knight.'

I consider this a reasonable figure.

At the current exchange rate it is no doubt exactly equal to thirty pieces of silver.

The six shillings and threepence would be for broken strings on his violin.

Cousin Lewis is nothing if not his father's son.

The other bit of news is perhaps more interesting.

His Majesty, my Sovereign Lord, King James, has received a formal letter from his dear brother King Philip III of Spain conveying Spain's wish that Don Guattaral be done to death in England.

No reason was given, to my knowledge.

Perhaps King Philip has too many innocent men of his own for execution?

For myself, I might laugh if my lungs still had power left for it.

I trust the prospect of this task gives King James no sleepless nights.

54

There will be no public trial.

There will be no trial at all.

Wilson could find no new treason. Their Lordships of the Privy Council took evidence from such members of my expedition as volunteered. None of that can have amounted to much. I have nothing to answer for, and they know it.

Does Sir Walter Ralegh go free then?

Will his Majesty permit him to live out his last days in peace as a country gentleman, tending his garden, minding his own business, ordering his estate, with his wife and his son to comfort him in his old age?

Not a bit of it.

No new treason to be found?

What matter?

The *old* treason will do.

All this I learned today from Allen Apsley, Mr Lord Lieutenant of the Tower. A decent fellow, with honour enough to be obsolete. He seems not to relish what is happening. Yet he does his duty, Mr Apsley. He serves the King. As I do. An honest soldier. May no black fate befall this honourable Lieutenant for his courtesy in telling his poor prisoner the truth.

The truth.

The truth is exquisitely neat. It is also disgusting.

Some excellent judicial brain has been employed to remind King James that Sir Walter Ralegh stands already quite properly attainted of high treason.

There is therefore no need for the aforesaid traitor to be tried and judged guilty or innocent concerning any crimes committed since.

Sir Walter Ralegh's 'recent offences against Spain' can be brushed aside as an irrelevance.

Legally, lawfully, constitutionally, it is all in order for his Majesty to revoke his limited reprieve and to issue a simple warrant for Sir Walter Ralegh's immediate execution according to the death-sentence passed on him at Winchester in 1603.

Simple.

Simplicity itself.

The simplicity of a viper.

I smell it. I smell genius, brilliance, philosophy.

I smell another old friend.

I smell Bacon.

Apsley says that Gondomar has gone off to Spain in a fury of impotence and belly-ache. Things haven't turned out as he wanted, and everyone knows. Stones were thrown at the Count's carriage as he passed through the streets. God bless us. There must be a few other left-overs from Elizabeth's day still alive and troublesome in London.

My son, remember this well.

Your father, Sir Walter Ralegh, was condemned to death for being a friend to the Spaniards. He is now to lose his life for being their enemy. *And all on the one sentence.*

That is the way of this world.

As the Indian said: It is a place apart.

Nothing to find here after your own heart.

Apsley says I might have a week left. Maybe less. Most certainly no more. There will have to be some sort of formal pantomime. The Lord Chancellor conveying the King's pleasure. Mr Attorney General, Sir Henry Yelverton, declaring the legality of it. And all to be done in private, of course, and quickly, behind closed doors. They won't want to give me the chance to open my mouth much before they cram the clay in and stop it for good.

Bacon. Of course. Francis Bacon. Apsley admits that all London knows it was Bacon who advised the King how to be rid of me with the minimum of fuss. Coke wanted a trial. James dismissed him. It was Bacon who murmured that I was already a *man dead in law*. He reminded the King that I had only existed these last fifteen years thanks to his Majesty's mercy and forbearance. That this Sir Walter Ralegh is thus a ghost. That his dispatch will not be so much as an execution; more an *exorcism*. Buckingham told Clapton the story, admiring its capital wit. It's common gossip now. To be sure, not everyone likes it. But the beauty of Bacon's reasoning is cause for much wonder.

He's come far, Francis Bacon. He'll go farther yet. His Majesty will assuredly reward this most subtle and simple of Lord Chancellors. For myself, I might claim that I never underestimated him. No more than Bacon ever underestimated himself. He penned a charming little autobiographical essay once. '*Ego cum me ad utilitates humanas natum existimarem*,' it began. 'Since I first thought myself born to be of advantage to mankind . . .' (Carew, take heed. Always put on Latin when tempted by the insanity of self-exaltation.)

So here we have another fine example of Bacon's birth being of advantage to mankind. I can remember others. He started by exerting himself most diligently to gain the favour of my Lord Essex. Essex, impressed, did his best for him. He told the Queen he'd make a grand Attorney General. Elizabeth refused. I can say it now: Elizabeth never liked Bacon. She said he stuttered like a new-clipped crow. Essex then sought to have Bacon made Solicitor General. The Queen again resisted, despite all manner of coaxing and tantrums from her great boy. Essex was embarrassed. He sweetened Bacon's disappointment with many gifts – a parcel of lands near Twickenham, in particular. Then, when Essex went mad and was tried for his treasons, his protégé forgot all this kindness and remembered mankind. Essex was doomed, but it was Bacon who secured that execution. Coke made his usual mess of the case for the Crown. He kept allowing the plain thread of the evidence to escape with his rhetoric. It was Bacon who stepped forward, zealously, cleverly, bringing things back to the point: the point of the axe for his gibbering patron's poor neck. His performance was stunning and clear-cut. I never heard anything to equal it. Not for truth, not for treachery. If any man killed Essex, apart from Essex himself, it was Sir Francis Bacon. He gave his friend in need a helping hand right up the steps to the scaffold.

O yes. A born advantage to mankind.

A most splendid philosopher.

But there are more things in heaven and earth . . .

All the same, I must bow to your skills, my Lord Chancellor.

How well, dear old friend, you dealt with those awkward pestering questions of mine in Gray's Inn gardens!

'Should I not try and purchase a pardon before sailing for Guiana?'

To which you: *'Not at all. A pardon is a mere formality. The King has made you his Admiral. You have freedom to sail and power of life and death over those who sail with you. Such Commission is equivalent to a pardon.'*

To which I, still troubled, knowing you well, demanded: *'Specifically, then, does it cancel out my conviction and sentence for high treason?'*

You shut your viper eyes, Francis Bacon, when I asked you that.

Can it be that you have sufficient sensibility left in that hailstone heart, that diamond mind of yours, that you prefer not to look upon those you intend to betray?

Surely not?

I do you an injustice, my Lord Aristotle Junior.

You looked keenly and openly on Essex when you ruined him.

Your nerves are in perfect working order.

You must just have been tired, or bored, or both.

You will perhaps forgive me for supposing that you ever had anything resembling a soul, or even a miniature conscience.

Pardon me also for still hearing in this foolish head of mine your shut-eyed words then:

'Your Commission as Admiral seems to me as good a pardon for all former offences as the Law of England can afford you!'

As you see, sir, your old friend is afflicted with this terrible and incurable disease of remembrance.

I feel confident that your own mental health is far superior.

Apsley just allowed me an hour's conversation with the Indian. (He remains in the cell next to mine. God knows what will happen to him. I have written to Bess suggesting that she might find him service in some gentleman's company if – as I dare to suppose – he is set free from the Tower once I am safely disposed of.)

I told Christoval the news.

That he would see what he had come for.

That I must die.

He said: 'Would it make any difference if I told Elizadeath the truth about Don Palomeque?'

'No,' I said.

He thought this over.

He said: 'I see.' He was looking hard at me. At last, he said: 'What if I named all those Spaniards who owned gold mines out there in Guiana? The ones I told you about, you understand? Pedro Rodrigo de Parana . . . Hermano Fruntino . . . Francisco Fachardo . . . You know what I mean?'

I knew what he meant.

It was good of him.

I shook my head.

'No,' I said. 'There is nothing that can save me now.'

True.

Nothing can save me from Elizadeath.

But it was more than good of the Indian, what he offered.

We sat in silence for a while. I smoked a pipe of tobacco. Then he said: 'I want to tell you a story. It is a legend among my people. It is about the song of the Sun God. Before there were men in the lands of the Chibcha, there were birds, and all the birds knew that there was one song sweeter and stronger than any that they could sing. It was the song which can only be heard in the topmost heights of the sky, in that blue empty place where the Sun God lives. All the birds desired to hear that song. If they could hear it, only once, then they too might be able to sing it. The smaller birds never even dared to try to reach so high. But the great birds tried. They flew higher and higher, until their wings grew weak, and they could rise no more. They all failed. The last to try was the condor. His wings were wide, he was very strong, he was the bravest of all the birds. He soared far out of sight. Yet even he could not reach the home of the Sun God, although he came very close to it before he fell back to earth again. So the greatest of the birds, the mighty condor himself, had failed. But that is not the end of the story. You see, when the condor took

372

off on his flight a small brown bird had hopped on his back. It was a bird so light and insignificant that the great condor did not even feel the weight of it. And when the condor had to give up his struggle, and fell back down, the little bird flew on by himself, on his own wings. The condor had come so near to the home of the Sun God that the small unimportant bird, being fresh and unwearied, had no trouble in flying the short distance that still remained. He flew into the palace of the Sun God, and he heard the Sun God's song. He lay there for a long time, hidden in a corner, singing the song of the Sun God over and over in his own heart until he knew it note for note, quite perfectly. Then he spread his wings and drifted gently down to earth. It was not difficult. It is easy for the smallest and weakest to fall down on the currents of the wind, even though the most powerful cannot fly the same distance upwards. Over and over again, the brown bird sang the sweet song of the Sun God to himself. But he was afraid. He was afraid that when the condor found out what had happened he would kill him, having done all the work and yet never heard the Sun God's song. He was afraid that the other birds would be jealous, and he had good reason for that, since all he had done to win the song was to ride on someone else's wings. So he hid himself. He hid himself in the thickest bushes he could find, and to this day he lives like a hermit, seldom seen, although sometimes heard. And to this day the sweetest and strongest song in the world is the song of this creature.'

'Its name?' I inquired.

The Indian shrugged.

'Some call it the hermit thrush.'

'And others?'

'The mocking bird.'

'I shall call it the hermit thrush,' I said.

Later. A game of chess with Apsley. I was thinking of Christoval's story. I still managed to win.

As Apsley put the ivory pieces away, he remarked:

'Once the game is over, the king and the pawn go back into the same box.'

I handed him a knight he had overlooked.

55

It took them only an hour. Which was apt. Because adding the two minutes it took me to limp the length of Westminster Hall, and the other two minutes to limp out again, that makes sixty-four.

One minute for each year of my life.

Quite poetic.

I am to die tomorrow at nine o'clock.

It was Wilson who came with the summons. He looked very spruce. His teeth, when he smiled, were still yellow, but his breath not so bad. Apsley, noticing me noticing this, looked ashamed and embarrassed. He need not have done. As Lord Lieutenant of the Tower, he has his little duties to perform. I am well aware that he must read these papers, and have them copied. I am glad to have done the State some service in this matter of dental hygiene amongst Government intelligencers. More importantly, on a personal note, Apsley has now given me his word that the originals of these my final writings will be passed on to Bess once I am dead. I record my gratitude for that. I pray again that no harm befall this gentleman for his charity towards me. He has done nothing I would not have done, had our rôles been reversed. And that does not make him a traitor. Unless Christian kindness be construed as treachery these days?

The hearing was begun at ten o'clock.

In the King's great hall at Westminster, as I say.

Apsley read over the writ of *habeas corpus*. He found it in order. He delivered me into their charge.

Seven judges present. And two observers.

The judges:

His Majesty's Attorney General, Sir Henry Yelverton.

His Majesty's Solicitor General, Sir Thomas Coventry.

Sir Henry Montagu, Chief Justice of the King's Bench. (Coke's replacement.)

Justice Sir Robert Houghton.

Justice Sir John Croke.

Justice Sir John Doderidge.

The seventh, of course, Francis Bacon, my Lord Chancellor. Bacon sitting on the King's white marble bench. Bacon never looked at me once. He was busy with papers. Some of them – who knows? – may even have been concerned with my case. But more likely he was working on his own philosophy.

The two observers:

George Abbot, my Lord Archbishop of Canterbury.

James Hay, Viscount Doncaster, a Scot. (I knew why he was there, as a sort of courier. In his youth he was one of James's favourites. His job today was to act as the King's eyes, then report to the King.)

His Majesty, but naturally, not present. It is the hunting season. He'd be occupied in pursuit of other game.

I stood leaning on my cane until Bacon made his entrance.

Then they gave me a fine black stool to sit upon.

Yelverton began the proceedings. He called on the Clerk of the Crown – a Mr Fanshawe, I believe – to remind all those present of my previous conviction and the judgement then passed upon it. Namely that long before, in the presence of divers noble personages, I had been legally convicted of high treason at Winchester, and was then and there sentenced to be hanged, drawn, and quartered.

That done, Yelverton said:

'My Lords, Sir Walter Ralegh, the prisoner at the bar, was fifteen years ago convicted of high treason, as you have heard. High treason, my Lords, committed by him against the person of his Majesty and the state of this kingdom. He then received the judgement you have also heard: the judgement of death – to be hanged and drawn and quartered. His Majesty of his abundant grace has been pleased to show mercy upon him till now. But now that same justice calls for due execution. Sir Walter Ralegh has been a statesman, and a man who in regard of his parts and quality is to be pitied. He has been as a star at which all the world has gazed. But stars may fall . . . Nay, my Lords, they *must* fall when they trouble the sphere wherein they abide!'

This pretty speech completed, I was required to hold up my hand. Which I did. The Lord Chief Justice, Montagu, then asked politely if I had anything to say for myself why execution should not be awarded against me.

I stood and said:

'My Lords, all that I can ask is this – that this judgement of death which I received so many years ago will not now be strained to take away my life. It was his Majesty's pleasure to grant me a Commission in a voyage beyond the seas. I was given the power of life and death over others. Under such favour, my Lords, I presumed I had possession of a pardon. I was, after all, granted leave to depart from this land and undertake a journey to honour my Sovereign and to enrich his kingdom with gold. In pursuit of that honour, I have lost my son and –'

Montagu interrupted me.

'None of this is to the purpose. We do not sit in judgement on your voyage.'

Coventry said: 'In any case, the issue of your Commission cannot help you. Treason can never be pardoned by mere implication.'

Yelverton said: 'Besides which, I have a copy of your Commission here before me. There is not a single word in it which could even be said to tend towards pardon.'

I looked at Bacon.

He did not look at me.

'So be it,' I said.

There was a silence.

Then I said: 'I am satisfied, my Lords, that nothing I can offer in my own defence will be considered to the point. I submit myself therefore to your judgement. I put myself upon the mercy of the King.'

Bacon wrote even more busily. I fancy I must have surprised him by capitulating so soon in this matter of the voyage implying pardon. To be honest, it was part despair and part pride which inspired my swift submission. The despair of my being aware that he would welcome the chance to put the knife in my back as he had put it so often into others. The pride of my standing there knowing and declaring by my silence that the swine was well-named.

Yelverton said: 'Sir Walter, you are wise not to argue the toss.'

I nodded my thanks for this compliment. 'I would add only one word.'

'What is it?'

'Hope,' I said.

'Hope for what?'

'Compassion,' I said. 'I might hope for the King's compassion, might I not? Concerning this judgement which is so long past. There are some here, my Lords, even amongst yourselves, in this very hall, who could bear witness that I had hard usage in that trial of mine.'

Montagu stared at me. Then he looked up at the rafters. 'Sir Walter Ralegh,' he said firmly, 'you must remember yourself. You had an honourable trial. You were justly convicted.'

I said no more.

'My Lord the King's Attorney has called you wise for not arguing the toss concerning your late voyage to Guiana,' Montagu went on. 'You would be even more wise if your submission ran to confess that your former treasons were well proved, and that the sentence then pronounced against you was no more than your guilt deserved.'

I said nothing.

Montagu sighed. Then he drew himself together.

'Sir Walter Ralegh,' he said, 'I am here called to grant execution upon the judgement given you fifteen years since. All that time you have been as a dead man in the law, and might at any moment have been cut off, but the King in mercy spared you.' He cleared his throat. 'You speak of hard usage. Well, sir, it might indeed seem hard to some if you were now to be executed in cold blood. But it is not so, and you know it. You understand very well that your new offences have stirred up his Majesty's justice, to cause him to recall his reprieve, and to revive your former sentence.'

He paused for effect. I think he was enjoying the sound of his own voice echoing in that vast hall, the largest in England, usually so crowded for proper trials, but this morning so empty.

'I know you have been valiant and wise in the past,' Montagu went on. 'And I doubt not but you retain both those virtues. Now you shall have occasion to use them. In the past your faith was

377

sometimes called in question, but I am resolved that you are a good Christian. Your *History of the World*, an admirable work, testifies as much.'

He glanced at my Lord the Archbishop, who inclined his head.

James Hay pursed his lips. He didn't like this. On reflection, it was perhaps the bravest thing my judges did. They must have known that the Scot would tell the King. And that James had found my *History* not at all 'admirable'. 'Too saucy in censuring princes', I think that's what his verdict was. He had the book banned for a while, and when it was released again the printer took my name off the title page.

Montagu rambled on. 'Fear not death too much,' he said. 'Nor fear death too little. Not too much, lest you fail in your hopes. Not too little, lest you die presumptuously. And here I must conclude with my prayers to God for it, and that he shall have mercy on your soul, for execution is now granted, and I command that you be taken from this place, and that at nine o'clock tomorrow you shall be —'

I had shut my eyes.

The Lord Chief Justice stopped abruptly in mid-sentence.

When I opened my eyes I saw Bacon leaning down from his white marble bench. He looked like a bent archangel. He was handing Montagu a piece of parchment. It was not the parchment he'd been scribbling on. I heard it crackle as Montagu took it. The parchment bore the seal of the kingdom: a great gold and purple blob on a sheet of yellow. I expect Bacon had been keeping it warm in some deep pocket of his robes all the time of the hearing. I suspect also that his sudden production of this missive came as no startling news to their Lordships. Just another of the King's little Scottish tricks, his small dramas, his ironies.

Montagu put on his spectacles.

He said:

'Here is the word of his Majesty the King. Signed and sealed. Delivered by his right trusty and well-beloved counsellor, Francis Lord Verulam, Lord Chancellor of England.'

He read aloud from the parchment:

'James, by the grace of God, King of England, Scotland, and Ireland, Defender of the Faith. We, by this present writing, do pardon, remit, and release Sir Walter Ralegh, Knight, from the manner of execution according to his former judgement at Winchester – namely, that he was to be hanged, and drawn, and quartered. Our pleasure is, instead, to have the head only of the said Sir Walter Ralegh cut off, at or within our Palace of Westminster.'

I will say this much for Montagu:

He did not play the clown.

He read out the rigmarole straight, in a sober unvarying voice, where he could have paused after that bit about pardon, remit, and release . . . Just to torture me a second with the prospect of a little more life.

Silence.

Were they expecting me to applaud?

More silence.

I heard the cry of a rat-catcher in the street outside. He was singing the rat-catcher's song. I cupped my ear to listen to him:

> Rats or mice, ha'ye any rats, mice, polecats, or weasels?
> Or ha'ye any old sows sick of the measles?
> I can kill them!
> And I can kill moles!
> And I can kill vermin that creepeth up and creepeth down,
>   and peepeth into holes!

A long time since I've heard that song. Perhaps I only imagined it? No one else in the great hall showed any sign of having heard it. Yet I swear I did. And that the rat-catcher had a broad Devon accent.

Yelverton rapped with his staff.

'Does the prisoner understand?' he demanded irritably.

Bacon had gone back to his writing. He crossed something out. Then he added some commas in another place. He did not look up. He never said one word, nor looked once in my direction, the whole time.

I stood erect.

Then I said:

'My Lords, let your record show that the said Sir Walter Ralegh, Knight, has perfectly heard and very well understood the *pleasure* of his Majesty.'

Bacon covered his lips with his hand. If he smiled, no one saw it. Did anyone ever see Bacon smile? I didn't.

The rest of my noble judges did not smile. My words appeared to have frightened them out of their wits.

'Amen,' cried Lord Chief Justice Montagu, at last. 'Execution is granted. God save the King!'

I bowed.

I dropped my cane with a clatter and let it roll.

I turned.

I limped away without it from Westminster Hall.

As I said, that took two minutes.

I walked as well going out as I did coming in.

As well, or as ill.

So the cane made no difference. No difference at all.

I am here in an upper chamber of the Gatehouse. The Sheriffs of London have guard of me. This place was once the old monastery of Westminster. To be sure, my room is monastic enough. A well-scrubbed floor, a trestle table, a hard bed. From the one tiny window, if I looked down into Old Palace Yard, I could see the carpenters at work constructing a scaffold for my final use tomorrow. I have no wish to watch them. It is raining. The unfortunate fellows no doubt are getting soaked to the bone. I have a fire. I can hear the sound of their hammers. Apsley instructed the Sheriffs to allow me pen, ink, and as much paper as I required. I do not think I shall need the great pile they have brought.

I dined well. The porter served me roast beef, green peas, turnips, and artichokes. There was a quince pie to follow, baked (so he said) by his wife. He offered me wine. I prefer not to drink it.

Three o'clock. The bell called Great Tom has just boomed it out from the clock tower.

A wet, a windy, a wretched afternoon. I can see that the darkness will come early. I shall have candles lit. I always liked to write by candlelight. I always liked the winter smell of wax.

I have sent word to Bess. She knows where I am. The Sheriffs say she can visit me tonight. I asked her not to bring Carew. It is better that way.

*

All this paper . . .

It silences me.

For the first time in my life, I find it difficult – if not impossible – to write.

What can I say that's not been said?

To whom should I address myself?

I waste time. I sit and smoke my pipe and stare into the fire. I hear the hours strike, and the rain against the windowpane. They have ceased that damned necessary hammering. I should be exerting myself to write some kind of public statement, something my friends might have published if my speech on the scaffold tomorrow is cut short.

Short or long, it will be cut all right.

This time tomorrow I shall be dead.

I can afford to waste time, for time will soon waste me no more.

For the first time in my life, I feel *free*.

'Stars must fall . . .'

Quite a decent phrase, that one of Yelverton's. I wonder where he got it from. Sounds like a quotation. Marlowe, maybe. Or Kyd. Too good for Kyd. Shakespeare? No, not good enough for Shakespeare.

Dead.

All dead.

Marlowe, Shakespeare, Kyd.

They broke poor gentle Thomas Kyd on the rack. I am spared that, apparently. I am spared the dagger thrusts through the eyes which dispatched poor Marlowe. I am spared the anti-climax, even, of dying at home in my bed, a man of property, like the great upstart from Stratford. (He must have lain dying that month I stepped forth from the Tower two years, two lifetimes, ago. Wat said Ben Jonson got him drunk on a visit to that vulgar house of his, New Place, and that Shakespeare slept it off under a tree all night in the rain, only it was a thin tree, and S. then took to his bed with a fever. I don't believe it. Drink only ever *sobered* Mr Shakespeare, and God knows he was always sober enough without.)

Dead, anyway, all of them.

All of *us*.

So here's the chance to say I forgive the worst and the best, the star that out-shined us all, the only one clever or unlucky enough to die without poetry or violence or drama, at home in his second-best bed.

I mean: Mr W.S. And I mean forgive him specifically for mocking me as that character called Don Armado in his *Love's Labour's Lost*. A muddled patchwork piece, in my opinion. Essex loved it. So did the Queen, when it was done for her at the Christmas revels in '97. At least, Shakespeare allowed his fantastical Don Armado the last speech in the whole stupid farce. 'The words of Mercury are harsh after the songs of Apollo. You, that way: we, this way.' Which also happen to be some of the better lines in the wretched production. Only now we all go the same way. And that's no jest.

I wonder which particular star my Lord the Attorney General can have had in his mind?

Mercury?

In astrology, according to Dr Dee, Mercury signifies subtle men, the ingenious and the inconstant. Rhymers, I remember him saying, poets, advocates, orators, philosophers, arithmeticians, and busy fellows generally.

'The words of Mercury . . .'

I don't intend to utter many more.

In any case, Yelverton probably meant *Lucifer*. As proud as Lucifer, that one who was damned and ruined by his pride. Lucifer, after all, is the most notable star anyone ever thinks of as *falling* . . . It's in Isaiah somewhere: 'How art thou fallen, from heaven, O Lucifer, son of the morning!'

And Coke called me Lucifer. And so did Howard.

In fact, it was my star part in that other farce at Winchester.

I write drivel. I know it.

Stuff about plays and nonsense about players. Because my life on the stage of this world has been a play, and I have played in my time many parts, but always the actor, the actor, not the man of action, the actor. And so on. I've said it all before.

What tedium.

I heard Edward Alleyn once. Drunk. Playing Faustus. He got stuck. He must have forgotten his lines. He just stood there, centre-stage, shouting over and over again:

'See see where Christ's blood streams in the firmament!'

Shouting louder and louder each time. He must have roared it all of six times before he was prompted. It was very effective, all the same. No one laughed. By the fifth scream, everyone in the audience at the Fortune could see that blood streaming.

But I have no great line to get stuck with.

I sit here repeating banalities like a fool.

The porter brings more coals. The fire is already too much.

It's dark. The candles are nodding in their cowls.

I ought to be writing and rehearsing that last speech. The speech I might not even be granted the chance to deliver. It's the condemned man's right. It's traditional. But, with King James for curtain-master, who knows?

Let's face it. I haven't the heart.

And it would be rather good to say *nothing*, would it not?

Good. Yes. To deny them their oration. To go tight-lipped to the axe. To die in silence.

But vain.

Prouder than Lucifer.

My last and most devilish pride to overcome.

I have to say something. Anything. The best I can say. Which won't do. Which will have to do.

God help me.

What?

I give thanks to God. He answered my prayer. I have suffered two most welcome interruptions. Now I am inspired. Now I know what I must do, what I must say.

The first inspiration came in the shape of a clergyman. A round, plump, busy shape. Bustling in with a copy of Cranmer's *Book of Common Prayer* held outstretched in his hands as if to ward off some malevolent spirit.

I gathered I was the spirit in question.

The young cleric introduced himself. A Dr Robert Tounson, King's chaplain, and Dean of Westminster. He had come, so he said, to encourage me against the fear of death. It was part of his usual priestly duties. A mission he performed for all men about to leave this world.

I offered him my chair. He sat down, flicking dust from black pumpkin breeches. I stood with my back to the fire. It was pleasant, the heat against my buttocks.

'*I am the resurrection and the life,*' Tounson said.

'*Saith the Lord,*' I said. '*He that believeth in me, though he were dead, yet shall he live: and whosoever liveth and believeth in me shall never die.*' I lit my pipe, smiling. 'You see, sir, I know a little religion . . . But are we not premature? This is the beginning of the Order for the Burial of the Dead. I have not yet achieved that translation.'

'Quite so, quite so,' Tounson muttered impatiently. 'I offered those comfortable words of Our Lord vouchsafed to His disciple St John merely to introduce the subject.'

'Which subject?' I said.

'Christianity, sir. The state of your soul.'

I blew a smoke ring.

'As you see, it could be worse, my dear Dean.'

'Men have called you an atheist –'

'Men were wrong. *I believe in one God the Father Almighty, Maker of heaven and earth, and of all things visible and invisible. And in one Lord Jesus Christ, the only-begotten –*'

'Amen,' Tounson interrupted. 'I see that you know the creed. I did not doubt that. But what men say with their tongues does not always chime with what they think in their hearts. What is your true faith, sir? Your religion?'

I blew no more smoke rings.

I said:

'I am a Christian. I shall die as I have lived, in the only faith I have known, which is the faith professed by the Church of England.'

Tounson blinked.

'Sir Walter, I confess that you surprise me. I had heard much of your scepticism.'

'To doubt is not to deny. All men, if they are honest, must admit to doubt. This time tomorrow I shall have my doubts, with all my other sins, absolved and washed away by the most precious blood of our Saviour Jesus Christ.'

'Amen to that,' said Tounson. 'Yet it seems to me that there is something in you which makes light of death.'

'I have never feared it.'

'There! You speak too proudly, sir, too cheerfully. Why, the dear servants of God, the saints themselves, meeting their ends in better causes than yours, have shrunk back and trembled a little!'

'My flesh may tremble,' I said. 'My soul does not.'

Tounson picked at the ruff at his neck. 'Yet you die by the axe! You die the death of a traitor!'

My pipe had gone out. I lit it again with a coal plucked from the fire with a tongs.

'I shall die by the axe,' I said. 'Sir, that manner of death might seem grievous to others. For myself, it holds no terror in particular. It is a swift death, and a clean one. I would rather die that way than of some slow burning fever.'

'But your treason, Sir Walter –'

'Mr Dean, I shall die a sinner. I have lived, as all men live, a life full of sin. I pray God to forgive me. But I shall not die a traitor, because I have committed no treason. I know that. God knows it.'

Tounson looked uncomfortable.

'You intend to proclaim this on the scaffold?'

'I shall stand upon my innocence in the fact.'

'And deny the King's justice?'

'It is not for me to fear or to flatter kings. I am now Death's subject. The great God of heaven is my Sovereign.'

Tounson sighed, shaking his head.

'I see I waste my time with you, Sir Walter . . .'

'I trust not.'

'But if you intend to die –'

'I shall die as well as I can, with God's help, and there's an end to it.'

'You speak like a stoic.'

'Then you mishear me. We are both of us Christians, Mr Dean. You will bring me the Holy Sacrament in the morning?'

Tounson's mouth fell open. Then he nodded.

'Thank you,' I said.

Tounson got up in a hurry. 'You will forgive me. But I have many duties. This is quite a busy week for me, you know.'

'I sympathize.'

'Today is a Feast Day. St Simon and St Jude. And tomorrow is the day of the Lord Mayor's Show.'

'Indeed? I had forgotten.'

'Yes, Well . . .' Tounson clasped his prayer-book to his breast. 'Sir Walter, I shall pray for you,' he muttered.

'I thank you,' I said. 'I shall pray for you also, Mr Dean. I shall pray especially that despite your many duties it does not slip your mind that you are God's servant.'

Tounson stared at me, frowning.

'The Sacrament,' I said. 'Tomorrow at dawn.'

The King has been ill advised. That is, if it was his Majesty's hope to be rid of me quietly.

Tomorrow is the day of the Lord Mayor's Show.

All London rises early to watch the procession. There will be crowds up from the country too, no doubt. The beheading of Sir Walter Ralegh will provide a splendid prelude. I can be sure of a good audience, at least.

The Feast Day of St Simon and St Jude. That's appropriate also. Our Lord's most obscure apostles, martyred together in Persia. Simon was nicknamed the Zealous. Nothing else known about him for certain. Jude was of course the other Judas. The Judas who was *not* Iscariot. The patron saint of the desperate, the intercessor in lost and hopeless causes. I sit here in fine company, you see.

My second inspiration I owe to Apsley. No sooner had the busy Dean gone than the door of my chamber was unlocked again.

It was Christoval.

He has been set free from the Tower. He is to be given lodgings for this one night in some other room of the Gatehouse. Tomorrow he is to be allowed to witness my execution.

The Sheriffs permitted us just five minutes of talk.

That proved sufficient.

'What will you do after tomorrow?' I asked him. 'I have been trying to find you service –'

He shook his head. He told me that arrangements had already been made. Count Gondomar's agents will escort him in his travels to Madrid. Thence he will go back to Guiana on some Spanish vessel.

'I understand,' I said. 'They will use you as a witness. Your destiny now is to spend the rest of your life singing the one song: the fall of Don Guattaral!'

He smiled.

Then he said:

'I shall hide in the thickest bushes. Amongst the trees around Lake Guatavita. Where the leaf grows. As for singing, I never had any voice for that. Nor shall I shout. But, be sure, I shall tell your story to any who will listen.'

'Like the mocking bird?' I said.

'Like the hermit thrush.'

When the Sheriffs' men came to put an end to our interview, Christoval held out his right hand.

I grasped it.

He said:

'I told you once, long ago, that I came to see Guattaral die. I shall be there tomorrow, by the scaffold. But I shall not see Guattaral die.'

'You will shut your eyes?'

'No.'

'I am glad of it. Life is perfected by death, you told me that too, and it is true. But what do you mean? There is no escape, no avoiding it. You will see Guattaral die.'

Christoval shook his head slowly.

He spoke his last words to me in English.

'I shall see more than I came for,' he said. 'I shall see the death of Sir Walter Ralegh.'

Dean Tounson's visit told me that I must speak out.

Christoval's that I must speak out in plain language.

He learned to say my name.

I must learn no less.

Midnight.

Bess came. Now she has gone.

I can hardly write about this.

We are good at our goodbyes, my wife and I. We must have said more farewells than most in marriage.

Yet this last goodnight tonight was graceless. We sat side by side

387

on the bed. I held her close in my arms. I asked her not to be there tomorrow by the scaffold.

She protested.

'You have suffered enough,' I said. 'I beg you, Bess. Do not see this. Remember me living.'

She wept. I kissed her tears away. I turned our talk to gooseberry creams and sweet strawberries. Bess gave me her promise at last. She would not watch me die.

Then she said:

'Wat, it would have been different, wouldn't it? If Damerei had lived –'

It was my turn to weep. 'I don't know,' I said. 'I can't say, Bess. Perhaps the truth is I was not a man for marriage.'

'But Damerei – He slipped through my fingers like a bird, Wat. Like a bird. Like a fledgeling. That little heart. I can still feel it beating. O my poor chick, my bantam –'

I stopped my wife's lips with a kiss to comfort us both.

Then I said briskly:

'It was God's will, Bess. You take good care of Carew.'

She promised that she would. She said she would entrust him with my papers when he was old enough. 'He will need to be a hundred,' I remarked.

Bess managed to smile.

Then she said shyly: 'Wat, I have read what you wrote. Every word of it. About yourself. About the Queen. About me.'

'Forgive me, wife. I fear I was often confused –'

'No matter. Wat, I read what you said. I read it as you wrote it, with the heart. And I know now what I always knew. That Bess Throgmorton married a true man. A true man, and a truthful. I love you *more*, Wat, now I have read those writings.'

I could not see her face for the tears in my eyes.

I said:

'Then you love me more than I could ever love. God bless you.'

I said:

'Bess Ralegh.'

'Swisser Swatter,' she said.

'Remember him, Bess.'

'I shall remember him. I shall remember you, husband.'

Then she told me that she had received a note from the Privy Council, giving her permission to bury my body.

I answered her smiling.

'It is well, Bess, that you may dispose of it dead. You did not always have the disposing of it when it was alive.'

My last written words. I have inscribed them in my Bible. A poem. I began this poem, years ago, for Bess, that first night I met her. It was the one beginning: 'Nature that washed her hands in milk . . .' The end of that poem I could never get right. It needed my end to right it. It is right now. By the simple addition of two lines at the end of its last stanza it has become a poem in itself. I think it will do. It stands. I must sleep now to be ready for tomorrow.

> Even such is Time, which takes in trust
> Our youth, our joys, our all we have,
> And pays us but with age and dust;
> Who in the dark and silent grave,
> When we have wandered all our ways,
> Shuts up the story of our days.
> But from this earth, this grave, this dust,
> My God shall raise me up, I trust.

56

The Execution of Sir Walter Ralegh
with his Speech
immediately before he was Beheaded
(*as collated from contemporary accounts by his son Carew*)

Upon Thursday the 29th of October, 1618, after he had received Communion in the morning, and eaten his breakfast heartily, and smoked tobacco, and made no more of his death than if he had been about to take a journey, my father Sir Walter Ralegh was conveyed by the Sheriffs of London to a scaffold in the Old Palace Yard at Westminster.

The time was about nine o'clock.

The weather was bright, cold, and frosty.

There were great crowds, with many gentlemen present.

My father wore a hair-coloured doublet of fine satin, with a black wrought waistcoat under it, a pair of black taffeta breeches, a pair of silk stockings of ash colour, a long black velvet gown, and a high-crowned hat with a peacock's feather in it.

He appeared upon the scaffold with a smiling countenance.

After a proclamation of silence by an officer appointed, my father put off his hat, and he addressed himself to speak in this manner:

'My honourable good Lords, and the rest of my good friends that come to see me die, I thank God of His infinite goodness that He has vouchsafed me to die in the light, in the sight of so honourable an assembly, and not alone in the darkness.'

Then, perceiving that some of his friends, including my Lord Arundel, were leaning from high windows and that they could not easily hear him, his voice being weak, my father called out to them:

'I shall seek to strain my voice, for I would wish to have all your Honours hear me.'

But my Lord Arundel called down:

'Nay, sir. We shall rather come down to you upon the scaffold.'

Whereupon the Earls of Arundel and Oxford and Northampton, and other men of distinction but lesser rank, were permitted by the Sheriffs of London to join my father Sir Walter Ralegh upon the scaffold. He saluted every one of them severally, then began again to speak.

'As I said, I thank my God heartily that He has brought me into the light to die, and has not suffered me to die in the dark prison of the Tower. I thank God also that my ague does not afflict me at this time. I prayed that I might be spared it. That prayer has been answered, I believe.'

Then my father denied all the charges of treason laid against by King James and the Privy Council.

He said:

'For a man to call God to witness to a falsehood at any time is a grievous sin, and what shall he hope for at the Tribunal Day of Judgement? But to call God to witness to a falsehood at the time of death is far more grievous and impious, and a man that does so cannot have salvation, for he has no time for repentance, and there is no hope for him. Very well. I call to God to witness, as I hope to see Him in His kingdom, which I trust will be within this quarter of this hour, that I, Sir Walter Ralegh, was never a traitor to King James. I am guilty of no treason. I never was. If I speak not true, O God, let me never come into Thy kingdom!'

My father bowed his head.

And then he cried:

'It is not for me to fear or to flatter the King! In this I speak now, what have I to do with kings? I have nothing to do with them. I have now to do with God, therefore to tell a lie now to get the favour of the King would be something worse than vanity. I am Death's subject, and the great God of heaven is my Sovereign before whose tribunal seat I am shortly to appear. I say again to you most solemnly: *I was never a traitor*. If I speak false, let the Lord blot out my name from the Book of Life!'

My father paused.

When he went on he spoke of what had happened since his sailing back from Guiana, and all the charges and suspicions which had been laid against him then. He spoke of Manourie and Stukeley and how they had betrayed him. He held his head high.

'I confess,' he said, 'I did attempt to escape. I knew it would go hard with me. I desired to save my life. And I do likewise confess that I did dissemble and feign myself sick at Salisbury. But I hope it was no sin. The prophet David, a man after God's own heart, did for the safety of his life make himself a fool. He let his spittle fall upon his beard, and went upon all fours like a beast, to escape the hands of his enemies. Yet it was not imputed to him as a sin. I intended no ill against King James by doing likewise. I intended only to prolong time until his Majesty came, hoping for some commiseration from him.

'I forgive the Frenchman and Sir Lewis Stukeley. They betrayed me. I forgive them for that betrayal. I have received the Sacrament this morning at the hands of Mr Dean, who stands here now beside me, and taking the Sacrament I have forgiven all men their trespasses against me, even as I pray God to forgive me mine. Yet, touching upon this Sir Lewis Stukeley, my kinsman and keeper, I believe I am bound in charity to warn others against him. He is no honest man. But I ask God to forgive my cousin the wrongs he has done me, as I hope to be forgiven my own wrongs.'

The Sheriffs grew restive.

My father said:

'A little more. Only a little more, and I shall be done.'

Then he told, in simple fashion, the story of his last voyage to Guiana. It was at all material points the same as he has told it in these papers, so I shall not repeat every word he said. Sufficient to report that this story came as news to many in that great throng about the scaffold. For there were some there who had believed that he did not even return of his own free will to England, and others who thought that he had all along intended to fly away, but when my father came to the end of his account all men knew otherwise. Not just by his own word either, for he turned suddenly to Lord Arundel.

'My Lord, I am glad that you are here. Your Lordship stood with me in the gallery of my ship at my departure. And I remember how you took me by the hand and said you had but one thing to ask me. "Tell me freely and faithfully," you said. "Do you intend to return home, Sir Walter? Whether your voyage has good fortune or ill, will you come back to England?" And I gave your Lordship my hand, and I said: "Whatever happens, I give you my word I shall return." I gave you that pledge, and I have kept it.'

'You did,' said Lord Arundel. 'It is true. I remember it perfectly.'

My father bowed.

Then he spoke of other minor matters that troubled him. He had heard it falsely said that he carried vast sums of money abroad with him. He had heard it falsely said that he intended to abandon his own men upriver in Guiana. He had heard it falsely said that he stinted dying sailors of a little water.

These things are trivial. What interests me is that my father Sir Walter Ralegh thought them not trivial even in his own extremity. It mattered to him that the least lie should not go uncorrected. He stood there, a stride away from death, and went over the account books of the *Destiny*, piece by piece, point by point, pound by pound.

When he had done, he smiled and said:

'I am now at this instant to render my own account to God, and I swear as I shall appear before Him, all this that I have spoken is true.'

The Sheriffs now stepped forwards, thinking the speech finished.

But my father held up his hand.

'I have one more word to say. It concerns my Lord of Essex.'

There was silence then.

There was silence. There was stillness.

No one had expected this.

Then my father said:

'Many lies and slanders have been told against me in my time, but there is none that makes my heart bleed more than this. It is said that I was the persecutor of my Lord of Essex, and that I rejoiced in his death. It is said that I stood in a window to watch him when he suffered, and that I puffed out tobacco smoke in disdain of him, to mock him.

'God be my witness, I did no such thing. These eyes of mine shed tears for him when he died. And as I hope to look God in the face hereafter, I swear that my Lord of Essex could not even have seen my face in his last moments. For I was far off in the Armoury. Where I could see him, but he saw not me.

'I confess I was indeed of a contrary faction. But I knew my Lord of Essex for a noble gentleman. I bore him no ill will. I pitied him.

'After his death, it went the worse with me. I got the hatred of many who had claimed to wish me well in better days. And those who set me against him, to their own advantage, afterwards set themselves against me, for the selfsame reason. They were my greatest enemies, perhaps. I shall not name them. Those still living will know who they are. And God knows the hearts of them all, the living and the dead.

'My soul has been many times grieved that I was not nearer my Lord of Essex when he died. Because, as I was told afterwards, he asked for me on the scaffold, and desired that we should be reconciled.'

Some say that my father's voice shook as he said this. But most are agreed that it did not. Captain Samuel King, my father's oldest friend, has told me that in all the time my father was upon the scaffold there appeared not the least alteration in him, either in his voice or his countenance. And the Indian, Christoval Guayacunda, who had also befriended my father, remarked to me that although he could not follow or understand many of the things my father said, yet he knew that his spirit never faltered. Indeed, he seemed as free from all apprehension of death, said the Indian, as if he had come there rather to be a spectator than a sufferer.

My father Sir Walter Ralegh then said:

'And now I entreat you all to join with me in prayer to that great God of heaven, whom I have most grievously offended while I lived. For I have been a man full of all vanity, a great sinner of a long time and in many kinds, my whole life's course a course and curse of pride. I have lived a sinful life in sinful callings. For I have been a soldier, a captain, a seafaring man, and a courtier, which are all places of wickedness and vice. And the temptations of the least of these were able to overthrow a good mind and a good man.

'I ask you all to join with me in prayer that God, as I trust, will forgive me, and that He will receive me into everlasting life.

'So I take my leave of you all, making my peace with God.'

My father knelt in prayer, and many knelt with him.

Then proclamation being made by the Sheriffs that all men should depart from the scaffold, my father prepared himself for death, giving away his hat and wrought black nightcap, and some money to such as he knew that stood near him. And then taking his leave of the Lords, knights, and other gentlemen, he turned once more to my Lord of Arundel, thanking him for his company, and entreating him to desire the King that no scandalous writing to defame him might be published after his death, saying further unto him:

'I have a long journey to go, and therefore will take my leave.'

Then putting off his long gown and his doublet, he called to the headsman to show him the axe.

The headsman was nervous. He hesitated.

'I pray you,' said my father, 'let me see it. Do you think I am afraid of it?'

Then the headsman gave the axe into the hands of Sir Walter Ralegh. And my father ran his thumb down the edge of the blade.

'This is a sharp medicine,' he said. 'But it is a medicine which will cure all diseases.'

Then he went first to the one side of the scaffold and requested them all that they would pray to God to assist him and strengthen him, and then turned to the other side and did likewise.

And the executioner knelt.

He kneeled down and he asked Sir Walter Ralegh for his forgiveness. Which my father freely gave, laying both his hands upon the man's shoulders.

And the executioner threw down his own cloak because he would not spoil my father's black gown.

My father stretched himself out along it and laid down his head upon the block.

But Dean Tounson found fault with this.

'Sir Walter,' he said, 'you face westward. It is not the customary position. You should lie facing east, in honour of Our Saviour Jesus Christ.'

My father, rising, said:

'It is no great matter which way the head lies, so the heart be right.'

But when he laid down his head upon the block again, his face was towards the east.

The headsman now approached him and offered him a blindfold.

My father said:

'Do you think I fear the shadow of the axe, when I do not fear the axe itself?'

With which words, Sir Walter Ralegh declined the blindfold, lying there upon the block with his eyes open.

Then:

'Sir,' he said to the executioner. 'Grant me one moment of prayer and meditation. When I am done, I shall stretch forth my hands and you may strike.'

This was granted.

But the executioner was frightened.

And when my father stretched forth his arms nothing happened.

My father saw his executioner trembling.

He gave the man time to recover. Then once more he spread wide his arms.

But still the headsman could not or would not do his office.

Then my father cried out in a great shout of command:

'Strike, man, strike!'

The axe flashed in the sun.

The axe came down.

The first blow was not good. Yet my father's body did not flinch a whit.

The axe came down again.

It struck off his head.

Then the executioner held up my father's head by his white hair.

The executioner should have called out:

'This is the head of a traitor!'

But the executioner said nothing. And the crowd was silent.

Then a voice cried out from the crowd, and the voice cried:

'We have not such another head to be cut off!'

The large effusion of blood which proceeded from my father's veins amazed the spectators, who conjectured that he had stock enough left of nature to have survived many years, though he had been now near to three score years and ten.

Sir Walter Ralegh behaved himself at his death with so high and so religious a resolution, as if a Christian had acted a Roman, or rather a Roman a Christian. And by the magnanimity, which was then conspicuous in him, he abundantly baffled their calumnies, who had accused him of atheism.

My father's head was then put into a red leather bag, and his wrought velvet cloak was cast over his body, which was afterwards conveyed away in a black mourning coach of my mother's.

57

Lady Ralegh: a letter addressed
'To my best brother, Sur Nicholas Carew, at Beddington'

I desiar, good brother, that you will be pleased to let me berri the worthi boddi of my nobell hosban, Sur Walter Ralegh, in your chorche at Beddington, wher I desiar to be berred. The Lordes have geven me his ded boddi, though they denied me his life. This nite hee shall be brought you with two or three of my men. Let me here presently. God hold me in my wits.

E.R.

58

Epilogue by Carew Ralegh

My father's body was buried in front of the Communion Table at the Church of St Margaret's, Westminster. My father's head was embalmed and preserved by my mother until her own death, at the age of eighty-two in the year of Our Lord 1647. God held her in her wits for the twenty-nine years of her widowhood.

It falls to me now, on this, the forty-second anniversary of the day of Sir Walter Ralegh's execution, to round out his story with a few words regarding the fates of other persons mentioned in these papers.

First, Sir Lewis Stukeley. And here I must mention something my father got wrong. Namely, that he accepted the common story that this man was the *son* of Captain Thomas Stukeley, of infamous renown. I have done some research on this subject. Lewis Stukeley appears to have been only the previous traitor's *nephew*. It is not very important. But I like to get things right. Whatever Sir Lewis Stukeley pretended to himself and made others believe, the two men were not truly father and son, and that's a fact. Anyway, the said Sir Lewis, having received his £965 6s. 3d. from the Exchequer, found himself shunned and reviled by all men of honour. He was scorned as 'Sir Judas'. When he tried to seize the *Destiny* itself, and went to my Lord Howard, the Lord Admiral of England, in pursuit of this claim, it is said that the old Admiral addressed him thus: 'What, thou base fellow! *Thou* – the scorn and contempt of men! How dare you presume to come into my presence!' And that the Admiral took his staff to Stukeley's back, and drove him from his house. Stukeley complained to King James, protesting that all England appeared to condemn him. King James is said to have answered: 'What would you have me do? I cannot hang every man who speaks ill of you. There are not trees enough in my kingdom!' Charged and punished for counterfeiting coin, Stukeley was then imprisoned in the Tower. On his release, not daring to show his face even in his native Devon, he sought shelter on the Isle of Lundy in the English channel. He died there, raving mad, within two years of his betrayal of my father.

Sir Francis Bacon's fall came six months later. Arraigned on twenty-eight separate charges of bribery and corruption, he confessed them all, was stripped of his seal as the Lord Chancellor, and on 3 May 1621 was sentenced to be fined £40,000 and imprisoned in the Tower at the King's pleasure. Bacon was kept in the Tower a mere four days, but his York House was given to Buckingham, and the Parliament passed judgement that he was never again to be allowed to hold any office, place, or employment in the kingdom, nor to sit in the Lords, nor to come within the verge of the Court. He died, a broken man, some five years later, of a chill caught when he stuffed a chicken's corpse with snow to see if the snow would prove an antiseptic. Bacon left more than £20,000 in unpaid debts. He also left a certain work of philosophy called the *Novum Organum*. I have not read it. But King James, who tried to, is reported to have remarked that it was like the peace of God, i.e. it passeth all understanding.

Count Gondomar, replaced by a new Ambassador, and all hopes of the Spanish Match finally extinguished, found no favour with Spain's new King, Philip IV. He died, in poverty and disgrace, at Castile, the same year as Bacon.

King James himself died on Sunday 27 March, 1625, being fifty-nine years old, and in the twenty-third year of his reign. He had been taken ill while hunting at Theobalds, and his agony lasted only fourteen days. Some say that Buckingham poisoned him, his 'sweet Steenie'.

Buckingham was murdered three years later, thirty-six years old, stabbed with a knife through the heart by a disaffected sailor, John Felton. But Felton's knife only forestalled the axe of the public executioner. The Commons had already taken the offensive against Buckingham. As an evil counsellor of the King. As an arch-traitor to the country. Even King Charles I could not have saved him.

Of the recent Civil Wars I will say nothing. Only that James's son King Charles was executed in front of Whitehall about a quarter of a mile from where my father had suffered the same fate some thirty-one years previous.

Cromwell is said to have considered my father a hero.

Myself, I had no liking for Cromwell.

Nor do I think my father would have liked him.

I, Carew Ralegh, am now fifty-five years old. My father's friends and my mother's relatives provided for my education. I went to Wadham College, Oxford, yet proved no scholar. On coming down from Oxford, I was presented at Court by my kinsman, the Earl of Pembroke. But King James found in me my father's ghost. I travelled some years abroad, and have passed all of my life seeking to live according to the precepts handed down to me in my father's *Instructions*. I had that booklet published in 1632. It ran through six editions within four years. I shall never publish the rest of my father's papers. I confess I can see no merit in doing so. And I do not think that my father would have wished it.

I married well. My wife is Philippa, the widow of Sir Anthony Ashley. She brought me estates. She was wealthy. Our marriage has been blessed with two sons and three daughters.

Much of my life's energy has been spent in efforts to get back Sherborne. In this, I have failed. It is the residence of Sir John Digby, Earl of Bristol. But under the Commonwealth I was awarded £500 per annum out of that estate.

Now England has a king again. James's grandson, King Charles II. In February of this year, 1660, I was appointed by the King to my father's former office as Governor of the Island of Jersey. I was also offered a knighthood, but I have declined.

On my mother's death, the head of Sir Walter Ralegh came into my possession. I keep it in the same red leather bag. Sometimes – not often – I take it out to look at it. I find it harder and harder to recognize.

All the same, I have made provision that when I die this head is to be buried with me. It is, after all, a far better head than my own.